DATE DUE

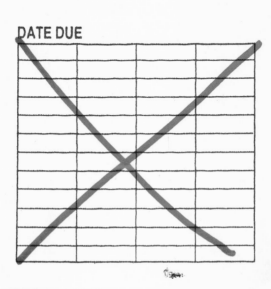

9-5-96

WEEDED

DEMCO

BLACK MARKET

BLACK MARKET

A NOVEL BY

Robert Tine

St. Martin's Press

New York

Design by Susan Hood

Library of Congress Cataloging-in-Publication Data

Tine, Robert.
        Black market / Robert Tine.
            p.   cm.
        ISBN 0-312-06907-3
        I. Title.
    PS3570.I48B58   1992
    813'.54—dc20   91-36076
                                                        CIP

First Edition: February 1992

10   9   8   7   6   5   4   3   2   1

For my brother Donald, a good man

Heartfelt thanks to my family and friends, who helped: Reagan Arthur, Emily Beck, Michael Bradley, Michael Carlisle, Thomas Dunne, Kate Edelman, Nona Hershey, Brian Kelleher, Patricia Partee, Amy Pershing, Phoebe Natanson, William Schwartz, Harold Tine, Rita Tine, Victor Tine, Carolyn Toloczko, Anne Vladeck, Brian Walls, Krisahn Williams.

All my love and my special thanks to my wife, Karen, who made the winter pass and the rains end.

Charlie Poletti, Charlie Poletti
Fewer Words,
More Spaghetti.

—Grafitto in Rome,
Summer, 1944

PROVENANCE

You always figure when you hear someone's name you know what that person is like, right? Take me. My name is Harry Leblanc and I'm not what you'd call striking. I'm not big or tall or small. I'm not young, but I'm not old either—forty-two. I look like everybody else.

You think you could describe someone named Peony Seagrave without any trouble at all. Tall and willowy and if she isn't English then she ought to be. Say "Peony Seagrave" to someone and right away you think of chintz and rose gardens and little dogs named Scamp. Well, you'd be wrong. My Peony Seagrave is a small, tough young woman with a lot of money.

There was a message on my machine. Peony said: "Harry. Come over to my place—the apartment—at six tonight. If you can't come, call. But I think you should come." I wasn't doing anything, so I went. Actually, I would have gone anyway because I like Peony and she's always doing something interesting.

Peony lives on Fifth Avenue in the eighties, a building with a lot of other rich people in it. She has always lived there; it's where she grew up. From every window there's a great view of the park, and from Peony's study you can look straight down on the Metropolitan Museum of Art. You might say that Peony grew up there too, like the museum was her backyard.

Peony's mother, also called Peony, looked like a Peony Seagrave is supposed to look—we've been through that—but Peony looks like her father, Jack. He was short, ugly, tough, and very, very rich. I never met the guy, but Peony told me that he used to brag that he had never had a boss in his life, except for a year or two when he was just starting out,

1

working for the railroads out West someplace. He saved some money from that job and went on to make a fortune in oil and textiles and any other damn thing he could think of. Peony says that he was proud of the fact that he made money *making* things, not the way those Wall Street guys do it, or used to do it, anyway. I don't know a lot about it.

Jack Seagrave's last words are recorded for history. He said, "Well, shit." The black box in his little jet picked that up as the plane, Jack at the controls, ran out of runway at Stanhope Cay, the island that Jack owned in the Bahamas. We don't know what Mrs. Seagrave said, but I'll bet it was something like "gracious" or "mercy." Peony wasn't along on that trip. She was in London and had just celebrated her twenty-sixth birthday. This was all about ten years ago.

She's a remarkable woman, Peony. At the age of twenty-six and the owner of a large sum of money, she decided to become an art dealer. And she didn't fool around; she wanted to deal in old masters. That is the art world equivalent of the Bigs.

Peony had some formal training—art history at Yale and that social-ite Sotheby's course in London—but better than that she had been going to the Metropolitan since the time she was old enough to toddle up the steps. Her whole life she had been looking, developing her eye. She looked at everything, not just pictures, but armor, furniture, tapes-tries, ivories, miniatures, everything. For years, Peony had been train-ing herself, educating herself. She read everything she could get her hands on. Like I said, it was like playing in her backyard.

And she had all that money—it made her professional debut a little easier. And it was quite a debut. Peony managed to get hold of a painting called the Mildenhall Madonna, by Luca Signorelli, that had been hanging on the walls of an English stately home called Milden-hall since 1791. It was the usual story—an old English family needed the money—and as Signorellis don't come on the market all that often, all the big boys wanted it: Sotheby's, Christie's, Wildenstein, Col-naghi, Agnew's. Peony got it. She plunked down three and a half million dollars for it, and after the usual moaning from the Brits about how they were losing yet another piece of their artistic patrimony, Peony sold it to a developer in Singapore. Funny to think of an Italian Renaissance Madonna in a Singapore high rise, but that's the art world these days.

Publicly the established names in the art world said that they wel-comed fresh blood and to the victor went the spoils and all that, but privately they all said as how you could do anything if you had enough money and that you didn't have to be any kind of genius to sell the Mildenhall Madonna. Never mind, Peony had arrived. She even made the front page of the *The Times.*

I got to Peony's right on time—I'm a very punctual person—and negotiated with the doormen for a while. They aren't nice to people they don't know. Peony cleared me over the house phone and was waiting in the hallway of her apartment (the elevators go right into the apartments, you know) with a drink in her hand. "Hi Harry," she said. "Thanks, Randall." Randall was the elevator operator and he was standing around in the background like he was hoping Peony would say "I've never seen this man before in my life," so he could have the fun of throwing me out.

She led me through the apartment—it's about the size of an airport—and into her office. There was no sign of the servants—I'm not sure how many she's got, but she said a lot of them are left over from when her folks were alive—or of the two very serious young men who are her assistants. They were probably at the gallery Peony has on Madison. Peony's office is a cozy room with a nicely carved fireplace and some works of art she likes but which don't fit together very well, I don't think, anyway. There was a George Inness Italian landscape, a Lautrec pastel sketch, an Epstein bronze, and a couple of those pre-Columbian figures I don't know anything about.

There was also an easel with a painting on it, covered with a cloth. Dealers always pull this. All of them, even Peony—maybe her more than most—have a taste for the dramatic. I knew at the right moment she would whip the cloth off the painting and say "Voila!" or something like that.

I like a martini at the end of the day, so Peony made me one and told me it was okay to smoke. Then she sat down in one of the big leather armchairs next to the fireplace. She is short and hard-looking, with a wide mouth and short, thin, reddish hair. To me, she looked just like the portrait of Jack that hung in the living room. She had one of those cultured Fifth Avenue–type voices, which I guess is to be expected.

"So," she said, "what have you been up to, Harry?"

"Nothing much. I'm thinking of going to Vermont."

"Vermont? What for?"

"Someone stole a signed Evelyn Waugh from the rare book room at the University of Vermont."

"I didn't know you did books."

"I don't usually."

3

"And Evelyn Waugh? What can that be worth?"

"Not that much, hard to tell. It's supposed to be a limited edition, fifty copies, signed and illustrated by the author. It's called *Basil Seal Rides Again*, but I happen to know that the edition got out of hand. The printer printed too many of them or something. Anyway, I like Vermont. So why not?"

"Cancel the trip, Harry." She stood, drained her drink and yanked the cloth off the easel. She didn't say "Voila!" but I could tell she was thinking it. "So?"

I took a good long, hard look at the painting. It was a portrait, small, bigger than a miniature, but not by all that much. It showed a doe-eyed young woman in an elaborate turban, an elaborately worked necklace, pearls and gleaming emeralds, at her throat. The background was a landscape, flat and green, some trees and what looked like, far off, a band of cavorting peasants. There was a signature sadness about the face of the woman, the kind of expression that tells you: this is what she really looked like, this was painted from life.

"So what do you think, Harry?"

"Nice."

"That's it? Nice?"

"Very nice."

"Tell me about this nice painting, Harry."

I put down my drink and hunched forward a little to get a better look. "Well, you know it's not my field, but I'll guess. It's Italian."

"Right."

"It's seventeenth century."

"Easy."

"Now I know that you're excited about this thing, so it's not some baroque painter that nobody but you has ever heard of. I'll bet it's a Caracci."

"Guess again." Peony was grinning. She loves games like these, mainly because she's so good at them herself.

"You're still excited. So if it's not Annibale Caracci then it's got to be Guido Reni. Am I right?"

"You are. It's about the finest Guido Reni I've ever seen and all you say is 'nice.'"

"Okay. I'll go one better. It's absolutely the finest Zozo Smith I've ever seen. How's that?"

Peony laughed, showing a lot of gum. "No, sorry, not this time. I'm

4

afraid that's not a Zozo Smith. It's the real thing and you'll never guess where I got it."

"I know exactly where you got it. You got it from some motheaten old Italian family, that's where you got it. And I don't want to know how you got it out of Italy. And I'll tell you something else, if you *did* get it from Italy then you really might be holding a fine example of the work of Mr. Zozo Smith."

Zozo Smith was a painter from Boston who worked a lot in the nineteenth century, copying Italian masterpieces. He was very good at it and made quite a name for himself. Back in his heyday he was often called in to make a copy of a painting an Italian noble family wanted to unload on the quiet. Sometimes these families replaced the pictures out of pride—they didn't want the other dukes and princes and counts to know they were broke—but more often it was to avoid prosecution for exporting art. It's been a crime in Italy since the 1860s, believe it or not.

The trouble was that over the years people forgot—or pretended to forget—what was a Zozo Smith and what was an original. There were lots of Zozos hanging on important walls that people said were Raphaels or whatever. Smith worked right at a time when Guido Reni was popular so I'll bet he turned out a couple in his time. I always meant to look up where he got that crazy name.

"It's not a Zozo and it's not a school-of, either," said Peony. "Harry, you can feel the real thing just as strongly as I can."

"No I can't. Where's it from that you're so sure?"

"The Mrs. Daniel Chapman collection."

"The who?"

Peony smiled. "Roberta Chapman. It's a small collection."

"Never heard of it."

"Very small. In fact, this is the entire collection. One Guido Reni."

"Oh, I get it. This Mrs. Chapman is some rich dame from Palm Beach who's tired of having an old master and wants the money so she can buy something by whoever's hot right now, right?"

"No. You are completely wrong. Mrs. Robert Chapman lives in New York, not fifty blocks from here. Uptown."

I had to laugh. "It would have to be more than fifty blocks, Peony, because fifty blocks puts you right in the middle of Harlem and I don't recall too many collectors of Italian baroque up there."

"That may be, Harry, but that's where it comes from."

"Peony, what the hell are you talking about?"

She sank back in her chair. "Harry, I'm not sure. It all started with Randall, you know Randall . . ."

"The elevator guy."

"Yes. A couple of days ago he took a day off work. He said that his grandfather had died."

I shrugged. "So?"

"So when he came back to work all of a sudden he started talking to me in the elevator, where normally he doesn't say anything to anybody. However, the next thing I know, he's talking about his mother and how she had inherited a painting from her father and that it was old and valuable." Peony sipped her drink.

"And?"

"And he wanted to know if I would take a look at it with an eye toward selling it. He said that his mother would come here with the painting." Peony shrugged. "Well, what could I say? Forgive me, but I was sure he was talking about a painting on velvet of Martin Luther King."

"Wait. You're telling me that Randall's mother showed up here with that Guido Reni?"

"In a Waldbaum's shopping bag."

"Jesus Christ!"

"Amazing, isn't it? She works at Beth Israel Hospital as a cleaning woman. She's nice. Honest. A little scared, I think. Randall is behind the whole thing, of course. I think if it was up to her, she'd just forget about the painting. She's no fool. I told her the painting was valuable and she knows that valuable paintings don't fall into the hands of black subway workers—that's what her father did—by accident."

"Stolen?"

Peony shrugged. "Well, that's what one would think right off the bat. Makes sense. Except when you think about it a minute, it doesn't make sense. We obviously aren't dealing with major art thieves here. You need an organization, you need contacts—all the things the Chapman family does not have. I don't need to tell you the ins and outs of stolen art."

"No, you don't. Was there a will?"

"No, but she's the closest heir, as best as I can make out. Establishing her claim to the painting isn't all that important right now. First I want to find out how her father got it."

"How does Mrs. Chapman account for it?"

"She didn't know. She just said that her father always had it. He kept

6

it wrapped in a closet. As you can see, it isn't in bad shape. It could use a cleaning."

"Have you checked it against any of the lists? Interpol or anyone like that?"

Peony waved dismissively. "You know those stolen art things are hopeless, but I checked anyway—hoped I could spare myself your fee—and there is one Reni missing. It was stolen from a church in Pesaro, in Italy, in 1979 and not heard from since."

"This isn't it?"

Peony shook her head. "No. The missing one is a Holy Family."

"Is there a catalogue raisonné for Reni? Is this one mentioned?"

"There is, but it's difficult to say if it's included. I mean, what is this anyway? A portrait? A classical figure? It could even be a study for a figure meant for a larger painting. I don't know what to call it, so you'll have to do some digging on the iconography."

"I will?"

"I'd like you to take this on. Assemble the provenance."

"Did you tell the Chapmans how valuable the picture is? How much do you think you could get for it?"

Peony narrowed her eyes and looked sideways at the painting the way a farmer appraises livestock. "Hard to say. Reni isn't everyone's cup of tea, the whole baroque era was under a cloud for so long, but baroque is back—I even heard that Sylvester Stallone is sort of interested in the period."

"Jesus! You're kidding."

Peony laughed. "No, I'm not. I think with the right kind of publicity—you know, lost masterpiece found in Harlem, that kind of thing—I might be able to get someone interested in it in the region of five to eight hundred thousand dollars. Perhaps a little more. There was a big Reni show in Bologna a couple of years ago, and the city of Florence just sold one from the municipal collection, but that went for just under half a million dollars. Of course, it was sold in Italy and would have to stay in Italy, so the price would be depressed. This one, though, is free to travel."

"Assuming it came into the Chapmans' hands legally."

"Of course."

"Did you tell them how much it was worth? Did they ask?"

"Randall asked. So I told them just what I told you. I didn't mention Sylvester Stallone, though."

"Jesus, he must have flipped."

"No. He just smiled and said, 'Mama, looks like you're going to have to quit your job.'"

"What did she do?"

"It was strange. She hardly moved a muscle. She just said that her father had always said that it was valuable."

"Her father was right."

"So. If we can establish their title and get some kind of history on the painting then they can sell it. Or rather, I can sell it for them. They'll make money, I'll make money, you'll make money, and the art world will be richer by one Guido Reni."

"Neat," I said.

FOR A WHITE person, the hard part about going to Harlem is not getting there, but getting out. Most taxis will take you there during the day, but they won't wait, and cabs never cruise the streets so you can be sure in advance that you won't get one for the return trip. The subway is direct and, if it's working right, fast, but it doesn't do door-to-door service and a lot of people, black and white, don't like to stroll the streets of Harlem at any time, day or night. Anyway, I was damned if I was going to rent a car to go uptown—for Manhattan dwellers owning a car is like other people owning yachts—so I took the subway and walked down 133rd Street to Mrs. Chapman's apartment, and no one gave me a second look even though in that neighborhood, for once, I didn't look like everyone else. I suppose I looked pretty much like a policeman, which isn't all that surprising seeing as I was one for so many years.

Mrs. Chapman undid about twelve bolts before opening her scarred front door. She led me into the living room and offered me a cup of coffee from the pot that stood on a chrome and glass coffee table. She seemed sad and moved slowly. Randall was there, too, leaning against the windowsill and glancing out into the street, as if on the lookout.

"I'm watching my car," he said. He seemed about as happy to see me as the last time we met.

"Milk and sugar, Mr. Leblanc?" asked Mrs. Chapman. She spoke in that modified Southern accent that so many older New York blacks have, even if they've never been any further south than Staten Island.

I took milk and sugar and settled on the sofa. "Do either of you mind if I tape this?" I pulled out one of those little cassette recorders from my pocket and placed it on the table.

Mrs. Chapman looked with worried eyes to her son. "What's it for?" demanded Randall.

"It helps me. I go over the tape a couple of times and maybe I'll hear something I didn't catch the first time. It's not, you know, like evidence or anything."

Randall shrugged. "I guess it's okay."

I turned on the machine. "Now, Mrs. Chapman, has this painting always been in your father's possession? Do you remember him having it when you were a little girl?"

"Yes. He always had it. Even as long as I can remember."

"Where did he keep it? Was it on display?"

"No. It was in the closet."

"He never showed it? Did he ever show it to anyone?"

Mrs. Chapman nodded. "Sometimes he did. Sometimes he would take it out and show it. He said it was real valuable and Mama always said if it was so valuable why didn't he sell it and Daddy would always say that it was his and he was going to keep it."

"What was your father's name?"

"James Holt."

"And your mother's name was?"

"Cynthia Holt."

"And she is no longer living?"

Mrs. Chapman shook her head sadly. "No, they both gone."

Randall broke in. "What's this for, all this?"

"We have to find out where the painting came from before you can sell it. Once we have established that your grandfather acquired it legally then you can sell it, the painting."

"Maybe you're calling my grandfather a thief."

"Of course not. Nothing like that." Well, of course, that's exactly what I was doing, but not in so many words.

"It was always in the house," said Mrs. Chapman. "Why would Daddy steal a painting? He was an honest man. And he worked hard."

"I'm sorry, Mrs. Chapman. Was he ever in trouble with the police?"

Randall sighed indignantly.

Mrs. Chapman shook her head. "Never once."

"And he never said where the painting came from?"

"No, sir."

"Did he ever show it outside the family? Was the painting a secret or something you weren't supposed to talk about?"

"Well . . . it was sorta secret. But we all knew it was there. I mean, it wasn't *real* secret. Sometimes he'd bring it out and just kind of show it to us all. Then there were other times Daddy would just show it to himself. I mean, you'd just find him here looking at it. I think it made him sad sometimes, like it brought back memories, bad memories that he couldn't let go of."

"Do you have any idea what memories? What do you think bothered him about the painting?" I couldn't help but wonder if it was just a periodic bout of bad conscience. Randall would kill me if I told him.

"I think maybe . . . maybe it had something to do with the army."

"The army? He was in the army? Do you know what he did in the army?"

Roberta Chapman looked at her son and then at me. I could see that she was puzzled by the question. "He was a soldier."

"Yeah," I said, "but do you know what outfit? What his job was?"

"He didn't talk about the army much. We always got the feeling he saw some bad things in the war."

"He was in the war?"

"Yes, Mr. Leblanc."

"Do you know where?"

Randall broke in. "He told me he was in Africa and Italy and at the end of the war he was in . . . Germany, I think."

I wasn't interested in Germany, not yet anyway. "Italy?"

"All over," said Randall.

On the tape you can hear me trying to keep the level of interest in my voice down. "Did he ever talk about being in Italy? Did he ever mention the painting in connection with his time in the service?" You didn't have to be an expert to see that Holt probably got the painting while on active service in Europe, more specifically, in Italy. I wasn't part of that big haul of looted art that turned up in Texas—God, how I wish I had been—but that was only the most conspicuous case of a light-fingered GI helping himself to some stolen art, and I had certainly been that route before. If Randall's grandpa had helped himself to the Reni from the ruins of a museum or villa—it wasn't the kind of painting you found in a church—then it was probably bad news for Roberta Chapman.

"I'm sorry," she said, "I just don't remember."

I snapped off the tape recorder. "That's okay, Mrs. Chapman. We'll figure it all out."

I STOOD ON the cracked front steps of the building hoping that I'd see a cab come down the street, but I knew I was more likely to see a gondola heading my way. Some kids playing in the street interrupted their game for a moment to stare at me.

"Cop," said one.

"Gotta be," said another.

Someone tapped me on the shoulder. I jumped a little and turned. It was Randall.

"You want a ride?"

And I thought he didn't like me. "Yeah, that would be great."

"Come on." He looked with distaste at the Harlem street. "I live in Queens. Nice house, barbecue out back." He felt for his keys. He drove a shiny, new Camry. "And I want you to sell that damn painting so I can take my mother away from this shit hole, you understand what I'm saying?"

I said I would do my best.

Rome, July 1944

1

Just after the beginning of curfew that hot night, the residents of the Via Foraggi in the old Velabro section of the city heard the rumbling engines of twenty heavy trucks echoing in the street. That quiet corner of Rome had been liberated.

The city as a whole had fallen to the Allies some weeks before, but until that night no liberating soldiers had strayed into the Via Foraggi except for a few who had lost their way looking for the Forum, which lay on the district's eastern edge.

It was not, however, the first time foreign soldiers had occupied the neighborhood. In the middle of the Velabro was a large municipal garage which had been the home to a transport unit of the German army, but it had lain vacant since the Wehrmacht had pulled out of the city in early June. The Germans had not been particularly welcome in the district, but they had been polite and orderly and brought with them some small economic benefits. All of the privates and NCOs had been housed in the Hotel Palatino Splendido, a careworn hotel a few hundred yards from the garage, and a German military paymaster had arrived every Saturday morning to settle the billeting and breakage bill. The local wine seller had done a good trade selling sour *vino sfuso* to the thirsty troops. Beyond that, the Germans had gone about their business and the residents of the district had ignored them.

The nationality of the liberators was unknown. While Romans had taken to referring to the occupying troops as *gli Americani* or as *gli Inglesi*, everyone was aware that the Allied force was not just American and English, but French, Polish, South African, and

15

Australian as well; more obscure nationals—New Zealanders, Indians, Brazilians, and, strangest of all, anti-Fascist Italians—were known to exist, but no one could identify them with any certainty.

Signor and Signora Benelli, proprietors of the Hotel Palatino Splendido, would be the first to learn who their liberators were, but that information would spread through the district in the minutes following the lifting of the curfew at dawn. The sign the newcomers nailed to the door of the garage was in English but even someone with a knowledge of that language would find the meaning obscure:

> V Army 169th Brig.
> 3rd Hvy Tran. Div.
> "A Co." Rome Region

The residents, hot and bored, hung out their windows and watched as twenty two-and-a-half-ton Chevrolet trucks and a few jeeps nosed their way slowly down the street. One by one, the trucks pulled into the garage while the others remained outside like farm animals, dumb and uncomplaining, waiting for their turn. Inside the garage, the trucks lurched two and fro easing themselves into tight parking spaces. The garage was without electricity and the trucks had blackout shields on their headlights. Progress was slow and there was much loud cursing and shouting of orders.

A sergeant ran up and down the rank of idling trucks. He carved a course in the blue-grey cloud of exhaust which hovered in the street. He shouted, "Which one of you fuckers got the generator?"

One of the residents of the district heard the accent and turned to his wife. "Americani," he said authoritatively.

Thin, sweaty Calvin Utterback hated the army in general and A Company in particular. "Generator," he screamed, kicking out at the truck nearest to him.

"Hey," said Private Stanley Leacock to the driver of his truck. "We got the generator, don't we, Jimmy?"

Private James Holt stared over the wheel of his truck at the tailgate of the vehicle in front of him. "Uh-huh."

Utterback jumped on the running board of Holt's two-and-a-half and leered through the window like a villain in a silent movie. "Holt! You got the motherfuckin' generator. I seen it loaded."

"Yeah, Sarge, it's in the back."

Utterback's face screwed in upon itself in rage. "Didn't you hear me, asshole? Didn't you?"

"Can't hear nothing in the cab, Sarge. Not with all these trucks on idle."

It was not the time for rational argument with Sergeant Utterback.

"Get the fuckin' generator out and get it in the fuckin' garage. Get it!"

James Holt took the truck out of gear and yanked up the hand brake.

"Yeah, Sarge. C'mon, Stanley."

Utterback trotted into the garage, muttering under his breath as he went. He hated the army; he hated the Supply and Transport Corps. He hated A Company. But most of all, he hated Private James Holt. He was also afraid of him.

IT TOOK AN hour for the company maintenance unit to string up the lights and another twenty-five minutes to get the generator to cough some life into them. It took another hour to get the depot more or less shipshape. All of this activity was under the direct command of the two sergeants on duty that night and the company complement of corporals and Pfc's. The company commander, Captain Thorpe, looked on. Normally, a menial task like this one would have been handled by Thorpe's second in command, but to the captain's great resentment, he didn't have one. The previous holder of that post, a second lieutenant, had come down with a debilitating case of dysentery in Naples and his replacement had as yet to show up, aground, it seemed, somewhere on the shifting shoals of military bureaucracy.

When the company sergeant, Donal McManus, pronounced his men present and more or less correct, Thorpe was relieved. He had already plotted his escape to the bar of the Grand Hotel. The truck crews stood in the middle of the garage under the bright white light of the naked bulbs and stared expectantly at their superior.

"Where's the billet, Sergeant?"

McManus glanced at the billeting slip on the clipboard he held in a pink, freckled paw. "Hotel Palatino Splendido, sir. That's what it says here, sir." He held up the board as if Thorpe might think he was making it up.

Thorpe sighed. He had hoped that there wasn't an assigned

billet yet and that the men would have to bed down in the garage. It would be faster that way and he could get the hell out of there. He wiped the sweat off his forehead.

"Do you know where this place is, Sergeant?"

"Sent the Benny to find it," said McManus apologetically.

"And where is it?"

" 'Bout a hundred yards down the road, sir." McManus knew that Thorpe wanted to leave; McManus wanted Thorpe to leave. If Manganaro came back while Thorpe was still there, then the captain might ask some questions. McManus knew it wasn't too likely, but, all the same, he would rather have the officer out of the way.

"Look, sir," said McManus, as if he had just had a brilliant idea. "Why don't you leave it to us? Me and Utterback can handle it."

"Well," said Thorpe quickly, "if you think you can . . ."

"Easy as pie, sir."

"Well, good." Thorpe smoothed his mustache. "Form them up and I'll speak to them."

"Yes, sir." McManus wondered why Thorpe was going through this charade, as all it would do is delay the captain's first sip a little. Thorpe's solitary and melancholy drinking was well known to the NCOs.

The company formed itself into orderly ranks and Thorpe cleared his throat. "Men," he shouted, trying to make himself heard over the persistent hacking of the generator, "this is your new home."

"Heard that one before," observed Stanley Leacock out of the side of his mouth. In the past month the company had had about a dozen new homes. They had lived in barracks, garages, hastily improvised tent camps, cellars, and holes dug in the ground. For the last week they had been camped in a stand of umbrella pines on the beach near Civitavecchia, the port city of Rome. That had been nice.

"Your *permanent* home," stressed Thorpe.

No one had ever heard that before. Even McManus, who always knew everything well in advance, looked surprised.

"You are now permanent party, Rome."

A warm, safe feeling spread through the ranks of tired men. They smiled wide, happy smiles. Permanent party status was the answer to a prayer. It meant that they would not be sent north to the combat areas; it meant that they were safe. A Company had been under fire several times, and apart from nuts like Sergeant Manganaro and old soldiers like McManus, every man in the outfit—including Thorpe—had hated it.

"Jimmy," hissed Leacock, "we might live through this thing after all."

"Yeah," said Holt. "If the army don't kill us."

Thorpe was pleased. He could see that for once his words were having some effect on the usually sullen and resentful men under his command.

"Permanent party," he said again, as if the words themselves could make him popular. "So I just want to tell you to behave yourself and do what you're told and you won't have anything to worry about. Sergeant?"

"Sir?"

"Anything else?"

"No, sir."

"Well," said Thorpe, "fine." He seemed faintly embarrassed, like a dinner guest who had just noticed that his hosts were yawning. "I'll be going."

"Everything'll be fine, sir. Don't worry about a thing."

"Very good, Sergeant," said Thorpe, with all the military bearing he could muster. A few moments later, Thorpe was driving away from the new home of his company, headed for the Grand Hotel where, he had heard, an officer always received a warm welcome. Better than that though, it was said that the Grand was the only place in the whole hot city that had unlimited supplies of ice.

"IS SIGNOR FIORITO," said Jack Benny, introducing McManus to the keeper of the Hotel Palatino Splendido, "and is Signora Fiorito. I explain who you is, Sergeant."

Sergeants McManus, Utterback, and Giacomo "Jack" the Benny, company translator, stood with the Fioritos in the shabby lobby of the hotel. The soldiers looked at the threadbare carpet and the graying, dusty wall paper and decided that there was nothing in the Hotel Palatino Splendido that even their lousy soldiers could wreck. While the three sergeants surveyed their grim surroundings, the Fioritos stared glumly. Signor Fiorito coughed and shifted uneasily.

"It's nice to meet you folks," said McManus. "I got fifty-six guys

19

and a requisition order on your hotel. Says here that you got thirty-nine rooms, is that right?"

Jack Benny translated quickly.

Fiorito said something and Jack replied. The two Italians seemed to fence back and forth in their own language, but McManus understood not a word. The three words he did know, *vino*, *birra*, and *segnorina*, were never mentioned. He wished he had Manganaro with him. Manganaro had an effortless command of the language, but that night he had business to transact.

"Fiorito say yes, he got thirty-nine rooms but four is taken with the old folks who living here all the time and they can no be bother. And Fiorito want to know who is to pay."

"No one is going to bother the old folks and the army is going to pay, but I don't know how much. How many showers and bat'rooms he got?"

There was another heated and lengthy exchange in Italian. Fiorito and his wife did not look happy.

"He say he got nine bathroom but one is for the old people, but he still say how much you pay."

McManus was annoyed now. "Enough. Tell him enough. That's all I know. The United States Army ain't going to cheat him, okay?"

The next burst of conversation was even more voluble. This time Signora Fiorito joined in, firing off a few spirited salvos of her own.

"C'mon, Jack," said McManus impatiently.

"They say how do they know? They say you gotta guarantee."

"Oh for Chrissakes, yeah, I guarantee. I guarantee everything, let's just get this show on the road, huh, you guys? I need three rooms for the noncoms, and the rest of the guys will have to double up." He turned to Utterback. "Cal, go outside and double 'em up."

Signora Fiorito chose that moment to begin a long peroration, a torrent of words that not even Utterback's bellowing from the doorway—"Line up by twos, you fuckers!"—could stem.

"Eh, sergeant . . ."

"Yeah?"

"She wants to know about the sheets."

"Sheets? What sheets? Ain't she got no sheets?"

"They have sheets, Sarge, but she want to know maybe they get dirty and fuck up and—"

"Jack, do me a favor and tell her to go hop in the bowl, would ya please? This is a hotel and the sheets are her fuckin' problem. Maybe later there'll be some bedding but right now I don't want to hear her bitchin' about the sheets, okay? Capeesh?"

Jack Benny told the Signora Fiorito that the army would pay.

This seemed to satisfy Signor Fiorito. He stood behind the reception desk and started taking keys from the slots and laying them out carefully. He set aside the rooms for the noncoms as McManus had asked, and while he didn't show it, he was rather happy. First the Germans, now the Americans. The war might be the making of the Hotel Palatino Splendido. A piercing shriek from his wife made him look up.

Quickly he took in the scene in the lobby. "Porca miseria!"

"Jack," ordered McManus, "tell him to start handing out the keys."

With trembling hands, Signor Fiorito gave a room key to Ernest Biggs and his roomate Alvin Whiteside.

"Thank you," said Whiteside shouldering his kit bag. "And evenin' to you ma'am."

"Che vergogna!" wailed Signora Fiorito.

"What's biting her ass, Jack?"

"She no like the men, Sarge."

"Fuck it," said McManus, "she'll get used to 'em. I did."

"Pick it up, assholes," yelled Utterback.

The privates and Pfc's of A Company filed by the desk and picked up their keys. Signora Fiorito, stunned and fearful, watched with tears in her eyes. Every one of her new guests was black.

As THE ALLIED forces had struggled north toward Rome, rumors of the ferocity of the black troops had flown before them. The extent of the savagery had been exaggerated, and they failed to distinguish between the various nationalities in that many-flagged army. The object of Signora Fiorito's fears was the black North African troops, the Goums, who did have something of a well-deserved reputation for atrocities. The Goums, it was said, were paid by the number of ears they presented to the paymaster of the Free French forces, who had nominal command over these fierce fighters. The Goums were not, as it happened, paid by the ear, but such stories gained such credence that they penetrated the hushed corridors of the Vatican itself. Pope Pius XII asked that the Goums not be billeted in Rome and his holiness's wish was granted.

But national distinctions were lost on Signora Fiorito. Ever since Italy had bombed and gassed Ethiopia into submission in the 1930s she had heard much about Negroes, none of it good. Black North Africans, black Brazilians, Kenyans, Sudanese, dark-skinned Indians, or a black support company in the United States Army—they were all the same to her: bloodthirsty savages who violated, killed, and then probably ate their victims. And now she had fifty such men under her own roof. She was sure she would not be safe in her own bed.

As soon as the company had checked in, Signora Fiorito retired to her room, locking the door and wedging a chair against it. She threw herself down on the bed and alternated between fits of crying copious, bitter tears and lying perfectly still and silent, listening to the shouts and horseplay of the soldiers and the pounding of the water in the baths and showers. It seemed to run forever.

She crossed herself. "Santa Maria, Madonna mia . . ."

McManus and Utterback settled themselves in the lobby to await the return of Manganaro. They lit a roaring Coleman lantern and played acey-deucey, passing a two-liter flagon of wine back and forth between them as they rattled the dice. McManus had already lost a buck and a quarter when Jimmy Holt and Stanley Leacock came down the stairs. They had showered and shaved and they wore clean clothes. Signor Fiorito, still stationed behind the reception desk, not daring to go to bed for fear that he would be murdered in it, shrank back from the two young men.

"Hey, Holt, Leacock, where the hell do you think you're going?"

"Going for a beer, Sarge," said Holt.

"Yeah," said Leacock with a grin, "we're going to look for the permanent party."

McManus turned back to his game and the wine. "Well, if you find it, make sure you let me know where it is."

"Will do, Sarge."

"And remember, duty calls bright and early."

"Got it, Sarge," said Holt.

As the two soldiers headed for the front door, Utterback leaned forward and hissed, "You gonna let 'em go?"

"Why the hell shouldn't I?"

"I wouldn't give that Holt nigger the time of day."

McManus took a swig of wine. "He didn't ask for the time of day."

"I hate that nigger. Hate him more than I hate the army."

McManus shook the dice in his hand and blew on them as if his fingers were cold. "Hate him all you want. But don't tell me you hate the army. Me, I love the army."

"Some life," said Cal Utterback.

"I belong in the army. A place for everything and everything in its place, that's my motto."

IN THE OUTDOOR bar for enlisted men in Piazza Poli, known as Polio Square, Holt and Leacock picked up two warm beers from the serving counter and settled at a beer-slick table. There were several hundred soldiers crammed into the small square, each drinking as much as he could afford. A pale blue haze of cigarette smoke curled into the bright white lights which illuminated the square like a night ball game. From the windows of the buildings bordering Piazza Poli hung dozens of Italians, watching the drinking men as if observing animals in a zoo.

"So Jimmy," said Leacock, "how's it feel to know you're gonna live through the war? I can't believe we got so lucky. I still can't believe it."

Holt drank half of his beer in one thirsty gulp. "Amazing."

"Maybe I'll come down and see you in New York when the war is over. How'd that sound?"

Holt smiled. "You better, 'cause I know I'm not going all the way the fuck up to Maine to see you. Cold up there. All my life I never heard of a nigger from Maine."

Leacock grinned. "Hell, I didn't know there was any other kind. I never left Maine till I joined the army. Hardly ever left Bangor."

"Glad you came?"

Leacock looked around at the hundreds of sweating, cursing soldiers. "No."

Holt laughed. "Me neither."

"So where the hell was Manganaro tonight?"

Holt shook his head. "Don't know."

"That guy is no good."

Jimmy Holt nodded. "Yeah."

"Better than that Utterback, though. That man is crazy. And mean too."

"Yeah." But Holt wasn't really listening. He was looking across the top of the heavy-bottomed glass beer mug, watching two soldiers making their way toward his table. They were stumbling against other soldiers hunched over their drinks, and they brayed with laughter as they wandered their erratic path through the crowd. A few of the soldiers they jostled looked up from their beers angry and ready for a fight—but they backed off. The two were heavy-shouldered, big-fisted, hard-looking men, the type who, drunk or not, would be difficult to take in a fight. The two were dressed something like British soldiers, in baggy shirts and long flappy shorts that ended at the knee. Holt couldn't quite place them. They were not British; they were too big and well fed. Australian, maybe, or New Zealanders. Whatever they were, they were drunk.

"I think McManus is okay," continued Leacock. "I mean, he's still a sergeant, but he's okay. He could have stopped us coming out tonight, but he didn't."

"Yeah," said Holt, not taking his eyes off the two big men. "Listen, Stanley," he said quietly, "I think we might be in for a little trouble."

Leacock looked around, following the line of Holt's gaze. "Oh man, would you look at the size of those guys?" He swallowed hard. "What do we do, Jimmy, leave?"

"When I finish my beer."

"Then finish it."

Holt tossed down the rest of his beer, but held onto the mug firmly.

"Okay," said Stanley. He started to stand up.

"Sit down, Stanley. I feel like having another."

"Jimmy, man, please . . ."

The two white soldiers were standing in front of them, towering over the table, smiling and swaying slightly.

"So," said one of them, "tell me what tribe you kaffirs are from." The accent wasn't British or Australian; it sounded to Holt like a mixture of both.

"You bloody kaffirs," said the other one.

24

Stanley Leacock didn't want a fight. "Listen, mister . . ."

"Shut up, kaffir. I'm talking to your mate. I said what tribe you from?"

"I look like an Indian to you, Jack?"

"You keep civil when you're talking to me, kaffir."

"Why," said Holt wearily, "are you bothering us?"

"Because where we come from, kaffir, black bastards like you aren't allowed to drink with white men."

"Is that so? And where the fuck do you come from?"

"From the Union of South Africa, you fuckin' munt."

"Now we know. Fuck off, Jack. You're bothering me. And you smell bad."

One of the South Africans reared back, his big fist traveling toward Holt's chin.

Jimmy jumped to his feet, slipping the heavy beer mug across the back of his hand like a pair of brass knuckles. He swung to his right, slamming the thick glass bottom of the mug into the temple of one of his attackers. The man wobbled a bit, then his eyes turned up in his head and he fell heavily to the ground as if his legs had been scythed out from beneath him. Jimmy whirled to meet the fist of the other man, blocking the punch with the beer mug.

The South African's hand slammed into the mug, shattering it. The glass slashed open the knuckles, tearing the skin wide and ragged, exposing the hard white-blue bones. The knuckles shone for a moment in the bright light and then were washed over with a great gout of blood. The man stared at his lacerated fist, then stuffed it into his stomach and doubled over.

"Aynah!" he screamed at the cobblestones. "You fuckin' kaffir. I am going to donner you—"

Holt kicked the man sharply in the shins, knocking him to the ground. As he fell, his wounded hand smacked sharply against the edge of the table, blood swirling into the spilt beer. He screamed in pain.

Jimmy grabbed Leacock. "Let's go, Stanley." The other men in the bar were staring dumbly at the two men lying on the ground, at Stanley and Jimmy, and at the blood which seemed to be everywhere.

From the darkness above them, one of the Italians shouted, "Forza!"

Holt and Leacock took off, dashing out of the pool of light and

25

into the black streets. They ran for a few hundred yards, not caring where they went, their heavy boots ringing on the iron-hard cobblestones. They realized they weren't being followed and slowed. Stanley Leacock stumbled to the side of a building and leaned against it, panting and laughing at the same time.

"Where . . . " he said between gasps for breath, "what the hell was that all about? Where did you learn to do that, Jimmy? Did you see them drop? Did you see the look on their faces?"

"I dunno. I never done it before."

"The army finds out how dangerous you are and you'll be in combat in no time." His voice echoed loud in the silent street.

"Don't tell the army."

"What the hell were they anyway? Africans? I thought that there was only Africans in Africa. Marcus Garvey and that kind of shit."

"Like I know anything about Africa."

"I was just standing there shittin' scared," yelled Stanley. "I never seen you move at all. Jimmy, man, you are dangerous."

The shutters above them flew open. "In somma, signori . . ." The voice sounded tired.

They looked up. The girl was young and the moonlight caught the shine of her dark hair and made her pale skin look luminous, almost ghostly.

"Hey!" yelled Leacock. "Miss! Miss!" His excited voice filled the street. "I'm Private Stanley Leacock and this is my friend James Holt, and let me tell you, miss, he is the toughest damn soldier in the United States Army!"

A reply drifted down from the balcony. The girl said something in Italian and laughed. Stanley felt his skin tingle.

"Hey miss, why don't you come down and have a drink with us?" Stanley tipped his hand to his lips as if drinking something cold and refreshing.

"Yeah," said Jimmy, "c'mon."

The girl laughed again and shook her head.

"Awww, please . . ."

An angry and obviously parental voice growled from inside the apartment. "Si, mamma," said the girl. "Vengo." She looked down at Stanley and smiled. "Devo andare."

"Wait!"

The voice barked again and the girl seemed to wince.

"Let her go, Stanley. You'll get her in trouble with her mama."

The girl vanished from the balcony, but her place was taken by an elderly woman swaddled in nightclothes. She looked down into the street and shrieked. "Negri!"

"Evenin' ma'am. I'm Private Stanley Leacock—"

"Va fa'n culo!"

"What?"

"Va fa'n culo! Va t'en e via!"

Leacock winced as the girl had done. "Tell your daughter, ma'am, tell her—"

"I think she wants us to go, Stanley."

Leacock allowed Holt to drag him a few yards, a flow of invective following them down the street. Stanley stopped and shouted back. "You tell her I'll come visit, okay?"

"Vai in mona di tua sorella!"

They walked back to the Hotel Palatino Splendido, getting lost more than once. Stanley Leacock never stopped talking. "What a night! We're gonna live through the war, you beat the shit out of two guys, we meet a beautiful girl . . ."

"And her mama," put in Holt.

"Well, she's gotta be nicer than her mama, right?"

"Stanley, fuckin' *Hitler* is nicer than her mama."

SIGNOR FIORITO WOKE with a start when Holt and Leacock came through the front door of the hotel. The two sergeants were still playing dice in their corner and the proprietor looked to them for protection should Stanley and Jimmy turn violent.

"Find the party?" asked McManus. His words were slurred.

"Sarge, it was better than we expected."

"That a fact," said McManus without interest, returning to his game. Utterback said nothing, though his scowl was eloquent enough.

Fiorito never took his eyes off Holt and Leacock, watching them closely as they crossed the lobby and started up the stairs. At the top, Stanley stopped and waved to Fiorito. "Good night," he said, "sleep tight."

In spite of himself, Fiorito waved back. He was glad his wife wasn't there to see it. Stanley grinned.

"You know, Jimmy, I think I'm gonna like this town."

"Yeah, you can tell by the people. They're *real* friendly."

2

Manny Farfalla had no friends. Lieutenants in the Army Provost Marshall's Office, Criminal Investigation Division, were rarely befriended by brother officers of other corps, nor were they beloved of enlisted men or NCOs, even those under their command. The Romans, with their usual mistrust of authority, Italian and foreign, steered clear of the *poliziotto americano*.

Farfalla's colleagues in the Military Police didn't like him much either. Lieutenant Vittorio Emanuele Farfalla was single-mindedly devoted to his job: "an extremely dedicated and efficient officer," was the official army line on him. At the bar of the Excelsior Hotel the men who wrote the reports on Farfalla translated their army prose into more human terms. Farfalla, they said, was a tough, pushy, son of a bitch. In the building known as the Insurance Company, the newly established seat of the Allied Military Government in the Piazza Venezia, Lieutenant Farfalla was known as "Sherlock the Wop."

The Insurance Company faced the old palace that had been home to Mussolini's government, the Palazzo Venezia. The AMG brass all had offices in the front of the building, rooms with tall, gracefully arched windows giving wonderful views of the stately square and the balcony of the old palace from which the former dictator had harangued the crowds. The Palazzo Venezia was better suited to the needs of the Allies than the Insurance Company, but the AMG had decided against using it, fearing that they would attach to themselves some of the odium of the Fascist regime. Officially, the liberators sought to be loved by the liberated.

Manny Farfalla, who had a tiny office in the back of the building overlooking the narrow, dark Vicolo dei Funari, didn't care if the Romans loved him, or hated him, for that matter. His enemies were not the Italians or even the Germans. Farfalla was fighting his own side: his job was putting American soldiers in jail. He was winning his war. In the two years he had been in the service, Farfalla had sent seven men to the gallows and another eighteen were doing life in army stockades, in Leavenworth mostly.

The Insurance Company was a blaze of light in a dark town. Electric power was rationed in Rome, to the Romans anyway, but the AMG and the hospitals and the officer-only hotels on the Via Veneto got all they needed. That night the Insurance Company was lit up like an ocean liner at sea, on a peaceful prewar cruise, but the atmosphere in the building was far from relaxed. Clerks sweated over their typewriters, cursing the oppressive nighttime heat and the crushing amount of work to be done. They were looming ream upon ream of paperwork, codifying and classifying the laws that would rule the sleeping city.

The Allied Military Government had set itself the task of undoing in a couple of months the damage done by more than two decades of Fascist rule. Italian politicians, the ones untainted by Fascism, were wrangling with Washington and London and with each other about how Italy was to be governed when the war was won. In the meantime, Rome needed a government. The AMG supplied it.

Farfalla was not the most senior policeman in Rome—there were three captains, two majors, and a light colonel above him— but he was the most active. Since arriving in Rome on liberation plus five, he had nabbed nine GIs. Two were being held on rape charges and a third faced second-degree murder; the other six had been various crimes ranging from simple theft to assaulting a superior officer. All nine were being held in the Rome municipal prison, which went by the odd name of Regina Coeli—the Queen of Heaven.

He had open-and-shut cases against his three most serious crimes. The murderer, an almost moronic hillbilly from West Virginia, was a kid so dumb he never should have been in the army, never mind given a powerful weapon and taught how to use it. He would get the rope. Although Farfalla was held to be an unfeeling man, the boy's fate disturbed him. A recruiting sergeant

29

somewhere or a rubber-stamp draft board was responsible for the dead Roman girl, but it was the hillbilly kid who was going to have to pay the penalty.

Farfalla thought that the two rapists should be hanged. They were sneering tough guys from Philly, and they had assaulted and beaten their victim so badly that she had been blinded in one eye. They were all swagger and could-give-a-shit and that annoyed Farfalla. He would make sure that they got the thirty years apiece that the Uniform Code of Military Justice prescribed in such cases. All Farfalla had to do was wait for the Judge Advocate General's Office to appoint a couple of courts-martial.

The other six crimes in his caseload were routine. Despite the grumblings of the Romans, who said that the Allies, specifically the Americans, were not nearly as well-behaved as the Germans had been, Rome was calm. True, there had been hundreds of Article 15 sentences handed down by company commanders—drunk and disorderlies, willful damage to government property, short term AWOLs—but these didn't concern Farfalla.

Manny was glad he didn't have responsibility for the British and Commonwealth troops. Few had committed serious crimes, but two had been murdered and a number seriously injured, knife wounds for the most part. A single unfortunate subaltern had been blinded with lye. All this was due to an idiotic leaflet that had been printed up by the British Army Field Security Office, designed to discourage the thousands of pimps thronging the streets. British soldiers had been instructed to hand pieces of paper to the procurers which read, in Italian, "I am not interested in your syphilitic sister." Sisters were sacred in Italy and reaction to such insults was swift and violent.

Farfalla was night duty officer at the CID Command on the second floor of the Insurance Company. It was a tedious shift with little for the officer in charge to do except to make sure that his clerk didn't fall asleep. Farfalla was two hours into his shift and the phone had only rung once—there had been a bust-up in Piazza Poli and a hopping mad South African major wanted some action from the Americans. Two of his soldiers, he said, had been jumped by a gang of GIs and what was Farfalla going to do about it? Manny told him it wasn't his pigeon—an expression he had learned from his British comrades in arms—and that the South African would have to take it up with the Public Security Officer, whoever that unfortunate gentleman might be.

In the first few days after the liberation, the phones had rung all night. Overzealous and imaginative MPs had called in to report imminent counterattacks by Panzer divisions, that a bridge over the Tiber was in the hands of fifth columnists, that a spy was operating a clandestine radio receiver. The tanks always turned out to be Allied, thrashing around on the outskirts of Rome, trying to find their way north; the fifth columnists were poor hungry Romans huddled under a bridge, daring to break the curfew to try and catch the muddy-tasting fish from the filthy river; the spy was inevitably some poor guy trying to listen to his radio using power filched from one of the lines that ran by his window.

Outside his office, Farfalla heard his clerk, Corporal Garber, fiddling with the dial of the table radio trying to pick up the 2:00 A.M. broadcast from Berlin. There was a gabble of Italian, followed by a frantic flood of a language Farfalla could not identify, then a loud clear rendition of "Between the Devil and the Deep Blue Sea," Axis Sally's theme song.

"Bingo," said Garber.

All over Rome—all over Italy—troops were listening to Axis Sally, also known as the Berlin Bitch. She had a low sexy voice and thousands of soldiers had spent hundreds of hours discussing what she looked like. The general consensus was that she was leggy and blonde, although a rumor had started that she was short and bald. It was widely held that her partner on the show, an amiable straight man known only as George, was a fag and a dope fiend.

"Hello suckers," said Sally, as her theme music faded away.

Farfalla heard Garber laugh. "You bitch . . ."

"Had quite a surprise last night, didn't you?" said Sally sexily. "I'm talking about the Fourth Infantry Division and the Twenty-eighth English Brigade hung up there by Arezzo. Four hours of shelling by our eighty-eights is a little hard on the nerves, isn't it fellas?"

Garber laughed again. "You *fuckin'* bitch."

George broke in. "Hey guys, did you hear about Corporal Richard Henderson of the Second Battalion of the 442nd Regiment out there in a little hellhole called Rosignano?"

"Pooor Richard," said Sally. "He stepped on an s-mine and had his guts blown out. Still, he managed to live for twelve hours and

31

in the end he just plain screamed himself to death. Nasty things, s-mines."

"And we've got plenty of them," said George as if reading a commercial. "In fact, there's one with your name on it just waiting for you."

"And tomorrow just might be your unlucky day, Sugar," said Sally huskily.

"But you know who won't be getting hurt in this war, don't you Sally?"

Sally laughed. "Of course I do, George—"

"Those rich Jew-boy draft dodgers in New York," said Garber quickly.

"Those rich Jew-boy draft dodgers in New York," said Axis Sally. "They're getting into bed with the wives and girlfriends of the men of the Fifth Army who are out there, stuck on the Gothic line, getting killed in the war the Jew-boys started but won't fight."

Garber, who was Jewish and from New York, laughed. "Then what the hell am I doing here, Sally?"

"We're going to play a little New York music for you guys. Think about the Jews and your women while listening to Tommy Dorsey and his orchestra playing 'Getting Sentimental Over You.'" The Dorsey theme song flooded out of the speaker, almost drowning out the ringing of the phone.

"Garber," yelled Farfalla, "get that."

Garber grabbed the phone with one hand and lowered the volume with the other. He listened for a moment then said very slowly and loudly: "Will - you - for - Christ's - sake - please - speak - English - please? English? Ingliss?"

Farfalla heard Garber throw the receiver down on the desk. "Benny!" he yelled, his voice echoing in the halls. "Goddammit! Is there a Benny around here somewhere please?"

There was no answering call from a Benny.

Farfalla leaned out of his office. "What is it, Garber?"

"Some eye-talian, sir. Speaking eye-talian," Garber said petulantly, as if the existence of a foreign language was an obstacle designed expressly to foil Corporal Nathan Garber. "And there's no Benny around to translate."

Farfalla picked up the phone and spoke in Italian. Then he listened for a moment or two, snatched a piece of paper from Garber's desk, and quickly scribbled an address. Garber had no ear for accents so he did not recognize the Italian Farfalla spoke as being heavily Sicilian. The man on the other end of the line, a *maresciallo* in the Carabinieri—an Italian cop—did. To the *maresciallo*, an Umbrian, Farfalla's accent was almost comically Sicilian, and he sounded like one of the slapstick comics he thought so funny when he was a child.

"Close the street and put men on the roof."

"Subito, tenente," said the *maresciallo*.

During the 11:00 P.M. to 7:00 A.M. curfew the close-packed Roman roofs became busy thoroughfares.

"Your officer must be there when I arrive."

"Certo, tenente."

Farfalla dropped the receiver onto the cradle, snatched up the piece of paper with the address, and pored over the giant map of the city pinned to the wall behind Garber's desk. The plan had been left behind by the Germans, so Farfalla traced a route along Viktor Emmanuel–Strasse, through a warren of streets to Navona-Platz and on to his destination.

"Hold the fort, Garber," he said, heading for the wide and stately staircase.

"Yessir," said Garber, already turning back to the radio and Axis Sally.

The motor pool outside the Insurance Company was surrounded by a barbed wire entanglement and guarded around the clock. The rule was that no vehicle could be left unguarded anywhere, at any time. All military vehicles had to be parked in one of the dozens of guarded lots scattered around the city. The official reason for this precaution was to prevent saboteurs and fifth columnists from planting bombs in them; in actual fact, there were no saboteurs, no fifth columnists.

Pfc Danny Salapska, the MP duty driver that night, was sure he knew the real reason for the regulation. The vehicles had to be guarded, he figured, to prevent the gindaloons from stealing them. The Romans, it seemed to him, would lift anything. The hordes of kids who thronged the streets were the worst. They could steal the watch off your wrist, your belt out of your pants, the socks off your feet, and you wouldn't notice.

As Farfalla emerged from the building, Salapska, who had been leaning against his jeep trying to stay as still as possible to avoid working up a sweat in the tremendous heat, quickly stubbed out his cigarette and rushed to meet his officer. He immediately started sweating.

"Calling it a night, sir?"

"Nope," said Farfalla.

Salapska was disappointed. If Sherlock the Wop had been going off duty then Salapska would have had a little freedom and a jeep. Not that he could have done much. He'd lost a big chunk of his pay that afternoon in a crap game in the MP billet, and he didn't have any of the black market goodies that would have bought him the attentions of a whore in one of the illegal but tolerated nightclubs which operated after curfew.

Still, he wouldn't have minded just cruising around the city in a jeep. The heat, even at that time of the night, was so oppressive that feeling the wind whip around him as he roared through the streets would have brought him some measure of relief. Salapska suffered terribly in the heat and could work up a sweat so powerful that it damn near drowned him. He was convinced that had he been drafted in August instead of February he could have been IV-F based solely on his extraordinary powers of perspiration.

He swung into the driver's seat. "Where to, Lieutenant?"

"I'll show you."

Salapska gunned the engine and waited while the guard dragged open the gate, pausing just long enough for a Benny to emerge from the shadows of the building and walk quickly to the passenger side of the jeep.

The Benny doffed his hat to Farfalla. "Good evening, Lieutenant," he said politely.

"Evening, Duke."

"I was wondering if you had need of me?"

Farfalla looked him over. The Duke was a Benny, and Bennies were the servants, interpreters, and spies hired by the Allied Military Government. None, as far as Farfalla knew, was actually called Begniamino, but because these men were slavish in their devotion to their new masters, answering every order no matter how trivial or demeaning, with a cheerful "va bene, va bene," the name had stuck to all of them.

"What do I need you for, Duke?"

"I know the city very well. I can help you reach your destination."

The Duke was an elderly man with close-cropped white hair and pale blue eyes, and he looked questioningly at Farfalla through silver wire-rimmed glasses. He carried himself straight backed, his shoulders squared, as if he had been an officer once himself, but he was dressed like an Edwardian dandy, fitted out, it seemed, for an afternoon promenade in Nice or Biarritz. He wore baggy white trousers and tight kidskin shoes, also a snowy white. His high-collared shirt was of the palest blue, and a narrow-striped silk tie was tightly knotted at his throat. He wore a double-breasted blue blazer with a fine gold pinstripe. His panama hat was old but well cared for.

The Duke spoke English clearly and with a faint British accent, French like a Parisian, and Italian like a Florentine. He was a Roman.

"I know where I'm going, Duke. Let's move, Salapska."

The driver slipped the jeep in gear and pulled out of the lot a little faster than he had to, the rushing wind on Salapska's damp skin bringing immediate relief.

Farfalla yelled directions as they roared through the streets. They made tight turns left and right, bouncing over rutted roads and shiny cobblestones until Salapska was sure they were lost. The beams from the narrow blackout slits on the jeep's headlights shot ahead of them, illuminating for a second or two the facades of the elegant old buildings, tumbledown apartment blocks and fragments of ruins. Salapska could not have found his way back to the Insurance Company if his life depended on it.

Farfalla shouted at him to make one more left. The jeep squeezed down a street hardly wider than an alley and into a fairly large square. Salapska knew they were there—wherever there was—because of all the meatball cops standing around. The policemen blinked in the beams of the jeep lights and one waved them to a halt with a kerosene lantern, as if signaling a train into a siding.

An officer stepped forward to greet Manny Farfalla. "Tenente?"

"Yes," said Farfalla. "Are you in command?"

"Ah," said the man, "you speak Italian."

"Si," said Farfalla. "E Lei? Chi è?"

"Scarfiotti, Luigi," said the young lieutenant. It was the Italian habit to report last names first when speaking officially. He snapped a smart salute at Farfalla, who returned it with a casual flick of his hand.

Manny noticed that the lieutenant was wearing several American decorations, among them a Purple Heart and a Bronze Star. The Carabinieri were some of the few Italian soldiers who had been allowed to fight alongside the Allies in Italy. Although they were a national police force, they were nominally under the command of the Italian army and had never been trusted by the Fascists. When the Nazis seized power in Italy, the upper ranks of the Carabinieri had been decimated—officers summarily shot and corpsmen shipped off to prisons and concentration camps. Men like Scarfiotti had come over to the Allies in droves, fighting their way up Italy in the Fifth Army advance. Now, however, police units were being taken out of combat and used for peacekeeping in the newly liberated towns.

"What have we got here?"

"A dead man," Scarfiotti said, "a black marketeer. No surprise."

Farfalla grunted. Everyone knew that the small Piazza Lancellotti, the square they were now standing in, was a center of the black market, as was the Via Tor di Nona, a narrow street a few hundred yards away.

"Let's take a look."

One of the policemen swung open the door of the nondescript apartment building and Scarfiotti motioned Farfalla ahead of him, like a headwaiter. The corporal with the lantern followed, and another man turned on the powerful beam of a U.S. Army flashlight. The only other illumination was an oil lamp which burned in front of a ceramic image of the Virgin high up on the wall of the building's dirty lobby.

Leaning over the banister of the steep stairs, peering down the stairwell like spectators at a play, were the inhabitants of the building. They were silent, watching, anxious, as if the first act was about to begin. Scarfiotti was watching too, carefully examining Farfalla, as if trying to commit his face to memory.

Manny was of medium height, slightly round-shouldered, and stooped. He had a pronounced hook nose, heavy-lidded eyes and deeply pock-marked skin. He was not a handsome man, Scarfiotti decided.

A few of the Italian policemen roughly shoved the tenants aside, clearing a path for the officers. The people allowed themselves to be manhandled, but they never took their eyes off Farfalla. For some of them, this was the first time they had seen one of their

36

conquerors up close. They drank in details: The well-cut uniform, good cloth. The good shoes. The pack of cigarettes bulging from his blouse pocket. These few general-issue items marked Farfalla as one of the rich liberators.

A policeman standing guard before a door on the second floor stood aside to let Farfalla pass. The apartment was a small one, made up of an irregularly shaped entrance hall, two small rooms, a makeshift kitchen, and a dingy bathroom. It was almost empty of furniture. There was a table scored along the edges with scorch marks where cigarettes had rested, a few bentwood chairs, and an armchair, the upholstery worn down to the stuffing. In the bedroom was a swaybacked iron bedstead, a bundle of gray sheets on a stained mattress. Hanging above it was a lurid rotogravure picture of Our Lady of the Seven Sorrows, a sword for each of the torments piercing the Virgin's heart. Her eyes were turned heavenward, as if she was silently asking her son why He allowed His mother to be subjected to such rough treatment. A dried sprig of olive branch, a souvenir of some long-ago Palm Sunday, made a brittle garland above the picture.

The corpse lay crumpled in the corner of the living room. Blood dripped from the man's right ear, slowly, as if from a broken faucet, and pooled on the dirty terra-cotta floor. He was a big man, with a layer of fat rising above his thick leather belt, the kind of corpulence you didn't often see in Rome, a city facing starvation. His clothes suggested a level of affluence higher than that of the average Roman. He had not been an elegant dresser, but his shirt was new and his cotton trousers showed no signs of wear. On his feet were a pair of British-issue army boots, the soles hardly scuffed.

Farfalla looked at the corpse and then nudged it slightly with the toe of his shoe, the way one might shove aside a dozing dog.

"Who was he?"

"He was called Falcone, Arturo," Scarfiotti said. "He was a small man in the black market."

"How do you know?"

Scarfiotti shrugged, a typically Roman gesture which suggested that the question was foolish, the answer obvious. "The police know about these things. We know who the criminals are, even if we can't prosecute them. It is the same in America, I think. Police work is the same everywhere."

Farfalla nodded shortly. Until he had been drafted two and a half years before, he had never had any contact with the police, except to ask directions and the couple of times he had paid them off when some of them came round to his father's liquor store looking for a little payola.

"It is known that he had dealings with the Germans when they were here, and now with the liberators, perhaps. Probably. It has only been a month, so we don't know much about his activities recently. The files have not been kept up-to-date." He sniffed dismissively. "He was a small man."

"If he was a small man, who are the big men?"

"There are several." Why, Scarfiotti wondered, did he have to deliver a lecture on the black market? Surely the Americans had files? Everyone knew who the masters were, even if they couldn't be caught. "Lorenzetti is the biggest. Vaccanni is another. In Trastevere there is Calvo, Mazzalupi . . ."

"And who did this guy work for?"

"The files say Lorenzetti. Most of them work for Lorenzetti."

Farfalla nodded and got down on one knee next to the body, as if he were about to propose. He gestured for a flashlight. Manny took Falcone's ear between his thumb and forefinger and folded it back. There was ugly bruising on the blunt ridge of bone behind the ear below the hairline, but it had not been caused by a blow. He looked into the ear and saw that a clot of blood had built up in the hole, although the monotonously regular dribble did manage to get through.

Farfalla stood up. "Tell me, tenente, how do you get so close to a man that you can stab him in the ear?"

Scarfiotti whispered, "Perhaps someone was telling him a secret."

"Did the neighbors hear anything?"

"They heard two men come up the stairs. They heard them talking. They heard one man leaving."

"Did they see anything?"

Scarfiotti smiled. "That's why you were called, Lieutenant. The man who left they say was an American officer."

"Who saw him?"

Scarfiotti turned to his sergeant. "Bring in the nonna."

An ancient woman, her face creased like old leather, was shoved into the room by a policeman. She glanced at Scarfiotti and Farfalla

38

but peered closely at the corpse, working her jaw for a moment or two as if building up a mouthful of spittle. Then she seemed to lose interest and shifted from the dead to the living, looking questioningly at Farfalla.

"Signora Dominichelli," said Scarfiotti, "there is nothing to be frightened of."

The old lady sat down and pinned back a stray wisp of hair that had escaped from her bun. She regarded Scarfiotti like a general who had just been insulted by a private. "Of course not. I have done nothing wrong."

"Signora," said Farfalla, "I understand that you—"

The old lady broke into a broad grin, but she hid her stained teeth behind a wrinkled hand. "Siciliano?" she asked. As if to emphasize her own proud Roman roots she slurred the *c*. *Sisheeliano*.

"Americano," said Farfalla.

"Ma parla com'un siciliano." You speak like a Sicilian.

Farfalla had no intention of being drawn into a discussion of his accent. "How do you know you saw an American officer leaving here tonight? Are you sure he was American?"

"Of course," she replied stoutly. "The Americans have won the war. First we had the Germans, now we have the Americans."

"But you also have the English, the Australians, French, Polish. How do you know you saw an American?"

"Boh," said Signora Dominichelli airily. "A me ci son' tutt'uguale." They are all the same to me. She paused for a moment, as if to consider her answer and add something of importance. "Do you have a cigarette?" she said after a moment.

Farfalla handed her a pack of Chesterfields. Her eyes glowed happily when she saw them. "Ahhh," she said happily, "O cessa fetta."

The Italians had slang names for all the American cigarettes. Camels were "the humped donkey"; Raleighs, "the bearded king"; Chesterfields, *O cessa fetta*, "the shithouse stinks."

Signora Dominichelli lit up and sucked the smoke deep into her lungs. She leaned forward and tapped Farfalla on the knee, treating him as if he were a wayward nephew paying a visit to her kitchen, rather than a foreign invader conducting a murder investigation.

"Dimmi, generale . . ."

"Tenente," corrected Farfalla.

Differences in rank made as much impression on her as differences in nationality. "Uguale . . . dimmi, when are you Americans going to send us some food?"

"I have nothing to do with that," said Farfalla curtly, "but I will give you something."

Signora Dominichelli's old eyes glittered. "Money?"

"No," said Farfalla, crossing to the shuttered window overlooking the street. "A book."

The old lady snorted in disgust. "A book?"

Manny yelled into the street. "Salapska, bring the book."

A few moments later Signora Dominichelli was paging through a loose-leaf binder, a dossier assembled by Farfalla in contravention of a dozen military regulations. Manny had investigated scores of cases in North Africa, Sicily, and Naples against American soldiers in which the witnesses had been locals. The trouble was that they couldn't tell an officer from an enlisted man, a North African Air Force sergeant from a subaltern in the Royal Engineers.

Farfalla had solved that problem neatly, if unofficially. He had swiped a camera from a signal corpsman and had photographed a variety of men of every rank and in all manner of Allied uniform. He concentrated on the Fifth Army. If he found a subject of lower rank than his own he simply walked up to him and said, "Time to have your picture taken, soldier."

The subjects struck martial or comic poses, or they just stood and grinned foolishly while Farfalla snapped away. Manny didn't care what they did as long as he got some good pictures of the badges and flashes on the uniform.

If Manny saw an officer of higher rank he either photographed him on the sly or asked to take his picture "for the folks back home." All over the Med, in Alex and Tobruk and Cairo and Messina, there were dozens of publicity-anxious officers paging through issues of *Yank* and *Life* and *The Saturday Evening Post* looking for their pictures.

Manny had quite a collection. Americans of every corps and rank, Ghurkas, Free French, Poles, British army, Navy, and RAF. As a joke, a private joke, Farfalla had included pictures of General Mark Clark, commander in chief of the Fifth Army, and General Alexander. "Just in case," he told Salapska solemnly.

The old lady turned the pages with great interest, smoking

cigarette after cigarette. She looked at every photograph in the book, sometimes for minutes at a time. She was enjoying herself, the center of attention on what had promised to be a long, hot, boring night. She peered closely at the picture of Mark Clark and declared that she had seen him somewhere, she just couldn't remember . . .

Scarfiotti was fed up with Signora Dominichelli. She was drawing this process out, playing with the American. Manny saw the ruse as well but was inclined to be patient. He knew that the longer he gave her, the better the chance of a precise ID.

"Yes," she said triumphantly, "I have seen that man before." She pointed at General Mark Clark's red Indian profile.

"Si, signora," said Scarfiotti. "You saw him in *Il Messagero*, the day after liberation." *Il Messagero* was the largest newspaper in Rome. Once it had been the house organ of Fascism. Now it was vociferously pro-ally.

"Of course," she said. "Now I remember." She smoked the last of Farfalla's cigarettes and realized, sadly, that the evening's entertainment was coming to an end. Hopefully she inquired if Farfalla didn't have some wine in his jeep and looked resentful when he said he did not.

"Ecco," she said finally. She poked a horned old fingernail at one of the pictures, denting it slightly. She sat back and exhaled mightily.

"You're sure?"

"Assolutamente."

Manny looked at the picture. It was a snap he had taken earlier that year on a dirty sidewalk in Naples. The young man was smiling broadly and giving the Churchillian V-for-victory symbol with both hands.

Farfalla pointed to the corps badge on the young man's shoulder.

"The same?"

"Si, generale."

"And this?" He pointed to the rank flash on his sleeve.

"The same."

Farfalla stood up and tucked the book under his arm. "Thank you, signora." He bowed slightly as he said it.

The old lady shrugged. "Boh," she said dismissively, "niente,

41

niente, generale." Scarfiotti told one of his men to show the old lady out.

"Was she of any help to you?"

"Yes."

"And now?"

"I'll find the American and have a little chat with him."

"Will it be so easy?"

"Yes."

"Is it always so simple?"

Farfalla nodded. "Yes it is, usually."

"Then you are very lucky," said Scarfiotti.

"No," Manny said, "they are usually very stupid."

"And what should be done with the body?"

There was little point in storing it in the morgue near the University of Rome. There were few American pathologists around, and the army courts paid no attention to the testimony of foreign doctors, no matter how expert. Besides, Farfalla knew that this was not a case that would be solved by science.

"NOK it," said Farfalla, speaking in English.

Scarfiotti looked puzzled. "What does that mean?"

"Send him back to his next of kin."

"And where shall I find them?"

Farfalla was heading for the door. "I'm sure you'll find something in your files, Lieutenant."

As Manny Farfalla guided Salapska out of the warren of streets, he thought about the old lady. She had been right on one count: the man she saw leaving the apartment had been an American soldier.

"Calling it a night, Lieutenant?" Salapska yelled over the engine and the rushing wind.

"Nope."

Shit, thought Salapska. "Back to the Insurance Company?"

"Yeah."

The old lady had been wrong about his being an officer, though. He was in the Quartermaster Corps. And he was a sergeant.

SERGEANT EDDIE MANGANARO walked slowly back to the jeep he had parked on the Via Zanardelli. He carried a musette bag containing three cartons of Old Golds, four dun-colored cans of what the army referred to as cheese, a pint of Long John whiskey, and an ice pick.

42

The cigarettes, cheese, and scotch were supposed to have been for Falcone. Instead, he got the ice pick driven firmly into his ear.

Not counting a number of Germans and Italians dispatched by Manganaro in Sicily using a variety of weapons, Falcone had been Manganaro's eighth murder. The Axis dead had earned Sergeant Manganaro a Bronze Star, the bar of that medal on his chest a detail that Signora Dominichelli failed to notice. The killing of Falcone had gained him nothing, except for the satisfaction of knowing that if you messed with Eddie Manganaro you ended up wishing you hadn't.

The other seven men Manganaro had killed had been soldiers too, in the gangster sense of the word, killed during the short, bloody war between Lucky Luciano and Sal Maranzano in 1931. Maranzano was dead, Luciano had served a stretch in Dannemora prison in upstate New York, and his faithful soldier, Eddie Manganaro, was alive, well, and serving his country in Rome, Italy. He was also very angry. The dumb guinea—Falcone—had screwed everything up. Manganaro stumbled down the dark streets looking for his jeep, cursing silently.

It was supposed to have been the start of a beautiful friendship. Manganaro was going to give Falcone the stuff he had in his musette bag, and in return Falcone was going to set it up that Manganaro met a guy named Lorenzetti, a guy that everyone said was Mr. Big in the Rome rackets. It was all going to work out perfectly. Falcone—a nobody, Manganaro saw that the moment he laid eyes on him—would get some goodies and he would also get in good with his boss for introducing him to Manganaro. If the right deal could be struck, then this Lorenzetti guy stood to get some very valuable merchandise that had once been the property of the United States Army. Manganaro would get a lot of money. Eddie wondered how anyone could argue with a deal like that.

Eddie now realized that he had things slightly wrong. Falcone had no intention of introducing the American to Lorenzetti. Falcone already had a very nice connection with a British supply sergeant, obtaining goods at very attractive prices—there was no reason to deal with the Americans. Besides, Falcone didn't trust them. The American government paid its soldiers too much money and gave them too much food and too many cigarettes; they always expected to make more money, to have things easier than anyone else. The British were poor, so they were happy to get what they could for their powdered eggs and a canned concoction called "meat and veg."

Manganaro had met Falcone in the dingy apartment as arranged and the American immediately started taking his merchandise out of the bag, arranging it on the table like a merchant dressing a window. When he had finished, he sat back and smiled.

"Not bad, huh?"

Falcone had been forced to admit to himself that the cigarettes and the whiskey—a drink he could not stand himself, but which would be worth a fortune on the *borsa nera*—were pretty good. What he didn't like was that Manganaro spoke good, if heavily accented, Italian. That meant that the American was not dependent on Falcone.

He also was offended by the cheese. It wasn't cheese at all. Cheese was rich and fragrant and came wrapped in straw or had a good hard rind. This American cheese came in a can; it was orange, smelled like paint, and tasted of nothing at all. Falcone's face had darkened when he examined the cheese, taking a bit of it, licking it off his big fingers. He was doing the right thing, he decided. He would frighten off the American, get rid of him somehow, take the whiskey and the cigarettes for himself, and give the cheese to his mother.

"What is this?" he asked, holding up the can of cheese.

"That's cheese," Manganaro said.

Falcone put the can down on the table. "Cheese?"

"Yeah, cheese." What? Hadn't this guy heard of cheese before?

"You stand to make a lot of money and you bring me this . . . *cheese?*" Falcone put the full weight of his indignation behind the word.

"Look, Falcone—" Manganaro felt his temper rising and he was doing his best to control it. "Falcone, paisan . . ."

"The whiskey, the cigarettes," Falcone said, "okay." It was a word he had learned recently and he found that it or its negative applied to almost every situation involving Americans. The cheese *non è okay.*"

Manganaro was beginning to lose it. "The hell with the cheese," he shouted. "Fuck the cheese. When do I get to meet your padrone?"

"When you think of something else to give me," said Falcone

evenly. "You go and try to think of a gift worthy of a man of respect."

"Who? *You?*"

"Si, io."

With great effort, Manganaro managed to control himself. "Look, Falcone, this is just the beginning. There's plenty of good stuff out there and believe me, you'll get your share. Believe me."

Falcone's eyes narrowed. "You say this is the beginning," he said portentously. "For you, maybe the end."

For a second, the Italian that Manganaro had spoken around the house with his mom and pop and the members of his extended family failed him.

"What the fuck is *that* supposed to mean?" he demanded in English.

Falcone didn't have to understand the language to get the meaning of the question. He smiled. "Maybe the Americans would like to know about you. There's an office, you know, in Piazza Santi Apostoli; you go there and tell them about Americans working on the black market. They give one hundred lire for every name." Falcone shrugged. "It's a lot of money today, one hundred lire."

"What? You crazy? You're as dirty as they come. What about your own skin, huh?"

"Ah," said Falcone, as if he were a skilled debater about to score a showy forensic point. "I am just a poor Italian trying to keep my family alive. You are an American soldier trying to sell stolen goods. I think maybe things would not be so good for you."

Fuck it, thought Manganaro. A guy like this couldn't be trusted. It was time to cut and run. "Hey, Falcone, paisan, don't turn me in, okay?" Manganaro did his best to sound like he was pleading.

The black marketeer shrugged and shook his head back and forth as if trying to decide what to do with poor Eddie Manganaro. "Maybe I won't," he said, secretly pleased to have humbled one of the arrogant Americans. "But you must make it worth my while. You have to give me some money. You give me some money and perhaps I won't say anything."

"I'll tell you what," said Manganaro, "I'll do better than that." He wore the relieved smile of the man who had cheated the hangman.

"Better than money?"

"Yeah, let me solve all your problems." He gestured for Falcone

45

to lean closer. "Listen," Manganaro hissed, as if about to impart a great confidence. Scarfiotti had been right.

Eddie got a look at his target. Falcone had a large, flat, fleshy ear. It looked like a hairy mushroom.

"You fuck!" Manganaro whipped the ice pick out of the bag and drove it deep into the center of the ear, the needle shaft following an easy route into the black marketeer's brain. Falcone looked very surprised for a moment and then died, tumbling out of the chair while Eddie held the handle of the weapon, yanking it out of Falcone's skewered brain as he fell. There was very little blood on the shaft. Eddie wiped it off on Falcone's dark trousers. Then he started stowing away the goods he had brought.

If Falcone had lived long enough to be amazed by Manganaro's astonishing aim with his lethal little weapon, then it was all the more proof that Falcone didn't know Eddie Manganaro. Manganaro had done the same thing to Joey Petrella in April 1931 and to a mobster named Buddy Linetti later that same year. Petrella had fallen for the "let me tell you a little secret" trick, but Linetti had been screaming and hollering in the back seat of a De Soto zooming along the Palisades Parkway. Despite his attempts to stop it, Linetti got the same unerring jab to the ear. The ice pick was Eddie Manganaro's thing.

He rounded the corner and found his jeep. Two MPs still wearing their olive drab helmets instead of the usual white—Rome was still considered a battle zone—were running the beams of their flashlights over the jeep, examining it nervously as if they were members of a bomb disposal unit and this was their first day on the job.

Manganaro's shoulders sagged a little when he saw them. It had been a terrible night already and MPs could only make it worse. But he needed his jeep and he was an old hand at handling the police. The harsh white beams of the flashlights rested on Eddie and he put his hands up to shield his eyes.

"You want to take the light out of my eyes, fellas? Can't see a thing."

They turned the lights to the ground. "This your jeep, Sergeant?"

"No, Corporal," said Manganaro smiling, "that ain't my jeep. That's the army's jeep. *My* jeep's in Brooklyn."

"A laugh riot," said one of the MPs. He snapped off his light and

46

rested a beefy fist on his hip. Manganaro came a few steps closer. Both cops were sweating heavily.

"You know you ain't supposed to leave a vehicle unattended," said the other MP. He was a corporal as well, but the younger of the two men. He spoke in a flat midwestern accent, and Manganaro could tell by the sound of his voice that he took his job very seriously. It was the older guy, Eddie decided, who would be more receptive to doing business.

Eddie looked contrite. "Yeah, I know . . ."

"I want your name, unit, and name of your immediate superior," said the kid as if he was reciting from the Uniform Code of Military Justice.

"Hey," said Manganaro to the older MP, "where'd you get the Boy Scout?"

"Shuttup, Sarge, don't make things harder on yourself."

"Hey look, I'm sorry, fellas. I was just kidding. Look, before you write me up, just let me tell you what's goin' on here."

"This'll be good," said the old guy.

"No, really. Listen, you guys."

"So, we're listening."

A carefully modulated note of sincerity crept into Eddie's voice. "It's like this. I had this pal, an Italian kid from Cleveland"—even Eddie said eye-talian—"and he got pasted down in the Liri Valley. All the poor fuck ever wanted to do was get to Rome and see his grandmother"—Eddie said "gran'mudda—"and his uncles and aunts and relatives and shit like that. He talked about it all the time. He never met his grandmother and it was like the kid's life's ambition, but like I said, he got greased down south."

The young MP had heard enough. "Look, sergeant—"

"Wait, lemme finish. So anyway, I'm Army Supply Force, right?" He slapped the badge on his shoulder. The MPs nodded. They had already noted the Quartermaster Corps wheel, key, and sword symbol.

"Yeah," said the young man, trying to sound hard-boiled, "so what?" The remark about the Boy Scout still stung; in fact, he had been a Boy Scout and was proud of it.

"Well, these people are fuckin' starving, right? So tonight when I come off duty I says 'What the hell' and zip over here to take some meat cans and shit to my pal's grandmother."

47

"What was this guy's name?"

"Buddy Linetti," said Eddie without missing a beat. "So anyway, the old lady asks me how her grandson is and I make up some bullshit about he had to bypass Rome and head up north but it ain't dangerous, because I figure why should I do the dirty work, let the army tell her the kid's dead already . . ." Manganaro shrugged. "So, if you want to write me up for that . . ."

The younger man looked suspicious. "If you're QMC, how come you were fighting? Most of you ASF guys are a hundred miles from the heat."

Manganaro looked indignant and slapped the ribbon on his chest. "You think I got the BS counting bedpans? I was Twenty-eight Infantry until I got jeep fanny. They bounced me up a stripe and into support. Now I got a scar on my ass six inches long, and I can't help it if I landed in supply. Can't blame a guy for that. Look," he said with a grin, "I'll show you the scar if it'll make any difference." He grabbed his belt buckle as if to undo it.

"You don't have to do that," said the kid.

"I thought the Twenty-eight was a Texas outfit," said the older cop.

"What? You never heard of replacement troops? Look, I know this was out of line, but shit fellas . . ." It was time to open negotiations and get rid of these two jokers. "Look, the old lady, the grandma, she don't smoke or drink and she's too old and stupid to figure out that smokes and booze is valuable here." He pulled the Long John from the bag. "So why don't you guys take it?"

"This a bribe, Sarge?" asked the older MP.

Manganaro smiled broadly. "Yeah, Corporal, it's a bribe."

The MP looked at the bottle, then at the former Boy Scout.

"Gus," said the kid, "I don't think we should get mixed up in—"

"C'mon, Gus," said Eddie, "you must be sick of that dago wine and that piss warm beer. Am I right?"

Indeed Gus was. "Oh the hell with it," he said. Scotch was a rare commodity for anyone but officers, and Gus had heard rumors that his unit was headed north for traffic direction duties at the front. A little scotch would be a welcome companion under fire. Gus grabbed the bottle. "Get the fuck out of here, Sarge."

"I knew you'd see it my way." Manganaro slung himself into the driver's seat of the jeep. He gunned the engine, pulled a wide U-turn and roared away. Every time the rough-sprung vehicle bounced on the cobblestones Eddie gave a little yelp of pain. His pilonidal cyst—a complaint known as jeep fanny—still hadn't healed.

3

The Duke was not a duke; he was a count. As Il Conte Sanseverio, he held a name that was old, if not particularly distinguished and, as counts go, of lesser rank than the great families of Rome; the Colonna, the Orsini, the Doria, and the Massimi. But until quite recently, Count Camillo Sanseverio had been accorded his measure of respect by the title-conscious Romans. He, for one, however, continued to bear his family name with pride and he was deeply offended when the gum-chewing American lieutenant who had hired him as a Benny said, "Oh. A count. Like Dracula, you mean."

There had been a time when such a remark would have made Camillo Sanseverio turn on his heel and walk away. But Il Conte desperately needed a job, as he, Camillo Sanseverio, papal Gonfaloniere, Barone di Sutri, Cup Bearer to the Camera Apostolica, Cavaliere d'Onore, was broke. So when the lieutenant made his little joke, Camillo did his best to raise a smile.

"The same title," he said, trying to keep his voice light, "but no relation, of course."

There had been money in the family once, a great deal. But Camillo's father had invested heavily during the building boom which had seized Rome in the 1870s. Large areas in the southern part of the city had been overbuilt with apartment blocks in which few people wanted to live. By the time the old count discovered the market was nonexistent, he found his fortune was as well. His only consolation in the fiasco was that a far greater family than his, the Borghese, had suffered immense, almost crippling losses.

The financial blow had been a hard one to endure, but the social bankruptcy had been cushioned by the Borgheses' losses—to be tarred with the same brush as that illustrious name mitigated the disgrace—so Camillo was able to make a good marriage in terms of bloodline. His wife, the Countess Beatrice—Baba, as she had been known—was the daughter of a landowning baron of Tuscan stock, and while she had been pretty and gracious, she had little in the way of dowry; the land had gone, in the main, to her brother. Baba died of influenza in the great epidemic of 1919, leaving Camillo and their only son, Alessandro, to inhabit the Palazzo Sanseverio in Piazza Margana. They did have a few servants.

It was Alessandro who had been meant to restore the family fortunes, and he had been doing his job quite well as a banker. In 1931 he married, for love, the daughter of a middle-class wine merchant of Italian origin, but long based in Paris. Gabrielle, Camillo's daughter-in-law, considered herself French.

In 1937 Alessandro had been dismissed from his post at the Banca di Agricultura for anti-Fascist activities. He was allowed to retire in peace to his home, but a year later, in 1938, he was unexpectedly arrested and sent as a *confino* in internal exile to a remote town in Basilicata, a region in the far south of the country. There he remained until the fall of 1943 when the Germans took over the country. Sandro was transferred to the Forte Bravetta near Rome. With liberation he had been released, quite literally, a broken man.

At half past five that hot July morning, Camillo Sanseverio made ready to leave the Insurance Company. He had been at work since seven the evening before and had been scheduled to go off duty at 3:00 A.M. But the Americans paid a man for the number of hours he was on duty rather than for the amount of work he actually accomplished. Each day became a trial by ordeal—how many hours of labor, or simple wakefulness, could Camillo's seventy-year-old body endure before he had to give in to fatigue? The Americans also paid something called "overtime" which could increase his earnings dramatically.

The most disconcerting thing about his job was the constant shifting in hours. Sometimes he worked days, and then, abruptly, he would be scheduled for long nights. He was constantly kept off balance, out of kilter.

At three that morning he was sure he could stand no more. His

51

shift was done. Overtime would have to wait for another day, when he was feeling stronger. Just as he was preparing to leave, though, Captain Goodyear thrust a batch of papers into his hand.

"Duke!" the captain yelled—Goodyear always seemed to yell—"I want you on this. The other Bennys can't write English worth a damn."

Like it or not, Camillo would earn some overtime that night. He looked wearily at the papers the captain had dumped on his desk. They were unevenly typed, in English, and hastily corrected in a scrawled hand. It was the latest list of price controls, this one concerning fresh produce, and while it carried the signature of the mayor of Rome, Prince Filippo Doria Pamphili, it was obvious that the orders came from Colonel Poletti's office. Charles Poletti was the head of the Allied Military Government in Rome, the absolute ruler of the city. He had installed the popular and impeccably anti-Fascist Prince Doria as mayor, but everyone knew that it was Poletti who governed.

The Duke smoothed out the rumpled papers and began to translate, writing out a list of vegetable prices in his precise hand. At his feet, stretched out on the cool marble floor, an American sergeant snored. It was so hot in Rome that summer that every American seemed to prefer sleeping on hard, cold marble than in a comfortable bed. The Duke would come upon sleeping soldiers in the most peculiar places: in every corner of the Insurance Company, particularly in the wide portico in the front of the building, slumped under the arches of the church of San Marco, in the courtyard of the Palazzo Bonaparte on the far side of the square.

He worked his way down the list. His English, learned from an extremely English nanny before the turn of the century, was excellent, but the names of the vegetables taxed his skills. There had been very little talk of spinach and carrots in the salons he had frequented in London and in the British-owned villas surrounding Florence. In those far-off days—he found it hard to believe now that they had ever existed—the talk had always been of art and opera, music and theatre, horses, gossip, hunting.

And Camillo was so tired. For a moment he fell asleep at his desk, pulling himself back to weary consciousness just before his head came to rest among the papers. His eyes blurred, and he had to take off his glasses and rub his eyes vigorously. There were dark red tear-shaped welts on either side of his nose where his spectacles rested.

Every fifteen minutes, Captain Goodyear appeared and shouted, "Finished yet, Duke?"

"Not yet, Captain."

"C'mon Duke. I gotta get that thing out."

Goodyear's voice echoed through the building—he had only been on duty since midnight and was still in fine voice. Every time he shouted, the sergeant under Camillo's desk shifted and almost came back to consciousness. Once he had opened one eye and hissed, "Oh for Chrissake . . ."

The Duke pinched the bridge of his nose and then forced himself to concentrate again. Cucumbers were . . . *cetrioli*. They were now priced at ten lire a kilo wholesale, twelve to dealers, and thirteen to the general public. Citrus fruits—*agrumi*—were forty-six lire a kilo wholesale, forty-eight to dealers and fifty retail. The Duke sighed. Why did they bother? There were no lemons or oranges in Rome, not on the open market anyway. If you wanted *agrumi* you had to shop on the black market and pay thirty lire each, never mind by the kilo.

But Camillo labored on, finally finishing the last line: *Per ordine Sindaco di Roma, F. A. Doria Pamphili*. The Duke thought sadly that he had once had a nodding acquaintance with Prince Filippo; he used to see him often at the Cìrcolo della Caccia, but Camillo had long since let lapse his membership in Rome's most exclusive club. He noticed that Filippo Doria Pamphili had tipped his hat to the new democratic age by leaving his princely title off his orders. Perhaps, after the war, there would be no titles, no aristocracy, papal or royal. It didn't really matter to Camillo. He knew the Sanseverio line would die with his son.

Goodyear glanced at the translation when the Duke laid it on his desk.

"Can you read my writing, Captain? I am unable to type, so . . ."

"Great, Duke," shouted the captain unhappily, "just great. Now I'm going to have to get someone to type this thing."

"I apologize, Captain."

"Aww, forget it," said Goodyear without looking up. "What's this word?"

"Ortofrutticolo," said the Duke very slowly.

"Wait a minute, wait a minute. How do you spell that?"

The Duke spelled the word for Captain Goodyear, and as he did he reflected that something very strange had happened in his life. It had never occurred to him, never in his wildest dreams, that he would one day spend hours in the depths of the night discussing the price of fruits and vegetables with an officer of an occupying army. It was not the sort of thing he had been bred to. But then, what had he been meant to do with his life? To hunt, to play cards, to chatter with other members of his class, to be an officer himself, but an officer of an army that was never meant to fight a war. A useless life, really.

Goodyear wrote *ortofrutticolo* out in large block letters. It seemed to Camillo that the captain was not well acquainted with the act of writing. It was almost as if he had to hold his pen with both hands, the tip of his tongue showing between his lips, a schoolboy look of concentration on his face. For a moment, Camillo could see beyond the captain's rank and uniform and noticed that, indeed, Goodyear was little more than a schoolboy, a young man, with the schoolroom not many years behind him, now a conqueror.

"Screwy language, huh, Duke?" he yelled when he had finished laboring over the unfamiliar word. "Beats the hell out of me how you guys speak it."

The Duke managed a smile. "We speak it often at home."

"Yeah, I guess so," said Goodyear, wondering if the old Benny was making fun of him. "Dis-mis, Duke."

Camillo, Conte Sanseverio, bowed stiffly from the waist. "Good-night, Captain."

"G'night, Duke," shouted Goodyear.

Trembling now with fatigue, Camillo made his way down the wide flight of stairs, picking his way through the mounds of sleeping privates and NCOs sprawled on the landings. In those minutes before dawn the Insurance Company slowed down. Work still went on, listlessly, in a few brightly lit rooms, like a slow pulse, just enough to keep a sleeping body alive. A typewriter clacked somewhere, but without the early evening brio, and a phone rang again and again until an unhappy, sleepy voice answered it. The Duke listened a moment. "How the hell should I know, pal, *you* figure it out." Then came the sound of a telephone receiver clattering down.

It had always struck Camillo that the Americans had two voices. One was perpetually angry, stern and unforgiving. The other was exuberant and playful, "kidding," they called it, or "joshing." The playful voice was a pleasant one, the kind of voice a puppy might have, if a puppy could speak; the angry voice was harsh, like the bark of a no-nonsense watch dog. There was no middle ground in the voice of the American military.

The Americans had none of the extremely proper, cold, *politesse* of the Germans. Camillo remembered the German SS lieutenant who had been so apologetic, hoping that "il Conte"—titles still carried a lot of weight with the Germans—had not been upset by Signora di Porto's weeping.

The di Portos—an ancient Roman Jewish name—had lived in the palazzo next to Camillo's, on the edge of the ghetto. He had arrived home in the gray light of an autumn evening in 1943—he had spent the day searching for coal and had found none—in time to see Signora di Porto and her daughter being hustled into a truck. Leone di Porto, the signora's son, lay in a puddle of his own blood, shot while resisting arrest. Alonzo di Porto, Signora di Porto's husband, once a very important jeweler in Rome, had long ago been taken away.

Alonzo di Porto flashed through Camillo's mind. Gabrielle's engagement ring had been chosen out of a tray at di Porto's luxurious shop on the Piazza di Spagna. Camillo remembered that the ring had been costly, but by no means the most expensive, and yet di Porto himself had emerged from his office to handle the transaction personally, fawning and flattering, not because he needed the Sanseverios' custom, but as a neighborly gesture, something that would restore a bit of Camillo's lost pride. Di Porto was much richer than any Sanseverio had ever been.

When Signora di Porto had been taken and her son killed, Camillo had assured the SS officer that the scene had not upset him, treating abduction and murder as if it had been a minor breach of etiquette, like a waiter spilling the soup. The lieutenant saluted and clicked his heels, just as the gallant officers did in the German films so popular in Rome at the time.

Once Camillo was upstairs, in the cold, ornate salone, he realized, to his shame, that he had acted like a coward. He should have said something, shouted, protested. But he hadn't. He had let

Signora di Porto go to her death not knowing that he . . . Alessandro would have said something.

It was about that time that Alessandro had been transferred from Basilicata to Forte Bravetta.

The British were, as Camillo expected, reserved. Shortly after the liberation, Camillo had found a British major wandering in the thicket of streets of the Campo Marzio. Plainly, he was lost.

Camillo had volunteered. "Perhaps I may be of some assistance."

"Pantheon," the major had said in a voice that Camillo had heard before. It was the voice of the British upper classes, a tone reserved for Indians and Babus and blacks, the people of the Empire known collectively as wogs. Camillo had given the officer directions, hesitated a moment, and then said, "Before the war I knew a Lord de Sayles extremely well."

The major, in peacetime a solicitor in the provincial town of Aylesbury, had never heard of Lord de Sayles—not that he should have. De Sayles was an English lord with a lot of money, a tendency toward Catholicism and because of that, a taste for such unfashionable baroque painters as Ricciolini, Nessi, and Reni. But the British major viewed with suspicion and distaste any eyetie who claimed friendship with a member of the British aristocracy. The major wondered if this was not some new and rather abstruse way for the little dago to suggest an assignation with a *segnorina* of his acquaintance.

The major's eyes had flicked over Camillo's threadbare but correct clothing. "Did you? Lord de Sayles, eh? Jolly good." Then he had walked away.

The Duke had sighed. If he could get in touch with Quinnie, as Lord de Sayles had been known, he was sure that he would help him. But Camillo had no idea where his friend was or even if he was still alive. He had not seen de Sayles since 1937. . . .

THE WARRANT OFFICER on duty at the main desk of the Insurance Company was a big, red-faced man named Haley. Of all the soldiers who worked at the AMG headquarters, Haley was the Duke's favorite. He knew him to be a good-hearted man.

Haley had just come on duty and he smelled of shaving soap and bay rum, a clean, American smell, the Duke always thought. The big warrant officer had two electric fans trained on his desk, but there were already dark darts of sweat staining his shirt, running down from his broad shoulders towards his belt, like suspenders.

"Mornin' Duke," said Haley.

"Good morning, Mr. Haley." Warrant officers were always called mister.

Haley was sipping coffee from a tin mug. It was black and watery American coffee, not at all like the thick, dark, invigorating brew Italians love so much. But it was real coffee, not the mixture of barley, acorns, and ersatz coffee syrup from Germany that Italians had been forced to endure since the beginning of the war. The aroma of Haley's coffee was intoxicating—real coffee was an unheard of luxury in Rome, far more rare than the citrus fruits the Duke had spent the night pricing. In the back of his mind, Camillo heard the voice of his English governess, Miss McNutt. He heard her voice clearly, though she had left the employ of his family fifty years before and had been dead for thirty. "Don't stare, Camillo," said Miss McNutt, "it's not good manners."

But Camillo was staring, staring at the velvet black coffee in Haley's cup. The soldier noticed and smiled. "Hey, Duke"—in common with most Americans, Haley said "dook"—"you want a cup?"

Count Camillo Sanseverio dearly wanted a cup of real coffee but breeding required that he not seem overanxious. "If it would not be too much trouble . . . perhaps, yes, I will have a cup of coffee, Mr. Haley."

"Fuck no. No trouble." Haley had a two-pint thermos of coffee on his desk. He grabbed a mug from the desk behind his and slapped it down in front of Camillo, like a bartender in the western films Camillo had taken Sandro to see when he was a boy.

"Sully won't be in till oh six hundred. You can use his cup." He poured the coffee into the mug. "Drink up."

Camillo put the cup to his lips and sipped. There was no sugar in the coffee but it tasted wonderful, and he savored it like a connoisseur sampling a rare vintage from a great cellar. It was not Italian coffee, but it tasted of plenty and hope and of a future happier than the past.

Haley looked out into the piazza. Olive drab mounds, sleeping soldiers, lay strewn about like corpses. It was growing light.

"Gonna be a scorcher, huh, Duke?" He gulped down some coffee and grined. "Helluva thing. Hotter'n hell in this town and here we are drinking hot coffee." Haley slugged back some more. "But you know how it is, I just can't get started in the morning without a couple of cups of java."

"Java?" said the Duke.

"Yeah, you know, java. That's what we call coffee. Like the song. 'I love coffee, I love tea, I love the java jive and it loves me . . .' " Haley sang tunelessly. "It's a song."

"Yes," said the Duke, "of course."

"Yep. Gotta have java in the morning. Gets your motor running."

Motor running, thought the Duke. It was obviously a slang term meaning to get started, to be able to face the day. "It is the Italian habit also," he said. "Italians drink a great deal of coffee, or at least they did before the war."

Haley poured his coffee down his throat, the action of a man who has never known scarcity. Camillo sipped at his as if it was communion wine.

"Yeah," said the big American, his gaze returning to the piazza, "I hear there ain't too much of anything around these days. It's a damn shame too, you know, Duke? You guys just shouldna got mixed up with Musso and the krauts. It was a mistake and now you gotta take the rap."

"The rap?"

"The blame."

"The rap," Camillo repeated, committing the word and its meaning to memory. He was an avid collector of Americanisms, hoarding slang terms and expressions like an anthropologist studying a remote and primitive tribe. Sometimes when Sandro was awake and feeling up to it, Camillo would entertain him with the words and phrases he had learned. Now he had "java," "get your motor running," and "the rap" to add to "hep," "cool," "in the ball park," "chewing the fat," and a host of others.

Haley topped off their cups. "Yep, you shoulda stayed away from Musso," he said sadly. "I like you guys."

"It was unfortunate," said the Duke. "My son . . ." Camillo felt the fatigue and the unaccustomed luxury of the coffee, and he grew talkative.

"How many kids you got, Duke?"

"Just one. My son."

"That's great," he said, his red face beaming. "Me, I got six. All boys. Dave, Wally, Bill, Jim, Pete, and Steve." He took another gulp of his coffee. "Me, I'm regular army," he said, as if that explained his astonishing ability to produce sons.

"You must be very proud," said Camillo. He had decided that he would not mention that his only son had been imprisoned and tortured for trying to stop his countrymen from getting mixed up with Musso.

"You bet I'm proud," said Haley, as if challenging any man to say different. "And let me tell you something, Duke, every god-damn one of 'em is going to college. They ain't gonna end up ignorant dogfaces like their old man. No sir. They're gonna make something out of their life, be a doctor, lawyer, something like that."

College, the Duke already knew, was what Americans called university. He also knew that they had an almost mystical faith in education.

Haley drained his cup. "Well, Duke. Gotta fight the war." He pulled Camillo's time card out of a file on his desk and glanced at it. "Lessee, you come on yesterday at nineteen hundred and you're heading out at"—he glanced at his watch—"oh five forty-five. Pulling some overtime, huh Duke? Hell, I'll put you down for a full twelve hours on the job. It won't kill the paymaster to shell out for an extra hour and a quarter." He signed off on the card and thrust it back into the file.

The Duke was moved, so touched that he failed to notice the term "shell out" as a synonym for payment. A lump came to his throat.

"You are a good man, Mr. Haley."

Haley laughed, deep and hearty, the laugh of a happy man. "Hell, Duke. It ain't *my* money."

Camillo Sanseverio walked home very slowly. The curfew had been lifted, and the Romans who had been shut up in their steam-ing flats all night were now streaming into the streets. The women gathered at the few functioning fountains to get water or stood in lines at the food distribution centers. The children—there were no schools functioning—were just setting out for another day of roaming the city, shining shoes, or pimping, or simply begging for money, cigarettes, gum—something one chewed simply for the sake of chewing, a process which mystified Camillo. The few men who had jobs would go to them. The rest would gather on the

59

shady sides of the piazzas, shifting with the shadows, and argue and complain, about the king, about Badoglio, about the Germans, the Fascists, the Americans, the war.

Palazzo Sanseverio was in the Piazza Margana, near the ghetto and not far from the Insurance Company. It was a small palace as palaces went, made up of some three dozen rooms distributed over four floors. It had been built in the early seventeenth century by the first count, a gentleman also named Camillo, who had held some obscure but extremely lucrative post in the Papal Chancery. He had sold his office—the laws of simony did not apply to lay officeholders—and had had himself ennobled during the pontificate of Innocent IX, one of the few lasting achievements of a reign that had spanned just sixty days.

Just visible on the façade of the palazzo was a faint black and white mural depicting events in the life of Scipio Africanus, an ancestor the first count claimed, without any evidence, as the founder of the family. Baedecker's *Rome* judged the Palazzo Sanseverio "characteristic of its time, but of small architectural distinction." The guidebook did admit, grudgingly, that the ceiling of the *gran salone,* painted by the artist Francesco Albani (Castor and Pollux watering their horses at the Spring of Juturna) was "fine." The book concluded its brief entry with: "Application to view the *salone* and a small collection of pictures must be made, in writing, to the owners." Quinnie De Sayles had made application and so was born Camillo's great friendship with the English nobleman. When he had seen the fresco on the ceiling of the salon, he had exclaimed, in a voice heavily weighted with Eton, Oxford, and homosexuality, *"Magnifico! Veramente magnifico, mio caro Camillo!"*

From the pocket of his jacket, Camillo Sanseverio produced the key to the Judas gate, the tiny door scarcely large enough to admit a man, set within the greater gate of the palazzo. The key had weighted down his pocket all night, as if he had been carrying a revolver. The key was huge and black wrought iron and looked like the key clutched in the stone hands of St. Peter in the statues of the saint scattered around the city. It turned the ancient lock eight times before sliding back the bolt.

There had been a time when the porter or his wife would have come scurrying from their little apartment just inside the door. But they, along with the other servants, were long gone.

Camillo climbed the long wide stairs to the *piano nobile* and wearily removed his jacket. He mopped his brow and sat down heavily in one of the gigantic gilded *saloni* and stared out of habit at the Albani fresco on the ceiling. The two figures of Castor and Pollux looked strong, young, and virile; their majestic mounts were powerful, hot-blooded, and impatient; a few Roman maidens, fleshy, graceful, and coy, peeked out at the twins. Camillo had come to hate the pretty picture: it mocked him, the pretensions of his family, and his own humiliating circumstances. He wished there was some way of getting the damn thing off the ceiling and selling it to Lord de Sayles.

Camillo closed his eyes. In half sleep he heard the clicking footsteps of his daughter-in-law as she made her way along the long gallery to the stairs. He could imagine her walking with her basket on her arm, going out for food for her family like a good simple woman from Testaccio or Trastevere. But his daughter-in-law was a *baronessa*, his son a *barone*, and her menial tasks, like Camillo's own, were made more degrading by the condition of noble birth.

Camillo, Count Sanseverio, thought of the goodness of Mr. Haley, the pain of his son, the humiliation of his daughter-in-law and snuffled a bit, holding back a tear of self-pity. Then, slowly, he fell asleep in the chair, slack-jawed and old, snoring slightly beneath his fine fresco.

4

Their paths had crossed and recrossed in the eleven days it had taken to fly to Rome. Major John Howe had first seen the young lieutenant on a foggy morning at an American air base, Polebrook in the north of England. The young man—Howe guessed that he could not have been more than twenty-three—had been just one of a dozen officers and a single Pfc standing on the runway hardstand waiting for the morning mist to burn off. It was far too early in the day for conversation—they were all strangers to one another anyway—so they stood in awkward silence, doing nothing or, like Howe, reading. His book was Stendhal's *Rome, Naples, and Florence*, a title which mystified him as he was two hundred pages into it and Stendhal had yet to progress beyond Milan.

The most noticeable thing about the young lieutenant, apart from his superbly cut uniform, was that he left the group for a moment and returned with a mug of coffee. He drank it impervious to the envious stares of the other men and, when finished, handed the empty cup to a passing Air Transport Service mechanic as if the airman was a waiter and the lieutenant a guest at a cocktail party.

There was a dreary three-day wait in Gibraltar, and Howe spent his time writing a lengthy letter to his wife and worrying about his son, who was somewhere in the Pacific with the navy. When Howe was notified that the next leg of his journey was about to begin, he found that all of his original companions from England had disappeared, except for the Pfc. Even he vanished at Oran, the next stop, but after a five-day layover, the elegant lieutenant reappeared and traveled with Howe to Algiers, then Bizerte and on to Messina. There was no sign of the lieutenant on the plane ride from Messina to Naples, but he did materialize for the final leg, the flight from Naples to Rome. The major and the lieutenant never exchanged a word.

As the bruised Dakota gradually lost altitude coming in for a rattling landing at the military field at Salaria near Rome, Major Howe twisted on his hard bench seat to see if he could catch a glimpse of the city from the air. He had hoped to see the dome of St. Peter's or the Colosseum, but all he managed to catch sight of was a sliver of ochre-colored city slipping away under the wing of the plane. Then, with a juddering thump, they were on the ground.

A green and black Rome city bus driven by an American soldier ferried the passengers to the center of town. The major was disappointed with his first sight of Rome. The outskirts were drab, a procession of grim apartment blocks punctuated here and there with tatty-looking public buildings built in the overblown Fascist style. In order to keep the main northbound road open, the bus circled the city, approaching from the south and thus affording Major Howe a view of the Colosseum. He was reassured: it was as grand and as glorious as he always imagined it would be.

A few moments later the bus passed the white marble bulk of the Monument to Victor Emanuel and stopped in front of AMG Headquarters.

"Insurance Company," shouted the driver, "last stop."

The new proconsuls of the city of Rome clustered around the main desk of the Insurance Company. Warrant Officer Haley, with a noncom's eagle eye for rank, spotted the gold oak leaves on Howe's shoulders, passed a quick and practiced eye over the other new arrivals, determined that Howe outweighed everybody else, and dealt with him first. He reached past the proffered orders of a captain and took a sheaf of papers from Howe's hand.

"Welcome to Rome, major."

"Thank you, Mr.—"

"Haley, sir."

As Haley thumbed through the orders, Howe mopped his brow with a handkerchief.

"A real scorcher today, sir. But you'll get used to it." Haley looked at the orders carefully. So, he thought, this was Howe,

Major John C., Office of the Army Judge Advocate General. The law had come to town at last. It would please Sherlock the Wop, and Haley made a mental note to tell him. He consulted his assignment book.

"Okay, Major Howe, we got a nice room for you over at the Excelsior Hotel. There's a jeep and a driver outside'll take you up there." Haley slammed a rubber stamp down on Howe's orders. "Enjoy your stay."

"Just one thing," said Howe.

"Yessir?"

"Where is my office?"

Haley noted that Howe had a slight southern accent. "Second floor of this building sir. Next to the CID station. But there ain't nobody up there, sir. I mean, there's a corporal, clerk-typist, but you're the first JAG officer to show up, and mostly he's been sitting on his . . . seeing the sights. Name of Malinsky." Haley mentally added that Malinsky was a snotty, difficult pain in the ass. "Prob'ly better you go to the hotel first, sir."

"There's no hurry?"

Haley smiled. "No, sir, everything under control." Haley wanted to say, hey, relax, the war's over, for us anyway . . .

"C'mon," muttered the tired, sweaty captain behind Howe.

"Please tell the corporal that I have arrived."

"Will do, Major. Welcome to Rome, Captain . . ."

A few minutes later, Howe found himself in a luxurious suite at the Excelsior Hotel. On the Louis Quatorze writing table were a bottle of Dimple Haig, a basket of fruit, an ice bucket, and an invitation to attend a reception that evening at the Palazzo Barberini. His hosts were Colonel Charles Poletti and Prince Filippo Doria Pamphili. It was now just after ten o'clock in the morning and Howe wondered what he should do next; he wondered, in fact, what he was doing here in the first place, in Rome, in the army for that matter. He was fifty-six years old, in civilian life an attorney with the prospect of a judgeship in the next year or so. He knew nothing about the military, but he was fastidious and conscientious, so he decided to bathe, put on a fresh uniform, and then seek out Corporal Malinsky. It wasn't much of a contribution to the war effort, but it was all he could think to do.

Lieutenant Austin Kinney, the young lieutenant on Howe's journey from England, was also quartered at the Excelsior Hotel, but he had not been assigned a splendid suite. Rather, as befitted his rank, Kinney had been given a small room high up under the eaves. It was very hot, the bed was narrow and lumpy, and he shared a bathroom, down the hall, with a dozen other young officers. Austin Kinney was used to better things, even in the army. He had no hesitation about what to do next. He was going to get his billet changed.

The elevators were filled with majors and colonels, including, Kinney noticed, the studious-looking old guy who had been on the plane. The other officers in the paneled lift were not new arrivals, and they flaunted their knowledge of the city and its customs in loud voices, showing the greenhorns among them that they knew the lay of the land.

"I found a guy giving one sixty-five to the dollar," said a jowly major.

A companion, also a major, one-upped. "Hell, yesterday I found a guy offering one seventy."

A colonel at the back of the elevator trumped, "Christ, my guy gives one seventy *and* he took a check."

The three men laughed heartily. They were plainly enjoying their war. Listening to them, Austin Kinney had the feeling that Rome just might be the place for him.

Kinney had been born to great wealth, but as he was currently on the outs with his father, Lex Kinney, a well-known finance man in New York, Austin had been forced, temporarily, to make his own way in the world. The war, the army of the United States of America, and his lowly position in both, had not cured Austin of his well-accustomed desire for the good life. He could not buy rank, but he could buy the trappings of rank—and that he did.

There was something about Lieutenant Austin Kinney that made other lieutenants and even newly minted captains think that they ought to salute him. Often, Kinney's elegant form had swept past, leaving a lieutenant of artillery or cavalry staring after him, his right arm half-cocked, midway in a snap to the forehead. It was the cut and cloth of Kinney's uniform that caused the confusion. His clothes were not army issue but had been made for him by a tailor on Cork Street in London, the material, fine wools, cottons, and gabardines provided by Kinney, spoils of his carefully manipulated position as a requisition and supply officer at an Eighth Army base in Huddersfield in the north of England.

Kinney had not been liked in Huddersfield, not by his immediate superiors nor the men under his command, but that hadn't bothered him. He found that he was popular with attractive, unfettered women and with senior officers, two sections of the population important in time of war, agents of preferment more powerful than an Academy ring or a Silver Star. Heroes and West Point shavetails were out getting shot at, while Kinney—undistinguished Austin Kinney—was weekending at the Connaught and dining at the Ritz Grill and Boulestin's.

England was far behind him now, though, but that didn't bother him. London was drab and tired after five years of war and, alarmingly, a young woman of his acquaintance had been dropping uncomfortably broad hints about marriage. It had been with some relief that he had assumed a sad and wistful look, told her that duty called, and took the first plane out.

In the lobby of the Excelsior, surrounded by well-tailored army brass, Kinney didn't stand out as much as he did in dour, damp Huddersfield, but the Italian concierge at the reception desk took in the cut of the uniform and Kinney's manner and recognized him as a man worth cultivating. The concierge was as attentive to the lieutenant as he would have been to a lieutenant colonel.

"I can help you, sir?"

"I'd like to speak to the officer in charge."

"Captain Slade is very busy, sir. Perhaps I—"

"Please tell me where I can find him."

The concierge knew what this was all about. The lieutenant did not like his room. Lieutenants never liked their rooms. Unfortunately, there was nothing he could do for the young man. Captain Slade kept the choice rooms under his control, and a sudden change in the lieutenant's billet would be noticed.

"Change money," said the concierge in a low voice. "I give one hundred sixty lire for the dollar. Cash."

"How about one eighty and by check," responded Kinney.

The concierge looked at the young man with respect. He was not one of those Americans in Rome fat and ready for the slaughter. "One hundred seventy-five."

"Take a check?"

"One hundred eighty for cash."

Kinney nodded. "Deal."

"How much cash?"

"One hundred dollars."

"I will come to your room."

"I might be changing my room. I want to see this Captain Slade."

The concierge sighed. The lieutenant would not be changing his room, but there was no harm in his seeing Captain Slade. The captain was not as busy as he pretended to be.

"Who the hell are you?" Slade demanded when Kinney walked into his office. Slade was pale and balding and had a slope of fat hanging over his belt. By middle age he would be very fat. He was an accountant by trade, a job which in no way qualified him to run a first-class hotel—the Army did not expect the Excelsior to turn a profit, and that was the the only skill Slade knew. The staff, who had run the hotel faultlessly under the Germans, though, now continued to do the same under Slade and the Americans.

Kinney saluted smartly. "Kinney, sir."

Slade pushed his chair back from his desk and looked at his visitor.

"Kinney," he said, as if tasting the word. "Austin Kinney."

"Have we met before, Captain?"

"Nope. But I've heard of you. A friend of mine used to get his cigars from a fellow who got them from you."

"That a fact?" Kinney settled himself on the edge of Slade's desk and slipped a silver cigarette case out of his breast pocket. He offered one to Slade, who took it and lit up.

"That's a fact, Kinney. And pretty good cigars they were too, yes. Havana. Havana, Cuba," he said, as if Kinney might confuse it with some other Havana. Slade blew on the tip of his cigarette and then held it close to his eyes, reading the name stamped on the paper. "Sullivan and Powell. These are pretty damn good smokes too, Kinney."

"It's spelled Powell, Captain. But it's pronounced 'pole.' You know how the British are."

Slade didn't seem to mind being corrected. He chuckled. "Nothing too good for Lieutenant Austin Kinney. Tell me, your old man the banker?"

"Yes he is, Captain."

Slade nodded. "And nothing's too good for Lex Kinney's boy, right?"

"Life's too short for anything else, Captain."

"Yes indeedy." Slade leaned forward and slumped on his desk. "Let me guess, Lieutenant, you don't like your room, do you? Where'd they put you?"

"A shit hole on the top floor, Captain."

"And you'd like something a little more comfortable, right?"

"Yes I would, sir."

"And what would you do to get it, Kinney?"

"Is the captain in the market for anything in particular?"

"The captain is in the market for rotation home, Lieutenant, but I doubt that not even the lieutenant could arrange that."

"That's right, sir."

"But because I'm an understanding man, I'll arrange something nice for you on the second floor, view of the Via Veneto. That's like living on Park Avenue, son."

"Captain, I've been living on Park Avenue all my life."

Captain Slade chuckled. "Yeah, but this time it's gonna cost you something."

"How much?"

"Three hundred."

Kinney nodded and took a wad of bills from his trouser pocket. He counted out six fifties and laid them on the desk. Slade placed a buff-colored folder over the money and watched as Kinney returned the rest to his pants pocket. "How much you got there, Lieutenant?"

"Enough, Captain—enough to see me through a while."

"I'll bet you've got another three hundred in that roll. Probably got another stash in your room."

"Nothing wrong with that."

Slade laughed and shook his head. "Nothing wrong with that, the man says. I think maybe there is. Here we got a shit-ass little lieutenant carrying around two, three hundred in cash. A lieutenant who just happens to be Army Supply Force, Quartermaster Corps, who happens to get paid a lousy couple a hundred a month."

Kinney ground out his cigarette. "Let's just say I'm careful with my money."

"How much you think your ass is worth to the CID?"

"Nothing," said Kinney. "Why should the CID be interested in me?"

"C'mon, Kinney. You work for the QMC. You got plenty of dough. You dress like Patton . . ."

"Then tell the CID about Patton. He's a bigger fish." He slipped off the edge of Slade's desk and stood upright. "So when can I change my room?"

"Don't rush me, sonny." Slade drew on his cigarette and then stubbed it out. He picked up a pale green billeting slip and scratched his pen across it. "See the man at the desk."

"Thank you, Captain." Kinney saluted smartly, as if Slade had just pinned the DSC on his chest.

"You are some kind of operator, Kinney."

"Just trying to win the war, Captain."

Slade laughed. "How come I got the feeling you're a side all to yourself?"

"We're all Americans, Captain."

"Beat it, Kinney."

MAJOR JOHN HOWE and Corporal Adam Malinsky walked into the hallowed quiet of the church of San Stefano Rotondo, their military heels noisy and intrusive in the silence. Howe would rather have gone to the Pantheon or St. Peter's but had tagged along when Malinsky had mentioned that he was going to see this macabre Roman church. Malinsky, who had been going off duty when Howe arrived, had politely sneered at the major's sight-seeing plans.

"Sad to say, Sir, but St. Peter's is today the scene of a requiem for the fallen of the Polish Corps. Ticket holders only."

"Perhaps I can get a ticket."

"Extremely unlikely. Sir."

Malinsky did not emphasize the "sir," the universal signal of the contempt an enlisted man felt for an officer. He preferred a sudden and complete stop before and after "sir," thinking that form far more offensive. At the University of Chicago, Adam Malinsky had been a very effective member of the debating team.

"But the Sistine—"

"Open only Tuesdays and Thursdays. Sir. Today is Wednesday. Sir."

"And the Pantheon?"

"Closed indefinitely. Sir."

"The Forum?"

Malinsky looked at his watch. "Closes at noon. That's nine minutes from now. Sir."

"And where are you going, Corporal?"

"San Stefano Rotondo. Sir."

"And where is that?"

"On the Caelian Hill. Sir. A few hundred yards from the Church of Santa Maria in Domnica. Sir. Or, to give it its more popular name. Sir. The Church of Santa Maria Navicella."

Howe didn't know the church by either its formal or familiar name.

"Perhaps I could tag along."

Malinsky's face closed flat like a venetian blind. "With me. Sir?"

"If it's no trouble, Corporal. If you don't mind."

It was no trouble, and Malinsky minded a great deal, but even he realized that he couldn't get away with saying so, no matter how diffident and polite Major Howe might seem to be. He sighed and said that it would be an honor to have the major accompany him. They walked the sweltering streets, Malinsky sending a pack of street kids—screaming "Caramelle!" as if it were a war cry—scattering with an authoritative "Va t'en ne via!"

"You speak Italian, Corporal?"

"Just a few handy words and phrases. Sir."

Malinsky claimed that he didn't speak German either, but with a series of handy words and phrases he talked an alarmingly Teutonic nun into admitting them to the church attached to the convent.

"I gather," said Howe, "that as a member of a religious order she does not qualify as an enemy alien."

It was all Malinsky could do to prevent himself from rolling his eyes heavenward. "No. Sir. She does not."

Malinsky was surprised to see Howe dip his hand in the holy water stoup and make the sign of the cross as they entered the church. The major was a southerner and Malinsky never thought of southerners as Catholics. He suspected that the major thought it was the polite thing to do.

Corporal Malinsky claimed he had never been in the church before, but he seemed to know all about it.

"San Stefano Rotondo was built by Pope St. Simplicius in 468," he said, his reedy voice echoing professorial in the great white space. "It is said to be a copy of what was thought to be the Holy

Sepulcher in Jerusalem. The walls were frescoed in the seventeenth century by Pomarancio and depict the most gruesome of the martyrdoms undergone by the saints of the early Christian Church." Malinsky thrust his face up close to a fresco of Saint Lawrence broiling on his red-hot grill. Malinsky chipped at the paint with a fingernail. "Plaster rot," he said.

Everywhere Howe looked he saw a frieze of atrocities: flayings, beheadings, slow and terrible tortures. "I suppose," he said, "that given the date you mentioned the idea was to impress the Counter-Reformation movement that there were still privations to be undergone for the Church. Would you agree with that, Corporal?"

Malinsky looked at Howe warily. "That would be one interpretation. Sir."

"What I mean to say, Corporal, is that these paintings would have been executed about the time the new orders—primarily the Jesuits—were setting out to reconquer the world for the Church. I would imagine that the purpose of these paintings was to inform the new soldiers for Christ that there were still tortures to be undergone—in China, in the wilds of Canada, South America, even Protestant England."

Malinsky's eyes narrowed. "Studied a lot of Church history, have you. Sir?"

"Just an amateur's interest, Corporal." Major Howe stopped to look at the martydom of St. James Intercisus. He was being whittled down, limb by limb, until he was a collection of bloody parts on a bright Persian landscape.

"The artwork is, of course, of no interest at all," said Malinsky with a sniff. He added, "Sir."

It hurt Malinsky to say that, as the Italian baroque was the area he had specialized in while getting his master's in art history at Yale, and it was the field in which he planned to make his academic reputation. Yet he could not resist taking the major down a little, letting him know who was the intellectual boss around here.

"No, Corporal?"

"It's nothing more than cheap propaganda." He cleared his throat noisily. "The mosaics in the side chapels are depictions of Saints Primus and Felician and date from the middle of the seventh century."

"Amazing," said Howe.

"Architecturally, of course, the building is something of a pa-

71

limpset in that there are a number of styles in play here. The most interesting thing we can see here—"Hang on to your hat, Major, thought Malinsky, because here comes the hard part—"is the slight pulvain in the abacus." Malinsky did honestly expect the major to look bewildered by this bit of jargon. He was disappointed. Howe looked to the spot above the capitals of each pillar—the abacus—and saw that there was a slight swelling of masonry there—a pulvain.

"Yes, that's clear, Corporal. But what's its significance?"

"It denotes, ah, the influence of the Byzantine architectural orders. Sir."

Malinsky looked at the Major with something approaching respect. He was the first soldier in Rome to discover that Major Howe was not to be underrated.

GABRIELLE SANSEVERIO SAT in a deep armchair in the *gran salone*, the same chair Camillo had rested in when he had come home from his work at the Insurance Company. Camillo had been sleeping for hours in his bedroom. Sandro, Gabrielle's husband, was probably on the verge of waking up.

The chair was an eighteenth-century piece, part of a set commissioned by some Sanseverio to complement the fresco on the ceiling. Each was covered in tapestry and each depicted a scene from the myth of Castor and Pollux. The one in which Gabrielle now sat showed Zeus creating the constellation Gemini in honor of the two young men. The family had always thought the chairs to be very valuable.

They were not. The pieces had been refused by the antique dealer Camillo had summoned from the Via del Babuino in the early days of the war, and it took the man's experienced eye but a few minutes to discover that the tapestry covering was not Gobelins as had always been thought in the family.

"School-of," he said apologetically, although inside he was relieved. With a war on who would want to buy eighteen tapestry chairs, Gobelins or not? No one, not even the great collectors were buying now.

Gabrielle hunched in her school-of chair, her knees drawn up to her chest, her feet hooked over the edge of the seat cushion. Her arms encircled her slim legs, like the bands of a barrel holding together the staves. She huddled in the chair, as if the elegant room still held the biting chill of the previous winter instead of the uncomfortable damp of the summer heat. A very fine band of sweat shone on her upper lip, and the delicate curls of soft hair which brushed her long neck stuck to her skin.

Even in poverty her fine-boned, pale beauty was striking. Her eyes were blue and round, questioning, her hair blonde and smooth, artlessly twisted at the base of her neck into a loose bun. Her body was slight and delicate.

She could not leave the palazzo without being accosted by soldiers who, used to easy and mercenary sex, assumed she was for sale. That morning, as Gabrielle had walked down the Corso Umberto the soldiers gathered on the street corners and in the cafés had whistled and stamped their feet as she passed. Some pretended to swoon, and some said, "Oh, baaaby . . ."

One had been even more forthright, threatening. He had stood in her path on the pavement, planted solid like a statue. "Five bucks," he said. It was five times the going rate. To the Baronessa Sanseverio it was a great deal of money.

She had pushed past him, but he followed. "Ten bucks." He had tried to thrust some soiled bills into her hand. She broke free.

"Okay, bitch. Twenty and that's it."

For a moment, she had felt the words rising in her throat. She could hear herself saying it: All right. Come on then.

Gabrielle could see herself taking the soldier by the arm and steering him into a hotel—there was one in the Piazza San Ignazio—walking with him the way she had seen the whores do it, proprietary and proud. She could see herself taking him upstairs, stripping off her light cotton dress, kicking off her sandals, throwing herself on the bed. And when it was done, she thought, she'd have twenty dollars. Maybe she would have more. Maybe she would steal his wallet.

She had heard a voice. It said, "Scram, Private." A military policeman was staring at her, peering into her face, sweat dripping into his eyes. "That soldier bothering you, miss? You okay?"

"No," she said. She walked away quickly, trembling.

Lying next to the chair was a string bag containing a grayish loaf of bread and some tins stamped with the seal of the United States Army. The ration distribution center for her district was in Piazza San Lorenzo in Lucina, a long, hot walk away. There had been a queue, a crowd of people milling around. They were servants and the wives of workers and deportees and soldiers who had not come back from the Fascist wars. There were sleepy-eyed whores.

"Why is she here?" A hard-faced signora kept an eye on Gabrielle, grumbling in her ugly Roman dialect. "She's got money written all over her face. She's taking bread from the mouths of our children. *Sporca puttana.*"

Gabrielle pretended not to hear, as a lady was supposed to do, but the woman kept it up for the entire two hours it took to get inside the shop and make her scanty purchases. Sometimes she spoke to Gabrielle directly, other times she addressed other members of the crowd, trying to enlist allies.

"I call it a disgrace. Why don't she buy food for herself and leave this for those that need it? There's not enough to go round, never mind for people like her . . ."

Gabrielle sat in her chair, her eyes slowly tracing the delicate lozenge pattern set in the marble floor. Soon Sandro would be awake. Random thoughts shot into her mind, and in her fixed stare she saw events from her past, sudden and vivid, as if lit by a white blade of lightning, followed by a gloom made darker by the clarity of her memories.

She recalled the day Sandro had come home from the bank, saying he had been discharged. He had made light of it, announcing that they should have a bottle of champagne brought up from the depleted cellars to celebrate his freedom. He also said that they would be forced to live on their investments, "for the time being." She remembered Camillo's eyes, blue and fearful, in the background. Then he had been an old man, an old man who had abdicated his position as head of the family to his son.

She remembered the night they came to take Sandro away. The Fascisti had said that Il Conte had to come with them. For several minutes there had been confusion. Camillo was Il Conte, and what had the old man done?

"It doesn't matter," Camillo said, "I am quite prepared to go with these . . . gentlemen."

But Sandro had insisted. They wanted Il Barone, not Il Conte. There had been some hurried consulting of lists and some telephoning, and they discovered that Sandro had been correct. The Fascists had nothing against the count, it was the son they wanted.

Sandro had told his wife and father that they were not to worry. The Squadristi had hustled him away. The OVRA officer told Camillo to be careful. "Next time we'll come for you, old man. And then for her." He jerked a thumb as red and as thick as a carrot at Gabrielle and looked at her crotch.

"Get out of my house," Camillo said.

"Times have changed," said the man from OVRA.

Then the war came and food became scarce. The servants melted away, fleeing to the countryside, returning to the green and fertile farmland where they knew they could find food, until the war descended on them and laid waste their fields and vineyards.

They received one letter a month from Sandro. He claimed to be well and not badly treated in his internal exile, his greatest trial being the dearth of books. They were not allowed to write back. Then his letters stopped coming.

Gabrielle and Camillo tried for weeks to find out where he was. They besieged Rome Fascist Headquarters in the Palazzo Braschi and National Headquarters in Piazza Colonna, waiting in the halls for hours, but they discovered nothing. Camillo appealed to his few influential friends, time and again, until they stopped receiving his calls and pretended not to see him when he passed on the streets.

Gabrielle had gathered what remained of her jewelry and tried to bribe the clerks at the Fascist party headquarters for information. This yielded results. Sandro had been transferred from Basilicata to Forte Bravetta outside of Rome. They also discovered that he had spent some time in the Pensione Oltremare, a grubby little hotel near San Lorenzo, an "interrogation center," the Fascists called it. Camillo and Gabrielle knew, or could guess at, the methods employed there.

He had been released in the weeks between the fall of Mussolini and the seizure of the city by the Germans. The teeth on the left side of Sandro's jaw had been knocked out and his pelvis had been broken. He had no nails on his right hand. "I told them nothing," he said weakly, "because I knew nothing." The Nazis, apparently, concurred. They did not bother to re-arrest him.

Gabrielle had put her husband to bed. He had been there ever since.

She stood and tried to smooth her creased skirt. It was time to see to him. But she lingered, kneeling to tear a corner from the loaf

75

of bread. It was soft and mealy, like modeling clay, made with dirty flour, gritty, mixed with sand. She jammed the bread into her mouth and felt a rush of saliva; she was always hungry these days. Later she would open the tins and be pleased when Sandro refused food and be irritated when Camillo took his small share. She would eat alone, in the kitchen.

Sandro was thin, his skin pale and papery. He scarcely moved in the big bed and his linen was sodden with sweat, adding to the sickroom smell, the dispiriting odor that told of someone having taken to his bed never to leave it.

"I was afraid you were out."

"I was. I went to get food."

"Please . . ."

Gabrielle went about her business with brisk efficiency, like a nurse in a charity ward. She lit a candle and waved the needle through the flame absentmindedly. It would not be well sterilized, but she couldn't be bothered with boiling the needle anymore. From a drawer in the night table she took a phial of morphine and with expert skill pushed the needle through the membrane, sucking the last of the brown liquid into the cylinder of the hypodermic. Watching the drug drain, she felt the hot pain of frustration. That was the last of their supply of the drug, and now she must address herself to the task of getting more. How many miles would she walk and how many ruffians would she have to deal with? What would it cost and how would she pay? Morphine was the rarest commodity in the city. It would have been easier if Sandro had become addicted to some rare alchemical substance like gold dust or powdered pearls.

She pushed up the sleeve of his pajama jacket, catching as she did so the damp smell of him, and pinched the vein in the crook of his arm. It was bruised and perforated, on the verge of collapse. He watched the needle puncture his flesh, ignoring the slight pain, staring the way a peasant gazes at a relic.

A tiny dot of dark blood welled up around the needle. Evenly she injected the morphine into him, pulled out the needle and folded her arm back, her mouth set in a hard line, as if to say, "There, now leave me alone . . ."

Sandro lay back on his pillows and his breathing became easier. The pupils of his eyes grew smaller and smaller and a slight smile appeared on his lips. The streams of sweat on his forehead dried rapidly, as if he had lain down in the hot summer sun.

"Do you want something to eat?"

Slowly, he shook his head, staring off at some point beyond her. Gabrielle watched him vanish into his own sweet world, and she watched with resentment. He could escape, but she was doomed to live here in the drab and hungry present.

5

Every time someone slammed a truck door or dropped a tailgate or gunned an engine, the sound boomed through the garage and made the thin glass window in the duty NCO's office shake. When it happened, McManus would look up from his papers and scowl through the rattling glass, drawing a bead on the noise maker like a sniper.

McManus felt terrible and the noise made his headache worse. The wine of the night before pooled sour in his stomach, his mouth was dry, his head hurt, and the sweat that seeped into his collar smelled of grape.

Calvin Utterback, who shared the office, was slumped over some papers on his desk, barely making a pretense of work. He didn't look well. Still, both men had had hangovers before; they would have them again—tomorrow morning, probably. The effects of drink, in this case, only exacerbated a more serious condition. Both men were worried.

Manganaro had come wandering in the night before around three, just about the time Utterback won the last of McManus's money in acey-deucey. Eddie Manganaro had been drunk too, and unhappy. His meeting with Falcone hadn't gone so good, he said.

"What happened?"

"It was bad, okay?"

"How bad?" demanded Utterback.

"Gimme some of that wine." Manganaro lurched across the table, trying to grab the bottle.

Utterback snatched it away. "How bad did it go, Eddie?"

Manganaro tried to tear the bottle from Utterback's hand and they had a little tug of war over it for a moment or two, until Eddie said, "Really, fuckin' bad, okay?"

Utterback released the bottle and Manganaro took a deep swig. He wiped his hand across his mouth. "It was a setup. A double cross. He tried to double-cross me. Me! Can you believe that?"

McManus paled. "And, yeah, so . . . ?"

Manganaro shrugged. "So, he's not going to do that no more."

Donal McManus's stomach lurched. A remark like that, from a guy like Manganaro, could only mean one thing. He took the bottle from Eddie, slugged back some wine, and belched unhappily. Utterback, slower on the uptake, didn't guess at the full weight of Manganaro's words. "So? Did you set something up?"

"No."

"So what you gonna do, Eddie?"

"I'm gonna go to bed."

"Bed!" Utterback's voice awakened Signor Fiorito, who dozed, still a sentinel, at his post behind the reception desk. He snorted and sat upright, rubbing his eyes.

Manganaro swung round. "Who's zat?"

THE WALLS OF the office shook and McManus looked up. Instead of seeing one of the maintenance guys grinning guiltily and shrugging over the jack he had dropped, McManus saw that the commotion had been caused by someone wrenching open the door of his office. The old wood had expanded in the humid heat and the force of the door opening had rattled the glass powerfully.

"Who the hell are you?" Then, in a gentler voice. "Lieutenant."

"Who are *you?*"

McManus stood up. "Sergeant McManus, sir." He tried to look into the young lieutenant's eyes, but the man wore heavy, horn-framed sunglasses with lenses so dark he couldn't make out his eyes at all.

The lieutenant turned on Utterback. "Who are you?"

Utterback got to his feet too, but slowly, as if he was a tired old man. "My name's Utterback, sir."

Something clicked in McManus's skull. It was like one of those cartoons where a light bulb comes on over your head. Idea. "Lieutenant Kinney, sir?"

The lieutenant raised an eyebrow. "*Austin* Kinney?"

"Yessir, that's right. We sure are glad to see you, sir." McManus waved a hand at the work floor beyond the office window. There wasn't a hell of a lot going on out there—he'd have to go out and shake things up—and he hoped that this Kinney didn't notice. "It ain't much but it's home, sir. Welcome to the outfit."

Lieutenant Manny Farfalla shook his head. "I'm not Kinney."

McManus's heavy, red face, a drinker's face, fell. "You're not?"

"Sit down, sergeants." Manny remained standing. "I'm Farfalla. I'm with the Army Provost Marshall's Office."

McManus's stomach jumped like a newly caught fish. APMO was a nice way of saying CID. "Yessir," he said as cheerfully as he could manage, "what can we do for you, sir?"

"One of the niggers acting up?" asked Utterback sourly.

Farfalla ignored him. "Where were you gentlemen last night?"

"When last night, sir?" parried McManus.

"All night, last night."

McManus forced himself to grin. "Nothing to do with us, whatever it is, sir. Hell, we didn't get here till late last night. Did we Cal?"

"Nope."

"What time did you get here?"

"Midnight. Roundabout."

"That a fact?"

"Yessir, it is," said McManus.

"Where did you come from?"

"Civit, Civit—I can never say the name of that place. On the coast, you know. 'Bout thirty-five, forty miles."

"Civitavecchia," said Utterback unexpectedly.

"Uh-huh. And what did you do after you got here?"

McManus's eyes narrowed. "Like to tell me what this is all about, Lieutenant?"

"No, I wouldn't like to tell you what this is all about, Sergeant."

McManus nodded. Figured. "Let's see. We pulled in around midnight. We took over the depot and then we took 'em, the men, to the billet."

"Then?"

"Me 'n' Cal and a staff sergeant played some acey-deucey and drank some."

"That's right," said Cal Utterback.

"Till what time?"

"Late," said McManus. "Tell you the truth, Lieutenant, I was a little in the bag when I turned in. All I know is that morning came fast. Too fast." McManus guffawed hopefully.

Farfalla looked enquiringly at Utterback. "Sergeant? Can you be a little more precise?"

"Was almost dawn," said Utterback. "Say, oh, 'bout four, four-thirty."

"What's the name of the other guy, the staff sergeant?"

"Manganaro."

"Italian boy?"

"I don't know about the boy part, sir. But yeah, Eddie's eye-talian." McManus noted that the CID guy wasn't taking notes. In his experience, CID guys always took notes. Donal allowed himself a little hope. If this guy was serious, he'd be taking notes, right?

"Mind if I take a look at your morning report, Sergeant?"

"Not at all, Lieutenant." McManus handed over his clipboard with the carbon of the DA 1; the original had already gone to Thorpe, and Thorpe had already gone to lunch. To an old-time NCO like McManus a morning report was a sacred thing, a minutely detailed record, one produced every day by every unit in the forces; morning reports always had been and would always be, like God and Heaven and Hell and other entities too mystical to contemplate.

The collection of dun-colored forms was a senior NCO's ultimate alibi. It proved beyond a shadow of a doubt that the company was all present, very correct; that every penny of company funds was accounted for; that McManus's little corner of the army was fighting and winning the war. Of course, every morning report, from Greenland to Burma said the same thing: everything is hunky-dory.

"Who was the big winner?" Farfalla asked, as he paged through the report.

"Sir?"

"In the game. Acey-deucey. Who won the money?"

Utterback grinned. "I was, lieutenant."

Farfalla smiled back. "Really? How much?"

"Six and a quarter, sir."

Farfalla stopped smiling. "That's not much money. Three guys playing for four hours. You took all that time to win six bucks?"

"And a quarter."

McManus smiled nervously. "It's a lot of money if it's all you got, lieutenant."

"I suppose. Took you so long, though. You guys didn't get bored?"

"No sir."

"Didn't get bored one of you, and maybe wandered away, to get a breath of fresh air? Take a walk? Go look for a girl? See the sights? Get some more wine?"

"Took a leak," said Utterback.

"Aside from that. None of you left the table?"

"Nope," said McManus.

"Strange it took you so long, doesn't it seem to you?"

McManus shrugged. "Never thought about it, sir. We gassed a little between rolls, you know."

The question didn't seem to interest Farfalla anymore. He tossed the morning report down on the desk. "So where's the other guy? Manganaro."

"Leading a charge on the station, sir. Ferrying supplies from the railroad."

"You got a warehouse?"

"Oh yes sir, right here. We're gonna be general dispersal for Rome. Things'll get busy 'round here in a couple of days."

"All classes?"

"Three, four, and five, sir." McManus grinned. "And maybe six, too."

Farfalla didn't think that was funny, but there again, he never thought much was funny. There were five classes of supplies in the army, each carrying a number, one to five. Class six was Quartermaster Corps slang for alcohol, which didn't figure in the official classifications.

"I'm glad you brought that up," said Farfalla. For one brief moment McManus hoped that the CID man was going to ask for a couple of bottles of scotch. There was nothing Donal McManus wanted more than to do Farfalla a favor. Farfalla, however, didn't drink. "Tell me about the black market."

You couldn't be in the Army Supply Force without being asked about the black market at some time or other, and McManus had long ago learned to deal with the question. He assumed what he hoped was a solemn and honest expression.

"Well, Lieutenant, I'm not gonna try and fool you that it don't exist. Every jackass knows that. Stuff gets on the market and I'll bet there are a thousand guys working it. Where they get the stuff I can guess, but what I know for sure is that they don't get it from me or anybody who works for me. Over the years, sure I caught some guys stealing but lemme tell you they're long gone."

"How do you deal with them? Reports?"

McManus shook his head. "I know it's against the rules, Lieutenant, but I don't work that way."

"Why not?"

"Never been serious enough. You get caught pilfering and you get a kick in the pants and a transfer. I find you doing anything serious, something that hurts the guys in the field, and then you get a personal escort to Leavenworth. Lieutenant, I got twenty-three years in the army so I don't take that shit."

"So you've caught guys stealing but you haven't reported them?"

"That's right, sir."

"Right there, that's enough to open an investigation, you know that?"

"Yes sir, I know that. But that's NCO justice and I know that the army allows a little bit of that. That's the way the army works."

Farfalla nodded. McManus was talking straight. The CID and the MP pool would have to be ten times as big if it was going to deal with every petty theft. "So I should just forget about it, right?"

"That might be best for everybody, sir."

"You know, Sergeant, you're the seventh supply sergeant I've spoken to this morning. And you know, every one of them said something like you just did. Sure, there's a market, but they don't know anything about it. The stuff's gotta be coming from somewhere, wouldn't you say?"

"I can't speak for the other guys, Lieutenant. I just know what goes on in my patch."

Curiously, all the other Quartermaster Corps sergeants could account for their movements the night before, ironclad alibis as strong as Utterback's, McManus's and this Manganaro's. The other sergeants had sworn that they were with their buddies, drinking, chewing the fat, playing cards. One or two, naively, admitted to being asleep, but the old pros like McManus swore that they had been awake and in company. Sleep was not a good alibi, even if it was the truth.

"Any other sergeants here?"

"Just us, sir."

"If you just got here, you won't be leaving for a while, right?"

"Our orders say we're permanent party now." McManus shrugged. "But that don't mean much. You know how the army is."

"Yeah." Farfalla wrenched the door of the office open and the glass walls shook. Then he turned back to McManus. "How come there are white noncoms in a Negro outfit? I thought they had colored up to top kick and white officers."

"That's what I'd like to know," said Utterback.

"This unit got clobbered at Anzio, Lieutenant, just before the breakout. They plugged us guys in where they needed us. They ain't bad boys. I don't mind."

"*I* mind," spat Utterback. "Niggers! How the hell am I supposed to go home and tell my folks I fought with a nigger outfit?"

It occurred to Farfalla that playing dice until the small hours on a sticky summer night followed by spending a day slumped over your desk wasn't exactly heroic. "Where's your billet?"

"Down the street. Turn left out of the gate. You can't miss it."

Farfalla nodded. "I'll be in touch."

"Hey Lieutenant."

"Yeah, Sergeant?"

"How did you know about the other guy, Lieutenant Kinney? How did you know his first name? He a friend of yours?"

Manny Farfalla shook his head. "Nope." He slammed the door behind him.

The two sergeants watched Farfalla as he made his way through the gloom of the garage and out into the blinding white light of the day. McManus pulled a damp cigar out of his breast pocket and lit it. "Cal," he said, "I hope that's the last we see of that guy."

Signor Fiorito, the ten-dollar bill Manganaro had given him concealed in his sock, confirmed that the three sergeants drank and gambled until dawn that morning.

"You saw them?"

"Si, signore."

"All the time?"

"Si, signore."

"Non dorme?"

"Io? Poco."

"Doesn't anybody sleep in this town?"

Fiorito answered with the Roman shrug: stupid question, obvious answer.

PROVENANCE

I'm an investigator and I specialize in art; stolen art, usually. Sometimes I track it down and then tip off the police; other times I try to get it back myself. I spend a lot of time researching provenance, figuring out who owned a work of art, how it was purchased and disposed of, and if it was all above board. Sometimes legality doesn't enter into it. Pretty frequently people want to know if their paintings had ever been owned by someone really famous. It's sort of like hunting for your ancestors in the hope that they'll turn out to be aristocrats. The better the bloodline on a work of art, the more valuable the thing becomes. Once in a while it turns a piece of junk into a gold mine, as we all found out when Andy Warhol's *tsatskes* came on the market. I also advise museums, collectors, and galleries about security.

I'm not a private investigator. You need a license for that and you spend most of your time doing divorce work, which usually involves being out in all kinds of nasty weather in the middle of the night, drinking cold coffee from paper cups. There's no real name for what I do. When I went to have my cards and stationery printed up, I considered calling myself a consultant but any damn fool can become a consultant just by calling himself one, and I bring a lot of knowledge and expertise to my job. People don't really trust "consultants"; at least, I don't think they do. Anyway, I settled for Harold A. Leblanc, and my address and phone number.

I was a policeman for twenty years and I started out like any other, in a patrol car. I was posted to the Nineteenth Precinct in New York, the East Side of Manhattan, known as the Silk Stocking district. It's the toniest and richest neighborhood in the city, probably the country;

maybe Beverly Hills is richer, I don't know. All those rich people introduced me to art.

You see, once in a while, we'd get a call to some apartment, sometimes places as palatial as Peony's, to check out a theft. Usually it was burglary or a lost wallet or a maid walking off with a TV set, but sometimes it was art. Even if it was something like a TV, those apartments always had a lot of art around. Rich people seem to buy art whether they like it or not. I guess it's something they think they are expected to do.

At the time, I didn't know anything about art, but it interested me. The Nineteenth also includes the Metropolitan Museum of Art, the Frick, the Whitney, the Guggenheim, and a couple of other museums, and so I took to dropping in when I had some time (did you know they let cops in free?) and I discovered that not only did I like art, it also— this might sound crazy—reassured me.

You see, even if you work in New York's nicest neighborhood you're still in New York. You see a lot of unpleasant things, and let me tell you when you see that stuff every day, day in day out, you get to developing a pretty low view of mankind. Art tended to show people in a better light. It told me that not everybody was dragging things down, trampling life in the dirt. Art—most of it, anyway—is beautiful. Even Goya at his blackest painted beautiful paintings. That always made me feel better. Call me a romantic.

Of course, later, when I studied art history I discovered that artists were as rotten as anybody else, maybe more so. Still, it was an end-versus-the-means thing with me. Caravaggio may have been a murdering, philandering, hotheaded prick, but he still produced great paintings. A charming murderer doesn't produce a charming murder, if you see what I mean.

I have a master's in art history from NYU paid for by the NYPD's education plan, and I spent fourteen years on the stolen art squad as a detective. I have to say I enjoyed it, and I met a lot of people in the art world—which isn't always so enjoyable, but that's how I got to know Peony. She called up once and said that she had been offered a painting by Zurbarán and she suspected that it was stolen. Some dealers would not have asked questions and sold it—you can get money for a Zurbarán—but with Peony, for obvious reasons, money is not the object of the game. She doesn't have to mess with stolen art. Anyway, turns out that she was right. The Zurbarán was hot.

That was my first really big case. I traced the thing all over the place, from New York backward to Nice, Zurich, and finally to a guy in Paris who bought the painting from a guy who stole it from a Spanish zillionaire's house in London. The painting had been taken out of Spain illegally. The thief figured that the owner was not going to make a big stink about a painting that shouldn't have been in London in the first place.

The NYPD paid for all that travel—and more on other cases over the years—and I built up contacts all over the country and in Europe, Asia, Latin America. After I did my twenty years on the force I took my pension and all that I had learned and set myself up in business. I'm not rich but comfortable, and because I live in Stuyvesant Town my rent isn't ridiculous.

After I spoke to Mrs. Chapman, Randall dropped me off on Fifty-seventh and Fifth and I decided to swing by Hacker's Art Books to see what they had on Guido Reni. I had studied the Italian baroque in college, but I have to say that period is not my strong suit. My own specialty is Northern European with an accent on the German Transcendentalists. I wrote my thesis on a painting by Kaspar David Friedrich that hangs in the Springfield Art Institute. I proved it was a fake. The people in Springfield didn't agree, but they wouldn't allow the painting to be taken down for chemical analysis, which I think tells you something.

I turned up an interesting book at Hacker's. It was a monograph published in 1957 by an associate professor of art history at Yale named Adam Malinsky. The title: *Problems of Attribution in the Works of Guido Reni, 1600–1642.* It was one of Malinsky's earliest works. Now he was the Grand Old Man of the art history department at Columbia. He publishes big fat art books that are assigned in every European survey course in the country; he even had a series on PBS— the whole nine yards. I don't know the guy, but that doesn't stop me from thinking he's a pompous pain in the neck.

I snapped a language tape into the cassette player and settled down with my smokes to read. I love language tapes. The Italian one, *Caffè e Conversazione,* deals with the life of two people, Signora Conti and Signor Rossi, who talk at length on subjects of paralyzing boredom. They always sound a bit sad, as if they longed to speak not of the *macchina* (Signora Rossi has terrible trouble with her car; if I were her I'd junk the damn thing) and the *stazione* (they seem to spend a lot of time at the railway station), but of themselves. I like to think that

Signora Conti and Signor Rossi yearn for one another and ache to confess their love but are imprisoned in the script.

The villain of the tape is the voice of the instructor who comes on every so often, he says, to explain, but I think it's to break up the Romeo and Juliet of the language instruction set. The instructor speaks in a strenuously clear American accent, one of those cheery-phony voices you associate with cult members. I half expect him to crack one day and intone; "We have a secret plan to take over the world. I am completely mad. Have a nice day."

So far, Signora Conti and Signor Rossi have only passed one remotely personal remark. Signora Conti: "I have a great deal of spare time in the afternoons." Signor Rossi: "That is a coincidence. I also have a great deal of spare time in the afternoons." I hope they get together some day.

Signora Conti and Signor Rossi were mournfully extolling the delights of train travel while I read about Guido Reni.

His reputation had risen and fallen over the years. For two decades early in his career he had been in Rome, enjoying great patronage and busy frescoing acres of wall space in palaces and churches. He was one of the best-known painters of his day, and the rich flocked to him for portraits, devotional paintings, and historical works based on classical themes.

A change in papal politics—a new pope, Innocent X, didn't much care for him—caused Reni to return to his native city of Bologna, where he stayed until his death in 1642. Even before he died, his reputation was on the decline. Between 1614 and 1642 he had lots of assistants, and they churned out trite and sentimental paintings, many of them signed by Reni but otherwise had nothing to do with him. A lot like some big-time artists today, but I won't mention any names.

Malinsky is blunt: "The number of paintings attributed to the master but untouched—indeed, unseen—by him is, quite simply, enormous."

Well, there was nothing trite or sentimental about the Chapman Reni. It could only have dated from the glory days in Rome.

Reni's star rose briefly in the nineteenth century, when the English adopted him. The "divine Guido" they called him and ranked him with Raphael. But after that brief flare-up of popularity, Reni sunk down to the footnotes for the next hundred years or so.

In 1954 his home town, Bologna, organized a huge show of Guido Reni's work, thus starting a favorite son on the long road to rehabilitation. Malinsky had seen the Bologna show and stated categorically that seven of the works weren't by Reni, or even "school-of," but fakes. Maybe he was right, but he put it very nastily—but that's Malinsky all over. "While acknowledging that a mere layman might have difficulties detecting the inconsistencies and weaknesses of these appalling paintings, one can only be shocked by the lack of ability demonstrated by the 'experts' who assembled this show. Reni is ill-served by such slipshod scholarship." The experts in quotes, that was Malinsky all over. He certainly knows how to piss people off.

Of course, you could see what was going on. Malinsky had staked out the Italian baroque and Reni as his little area of expertise. Baroque art wasn't popular in the fifties, so Malinsky had avoided crowded fields like the Renaissance and had taken on an unfashionable era, confident that it would come back into scholarly vogue. Having this big Italian show—which he wasn't asked to curate, obviously—come along and steal his thunder must have been a blow. I bet this monograph was answered by a baroque expert from Italy, which Malinsky probably responded to, only to be rebutted by the Italians, and so on. Of such things are reputations made in academia.

It was only much later, in the seventies, that Malinsky became a Renaissance man, in both senses of the term.

I put down the book and lit a cigarette. In the background Signora Conti and Signor Rossi were touring the local vegetable market. "Asparagus is not in season now," she said sadly. "No," said Signor Rossi, "unfortunately, it is not in season now." Did I detect a little bitterness in his voice, the cold realization that his love would always be denied him? "No," said Signora Conti. "It is far too late."

6

When Stanley Leacock got off duty that afternoon, he returned to the Hotel Palatino Splendido, showered, shaved, and put on a fresh uniform. He sliced a neat part into his hair and smiled at himself in the mirror.

"Hi," he said, "I'm private Stanley Leacock."

He wished he spoke some Italian. He searched through his duffle bag and found a can of Carnation condensed milk, a pack of Lucky Strikes, and two Baby Ruth bars. He stowed his loot in his uniform pockets and checked the cash in his wallet. Twelve dollars in cash and fifty lire in scrip, five ten-lira notes. He was about to leave the room he shared with Jimmy Holt but stopped, deciding to take another look at himself in the mirror.

"Hi, miss. I'm private Stanley Leacock. I saw you last night. Oh hell." He *wished* he spoke some Italian.

Ernest Biggs, one of the loaders, was sitting on the steps of the Hotel Palatino Splendido, feeling the warm afternoon sun on his face. He had gone off duty at the same time as Stanley, but he had no plans that night except some chow, some cards, and an early night. He grinned and whistled when he saw Stanley. "Look at you!"

"You seen Benny around?"

"Where you goin', Stanley?"

"I'm going on a date."

Biggs's grin got a little wider. "Who's the lucky lady?"

"A friend of mine."

Biggs whistled. "You work fast. You get here last night and already you got a friend."

"You know me, Ernest. I'm a friend to all."

"All the ladies . . . You take care, hear."

"You seen the Benny?"

"Maybe try the depot."

"See you later."

Biggs shook his head and laughed. "Look at you . . ."

Jack Benny was sitting on the tailgate of one of the trucks, looking alternately at a page of *Collier's* magazine, trying to figure out the words, and at a crate of Armour corned beef that had fallen off one of the trucks and split open. He was paying more attention to the meat than to the magazine. The loaders had kicked it aside, probably meaning to repack it later. When the time was right, Jack Benny was going to swipe a couple of cans and head for Tor di Nona and sell them. While staring at the *Collier's* article he tried to work out how much each can was worth: about sixty lire a kilo, he decided, and each can looked to weigh three kilos . . .

The depot was busy. Sergeant Cal Utterback was overseeing the unloading of a fresh shipment from the station, while Corporal Humphrey Joyce, the company clerk, made a list of what went where on the tall steel shelves that had been installed. They ran back into the gloom of the big storeroom and were already half filled. Supply shipments had been run into the garage all day, tons and tons of food and clothing, all manner of goods. It seemed to Benny that there was no limit to the wealth of the American army. What would a few kilos of meat matter to such rich men?

Eddie Manganaro stood in the middle of the garage, a clipboard folded in his arms, pressed against his chest like a breastplate. He did not look happy.

"What is it you got there, Cal?"

Utterback took some sheets of paper from his back pocket. "Number six says three hundred K rations, three hundred C, three hundred D, six hundred flour, six hundred edible oil, three hundred powdered egg, nine hundred sugar. That's two. You want three?"

Manganaro frowned at his own list. "Naww, let's stick to two for a minute. You sure you don't got three hundred pounds biscuit, five hundred powdered milk, and an even thousand bacon?"

"Yep. Not here."

"Jesus H. Christ. What's the number?"

"Three-ought-ought-six-four-slash-J. Loaded Alex."

Manganaro pantomimed throwing his clipboard in the air. "Fucked up again. Christ, it's gonna take a hundred years to straighten out this shit."

"Hey Sarge," shouted Sam Crosby, one of the loaders, "what do we do with this?" He had dropped the tailgate on one of the trucks and was staring at a wall of closely packed crates.

"What is it?"

"Well . . . we got some crates marked canned fruit, peaches. There's others say musical instruments. And there's a couple says scotch whiskey."

Manganaro started. "Scotch?" All of the workers in the depot slowed a little and shot sidelong glances at the treasure truck. Manganaro didn't have scotch on any manifest. "Cal, get that truck unloaded and bond the booze. Lock it up, bond it till I get this mess figured out."

"Aww c'mon, Sarge," said one of the loaders, "just a little. If it ain't on the manifest, who's gonna know?"

"Shuttup," barked Manganaro. "You give niggers hard liquor it's like giving firewater to the injuns. It'll drive you boys crazy. Next thing you know we'll have dark clouds all over Rome waving them straight razors."

Manganaro thought he was being funny. "Shit," mumbled Crosby, "I know where that shit's goin' first time some sergeants I know get alone with it."

"What did you say, boy?" yelled Utterback.

"Nothin'."

Utterback strode across the garage and stood over Crosby. "You sure?"

The whole depot was watching. Benny looked at the meat cans. If a fight broke out, he would have ample opportunity to make off with an armful of contraband.

"I asked you a question, nigger."

Crosby, a big man, drew himself up to his full height, his jaw clenched. "You got no call makin' names like that."

"I'll call you whatever the fuck I please, sambo," shrieked Utterback.

"Can it, Cal." McManus came out of his office. "Let's get some work done here. Move it! Eddie, what the hell is going on here?"

"Nothing, Donny, nothing at all."

"Good. Hey! We got a split crate over here. Someone get another box and repack it."

Jack Benny sighed.

"Hey Benny . . ."

"Hiya Stanley," said Jack Benny sadly. "You look ver' nice today."

"Hey Benny, you got a minute?"

"Sure Stanley, what you mind got on it?"

"I want to learn some Italian. I want to know how to say "How are you today?""

"You got a cigarette, Stanley?"

Leacock grinned and tore open a pack of Luckies. "Here you go. You need a light?"

"No, no," said Benny quickly. "I smoke later."

"So, how do you say it?"

"Ah, you say, 'Come sta?' or 'Come va?' "

"Which is better?"

"The same."

"Come sta."

The Benny nodded. "Yes, is right."

"How do you say, 'Hi, miss'?"

"Salve, signorina." The Benny grinned. "You gotta girl, Stanley?"

"Salve, segnorina!"

Jack Benny shook his head. "Stanley, I gotta tell you something. The Americans say always 'segnorina.' This is no good. In Italian, you say 'segnorina,' then you say 'whore.' You understand? This is no good. You gotta say 'signorina' or you make the bad face. It is not"—Benny paused, like a horse before a high jump—"polite." He smiled, proud of having used a strange word.

Leacock looked embarrassed. "Hell, I don't want to call her a whore. She's a nice girl, you know?"

"Then you say 'Salve signorina, come sta?' "

"Salve, signorina, come sta?"

"Good."

"How do you say, 'I was the guy in the street last night?' "

Benny had long since ceased trying to figure out what the Americans were talking about. All he did was translate what they wanted to say; what it meant was none of his business. He frowned as if trying to work out a complicated mathematical problem in his

94

head. "Ah, you say something like, 'Ero io nella strada ieri sera.' "

"Ero . . ." began Stanley.

"Io . . ."

"Ero io . . ."

"Nella strada . . ."

"Nella strada . . ."

"Ieri sera."

"Ieri sera."

"Good."

"Wait, let me try the whole thing. Salve, signorina, come sta? Ero io . . ."

"Nella strada ieri sera."

"Man, this is hard."

"Try. You get them."

"Ero io nella strada . . ."

"Ieri sera," coached Benny.

"Wait. Salve, segnorina—"

"*Si*gnorina," corrected Benny sternly.

"Damn. Salve, signorina. Come sta? Ero io nella strada ieri sera."

"Bravo."

"Whew. It ain't easy, is it?"

"You learn, Stanley."

"How do you say, 'I'm Stanley Leacock'?"

Jack Benny's meter clicked over. "Hey, Stanley, maybe you got another cigarette?"

Stanley handed over another Lucky. "Tell me how you say it."

"Is easy. 'Sono Stanley Leacock.' "

"Sono Stanley Leacock."

"Ver' good."

"Leacock," yelled Utterback. "If all you got to do is hang around talking to the meatball then maybe you better change into fatigues and get your ass in gear."

"I'm off duty, Sarge."

"Then get the fuck out of here."

It was a long hot walk to the center of town, and as he trudged along Stanley recited the words he had learned, like a monk telling his beads. He crossed the Piazza Venezia, threading his way through a stream of military traffic and into the streets beyond. He was sure her house was somewhere in the neighborhood, but where exactly he couldn't say. He wandered down one sunny street and then along another, peering at the street signs, but in his mind keeping up the chant, "Sono Stanley Leacock. Ero io nella strada ieri sera. . . ." Then he realized he was lost.

It was the height of the siesta hour, the streets burning hot and deserted. He felt the pricks of sweat edging his scalp. "Damn," he said aloud in the quiet street.

"Hey GI! You got caramelle for me?" A street kid was watching him from a scrap of shadow. "Maybe you got cigarette."

"Hey kid. Come over here a sec."

The boy was thin and dirty and he wore an American olive drab shirt and a pair of officer's pinks which had been cut off at the knee. His nose was running and he had malnutrition sores on his hands and wrists. The clothes hung on his scrawny frame, yet he ambled out of his patch of shade like a playboy leaving a casino.

"You got for me, GI?"

"Cigarette? You want a cigarette?"

"Gimme two, GI."

"Hold on now, you don't know what I want yet."

The kid laughed. "Ma, si. You wan' nice girl. Clean. Chip."

Leacock shook his head. "I want to know where Via Marcello is. You know, paisan? I'll give you two cigarettes if you take me there."

"Via di *San* Marcello, GI. Yeah. Come." He grabbed Stanley by the forearm. "Come. But first you give me cigarette."

"Nope. Not till you show me."

"One cigarette *qui*. One cigarette San Marcello."

"One now, one later, is that it?"

"Yeah."

Stanley figured that was fair. He took out his pack of Luckies, holding it high above his head. The kid jumped for them like a dog after a treat. "Hold it. One now, one later. Capeesh?"

"Si, si, va bene." The kid took out a cigarette and tucked it into the breast pocket of his outsized shirt. "Come."

"Yeah. I'm coming."

"What you name, Joe?"

"Stanley. What's yours?"

"Me, Lello. You got something for me? You want *sciuscia?*" He pointed to Stanley's faultlessly shined boots. "I make boot clean, real clean, polish. You want girl?"

"Nothing wrong with them boots, Lello."

"Gum? Juicy fruit? Spearmint?"

"I don't have no gum. Hey, Lello, how do you say 'What's your name' in Italian?' "

"What you name?"

"Yeah. In Italian."

"Come ti chiami."

"Slowly." Stanley stroked the air. "Slowly."

"Gimme one cigarette and I tell you all Italian."

"Okay." Stanley paid off his instructor. " 'What's your name?' "

"Come ti chiami."

"Come ti chi—"

"—yami."

"Come ti chiami."

"Giusto," said Lello.

"Salve, signorina, come sta? Ero io . . ." Stanley stopped in the street and thought for a moment. "Ero io nella strada ieri sera. Sono Stanley Leacock. Come ti chiami?" Leacock grinned down at the kid. "What you think, Lello?"

"I think you crazy."

Lello led Stanley around the block a few times and then, true to his word, deposited him in a street not five yards from where they had first met, the Via di San Marcello. It was a narrow street, lined with tumbledown apartment blocks, old and weathered, one looking much like another, but Stanley had no trouble identifying the building he was looking for. He looked up at the balcony where he had seen her and tried to recall what she had looked like. He could conjure up the white of her nightdress and the cool of her voice.

Lello knew from the private's face that they had reached their destination. He made one last stab at entrepreneurship. "Hey, Stanley, you look for girl? Women?" He pistoned a grimy finger through a thin fist. "I get for five cigarette."

"That's okay, Lello." Stanley pulled out his cigarette pack and paid off his guide. Without really thinking about it, Stanley peeled a ten-lira note off his roll and handed it to Lello. "Here you go, Lello. A little tip."

Lello looked at the faded, tissue-thin note and then at Stanley. He marched forward a step and gravely shook Stanley's hand like a general conferring a decoration. "Thank you, thank you, my buddy Stanley."

"Hey, Lello, forget about it."

Lello looked down at the note again and then, suddenly, seized Leacock's hand and kissed it.

"Hey!"

"Thank you, Stanley, thank you."

"Yeah, okay. Now scram, would you?"

Lello retreated a few steps and then snapped off a salute.

Stanley smiled and returned it. "So long."

He straightened his tie and walked to the door of the apartment building. Just inside the great door, to the left, was a sliding window and behind that, an elderly man, expectant and bored, like a teller in a bank. He looked at Stanley with suspicion. He was the first black man he had seen up close. He slid back the window.

"Desidera?"

"Afternoon," said Stanley. "I'm looking for a girl." He traced the curves of feminine hips in the air. "She lives in this building." Pointing towards the ceiling. "Upstairs."

The porter's face darkened. "No," he said shortly. He looked away.

Stanley smiled nervously and wiped the sweat off his upper lip.

"You don't understand. I just want to talk to the girl. She lives in this building."

The porter said something angry and slid the window shut.

"Please mister, I don't mean no harm."

He shouted through the glass, pointing toward the door. "Via! Vai via!"

Stanley walked back out into the street. Lello had found another shady spot and was sitting, waiting. He scrambled to his feet. "Hey Stanley!"

"What is it about this town, Lello? Everybody thinks we're the bad guys, like we were the Germans or something. Everybody thinks we're looking for whores. I don't get it."

Lello's dirty face brightened. "I get for you. Five cigarette."

Stanley Leacock squatted down until he was face to face with the kid. "Look, you want five cigarettes, I'll give you five cigarettes, but you have to do something for me. I want you to come inside and explain to that guy that I gotta speak to that girl. Just talk, you understand? Tell that guy I don't want to hurt nobody. Okay? Deal?"

Lello held up five fingers. "Five cigarette?"

"Yeah, five."

"Come." Lello marched up to the porter's window and rapped on the glass. "Senti . . ."

The man looked up from his copy of *Il Messaggero*, saw the urchin and the black soldier, and waved them away.

Lello puffed out his thin chest and barged into the porter's lodge, bellowing in Italian as he went. The porter jumped up from his desk and tried to swat Lello, but the kid was too nimble for him. There was a brief and heated exchange in Italian of which Stanley could make out only two words: "Stanley" and "cigarette." The latter seemed to calm the man. Lello emerged triumphant.

"He say okay. You give him two cigarette."

Leacock smiled and handed over the smokes. The porter examined them closely, as if they might not be the real thing, then put them in the desk drawer.

"Secondo piano, interna sei."

Lello grabbed Leacock's hand. "Come, Stanley."

"Wait. What was that about a piano?"

"Come, come." Lello dragged Leacock up two flights of stairs and knocked on the door of apartment number six.

"Okay Lello, you done enough. You can scram now."

"Attenda," whispered Lello, his ear to the door.

From within, a voice called. "Qui è?"

"Oh shit. It's her mama, Lello." The kid slapped him in the stomach.

"Sono Lello di Marco," he roared, "ed il mio grande amico Stanley!"

There came the sound of a lock turning and the rasp of a bolt being shot back. The door swung open. The woman was old, fat, and so short that Stanley thought she might be a dwarf. She looked impassively at the man and at the boy, as if being visited by a black American soldier and a street urchin was an everyday event.

"Sono—" said Stanley.

Without a word, without even changing expression, she closed the door.

"Wait!"

99

"Signora!" Lello pounded on the door. "Signora! Attenda! Un'attimo!"

The stout oak door hardly muffled the woman's irate voice. "Va t'en ne via! Vai! Vai! Andatene via! Stronzi maladetti! Porca miseria! Mortacci tua!"

Stanley's shoulders slumped and he shook his head. "Never mind, Lello . . ." He started for the stairs. The porter had been joined by his wife and the two of them looked with curiousity at Stanley as he passed.

"Thanks, mister," said Leacock, "thanks all the same."

"Ssst," hissed his wife. "Vieni qui. Venga . . ."

"What's she want, Lello?"

The woman spoke fast, glancing towards the stairs as she did so, afraid that the short old signora would come thundering down at any second and discover her treating with the enemy.

"She say that the old signora is for shit . . ."

"I know that."

"And she say him"—Lello jerked a thumb at the porter—"is a stupid old man and the signorina is no there."

Leacock brightened. "She's not home?"

Lello shook his head. "She . . ." He made a walking motion with his fingers and then held up his hand. "Pochi minuti, she there. Five minute, six minute, she there."

"She's out but she's coming back, is that it?"

Lello nodded vigorously. "Good."

"Then I'll wait."

"You give her three cigarette."

Leacock handed over the cigarettes and the woman smiled. "Grazie, generale."

Stanley and Lello waited longer than five minutes, long enough, in fact, for Lello to discover that Stanley knew none of a number of famous Hollywood actors, nor a single cowboy, not even an Indian. Stanley, for his part, heard a detailed description of the partisan raid on the German column in the Via Rasella and Lello's considerable, not to say pivotal, role in it. Lello was energetically acting out the Germans' falling grotesquely to the partisans' bomb when the girl came into the street. She glanced nervously at Stanley and then hurried for the gateway of the apartment building.

"Hey wait. Miss—"

"Signorina, attenda! Ti presenterò un amico, Stanley."

The girl stopped and shot a sidelong glance at Stanley and then put her head down. Stanley stepped in front of her, took a deep breath and said in a rush:

"Salve, signorina, come sta? Ero io nella strada ieri sera. Sono Stanley Leacock. Come ti chiami? Goddamn! I said it!"

The girl smiled and hid her mouth behind her hand. "Cosa?"

"Salve, signorina, come—"

"Ti prego, signore, lascimi." She tried to push by him.

"—io nella strada ieri—"

"Per favore . . ."

"Sono ti chiami?"

"Come," corrected Lello.

The girl smiled again and glanced at the porter and his wife.

"Dai," they urged, "dai, Elena. E un bravo raggazzo."

The girl stopped and hesitated. Then she put out her hand. "Mi chiamo Elena," she said softly.

Stanley pumped her hand. "Stanley. Elena, that's a pretty name."

"Stanley?" she said uncertainly.

Leacock grinned. "That's me." He turned her around and started walking her away from the apartment building. "I told you last night I'd come back. And here I am. I thought maybe you and me might take a little walk. You know, a walk . . ." He marched two fingers along his arm. "You know, a walk."

"Una passegiata," translated Lello, trailing behind them.

Elena shook her head. "Non posso . . ."

"Please? Five minutes?"

"Cinque minuti," put in Lello.

"Hey Lello, take a hike."

Elena glanced over her shoulder at her apartment building and then looked at Stanley. "Cinque minuti?"

"Yeah, just five minutes. There a park around here or something? Lello, there a park around here?"

Lello and Elena looked blankly at him. "Never mind, let's just take a walk."

They walked a block in silence, Lello keeping a discreet distance behind, like a chaperone. Stanley stole a look at Elena. She was short and thin—most Romans were nothing but skin and bone—with pretty curly black hair and very white teeth. He could see no resemblance between her and the gorgon who guarded the apartment. He guessed that the woman must be her grandmother. Elena's clothes were shabby but clean, and on her feet she wore the knitted clogs that most women wore. Shoe leather had run out years ago.

At the top of the Via Dataria they climbed a steep flight of steps and found themselves in a wide piazza giving a fine view of the city. To their right rose the bulk of a huge palace, guarded by two bear-kneed New Zealanders. An American army jeep was parked in the middle of the square and a couple of MPs lazed in the seats listening to the squawk of the radio. Like all soldiers, Stanley stopped involuntarily when he saw the two policemen, wondering if the smart thing to do would be to head back down the steps, the way they had come. But he caught himself. He hadn't done anything wrong, and he figured that it wouldn't do to look like a coward on a first date. He examined the palace instead.

"That's an awfully large building. What is it?"

"Palazzo Quirinale," said Elena. "Il Palazzo del Re."

She traced a crown over her head. "Il re e la regina."

"The kink," shouted Lello. "The kink and quin."

"The king and the queen's palace," said Stanley. "I never knew that there really was kings and queens. I mean, I heard about them in fairy tales and stuff like that, but I always thought that was just make believe. Just think, I'll be able to tell my mama I saw a real king's palace."

"Mamma?"

Leacock smiled. "Yeah, my mama back home in the United States of America. I sure miss her sometimes."

They walked past the jeep. The two MPs looked them over and then sniggered about something. Leacock frowned and looked away.

"Hey look. A park." Across the street from the palace was a little patch of green, a few stunted trees and an equestrian statue. "Maybe we can find us a bench and sit down." He led Elena to the park and they settled on a broken bench under one of the trees.

"Hot," said Stanley. He pointed to the sun.

" 'At," repeated Elena. "Fa caldo."

"Fa caldo."

Elena giggled and said something.

"Next time I'm going to bring a dictionary."

"Dizionario."

"Maybe you can teach me Italian and I'll teach you English."

Elena shrugged and shook her head.

"When I saw you last night, I knew you were the girl for me. You looked so pretty standing out there on the balcony."

Elena shrugged again.

"Awww well, it's nice just to sit here. You want a cigarette?" He pulled the pack out of his shirt pocket.

"Non fumo, grazie."

"That don't matter." He folded the pack into her hand. "Take it and give 'em to someone. Maybe your daddy or someone."

"Daddy?"

"Yeah, you know, there's Mama and Daddy."

"Papà?"

"Right. Papa. Mama and Papa."

"Papà."

"Papà."

"Giusto."

They were silent a moment. Lello sat twenty yards away, watching intently. He had seen Stanley give an entire pack of cigarettes to Elena, and it didn't look as if she was going to have to do anything in return. Every day the Americans became stranger and stranger.

"You work or something?"

Elena looked puzzled.

"Work?"

"Non capisco."

"Me, I'm a shoemaker, back home." He pointed to his boots and made a sewing motion. "My whole family, we got a shop to repair shoes."

"Ahhhh. Calzolaio."

"Is that what you call it? Calz—"

"—olaio."

"Calzolaio."

"Bravo."

She raised her legs off the ground and held them straight and stiff in front of her, showing her shoes. "Sono brutte queste scarpe."

"What are those made of? Yarn?" The soles were crudely carved from a block of wood and the woven wool nailed to it with tacks. "If I can get hold of some leather, I'll make you some nice shoes, with heels this long." He tapped the thick heel of her clog and held his fingers a few inches apart. "They'll be fine."

She said something and pointed to Stanley's own heavy boots.

"I'll get some leather. It don't take any hide at all to make a pair of ladies shoes." He looked professionally at her foot. "I'll bet you take a small shoe, 'bout a five." He pointed and held up five fingers.

"Cinque?"

He bent over and put one finger on her heel and another on her toe.

"Size five, right?"

Elena got the message. "Non cinque, trentuno." She traced a three and a one in the dust.

"Thirty-one!" Leacock laughed. "Back home that's an awful big shoe!"

They were silent again. Elena finally spoke. "Fratelli? Sorelle?"

"I don't know . . ."

"C'è mamma, papà, fratelli, sorelle." She raised her hand high to indicate the height of the father, a little lower for mother, and lower than that for brothers and sisters.

"Oh, I got two brothers and a sister." He held up two fingers, then one.

"Due fratelli, una sorella. Ci son' anche negri?"

Stanley shook his head. "I don't know what you're saying . . ."

She rubbed the skin on the back of his hand. "Ci son' anche negri? I fratelli son' negri? La sorella è anche negra?"

Stanley laughed. "Oh yes ma'am, we're all colored. God don't mix up a set."

A woman had ambled into the park, walking casually, but glancing around as if she was being followed. She carried a small brown cardboard suitcase, clutching it close to her breast. She walked past Stanley and Elena, paused a few yards beyond and then returned. She stopped in front of Elena and popped open the suitcase.

"Uova," she whispered. "Ne vuole?" Nestled in a bed of newspaper were six brown eggs. Elena stared into the case and then looked away.

"No grazie."

"Sei per trenta," said the woman.

104

"Hey, Elena, you want them eggs? Lady, how much?" Stanley reached for his billfold. "How much?"

The woman looked at the bills and upped her price. "Cinquanta per sei."

"No, no, no," protested Elena.

The woman held up five fingers. "Cinquanta. Uova. Buone, fresche." She held up one of the eggs as if displaying a gem from a jeweler's tray. "Guarda che roba . . . Cinquanta lire, poco, poco."

"Ladra!" yelled Lello, running up. He poured a torrent of irate Italian on her, heaping abuse on her and her merchandise. She waved him off like a pesky fly.

"Lello, tell her I want them eggs."

Lello took charge. The negotiations were lengthy and loud, the seller insisting first on fifty, then forty-five, then thirty-five lire for the six eggs. But Lello was resolute, arguing manfully that the old signora had better sell her eggs for twenty lire because now the Americani were here there would be eggs for everybody. Get some money while you can . . .

Finally: "She say, twenty-five and two cigarette."

"Fine." Stanley peeled off three ten-lira notes, but the woman denied having any change. Change? Who had change in times like these?

"Aww hell, take thirty."

"No cigarette," cautioned Lello.

The egg seller wrapped the eggs and handed them to Stanley. "Thank you, ma'am."

"Vai, brutta carogna," ordered Lello.

The woman made to slap him, but he danced away, shouting and giggling. "Via, stronza!"

Grumbling, the woman made her way out of the park. Stanley unwrapped the eggs and looked at them. "It's pretty sad when you gotta fight over a bunch of eggs. There's no food in Rome, is there?" He looked sadly at the eggs. "My family, we're pretty poor. There's lots of poor folks back home, but I don't think there's any so poor that eggs is something special."

He took an egg from its newspaper nest and handed one to Lello. "You don't mind if he has one, do you?" The boy took the egg, cracked it on the corner of the bench and sucked it raw into his mouth. He licked his lips and ran his tongue over his teeth. "Buono . . ."

"Yuck," said Stanley. He carefully folded the paper over the eggs and handed them to Elena. "Here. Take these."

She looked away. "No, non posso."

He patted his pockets, pulling out the can of milk and the two soft candy bars. "These are presents for you. Elena, I brought this stuff for you."

Lello's eyes grew wide at such a display of wealth. "Give me, Stanley."

"You had enough. These are for Elena."

"She don' wan'."

"How come?"

"She think you give her for fuck. Give me. I get nice girl."

Stanley took Elena's head in his hands, making her look at him. Her hair was warm and soft. "Hey, this is for you. Back home you take a present to a girl when you go out on a date. I'm not trying to pay you for . . ." He squirmed in embarrassment. "Look," he said gently, "please take this stuff. I don't need it. They give us plenty. Give the eggs to your mama and your . . . papà."

Lello remarked that she would be crazy not to take the stuff.

"Please, Elena . . ."

"Grazie," she said, her eyes downcast.

"No," he said, "Say 'thank you.' "

She smiled. "Thank you. Thank you Stanley."

"Hey, you like to dance?" He put his hand on his waist and swayed. He hummed a tune. "Dance? You like that?"

She smiled a bit more. "Ballare? Si, mi piace."

"Maybe we can go out dancing one night. You know this song: 'I can't give you anything but love, babeee . . .' "

"Babee . . ." sang Lello.

"Lello, get lost."

Lello slunk off.

"You know any songs, Elena?"

Elena looked up shyly. "Conosco una canzone, una canzone in inglese." She cleared her throat and then sang softly. "Stormy wedder, sin' my manni I ain' togedder . . ."

Stanley laughed and clapped his hands. "Hey! You speak English after all. It's raining all the time . . ." He sang loudly.

She laughed too, brightly and happily, and sang again: "Stormy wedder sin' my manni I ain' togedder . . ."

"Beautiful!"

"S'rain all de time . . ."

"Hey kaffir!"

Stanley looked up and winced. On the far side of the park stood three men, one of whom had his hand bandaged. Stanley swallowed hard. The three South Africans strode across the park toward them. "Hey, you fuckin' munt. Is that a white missie you have there? We're going to have to learn you, kaffir."

Stanley jumped up and grabbed Elena's hand. "C'mon, Elena. We gotta get out of here."

"Stanley, che successo?"

"C'mon, c'mon," he said urgently, pushing her along. He broke into a trot.

"Where you going, kaffirje?"

"Oh shit, oh shit," said Stanley. The MP jeep was gone. They crossed the street and ran to the gates of the palace. "Hey," Stanley said to the two New Zealanders, "you have to help us." The South Africans were trotting across the street.

"Fuck off," one of the sentries said out of the side of his mouth.

"Please man . . ."

"We're on fuckin' duty."

"Too right," said his companion.

"Hey kaffir."

"C'mon Elena." He grabbed her by the shoulder and together they raced down the steps. The South Africans' boots were ringing on the stones behind them, and they were yelling like hunters in full gallop.

"Jesus!"

"Stanley!"

At the bottom of the stairs one of the South Africans dove forward and tackled Stanley, pulling him down from the knees. Leacock landed heavily on the warm cobbles, but scrambled to his feet.

"Okay, you black bastard," said the one with the bandaged hand. "You haven't got your mate with you this time."

Stanley got between his attackers and Elena. "Why don't you just leave us alone," he said, his voice high and breaking with fear. "We don't want no trouble."

"We don't want no trouble," mimicked one of the men in a falsetto.

"All you munts are cowards."

"You'll fuck our boks but you won't fight our men."

"Stanley!" cried Elena.

"Stanley!" squeaked one of the men.

"Please man . . ."

The one with the bandaged hand stepped forward and swung. Stanley managed to get most of his head out of the way but he caught some of the punch. He staggered back a few feet. Elena didn't scream, she attacked. Nails out like a cat, she threw herself on the South African, carving three scarlet lines down the side of his face.

The soldier yelped in pain and threw her to one side. Stanley was up now, his fists out. He was resigned to getting beat up, but he was not going to allow Elena to be hurt by these thugs. He struck out and felt the satisfying connection of fist and belly. He grabbed Elena and pulled her down the street a few yards.

"Where you going, Stanley?" one of them roared.

"Let's go!"

Elena and Stanley ran fast, the South Africans in hot pursuit. Stanley tried to think. He had to do what they had done the night before, they had to lose them. Stanley and Elena crashed through a warren of narrow streets, the shouts of the South Africans echoing, bouncing off the walls of the close-packed houses.

"Where do we go? Where do we go?"

Elena tugged at his arm and pulled him into an alley. Then she stopped.

"C'mon," he yelled, "we can't stop."

"Guarda!"

Coming toward them, running through the alley was Lello at the head of a pack of boys. There were fifteen, perhaps twenty of them, each child a copy of Lello himself: thin, dirty, and dressed in the rags of a conquering army. The hoard of children were screaming like devils. Without hesitating they threw themselves on the three big South Africans.

"You little fuckers! Get off!"

The boys swarmed over the soldiers like rats, kicking, clawing, biting. Like bears attacked by terriers, the big men threw them off, but they came back, a half a dozen to each man, dragging them down. Once on the ground the boys danced around them, kicking

108

and taunting. Lello threw himself on the chest of one of them, grabbed the man by the ears and smacked his head against the ungiving cobblestones.

In a matter of seconds, though, the street was empty of children. The South Africans staggered to their feet, bodies and pride bruised. Then they discovered that their pockets had been picked.

7

McManus knew better than to park his jeep in the wide porte-cochère of the Excelsior Hotel, a privilege allowed only to senior brass. He swung the rattling vehicle into the guarded lot on Via Lombardia and signed in with the Pfc in charge.

"Fill 'er up, check the oil, and give 'er a wax job," Donal said with a grin.

The hot, bothered, unhappy private didn't think that was funny. "Only the third time today someone made that joke."

"Let a smile be your umbrella, that's my motto."

The attendant looked at the clear blue sky as if it was a personal affront. "Wrong time of year."

Some people, reflected McManus, have no sense of humor. He was waiting to cross the street now, and feeling better—no hang-over that morning, well, not much of one—and the wop at the Hotel Palatino Splendido had sworn to the CID guy just as he was instructed to. Maybe things would turn out okay. If only it wasn't so damn hot. He wiped a handful of sweat from his brow and waited as a line of Dodge trucks growled up the Via Veneto. The small Italian man standing next to him on the curb, a pimp, cleared his throat.

" 'Scuse please, sir . . ."

McManus didn't even look down. "Fuck off, greaseball." Then he crossed the street. The little man looked hurt.

The MPs on duty waved him through the revolving door and when he swept into the lobby he felt like he had passed from hell to heaven. His boots sunk into the deep, soft carpet, and all around him monkey-jacketed servants bowed and scraped—not to him, of course, but he appreciated catching their act—and from the marble lounge beyond the lobby came pretty sounds: the laughter of men and women, soft music from a string quartet, and the sweeter music of the rattle of ice and the chink of glasses. McManus shook his head. Not yet 9:00 A.M. and the brass were already hoisting a few. Now *that* was the kind of war McManus wouldn't have minded having a chance to fight. But best of all was the air: cool, smooth, sweet, rich, air-conditioned air. McManus drank it in like cold beer.

At the reception desk two concierges in their swallowtail coats and striped vests—they looked like diplomats—dealt with a colonel, two majors, a captain, and a civilian, and when those labors were done, ignored McManus, pretending they did not see him. He was, after all, only a sergeant.

McManus leaned across the reception desk as if it were a Hell's Kitchen bar. "Hey, Pepe, c'mere." He crooked a fat finger at the nearest flunky.

"Yes, sir?"

"What? Didn't you see me standing here?" At 250 pounds, McManus was hard to miss.

"I'm sorry, sir." The concierge doled out his smallest ration of civility.

"I'll bet. I'm here to pick up a lieutenant, Austin Kinney. You know the guy?"

Indeed he did. This concierge was the man who had exchanged Kinney's dollars at such a favorable rate. He was still wondering how much the lieutenant had paid Slade for his new quarters, a splendid two-bedroom suite on the second floor.

"Lieutenant Kinney is still at his breakfast."

"Is that so? Well you better tell me where he is, Pepe, because he's gotta report to his CO in about two minutes or he's gonna be in deep shit up to his ears, capeesh?"

The man frowned, nodded, and snapped his fingers. A middle-aged bellhop in a Paging Phillip Morris uniform scuttled over. He took his orders in Italian and headed for the lounge, McManus following.

"No," snapped the concierge, "you wait." He pointed to a spot on the far side of the lobby, like a teacher consigning the bad boy of the class to a corner. McManus retreated, grumbling to himself.

If it weren't for all the brass in the room, he would have given the little meatball a piece of his mind.

The bell hop reappeared a few moments later, leading a lieutenant and a full colonel into the lobby. McManus studied the two men closely. The bird colonel was a big man, about McManus's size, with a big sweet cigar sticking straight out of his face like the barrel of a field piece. He clapped Lieutenant Kinney on the back and spoke around the cigar, which seemed to be cemented between his big white teeth.

"Well hell, Lex Kinney's boy. Glad to meet you. Limey colonel I know says its going to be a long war so you might as well spend it among friends. Am I right?"

"You are, sir."

"Darn tootin'."

McManus looked with great interest at Lex Kinney's boy. He was as tall as the major but much slimmer, and stood as straight as if he were on a parade ground. He had blonde hair and pretty-boy blue eyes, long lashed. He smiled modestly at the colonel but McManus knew that smile. It said, "I'm a second lieutenant and you're a full colonel and, not that it matters much, a horse's ass."

"What you got planned for the rest of the day, son?"

"Reporting to my new outfit, sir." Kinney's tone of voice suggested that there was nothing he would rather do.

The colonel pulled the cigar out of his mouth and looked at it as if something of great import was inscribed in the outer leaf. "You play bridge, Austin?"

"Yes sir, I do."

"Well, there's usually a game or two going on up in Charlie Hamilton's suite. Junior officers aren't usually encouraged to partake, but for Lex Kinney's boy—Charlie knows your old man too. Maybe you ought to drop in some time, meet some of the fellows."

"I'd like that, sir."

"Good. Anytime. In the meantime, don't work too hard."

"I think they're going to be keeping me pretty busy, sir."

The colonel guffawed. "Just like the old man, eh? Always got the nose to the grindstone. Remember Austin, all work and no play . . ."

Austin Kinney grinned. "I read you, sir."

He slapped Kinney on the back. "Gotta go. Thanks for the smoke, son."

112

"My pleasure, Colonel." He snapped off a salute.

"So long, son." The colonel was secretly excited to have met young Austin Kinney. This war wasn't going to last forever and there was no better way to get started in civilian life than by having a connection to old Lex Kinney. There was a man who could make a guy rich if he decided he liked you.

McManus, knowing nothing of Kinney's pedigree, could only wonder at what he had witnessed. In his experience, colonels didn't have a lot to say to second johns unless the lieutenant had done something very, very wrong. *Thanks for the smoke, son!* Second lieutenants didn't offer bird colonels cigars—it was like offering a smoke, if not to Jesus Christ himself, then to John the Baptist, maybe the Virgin Mary.

But then, McManus was as experienced in measuring men as the flunky at the desk. Even if he hadn't witnessed the colonel's avuncular moment with Kinney, McManus knew at a glance that this was no ordinary second john. He was dressed in perfectly pressed suntans, looking as crisp and as handsome as a recruiting poster.

"Sergeant?"

"McManus, sir."

"Good to meet you." He returned Donal's salute like a field marshall.

"Likewise, sir."

"Let's get going," said Kinney, as if McManus had somehow been responsible for the delay.

"Jeep's across the street, Lieutenant."

"Go get it, Sergeant."

McManus looked doubtful. "Sir, I don't think them MPs on the door would . . ."

"Don't worry about them, Sergeant. I'm a guest of this hotel." Kinney spoke as if that would make a difference.

"Okay, sir." McManus bid good-bye to the cool air, wading through the heat to the barbed-wire lot. The steering wheel burned his hands and the seat was almost too hot to sit on. When he pulled the jeep into the shade of the porte cochere, Kinney was waiting on the top step wearing his cap and a pair of wire-framed sunglasses. The MPs didn't raise an eyebrow when they saw the jeep, and McManus had to smile to himself: Kinney was an operator and that wasn't such a bad thing. A good officer—not a sad sack of shit

113

like Thorpe—could make life easier for the men under his command.

As Kinney slid into the passenger seat of the jeep, McManus had further cause to marvel at the young lieutenant. The heat didn't seem to bother him, either. McManus was sweating buckets, but Kinney sat cool and unruffled, as if he had carried a nimbus of cool Excelsior air out with him.

"So Sergeant, tell me about the company."

McManus gunned the jeep past a couple of British trucks, crossed the Piazza Barberini, and muscled it up the Via Quattro Fontane, downshifting as they climbed the hill.

"We're doing our job, Lieutenant, but it'll be easier with you here." What the hell, he thought, kiss a little ass. Never hurts. "Captain Thorpe can't be everywhere." He added a silent: "thank God."

"Good man?"

But McManus wasn't about to trade the good graces of a captain for those of an unknown lieutenant, no matter how skillful an operator he appeared to be. "Oh yes, sir. One of the best."

"Where's he from?"

"Couldn't rightly say, sir. He's never told me."

"And the men?"

"They're from all over. Couple from New York, even got one from Maine." He mentioned Maine as if it was on the edge of an inaccurate map of faraway waters. "I'm from New York myself, sir."

"That's not what I meant, Sergeant. I meant, what are the men like?"

"Oh." He swung right on the Via Nazionale. "Sorry sir. They're okay. Like any bunch of guys, you gotta watch them otherwise you get a lot of goldbricking, you know. Depends on how you feel about nig—Negroes, sir."

Kinney turned to look at McManus. The sergeant, glancing at his pasenger, could see himself reflected in the polished lenses of the lieutenant's glasses. "Negroes?"

"Yes sir, this is a colored outfit. Didn't you know?"

"No. I didn't."

"I hope it don't bother you none. Me, I don't care. I know Eddie—Manganaro, he's the staff sergeant—he don't like it much. And Cal—Utterback—it sure as hell eats at him. But they ain't bad

114

boys. Pretty simple, some of 'em, but I guess you gotta expect that."

Kinney shrugged. He had no opinion about blacks, except that they were inferior to white people. In Kinney's world, Negroes were waiters, Pullman porters, boot blacks, at their most advanced, entertainers. None of them worth considering except for the quality of the service they provided. "Doesn't bother me, Sergeant."

"That's good, sir. Live and let live, that's my motto."

"Is it?"

"Yessir, it is," said Donal McManus emphatically.

KINNEY REPORTED SMARTLY if not on time, but Thorpe decided not to say anything about it in the interests of starting out on the right foot. The man Kinney was replacing had disliked Thorpe so much that the captain half suspected that his former second in command had actually welcomed his serious case of dysentery. Austin Kinney seemed at first glance to be a different type altogether, making amends for his tardiness by showing Captain Thorpe as much respect as he had the colonel in the lobby of the Excelsior Hotel.

"Good to have you aboard, Kinney."

"Glad to be here, sir."

For a moment the two officers eyed one another, each sizing the other up. Kinney knew nothing about his superior and Thorpe knew nothing at all about his new second in command. Thorpe had not even heard of that titan of New York finance, Lex Kinney.

Both men liked what they saw. Thorpe thought the lieutenant looked like a healthy, intelligent, bright-eyed, eager, respectful young man; Kinney thought that Thorpe looked like a nervous Nellie, a pushover.

"So. Just in from England?"

"Yes sir, that's right."

"So. How is old Blighty? Ha-ha."

Kinney smiled as if he appreciated a good joke as much as the next man. "Just fine, sir. A little cooler there, though."

"I can imagine." Thorpe's office was on the second floor of the warehouse, and his two windows caught a breeze which smelled of the scraggly pine tree in the courtyard of the building next door and the hot, dusty roofs just beyond.

"Where did they put you?"

"At the Excelsior, sir."

"I'm up the street at the Flora. I tried to get posted to the Grand, but nothing doing." This irritated Thorpe. The Flora was a first-class hotel—every bit as good as the Excelsior—but under the Germans it had housed senior officials of the Gestapo and had been the target of a huge partisan bombing late in the German occupation, the blast reducing the facade and lobby to rubble. The corridors and public rooms were now a noisy nightmare of workmen and power tools. Rare was the morning that Thorpe wasn't jolted awake by shouts and poundings, hard to take after an evening of heavy drinking.

"We should have a drink some time, seeing as we're neighbors."

"I'd like that, sir."

During the moment of silence which followed, a voice split the air, an apoplectic roar of anger, followed by a string of obscenities so penetratingly graphic and hurtful that Kinney could only imagine that they had been carefully worked out beforehand, in the author's spare time. Thorpe looked pained.

"That's sergeant Utterback down on the warehouse floor. He's a little tough on the men, but *he's* a good man. Hard worker."

"That's good, sir."

"Yes." Thorpe smoothed his military mustache as if reassuring himself that it was still there, on his upper lip, where he had left it that morning. "Plenty of hard work in this outfit, Lieutenant. This whole neighborhood makes up one of the largest depots in the theater. We're serving both sectors, front and behind the lines. There are transport companies, three of them, MPs, the Quartermasters, maintenance, APO, even the accountants to make sure we stay on the straight and narrow. Ha-ha. That's a big problem for us, you know."

"Staying on the straight and narrow, sir?"

"Well, yes—no. Security, I mean to say. Keeping the supplies secure. The Romans will steal anything and a lot of our job is making sure that they don't steal anything from us. That wasn't a problem you had to face in England much, they're more civilized there, of course. More like us, you understand. The Italians are kind of childish, can't seem to tell the difference between right and wrong." Thorpe paused. "You're not, er, of Italian extraction, are you, Kinney? I mean, Kinney isn't, I don't think, but perhaps on your mother's side."

"No sir, no Italian blood in my veins."

Thorpe looked relieved. "That's good. It doesn't do to get too close to these people. Sergeant Manganaro is, of course—of Italian extraction, I mean—and that's come in pretty handy, his speaking the language, but sometimes I think he's quite sensitive about it. Then, other times I hear him say things about the eyeties—well, you'd think he wasn't one himself." Thorpe managed to pull himself back on course. "Anyway, our watchword here, Kinney, is vigilance."

"I can appreciate that, sir." Kinney looked attentive, like an eager-beaver student hanging on his teacher's every word. It unnerved Thorpe slightly. He was pleased when there was a knock at the door and Sergeant McManus came into the room.

"Sorry to disturb you, sir, but we've got something downstairs you might want to take a look-see at."

"What is it, Sergeant?"

"A delivery we don't know anything about."

"Aren't we used to that?"

"Well yes sir, but this is a little different. Could cause trouble."

"Then send it back."

McManus paused a moment. "Well, sir, what happens if we were supposed to be expecting it but the paperwork hasn't caught up with us yet? Could happen that we'll get a disbursement on this but we'll already have sent it back, if you see what I mean, sir."

"What is this thing we're talking about, McManus? Why are you being so mysterious?"

"No sir, sorry sir. It's a refrigerator, sir, a big one."

Kinney leaned forward in his chair. "Captain, why don't you let me handle this?"

THE FREEZER, A white enamel square about the size of a garden shed, sat on the flat bed of a three-ton Chevrolet truck. It looked as immovable as an Alp. Five men sat on the tailgate of the truck, dangling their legs over the edge like kids playing on a bridge. When Kinney appeared, one of them hopped off his perch, saluted sloppily, and proffered a clipboard.

"A signature and she's all yours, sir."

Kinney riffled the wad of papers and found the unit designation to be correct. The forms seemed in order. A rubber stamp and an illegible signature on the last page rendered the documents official

117

but concealed their origin. He raised his eyebrows at McManus. "No one knows anything about this?"

"We sure as hell didn't order it, sir. And if we sign for it and it ain't supposed to be here, then it'll be a pain in the butt to get rid of, sir. On the other hand, like I told the captain . . ."

The driver shifted uneasily. He was anxious to deliver the freezer because if he failed to get rid of it then he would be stuck with it and, worse, responsible for the thing. "Look, Lieutenant, I'm here at the right place, right? You're A of the 169th of the Third, right?" He smiled. "Sir, it was meant to be."

Kinney laughed. "This thing make ice?"

"You'll have to ask the experts." The driver jerked his thumb at the guys on the truck. "Hey Bob, this thing make ice?"

"Hell yes. Make a ton of ice."

Kinney clicked his ballpoint and signed with a flourish. "Then we'll take it."

"I just hope this thing ain't for meat," said McManus warily. "The next thing you know, the thing'll go on the fritz or the power'll go out and we'll have a couple of tons of spoilage on the books."

"Meat?" The man called Bob hopped off the tailgate, dragging a heavy tool box after him. "Meat? Sergeant, you don't know your freezers."

"You do, I suppose?"

"Bob and his guys install these things," the driver explained. "That's what they're here for. Refrigeration is his life."

"This isn't a meat locker, Sarge. It's way too small. This here is the army's new two-hundred-fifty-cubic-foot portable. This baby replaces the old ten-thousand-pounder semitrailer. And don't worry about the power, this runs on a B & S two-stroke gasoline engine. It'll drop down to minus ten degrees Fahrenheit, no problem."

"Told you," said the driver.

"But what's it *for?* We always handle dry goods."

"Search me," said Bob.

McManus sighed. Sometimes he wished he was in the infantry.

8

The Italians may have thought the Americans were profligate wasters of food and other essentials, but the army considered itself a model of prudence and frugality. Within days of arriving in Rome, the maintenance division of the Army Service Forces had established itself in the light industrial zone of the city, just outside the Porta del Popolo on the Via Flaminia. Just as hospitals repaired men for return to active service, so the shops of the maintenance division reclaimed the scraps and junk of war for further use.

At the shoe rebuilding shop Stanley managed to cadge just about all he needed to make Elena a pair of shoes. There was plenty of top-grain leather around, as well as 12-iron leather for soles, pots of barge cement, upholstery and sail needles, waxed linen thread, steel shanks to support the heels, and millions of clinching nails. All he needed now was a last and some peace and quiet.

Jimmy Holt was stretched out on his bed, hot and tired after a long day's work. Stanley's industry disconcerted him.

"Where you been?"

Stanley smiled and dumped a canvas bag full of his gleanings onto the bed. "Look what I got."

Holt fingered the steel shanks. "What the hell are these?"

"Shanks," said Stanley proudly.

"And just what the fuck are shanks?"

"Don't tell me you don't know what a shank is."

"If I knew what the fuck a shank was, would I asked you?"

"Shanks are for making high heels. You can't make high heels without shanks, Jimmy."

"Well any dumb motherfucker knows that."

"I'm making a pair of high heels to give Elena. You seen the kind of shitty shoes girls wearing in this town? Made out of yarn? That's no shoe for a lady."

"Uh-uh." Jimmy lay back on his bed.

"But Jimmy . . ."

"Yeah?"

"I need your help."

Holt raised himself up on his elbows. "You're making a pair of high-heel shoes for Elena?"

"That's right."

"And you need my help?"

"Yessir."

"Get the fuck out of here." Holt laughed. "What kind of bull-shit is this? I don't know nothing about making shoes."

"No, listen, Jimmy, I need your help getting some of the tools. I need a straight pick, a light hammer, and a sledgehammer. That's all."

"Do I look like I run a hardware store to you, Stanley?"

"I just want you to come with me over to the depot when I ask Sergeant McManus, that's all."

"Wait. You're gonna use all that shit on your bed, plus a light hammer, plus a straight pick, plus a sledgehammer, all that to make a itty bitty pair of high-heel shoes?"

"That's right."

"You have lost your mind."

Stanley giggled. "You'll see."

"You're gonna just set there on your bed and make these shoes, is that right?"

"No, I'm gonna do it outside. See, I'll be using barge cement and that stuff'll kill you."

"Oh. *Barge cement.* Of course. Stupid of me." Wearily, Holt swung himself off the bed. "C'mon, Stanley. Let's go see the sergeant."

McManus was alone in the office at the depot, putting the finishing touches on the day's paperwork. A cigar smoldered in the full ashtray and when it wasn't in his mouth, McManus whistled, a jazzy rendition of "Glow Little Glow Worm." An old time noncom, he loved army paperwork—it made sense to him in a way that life did not. He stopped whistling, stuffed the cigar in his mouth, and leaned back in his chair when Holt and Leacock wrenched open the office door.

"Christ," said McManus, "I hate that door."

"Sarge, we come to ask you a favor."

"Stanley's come to ask you a favor."

"No passes, no furloughs, no lending money, and wipe your own ass." McManus puffed on the cigar, filling a good portion of the room with pungent smoke.

"Sarge. Stanley wants to borrow a straight pick, a light hammer, and a sledge hammer because he is going to make a pair of high-heel shoes."

"That's right, Sarge."

McManus glanced at them over his cigar. "You boys ain't been drinking have you? 'Cause if you has, give me some."

"Not us, Sarge."

"What? The heat finally get to you?"

"It's hot, Sarge, but it ain't that hot."

McManus closed his eyes and shook his head. "You know, this is supposed to be a simple job. The stuff comes in, we pick it up, we store it. A order comes in, we load the truck, we take the shit to where it's supposed to be. A place for everything and everything in its place, that's my motto."

"Yeah?"

"But I understand. I'm not so stupid. Nothing is as simple as it's supposed to be, right? Sometimes you get too much stuff, sometimes you don't get enough stuff. Shit gets lost. Outfits ain't where they supposed to be. I got a two-ton refrigerator out there I don't know what the fuck it's for. That's the army."

"I don't get it, Sarge."

"Me neither, Stanley," said Holt.

"What you trying to say?"

"What I'm trying to say, Stanley, is normal fuckups I understand. But what I don't get is how I got two guys in my outfit say they can make a pair of high-heel shoes with a pick and a sledge-hammer. This, I gotta say, don't make sense to me."

"Don't make sense to me either, Sarge," said Holt.

"You guys ain't working for the krauts, are you? You know, spreading fear and confusion in the rear echelons? That makes sense, because I mean, I'm confused and I fear you two have completely lost your fuckin' minds."

"I'm sane and sober, Sarge."

"Jimmy, you I don't worry about so much. But I think your friend Stanley here, he's a fuckin' nut."

"You give me the tools, Sarge, and I have you a pair of high heels in three hours. You'll see."

"He's going to make them out of barge cement," said Holt.

"Stanley, I don't want a pair of high heels."

"You know what I mean, Sarge. I'll show them to you in three hours, no time flat."

"Jesus Christ!" McManus threw up his hands. "Take the tools. Take a screwdriver and make a hat. Take a fuckin' chisel and make a bathrobe. Do whatever you want. Just don't lose 'em or break 'em."

"Thanks, Sergeant," said Stanley gleefully. "We won't."

Leacock took McManus at his word, raiding the well-stocked company toolroom and filling his bag with a variety of hammers, pliers, and shears. Jimmy shouldered the pick and the sledgehammer.

"So now what?"

"Like I said, we got to do this outside. At the racetrack."

"Oh yeah. I forgot. Barge cement."

The vast field, the Circo Massimo, once the great racecourse of ancient Rome, lay at the foot of the Palatine Hill, only a few hundred yards from the depot. In form, the Circo Massimo was still the great elongated oval of the old track, ringed round by the raised embankments where the spectators' stands once stood.

To visitors with a romantic turn of mind, a certain grandeur still lurked here—it was easy to imagine the pounding of horses' hooves, the cries of the charioteers, the roar of the crowd. But to soldiers who were not, in the main, a romantic bunch, the Circo Massimo was just a big, wide-open space where they could let off steam. They called it the racetrack because it looked like a racetrack.

When Stanley and Jimmy arrived, a couple of baseball games were underway on the wide turn at the western end of the course and some Poles were playing a spirited, noisy game of soccer in the back straight. From the *spina*, the raised grassy island in the middle of the course, a British officer with a couple of woods practiced drives, whacking golf balls towards the place where senators once sat.

"Where we going, Stanley?"

"Right here." Stanley heeled a divot out of the ground and placed the end of the pick handle in the dent he had made in the earth. "Okay, now I'm gonna hold the shaft and I want you to pound the pick into the ground with the sledgehammer."

Holt looked at his friend quizzically. "You want me to beat the pick into the ground so's the head is sticking up?"

"That's right."

"What for?"

"You'll see. Just make sure you hit the pick and not my hands."

Holt raised the sledgehammer and slammed it down on to the pick head. The handle sunk an inch into the ground. It took only a few swings for him to drive the shaft into the ground, the pick standing up like a T. Sweat streamed in rivulets down Holt's face.

"Okay," said Stanley. "That's good. See, Jimmy." He fingered the blunt metal edge of the pick. "This here's the last."

"Last what?"

"The *shoe* last. You need a good strong piece of metal like this to build a shoe on. This here pick is going to stand in for the shape, sort of, of Elena's foot. It'll have to be a square toe. I mean, it's not a real last, I'm going to have to fit it by eye, but it was all I could think to do it on."

"It's a start, Stanley. Now what do I do?"

"Your part is done. You can just sit and talk to me and beat the shit out of any of those fuckin' Africans show up."

Holt lay down on the ground and stretched out. He plucked a stalk of sweet grass and stuck it in his mouth. "They show up and you're on your own, my friend."

"Now you wouldn't do that to me, I know." Stanley had spread out the piece of leather and had traced eight forms on it in pencil. Expertly, he cut out the pieces with the shears. "See, this is the innersole. This is the vamp. And this is a quarter, and this here is the topline. Put 'em all together and you got a shoe."

"Fascinating."

Stanley laid the iron leather on the pick and folded it over the last. "I wish these people would leave us alone. I was afraid that Elena was going to get hurt, you know? How can we go round together if I gotta keep looking over my shoulder all the time? That's no date." He tossed a handful of nails into his mouth like peanuts, picked up his hammer and started tapping away, pausing now and then to glue down some leather with barge cement.

"Stanley," said Holt soberly, "I'm not saying anyone should run away from anybody, but if they show up again and you alone, or you with Elena, you get the fuck out of there. You don't be a hero."

Stanley said something around the nails clenched in his teeth. "What?"

Stanley spat the nails into his palm. "I said don't worry. I'm not like you. I can't beat up nobody with a beer glass."

"That. That was just luck."

"Bullshit. Never mind the beer glass, you had the moves too. How'd you learn to move like that?" Stanley put the nails back in his mouth and returned to his makeshift last.

"Boxing. I did some boxing."

" 'Ike 'Oe 'Ouis," said Stanley.

"Oh yeah, I was just like Joe Louis." Holt laughed. "Yeah. Still. It's bullshit anyway, boxing is. Getting the shit whaled out of you for nothing." Holt shook his head. "Life is hard enough without volunteering to get beat up. I quit. Coach was mad."

" 'Oach?"

"In high school. Wanted me in the Golden Gloves. I said no thank you. Man can get hurt that way. I played football too—man can get hurt that way too, but not like boxing. I like baseball. We kicked ass all over the city. New York City champs two years in a row."

Stanley spit out the tacks. "No kidding? What you play?"

"Pitcher. After we won the second time, my senior year, a man comes up to me and says he wants me to play pro."

"No shit?"

"Negro league. Bullshit."

"Some good players in the Negro league. Cool Papa Bell is a good player. Josh Gibson is a good player. Satchell Paige."

"Yeah," said Holt, "but *Negro league?* That's bullshit. There's no Jew league for Hank Greenberg, no eye-talian league for the Di Maggios. Yankees, Dodgers, shit, they got fans in Harlem. How come they don't got Negro ball players? If I can't play for the Yankees 'cause I'm not good enough, good enough. If I can't play 'cause of what I am, that's bullshit."

"Then you won't be playing baseball, Jimmy."

"That's what the scout said."

"So what you do after school?"

Holt shrugged. "I got a job."

"What'd you do?"

Jimmy smiled. "I worked for an ice company. I delivered ice all over the city."

Stanley sang: "Any ice today, ladies? It's nice today, ladies. How about a piece of ice today?"

"I wish that song had never been wrote. Every time you tell someone you worked for an ice company somebody sings that damn song. How about you Stanley, you make shoes?"

"Our whole family repairs shoes, makes shoes. Always have."

"That what you going to do when you get back?"

"Guess so. You?"

"I don't have plans yet. Lots of sleep, some good food, and not taking any orders for a long time."

"Sounds good." Stanley went back to building up the innersole of the shoe.

Holt lay back in the grass and watched a formation of B17s high in the blue sky crawl noiselessly over the city. Shouts from the baseball diamond seemed muffled by the heavy sweet summer air. Stanley tapped and glued and mumbled to himself or talked to the leather that was taking shape under his expert hands. Jimmy Holt fell asleep.

WHEN MANNY FARFALLA appeared at the head of the Via Tor di Nona, some of the proprietors of the makeshift stalls which lined the street made hurried adjustments in their inventory. Pairs of American-army-issue boots disappeared under tables; cans of C, K, and D rations clattered out of sight; packs of cigarettes were thrust into pockets. A man with a suitcase of OD shirts closed up and walked away quickly as if he had a train to catch. Those who were selling merchandise whose origins were unclear—a cartload of potatoes, a few loaves of bread—stood their ground. All the vendors watched warily as the *poliziotto americano* made his way down the street.

Via Tor di Nona was the center of the black market in Rome, and due to the preoccupation of the Allies with more serious matters, it operated openly. From time to time the Carabinieri paid a visit and the dealers fled down the street as if blown by a gale.

The Italian police didn't pursue—it was too hot—and they knew that a temporary disruption was the best they could hope for anyway. In a hungry city there would always be a black market. Throw the black marketeers off the Via Tor di Nona and they would circle like starlings and settle somewhere else.

American soldiers were rarely seen on Via Tor di Nona, but a natural, built-in prudence made the vendors hide their American merchandise. Everyone hoped the same thing—that Farfalla was there to sell or to pick up a girl or to soak in some local color. Maybe it was just that he was lost.

Manny walked through the crowd, threadbare women for the most part, there to ogle the food and clothing, not to buy. The inevitable street kids tried and failed to cajole the dealers into tossing a scrap or two their way. There were a few well-dressed women from the better neighborhoods buying food for their families with carefully hoarded bank notes. Here and there were women in maid's livery.

Farfalla stopped at every stall and stared through his dark glasses at the sellers. None returned his gaze. Halfway down the street, he chose a victim. Like most of the stall keepers on the street, the vendor was a farmer who trundled his cart into Rome in the hours before dawn, carrying a few oranges, some bunches of fat skin-split grapes and a pile of pasta—a tangle of fettucine, made with dark brown flour, characteristic of the region just to the south of the city called Ciociara. Gone now that Farfalla was there were the items of contraband sold by the farmer, on commission, for the black marketeers.

Farfalla looked at the man a moment, then picked up an orange. He appraised it for a moment, then placed it carefully in front of him, as if he had made a sensitive move on a chess board.

"Quanto è?" asked Farfalla.

"Tenga, generale, tenga," said the man nervously. Take it, take it. It was worth an orange—forty lire—to get rid of any official.

Farfalla dug into the skin of the orange with his thumbs and pulled the fruit open like a fan. It was a *tarrocho*, an orange with blood-red flesh. Juice streamed through Farfalla's fingers and dribbled onto the cobblestones. He ate a wedge—it was sweet and warm—and licked some of the juice from his fingers.

"Buona," he said.

"Grazie, generale." The stall keeper looked nervously to his right and left, watching his fellow black marketeers watching him. Their worried eyes flicked from the peasant to Farfalla and back again. Manny let the orange fall from his hands, and he could almost feel the crowd shudder as the fruit hit the dusty street. Americans! They *wasted* food! Two kids dove for the orange, scrabbling for it under Manny's feet. He placed a thick-soled boot on it and ground it into the dirt. Two thin faces looked up at him.

"Oh ma dai, signore. Ho fame . . ."

"I know you're hungry. But don't eat that, it's dirty. Take these." Farfalla scooped up four oranges like a juggler and tossed them to the boys. The urchins looked at the oranges and then to the stall keeper. Farfalla thought the boys looked disappointed with his gift, not knowing that the fruit he had trampled underfoot could be eaten while whole oranges had to be saved and sold. They had ceased to be food and had become a resource.

"You don't mind, do you?"

The farmer shrugged.

"Here, take a few more." Farfalla threw a few more *tarrochi* to the urchins.

The farmer looked away but spoke. "Ma dai, signore. Per favore. Sono povero . . ."

"You're poor? We're all poor," said Farfalla, "but we're still alive. But you know who's dead? Falcone, Arturo. He was stabbed to death. Did you hear?"

There was no reaction from the farmer. He looked as if he was wondering if being alive was the great thing Farfalla made it out to be.

"What's your name?"

"Angelo."

"Angelo, did you hear about Falcone?"

A shrug. "Si."

"And what did you think?"

Angelo shrugged again. "Boh."

It was a particularly Roman term which expressed a variety of meanings simultaneously: What do I care? I don't know. What did you expect? In all cases, Angelo was lying. He and every other vendor on the street was glad, extremely glad, that Falcone was dead, that he was never coming back, never to swagger down the street again picking up Lorenzetti's share of the daily take. Everyone was glad Falcone was dead, because he deserved to be dead, but no one was relieved. At the close of business that day another thug would come and take their money. Falcone used to help himself to fruit, just as the American had done.

"Angelo?"

"Si, signore?"

Farfalla leaned forward and placed his palm on the pile of pasta, but keeping his weight off it. "Are you an honest man?"

"Si, signore."

"And do you love justice?"

Angelo looked sadly at Farfalla. "I don't know. I've never met her."

Manny had the feeling that he was, this time, telling the truth. He smiled and put a little pressure on the nest of fettucine. There was a faint crack, like kindling catching. A look of pain crossed Angelo's face. Tears welled into his eyes. "Please sir, please."

"How do I find Lorenzetti?"

"I know no one of that name."

There was another crack. "Why do you lie to me? Why are you protecting him?"

"Please sir, please."

"Please what?"

"Please leave me be. I have three children."

"Tell me what I need to know."

"I know nothing."

There were plenty of people on the street—vendors, customers, kids—who would be glad to tell Lorenzetti that Angelo had informed on him.

Farfalla shook his head in disgust, took a step away from Angelo's stall as if he was leaving, then lunged back, smashing his fist into the pasta. The fettucine splintered and Farfalla walked away. Angelo muttered in thick dialect as how, on the whole, he had preferred the Germans.

Farfalla made one more stop on the Via Tor di Nona. Two stalls up from Angelo, Manny stopped and reached under the counter, pulling out a pair of boots he had seen hidden there a few minutes before. He shook them in the face of the young woman who ran the stall.

"Where did you get these?"

The woman looked straight into the dark glasses. "I found them."

"Confiscato."

"As you wish, signore." Farfalla could confiscate the whole stand if he chose, it wasn't money from her pocket. Her stand and everything on it was owned by Lorenzetti, and she was paid whether she sold anything or not. Besides, the boots weren't selling, they were too big. Americans had such big feet.

Farfalla walked up the street carrying the boots at his side, like a fisherman who didn't want to advertise an embarrassingly bad catch.

ON HIS WAY back to the Insurance Company, on the Corso Umberto, Farfalla was approached by a street kid, smaller than most. He was dressed in rags and had pulled down over his ears a piece of army-issue headgear known as a "cunt cap."

"I speak English very good," he whined. "One, two, four, seven, eight, six. Dodgers, Cardinals, Yankee, Giant. Fuck you. Eat shit." He paused expectantly and then prompted Farfalla. "Caramelle?"

Farfalla waved the boots at the kid. "I haven't got any. Go away."

"I speak English very good," the kid replied insistently. "One, two, four, seven, eight, six. Dodgers, Cardinals, Yankee, Giant. Fuck you. Eat shit."

"Va t'en ne via!" barked Farfalla. Some soldiers had taught the kid these words and he had turned them into a livelihood.

The boy hung back a bit, then caught up again. "I speak English very good," he yelled, his eyes blazing and his cheeks red. He had the insistence of a spurned lover. "One, two, four, seven, eight, six. Dodgers, Cardinals, Yankee, Giant. Fuck you. Eat shit."

It was hot. Farfalla was already annoyed with his failure to learn anything at the Tor di Nona market, so he did something quite rare for him. He lost his temper. He slapped the kid hard on the side of the head and immediately regretted it. The child was hardly more than skin and bone—he was as light as a kite—and he tumbled into the gutter. His two big brown eyes filled with tears and his mouth turned down like a clown's.

"Oh jeez, kid. I'm sorry . . ."

"Lieutenant!"

Farfalla spun around and found himself confronted with an elderly-looking major, white-faced with rage. "That was the single most reprehensible act I have ever witnessed. You are a disgrace."

"Yes sir, sorry sir." Farfalla was sorry, but he was also thinking that if that was the worst thing the major had ever seen then the major must be new to the war. The boy remained in the gutter watching attentively.

"You will apologize to the boy."

"I already have, sir."

"Again. And give him something."

"He asked me for candy, sir, and I don't have any."

"Good God, Lieutenant! Use your initiative. Give him some money so he can buy some candy."

"I'm sorry," Farfalla mumbled, handing the kid a twenty-five-lira note. The boy snatched the bill and scrambled to his feet, retreating a few yards lest Farfalla should change his mind.

"We are here to help these people, Lieutenant, and to accomplish that we need to gain their trust. To see a grown man, an officer in the United States Army, manhandling a poor unfortunate child—it makes me physically ill. When I saw what you did I felt literally sick to my stomach."

"Sorry, sir."

"Don't you *ever* do that again."

"No sir."

"Go away. You disgust me."

In order to salute, Farfalla clumsily transferred the boots from his right hand to his left. But the major ignored the salute, pushing by him and hurrying down the street.

The major had walked a block down the Corso Umberto and was in front of the church of San Marcello when he heard a voice behind him. "I speak English very good. One, two, four, seven, eight, six. Dodgers, Cardinals, Yankee, Giant. Fuck you. Eat shit."

"Oh dear," said Major John Howe. "Go away little boy. You shouldn't use language like that."

"I speak English very good. One, two, four . . ."

"Go away," said Howe crossly.

A nun emerged from the church and was crossing the little piazza, coming toward Howe and his unwelcome companion. "Sister, sister," he called.

The nun stopped and smiled pleasantly. "Si, signore?"

"Please help me. This little boy . . ." He gestured helplessly toward the child who was now tugging insistently at Howe's crisp trousers.

"Cardinals! Yankee! Giant! Fuck you!"

The nun understood at once and a massive bone-white hand shot out of the black shroud of a sleeve and smacked the kid hard, knocking him, cunt cap flying, into the street. She yelled something fierce in Italian and the boy, faced with a superior foe, jumped to his feet and ran.

"Ecco fatto, signore," she said with a bright smile.

"Yes," said Howe unhappily. "Thank you. Oh dear . . ."

9

"Holt!" McManus yelled. "Leacock! Get over here."

"Yeah, Sarge?"

"You guys like music?"

"I do," said Stanley.

Experience had taught James Holt not to appear to be too enthusiastic about anything the army might have to offer. "How come? You gonna sing us a song?"

"Now what kind of answer is that? I asked you a simple question: you like music or what?"

"I like it well enough."

McManus grinned. "That's what I figured." He ripped an order off his clipboard. "Get over to the station and pick up a piano."

"A piano?" Holt stared at the slip. "A piano? Jesus Christ, Sarge, it's a hundred and fifty degrees out there."

"Don't exaggerate. It's only about a hundred and ten."

"A piano? Awww, sarge . . ."

"Gotta fight the war, Jimmy. The army says you gotta move a piano, you gotta move a piano."

"Yeah? Where we supposed to take this piano? Normandy?"

"To the officers' club at the Plaza Hotel, and don't get smart with me, soldier. Move it."

"Sarge," said Leacock, "two guys, a *whole* piano?"

McManus was not an unreasonable man. "Take Whiteside with you if you think you need help. That fucker is big enough to move the whole thing by himself while you two sit in the shade playing checkers."

"So where is he?" asked Holt.

"You two still here? I swear to God I gave you an order about ten seconds ago."

"Let's go, Stanley. We get that piano over to the officers' club and we could shorten the war by months."

"Save thousands of innocent lives," agreed Leacock.

"Look at this, I got Gallagher and Sheen working for me. Get lost, you two."

Alvin Whiteside, at over three hundred pounds, took up much of the passenger side of the cab of Jimmy Holt's truck. His massive thighs looked as if they would split the material of his fatigue pants, and his sleeves, rolled up to his shoulders, revealed arms as thick as railway ties. He rested his huge hands—they looked like baseball gloves—on his knees and stared through the window of the cab. Stanley squirmed in the little space left to him and tried to nudge Whiteside over a little. It took more than a nudge, however, to budge Alvin Whiteside. That didn't surprise Stanley, but something else did.

"Hey! Alvin, you're freezing!" Stanley touched him on the forearm and then on the forehead like a mother checking her child for fever. "You're like a block of ice. How do you do that?"

"I was sitting in the doorway of the ice-box. When I get a minute of my own, I open the door and I set there awhile."

"Might as well," said Holt, "nothing in that freezer 'cept cold air." He gunned the engine of the truck and pulled onto the Via Foraggi, scattering a small flock of pigeons pecking in the dusty street.

"Yeah, it's driving McManus crazy," said Leacock.

The army had delivered the freezer and then declined to deliver anything to put in it. McManus dutifully fed the gasoline engine and kept the temperature in the unit down as low as it would go. He knew, with an NCO's unfailing sense of impending disaster that the moment he let down his guard and neglected the freezer the army would cause it to be called into service.

"I say we take our time on this getting the piano," said Holt. "No sense hurrying back and getting to do more work for the army, right?"

"Makes sense."

"Alvin? What do you think?"

"Fine." Whiteside was from the South. The word came out "fahn."

It was midafternoon and the streets were almost deserted. War, famine, conquering armies—no catastrophe, man-made or natural, could interrupt the Roman siesta. Only the kids were out.

"Caramelle!" shrieked one as the truck passed.

"In New York the streets are straight. Uptown, downtown. East side, west side. You always know where you are. Here you get lost when you turn the corner."

"It's real old, Jimmy. Elena told me, you know, that some of these buildings are thousands of years old."

"How do you know what she's saying? She don't speak English and you don't speak Italian. She was probably saying, 'Man, are you ugly.' "

"We get by. She's learned a few words of English and she's teaching me a little. Besides, I know she thinks I'm beautiful. I can tell by the look in her eye." He dug an elbow into Whiteside's hard body. "You know, Alvin?"

"I don't live in no city," said Alvin.

"Huh?"

"I get lost in any kind of city. I had to go to Yazoo City for th'induction and I got lost. And Yazoo City is a small town, they tell me." Whiteside's voice was deep and gravelly and sounded a note not unlike one of the company's trucks on idle.

"Yazoo City!" yelled Leacock. "Where the hell is that?"

" 'Bout sixteen mile from Bentonia."

This time Holt laughed. "And where the hell is *that?*"

"That's where I'm from."

"What state, Alvin?"

"Mississippi."

"Woah," said Holt. "Deep down South. Way down yonder, am I right?"

"Go any further and you'll be shrimpin' in the Gulf," said Whiteside with a smile.

"Lot's of Klan down there, right?"

"Yeah, enough."

"They ever mess with you, Alvin?" asked Leacock.

"You don't mess with them, they don't mess with you. You know your place, stay out of trouble. That's all."

"That is bullshit," said Holt emphatically. "Bull-shit." He

opened his eyes wide and rolled them. "Yassa massa, kick me in de ass a little mo', massa. I'm just a good colored boy and I'm gonna go an' pick me some mo' cotton, massa." He shook his head in disgust. "Shit."

"No disgrace picking cotton," said Whiteside calmly. "I done it myself."

"Jimmy, why are you giving Alvin all this trouble? You're from the north, like me, and you don't know what goes on down there."

"I'm not giving Alvin trouble. Just burns my ass, that's all. My grandaddy got the fuck up to New York City because he couldn't stand it down South. Georgia or some place."

"New York City ain't paradise, all I hear about it," said Whiteside.

Holt smiled. "That's right, Alvin. You want paradise, you gotta go to Maine. Wherever the fuck that is."

"Now you're talking," said Leacock. "It's paradise when there isn't snow on the ground."

"Snowed in Bentonia once. Didn't last long."

"Hey Alvin, do they, you know, put on white sheets and all that stuff? The Klan?"

"Yes, they do."

"And burn crosses?"

"Yeah."

"You seen it?"

Alvin Whiteside looked at Stanley as if he hadn't learned the simplest lessons of life. "When the Klan is out I stay home."

"But, you know, you must have seen it afterwards, after they left."

"Wasn't near to me. It was a white man they was burning out. A Catholic man."

"They don't like Catholics neither?"

"No."

"Two strikes on me," said Leacock.

"They'd have a fuckin' hot time in this town," said Holt, looking up at the extravagant baroque façade of the church they were passing.

"Does the Klan really wear them pointy hats?"

"Yeah."

Holt slapped the wheel and laughed. "It must be something to

135

see, all those rednecks dressed up in white sheets wearing those pointy hats."

"Makes me scared," said Whiteside solemnly.

"You? A man your size?"

"Stanley, size don't mean a thing when there's a mess of them. Those boys'll kill you, they feel like it. Hang you from a tree and it ain't no good going to the sheriff. He's the one doing the hanging."

"Some white fucker tries that with me and we both going together, you know what I'm saying?"

Alvin shook his head slowly. "You northern boys don't understand how these things is."

There was something sad, resigned in the way Whiteside spoke. Jimmy Holt had been pushed around in New York City, but he didn't just take it, accept it the way Alvin Whiteside did. And he had never been threatened with death, either. "You might be right, Alvin. I guess we don't know how it is."

"I guess we don't," echoed Leacock, thinking of safe, drab Bangor, where stiff Maine Yankees always called his father "Mister Leacock."

"Shit." Holt braked.

An MP stood in the path of the truck, waving it to a halt. A few street kids gathered, watching, as if expecting trouble.

"Hey, Joe! Gum? You got gum? You got caramelle for me?"

The policeman hopped up on the running board of the truck on the driver's side of the cab. "Where are you boys going?"

"We boys are going to the station."

"Then you boys are lost."

"We boys know that."

"Take a right here," ordered the MP.

"Okay." Holt put the truck in gear and edged it forward a few inches, hesitating.

"What are you waiting for, Private?"

"For you to get off the truck. That's a tight turn. You'll get your ass tore off."

"I'm staying. Make the turn like I told you."

"We in some kind of trouble, Corporal?"

"Yeah. You're lost."

"Could happen to anybody. No crime in getting lost."

"I didn't say there was."

136

Holt shrugged. The truck lumbered forward, but the turn was a tight one and he had to back up and take it a few inches at a time.

"C'mon, c'mon," said the MP slapping the roof of the cab, "you got room. C'mon."

The truck emerged from the warren of streets and into the open space of the Corso Umberto. Holt had to brake sharply to avoid cutting into a column of military traffic which rumbled along the street. Planted in the middle of Largo Chigi was a tall signpost bristling with military acronyms:

> ↖ UDF ADM HQ MAIN
> ↖ HQ 2 BASE AREA RAF
> ← Q MOVEMENTS ROME
> ← 104 BR. GEN. HOSP.
> N.A.F.F.I. →
> TERMINI STATION →

"See it, soldier? Bottom line?"

"Got it."

"Just follow the arrows and you'll be there in a jiffy." The MP dropped off the running board. "Now move it."

"Hey." Holt thrust his head out of the window of the cab. "Appreciate it." He pulled his head back in. "Asshole."

"Well," said Stanley. "It was fun while it lasted."

PART OF ROME'S main rail station had been damaged by allied bombing, but there was enough of the vast building left over to serve as both the Rome area Replacement Depot and the Railhead Supply Depot. Both were warehouses. The RSD stored goods. The Replacement Depot, the "repple-depple," stored men.

The huge main concourse of the station was alive with soldiers, all ranks, all nationalities, sent there while the army decided where they would go next. A red-faced Australian lieutenant wandered among the hundreds of men, yelling for members of his platoon. A group of King's Own Yorkshire Light Infantry, British soldiers with red knees and peeling faces, sprawled on their kit and sang, to the tune of Auld Lang Syne, "We're here because we're here because we're here because we're here . . ."

Hundreds of others jawed or slept or read or argued. They stared into space, smoking, waiting, and bored.

The Railhead Supply Depot was as busy as an anthill with scores of supply corps soldiers servicing the trucks backed up to the long loading dock. Leacock stayed with the truck, as Holt and Alvin went in search of their piano. They zeroed in on a sergeant who grabbed a handful of sweat from his forehead and dried his hand on his pants leg before taking the slip Holt thrust under his nose.

"Oh yeah. Piano. Come with me." He wandered into a forest of packing cases. In a corner sat a piano. It was no ordinary piano, but a specially designed "Victory Piano." It was the size of a small desk, lightweight, and painted the ubiquitous army olive drab. Holt had never seen one before.

"That is the smallest piano I ever seen."

"What? You expected a *real* piano?"

"I didn't personally expect anything."

"Smart of you. These things are on wheels."

"Good. C'mon, Alvin, let's move this thing."

"Sign for it, Private."

Holt signed. "All in order, Sarge?"

"Glad to see the fucker go."

Alvin got behind the piano and pushed it through the maze of merchandise as if he was piloting nothing more onerous than a baby carriage.

"You need help, Alvin?"

"I'm fine."

He wheeled the piano off the loading dock and onto the truck, the stiff springs hardly noticing the combined weight of man and musical instrument. Holt jammed chocks under the wheels, while Leacock tied the piano down with rope. The ramp that led to the RSD was jammed with trucks, and it took almost fifteen minutes for the Chevrolet to edge out to Via Nazionale. Leacock whistled through his teeth, Holt studied his map of Rome, and Alvin White-side stared fixedly at the tailgate of the truck in front of them.

"I'm going to take Elena dancing," said Leacock after awhile.

"What happens if you run into some of those fuckers again?"

"They can't be everywhere. Besides, Biggsy told me he found this bar where only brothers go."

"Jim Crow," said Holt sourly.

"No. Strength in numbers. He says it's real nice. We oughta take a look."

"Yeah, what about getting there? What happens if you run into those guys on the street, like last time?"

"I'll take Alvin along with me."

"I don't like fighting," said Alvin.

"Don't you *ever* get mad, Alvin?"

"No."

"Never?"

"No."

"Not even when someone fucks with you?"

"Nobody ever does."

Holt and Leacock laughed. "No I guess they don't," said Holt. "I sure wouldn't mess with man mountain, here."

"Jimmy used to be a boxer, Alvin."

"Boxing? I'da hated that."

"Smart man."

"You play anything, Alvin?"

"Baseball, some. Football in the winter."

"Football?" said Holt. "You just told us you don't like fighting. What the hell is football?"

"That's different. That's a game. It don't mean nothing."

Leacock laughed. "Can you imagine being on the other side and seeing this man come running at you? Boom!"

The truck broke free of traffic and they zoomed over the Quirinale Hill and down the Via del Tritone. The late afternoon parade of streetwalkers was just beginning to assemble. They lined the street from the Piazza Barberini and stood three deep all the way down the avenue to Piazza San Silvestro. They were waiting for off-duty soldiers—officers if they were lucky—who would take them back to their hotels. If they were there past the eleven o'clock curfew, then they spent the night with their client, returning to their apartment in the morning when the curfew lifted, bleary-eyed and hung over, but with money in their pockets.

Leacock surveyed the gaggle of whores—they ranged in age from fourteen to fifty—and shook his head in disgust. "Elena isn't like these girls, not at all."

"They're just trying to stay alive," said Whiteside unexpectedly. "You can't blame them for trying to put food in their bellies the only way they know how."

"Brother Whiteside has spoken," said Holt. Then: "Jesus Christ!"

He stood on the brakes and the truck lurched to a halt. Holt and Stanley were thrown forward. The piano shifted and creaked ominously. Whiteside didn't move. Holt jumped down from the cab and started yelling at the man who had stepped into the path of the truck.

"Are you fuckin' crazy? Jesus Christ! You coulda got yourself killed! You stupid—" Then Holt stopped. The man he was yelling at, a slight, white haired man in a tan suit, was black. "Who the fuck are you?"

"I'm Earl Talker," he said as if he expected Holt to have heard of him. Then he climbed up into the bed of the truck, lifted the piano cover, and played a few soft chords. The whores, and the soldiers, gawked.

Earl Talker stood before the keyboard, his eyes closed, an ecstatic look on his face. He played a soft melody, the untuned piano responding under his long fingers. He hummed along quietly with the tune.

"Hey, mister . . ." called Leacock.

Earl Talker opened his eyes and sighed. "That's the first time I've played a piano in three years."

"Well now you played it, get the fuck off my truck." Jimmy Holt was still jumpy from the near miss. "C'mon man, let's go." With difficulty, Talker pulled his fingers off the keyboard.

"May I ask you gentlemen where you might be taking this instrument?"

"You ain't in the army, are you?" asked Leacock.

"C'mon, man. I said move it. Come down from there."

Slowly, Talker started to climb down from the bed of the truck, putting out his arm to Holt. "Would you assist me, sir?"

"You got up there easy enough," Jimmy grumbled, helping the small man down.

"I wonder if you might be interested in selling me that piano."

"No," said Holt sharply.

"Who are you anyway?" asked Leacock.

"I'm Earl Talker."

"And what are you doing here?"

"I live here."

"What? Here? In Rome?"

"That's right."

"Are you crazy?" demanded Holt.

Earl Talker smiled. "Lady Molly says I am, a little bit perhaps."

Holt's eyes narrowed suspiciously. "Do you have an English accent?"

"Perhaps. Just a touch."

Traffic was beginning to back up behind Holt's truck. Horns were blowing and drivers were leaning out of their windows pounding the metal panels of the cab doors.

"Earl, get in the truck. Stanley, ride on the board."

"I would appreciate a lift home," said Earl Talker.

Holt started the truck, ground the gears, and then lurched down the street. The whores on the sidewalk looked disappointed that the show was over.

Earl Talker offered his hand to Whiteside. "I am Earl Talker," he said gravely.

"I'm Alvin Whiteside. Yessir." Holt noticed that Talker, like Whiteside, had huge hands. They were the only large thing about him. His height was so diminutive that his feet, encased in pearl grey spats, barely reached the floor of the truck. His shoulders were thin under the worn material of his suit.

"And who might you be, sir?"

"James Holt."

Stanley leaned into the cab of the truck. "Sono Stanley Leacock," he said with a grin.

"Con piacere, signore."

"And what the fuck are you doing here?"

"As I explained, James, I live here. I have since 1924."

"Are you English or American or what?"

"I am American. I am from Grand Rapids, Michigan. But I have lived abroad since 1921."

"Abroad?"

"Paris, Rome, the Riviera, London . . ."

"You were here when the war started? Didn't the Germans round up all the Americans? You lived here through the war?"

"Indeed. Myself and Lady Molly."

"Who's this Lady Molly?"

"She your wife, Earl?"

Earl Talker beamed, pride radiating from his worn features. He seemed to grow a few inches out of pure happiness. "My sweetheart," he said.

THE CONCIERGE AT the Plaza Hotel looked with distaste at the piano. He touched the keys and then rubbed his fingers on his striped vest.

Holt would not take it back, and much as he would like to have given it to Earl Talker, he knew that was out of the question. "It's a piano, isn't it?"

"Yes, but . . ."

"But nothing, mister. It's the only piano the army got in stock right now. You want a piano, you got a piano."

The concierge was not used to being talked to in this manner by black men. In fact, he had never spoken to a black man before in his entire life. An American major had told him to expect a piano, but this little thing would hardly blend happily with the elegant art deco decor of the bar-turned-officers'-club. But it was a piano and an American army piano at that. The major could not complain.

"Very well."

"Sign," said Holt.

The concierge sighed and signed. How he wished the Italians had won the war.

EARL TALKER WAS still in the cab. "It hurts me to see that instrument go."

Holt swung up behind the wheel and fired up the engine. "It's no great piano. What is it with you and that piano, Earl?"

"Every piano is a great piano, James, when you haven't played one in three years. For a musician, that is torture, pure and simple."

"Hey." Leacock leaned into the cab. "We gonna give Earl a ride home?"

"I'd like you gentlemen to meet Lady Molly. It is just about cocktail time, after all."

Holt clapped his hands. "Cocktails. I could go for a cocktail, how 'bout you, Alvin?"

"I don't know what that is."

"A drink. You know, a *drink.*"

"I don't drink. Never have."

"Figures. Where to, Earl?"

"What about Sergeant McManus?" asked Leacock.

"Hell, Stanley, we're still at the station."

Leacock grinned. "Damn. I forgot."

Talker lived in an old but well-kept palazzo near the river, a towering pile with wide windows and elaborately sculpted cornices. Muscled classical figures swarmed across the façade, seeming to bear the weight of the building on their strong stone backs. The old man led them into a gloomy entrance hall and then slowly up a flight of clean-swept stairs. Earl paused at every landing to catch his breath.

"The elevator stopped working in 1942," he explained, "and I'm still not used to the steps. I'm not," he said as if they knew him back when, "as young as I used to be."

"Take your time," said Alvin Whiteside. *Tahm*.

On the third floor, Earl took a key from his pocket and opened a set of wide double doors. "Lady Molly?"

There was an answering trill from somewhere deep in the apartment.

"I've brought some friends to meet you." Earl ushered the three men into the flat. The ceilings were twenty feet high, gilded, coffered, and bossed. A decorative cycle of nymphs and satyrs danced around the upper edge of the walls, the lower part lined with stained and faded brocade shot through with silver thread. In the space between were paintings, bright colors daubed on raw canvas and hung unframed.

"Lady Molly is quite the painter," said Earl.

The living room was dominated by the stately windows they had seen from the street, a tall, sculpted chimney piece and a black concert grand piano of stupendous size. It looked as if someone had parked a hearse in the room.

"Hey! What was all that about you wanting a piano? I'd say that's a piano, wouldn't you, Alvin?"

"I would."

Earl smiled sadly and sat down at the piano bench and played a few chords. Except for the muffled thump of the felt-lined action within the piano case, there was no sound at all.

"A silent piano?" said Holt.

Talker tapped his temple. "Not in here it isn't. I hear every note."

"You do, but it's bloody frustrating for the rest of us."

"Molly!"

The men turned. Molly was a tall, hefty woman in her fifties, her face dominated by a hooked nose and glittering green eyes. Her skin was wrinkled and sallow and the flesh around her neck loose and raddled. There was an inaccurate smear of deep red lipstick on her wide mouth, and her hair was dyed a coppery red, the color of an Irish setter. In Lady Molly's left hand was a stubby ivory cigarette holder, an inch of cigarette protruding. In her right was a bottle of Gordon's gin which she placed in the middle of a marquetry coffee table like an explorer planting a flag.

She extended a hand to Alvin Whiteside, her nails painted the same vivid red as her mouth. She wore ivory and ebony bangles from wrist to elbow and they clacked as she shook hands.

"I'm Molly Pringle."

"How do you do, ma'am. My name's Alvin."

"And this is James and this is Stanley. These gentlemen just delivered a piano to the Plaza."

Molly flung herself onto a velvet sofa and busied herself with the gin and some smudged glasses. "The beasts! Why didn't they bring it here?"

"Army property, ma'am," said Holt.

"Rot. This gin is the property of the British Army but some ass in the Inniskillings gave it to me. Told him that my father had been at school with his father, or something. A lie of course." She handed a cloudy glass to Holt. "Gin? No ice or anything, I'm afraid."

"Cheers," said Earl.

Jimmy sipped and shivered. Stanley wet his lips with his ration, grimacing. It was, he imagined, what drinking gasoline would be like. Alvin declined.

"I don't drink liquor, ma'am."

"Heavens. How do you get through the day?"

Earl Talker smacked his lips and drank deep. "These gentlemen seem a bit puzzled by our being here, Molly."

"What? In Rome? Through the war and so on?"

"Yeah. How'd you get away with it?"

"Goodness. Hundreds did. We left getting out a bit late—on purpose, I think, don't you darling? We thought, 'England in war time, how terribly drab and serious,' and, of course, they've never quite approved of me and Earl there, have they? You're all too young to remember the last war, before you were born I'd imagine, but I do and it was terribly serious and sad and the weather was filthy. That's how I remember it, you know, from '14 right the way through to '18 with nothing but overcast skies, pelting-down rain too. I'm sure we must have had *some* sun, but I can't remember any. Filthy food, too, even for those who could afford it. Of course, my father—a copper-bottomed shit, you can believe me—absolutely adored tightening his belt. Said it was the duty of the upper classes to lead the way. You can imagine he had a fit, my dear, when my oldest brother, Alcibiades, quite rightly, refused to go off to Flanders and get himself killed and went to China instead with some of his queer friends and died after eating a crustacean of some sort. Luckily Agamemnon—that's my younger brother—went into the Guards and got himself slaughtered just as a Pringle was meant to do, so Daddy died with a little smirk on his face. Mummy slipped off the hooks in '21, from relief, I think, at not having to put up with Daddy anymore, so everything came to me and my sister Iocasta—stupid names all of them, but not as stupid as mine—Clytemnestra—so she's called Bunny and I decided to call myself Molly, a good common name, like Molly who gets fucked in that book by the blind Irishman. What's his name? Everyone talked about him in Paris but I don't think we ever met him. Do you remember, Earl?"

"Yes," said Earl.

"What?" Jimmy Holt said. Leacock gaped, but Alvin Whiteside looked as if he heard this kind of talk every day of his life. He gazed placidly at the nymphs and satyrs.

"We said, the Italians are sensible people and they won't allow that ghastly Mussolini to drag them into a war. A lot of people said the same thing, so the declaration of war was a bit of a shock." Lady Molly gulped some gin. It seemed to give her strength. "But I knew some people and they agreed to turn a blind eye for a bit—"

"—and some money," Earl interjected. He put down his drink and caressed the mute keys of the piano.

"Yes. They were quite easy to bribe back then. Earl was in no danger, of course, being an American. He didn't have to worry until '41 when you Yanks came in." She fitted a cigarette into her holder as if loading a gun and lit it with a box of kitchen matches taken from the table in front of her.

"We just closed the door and didn't come out," explained Earl.

"That's amazing." Leacock shook his head as if unable to believe his ears.

"Yes. I suppose now it does seem so. There was nothing else to do except go to one of those wretched camps. I suppose I would have been all right, being English and having a title and so on, but the Fascists were beastly to Africans like Earl so we couldn't let that happen, could we? We should have left in '35 when they went down to Abyssinia and thumped that poor little man."

"They banned jazz," Earl said in amazement. "Called it subhuman. Jazz!"

"That really was the last straw," snorted Lady Molly indignantly.

In spite of himself, Stanley gulped the gin. The burning glow in his stomach was not all that unpleasant.

"African?" said Holt. "I thought you said you were from Michigan."

"That's what Lady Molly calls people of the Negroid race."

"And so you are. So you all are. Noble African men transported from your homeland. In chains. By whites. They call you barbaric! Nonsense. Look at him"—she waved a hand at Whiteside, her bangles clattering—"pure Dyola. Perhaps Fulani. Broad shoulders. Deep, deep lungs. Coal black. Steatopygous buttocks. See it a mile away."

"What?" Holt said.

"Lady Molly has made something of a study of race."

"Now darling, don't go making me sound like Gobineau or that ghastly Austen Chamberlain."

"I don't understand," said Leacock, "how did you live all that time, here in your apartment? How did you eat?"

"Oh," said Lady Molly matter-of-factly, "there was a pimp named Bianchi—I think he was a queer too, so he wasn't exactly on the right side of the law—and he'd come periodically and turn some of my jewelry into food. He took a healthy share for himself, of course. If he'd denounced us he wouldn't have gotten a sou— the OVRA would have taken it all. The beasts."

Lady Molly drew heavily on her cigarette. "Oddly enough, things got a bit easier when the Germans came. The Romans absolutely loathed them, my dears, and while there were some bad apples, most people wouldn't denounce their neighbor's cat, leave alone two harmless souls like us. And, of course, by then, most people were in the same boat—half the city was hiding the other half, or so they said. Curiously, the Vatican was quite helpful. I've

146

never trusted those bastards, you know. So repressed—you just *know* they want to fuck everything in sight. Boys, mostly, too, I'll be bound."

"You just stayed indoors for three years." Holt was incredulous. "Didn't you go crazy?"

"Well, it's quite a big flat, you know, and there's a terrace. Quite secluded. Of course, the whole neighborhood knew we were here—there are no secrets in a Roman street, you know—but the Germans were such fatheads. More gin?" Molly waved the bottle and tapped a skein of ash on the marble floor. "Of course, it was hardest on poor Earl. Couldn't play the piano, you see. The boche weren't that stupid. It would tend to give one away rather."

Earl stood and lifted the lid of the piano as if opening a coffin. "In the spring of 1943 I desecrated this instrument." The interior was a tangle of thick copper wires cut from their moorings and curled back on themselves. A single bass wire stood up, sharp and jagged, like a broken fang. "I could play, but I had to remember how the notes sounded. Now, of course, I regret it. When I saw that piano on the back of your truck I had to stop you . . ." Earl looked into the piano case, as if staring into an open grave.

"Maybe we can find Earl a piano," said Leacock.

"Yeah," agreed Holt. As he spoke he wondered where the hell they were going to find Earl a piano.

"That would be marvelous, wouldn't it Earl? Earl has a whole sheaf of compositions he's written but he hasn't heard—heard properly, I mean; he's heard them in his head, of course—and I haven't heard them at all."

"I would deeply appreciate a piano," said Earl, his voice quavering.

"Well, we'll look around." Holt slugged back his gin. "We better be going . . ."

"Oh dear, you must stay. I think we have a bit of food or something." She closed one eye and squinted at the level of liquid in the bottle. "And we've still got a bit of gin."

"We can't, ma'am," said Stanley. "We gotta go or we're gonna get in trouble."

"All these rules. Well, do come back. We're always here."

"Good evening, gentlemen," said Earl Talker.

GIDDY WITH GIN, Holt and Leacock laughed most of the way back to the depot. "Did you ever see anything like that in your whole life?"

"Man, I couldn't understand half of what the lady said. How come she's called Lady Molly anyway?"

"And Alvin, what did she call your butt anyway?"

"I don't know. But Mister Talker sure was a nice man."

PROVENANCE

The army's got this place, Fort Benjamin Harrison in Nebraska, where they store the records of every soldier who served in the Second World War, and while it might sound funny, those documents are classified. As far as the army was concerned, I certainly had no business seeing James Holt's service record even if after all these years you might say, what the hell difference does it make?

With twenty years in the New York Police Department, I've met my share of prosecutors and some of them owe me favors for a little assistance rendered on the witness stand. Some people would call these favors "perjury" but me and every cop I've ever met prefers to think of it as stretching the truth a little to make a prosecutor's case a little stronger so they can put a piece of shit away for the time he deserves. I'm kind of conservative on the law and order issue.

Anyway, I called an assistant DA who owed me a few from way back and asked him if he'd request the service record of James Holt. Those documents aren't all *that* classified and I figured that a New York DA would get some results. If that didn't work I was going to have to get Mrs. Chapman to make a request under the Freedom of Information Act, and that would take forever. My pal Sid, the assistant DA, said, "Anything for you, Harry," and made the call. It's nice to have friends.

Of course, this being the army we were dealing with, there was the usual run around for a couple of days until Sid got on the phone to some colonel and told him that the army was holding up a major investigation—mine—and would the army kindly get a move on or Sid was going to give the story to the papers. The army hates that—they know that there is such a thing as bad publicity.

Did I mention I was in the service? MPs, what else, right? I got drafted in '68, if you can believe it, but where I'm from—Queens—it might as well have been '58. I was a crew cut kid who came from a family where the flag was hung out on every major holiday and, because we're French Canadian by background, on Lafayette Day too. Bet you never heard of that one. I didn't like the army but I didn't mind missing the sixties. Everybody dressed so sloppily.

I didn't go to Vietnam. Traffic control on Diego Garcia. Hey. They send you where they need you.

Eventually, Holt's records were faxed to Sid, who faxed them to me.

I've never seen any report anyone has ever written on me, but I'll bet one word—methodical—kept on showing up. In the army I bet they called me methodical, same on the force, college, the Boy Scouts. I'll bet my mother probably has called me methodical. I'll have to ask her. Anyway, I don't think methodical is such a bad thing, even if it does make you sound a little dull.

When Sid called and said he was sending over the material, I told him okay and went into my kitchen and made a pot of coffee. When the paper started scrolling out of the machine—why do those things always remind me of player pianos?—I didn't stand over it, getting the highlights. I methodically waited until all the sheets were in; then I carefully cut up the pages and put them in order.

Then I put on the greatest hits of Signor Rossi and Signora Conti, poured myself a cup of coffee, and sat down with a full pack of cigarettes and an empty ashtray. Sorry. Can't help it.

Signor Rossi and Signora Conti were at a museum. I guess they were using up some of the free time they have in the afternoon but I bet they would rather have checked into one of those motels that advertise Fur Chambers and XXX Movies Free. They didn't dare, though. So they went to the culture well instead.

Signor Rossi was an art snob. "I find the colors in this picture quite pleasing," he said. He didn't identify the work, but I'll bet it was one of those lousy overpriced impressionists. I can't stand a lot of them. Too cute. Renoir—cut me a fucking break!

Still, I was glad that Rossi didn't start with that art-speak, you know, "simultaneity of space," or "I can respond to the image but not to the information." That stuff drives me crazy, and I think it was invented to shut the average Joe out of the art world. The critics and artists today, they want to turn art into their private preserve, just for them, like a real exclusive country club where everyone wears black clothing.

Signora Conti was much more my type. "This painting makes me feel happy," she says at one point (bet it was a Breugel). I really wish I knew what she looked like.

Old army records are hard to read because they're stored on old-fashioned microfilm. The writing is white and the paper is kind of army brown, like old film negatives. Come to think of it, that's probably what they are. The originals were photographed—pre-Xerox, you know—and nobody ever bothered to develop them. The two faxings didn't help much either.

Holt's AGCT, Army General Classification Test, gave him a score of 118 which meant he was pretty smart (by army standards). Anyone scoring 110 or higher was automatically recommended for OCS, if you were white, that is. It was strange to see "Negro" typed on the line marked "race." Nowadays, for white people anyway, it's hard to believe that those times ever existed. It's probably a whole lot easier to believe if you're black, though.

Holt was inducted into the army on April 11, 1943, at Whitehall Street, way downtown, near the Battery. I was inducted there myself.

He was sent to Fort Eustis, Virginia, for basic, and while there was nothing on his sheet that suggested he was the next Audie Murphy, he didn't screw up either. When basic was finished he was sent to Fort Ord in California, a buck private in the catering corps. Then began the usual army to-ing and fro-ing: Twin Falls, Idaho; Evansville, Indiana; Mansfield, Ohio; McAlester, Oklahoma; Kansas City—all over the map. Why he was shunted into transport it didn't say, but he did his heavy driving training in, of all places, Miami. He never distinguished himself, good or bad.

I think I can imagine what it must have been like for him. He was a smart kid and he came from Harlem. People tell me it was a safer place back then, but it still was no bed of roses, so I'll bet James Holt wasn't just smart, he was street smart too. I imagine him as being like his grandson Randall—angry and nobody's fool.

He shipped out from Fort Dix, direct to North Africa. His unit served in Bizerte and Benghazi and then got sent into Sicily. He was there for two months and then was yanked back to North Africa in late '43. Holt and his unit got to Anzio right there at the beginning, January 1944. From there he was sent someplace I've never heard of, Civitavecchia, and then to Rome and things got interesting.

Holt's service in Rome was summarized in a single laconic line:

7/44–9/44. Rome region. IV. A/179th, 3rd, Vth. (Art. 15/AW 103. 15-2. See attached.)

I wasn't quite ready to see attached. I wanted to think a moment. Methodical, that's me.

Private Holt had got himself in a little trouble, not serious trouble, not enough to get on his permanent record. Article 15 of the Uniform Code of Military Justice was an old friend of mine. It was also known as "company punishment," a penalty inflicted at unit level for crimes not serious enough to warrant a formal court martial, although if a soldier felt he was innocent of the charge he was entitled to request one.

James Holt didn't. He took his medicine and didn't complain, not even about the AW 103, a penalty known as "bad time." What that meant was that Holt had to forfeit pay and make up work to compensate the army for the length of time of his offense—in other words, if you went AWOL for three days, you didn't get paid for those three days and you had to work for three extra days without pay to make up the time. This over and above his punishment under Article 15. The 15-2 was the punishment designation—fifteen days restriction to barracks and two hours extra duty every day. Small potatoes, really.

I turned to the attached. Holt, it seemed, *had* been AWOL for two days in August 1944. The criminal record contained a note:

Precis of statement made by Holt, J. Pfc. in presence of APMO Investigator Farfalla V.E. Lieut. and JAGO Howe, J. Maj.

The accused states that he had been drunk and incapable following events of 8/30 (see attached) and had been in the presence of civilian personnel (confirmed per Farfalla) for the duration of his absence. He further states that he has no knowledge of the events of 8/31, 9/2, or 9/3. Per JAGO: rec'md punishment per Art. 15 UCMJ.

Now this was strange. What were two heavyweight legal types doing concerning themselves with something trivial like a soldier's AWOL? And what were the events of 8/31, 9/2, and 9/3? And why did Holt go on a bender in the first place, unless it was just that he was generally pissed off with the army, which is always a possibility.

There was no explanatory note attached. *Damn.*

The rest of Holt's dossier was straightforward. There were a couple of other postings in Italy and then he got sent to Austria. Randall had said Germany, but he wasn't sure about it. Germany. Austria. Close enough. The little bit of trouble in Rome didn't affect his discharge, which was an honorable. He demobbed at Whitehall Street, right where he went in.

I sipped my coffee and smoked a Merit (ridiculous name) and then turned back to the statement and reread it. Then I saw something I hadn't noticed before. At the bottom of the sheet, so badly reproduced that at first I thought it was a smudge, were the words: "Recording sec'ty. Malinsky, A. Cpl." Now, there was a coincidence. I took off my glasses and put the papers down on the desk in front of me.

"These paintings," said Signor Rossi, "are of great historical value." The guy was beginning to get on my nerves. What, I wondered, did Signora Conti see in this jerk?

10

Behind the Hotel Palatino Splendido was a garden where, in more prosperous times, guests took breakfast or an evening aperitif. Like the rest of the hotel, the garden had been neglected. The grape arbor had grown so thick it was now a tangled green roof which cast the garden in deep shadow, no matter how bright the summer sun. A persistent bouganvillea had forced its way through to the light, but the rest of the vegetation had died in the gloom, leaving brown, brittle, dusty corpses. The gravel path was unraked and mixed with several decades of cigarette butts and bottle caps. Wooden crates filled with empty mineral water bottles were a stacked ziggurat in a cobwebbed corner. The cane chairs where fin de siècle tourists in leg-of-mutton sleeves had once sat drinking caffè latte and consulting their Baedekers and Murrays had no seats now, and the few cast iron chairs and tables bled rust through grayed white paint.

But the garden was cool and quiet and secluded and so became the Rome branch of an exclusive club: Father Mousecat's Home for Children—as proclaimed by the sign that Manganaro had nailed to the gnarled stem of the vine.

Manganaro's first foreign posting had been a jerry-built transit camp on England's south coast. Over the door of his barracks had hung the meticulously lettered sign, its author and meaning unknown. Manganaro had enjoyed his seven weeks at the transit camp, as Father Mousecat's Home for Children had been the unofficial club for the camp's gamblers and Eddie had made a steady hundred dollars a week running a variety of games of chance.

When he received his orders for North Africa, he pried the sign off the lintel and stuffed it into his pack, carrying it with him—talismans are important in times of war—establishing a Father Mousecat's Home for Children in every post he occupied. The latest Father Mousecat's Home for Children was the exclusive preserve of Manganaro, McManus, and Utterback.

The three white sergeants gathered there when the day was done, talking in the shadows and drinking cold wine from the freezer. McManus continued in his stewardship of the still-empty machine, and he was in charge of chilling the wine too—a delicate task, as the wine froze and smashed the bottles in a matter of minutes.

"So," said McManus puffing on a stogy, "you know what he fuckin' says? Fuckin' 'Thanks for the smoke, son.' " He sloshed down some wine and wiped his mouth with the back of his hand. "Can you fuckin' beat that?"

"Fuckin' a-mazin'," said Manganaro.

"I kid you not." McManus's voice came forcefully out of the gloom.

"Aw, who gives a shit?" Utterback said. "They're all assholes anyway, the officers. Second john, full fuckin' colonel, fuckin' general. Assholes." Utterback was passing through the petulant stage of drunkenness. "And niggers too. Fuck 'em."

"You're good company tonight, Cal."

"And fuck you too, Donny."

McManus sighed in the darkness.

"You know what I want to know," said Manganaro, "what I want to know is how is this Kinney going to affect business." He belched. "That's what I want to know."

Utterback made lip noises. "Business? Business? We don't got a business." His face was lit for a stark second as a match flared. He lit a cigarette and drew deep.

"Give it time, Cal. Give it time."

"I don't see you doing a fuck of a lot about it," said Manganaro angrily.

"Calm down, girls, calm down. We gotta think about this. This fuckin' town is starving and we got the goods, right? We're sitting on a fuckin' gold mine."

"That's right," snorted Utterback. "Sitting on it. And who do we have to thank for it? Mister Meatball himself here."

"Hey, fuck you, Cal."

"Fuck you, Eddie." Utterback jabbed a finger at Manganaro, as if poking a hole in the darkness.

"Okay, for Christ's sake, cut it out. We gotta think. All we need is an organization. The supply paperwork is so fucked up that the army doesn't know half of what it's shipping. If we can connect with the right guy . . ."

"We can't sell it ourselves. We need a middleman."

"What the fuck for?" demanded Utterback.

"Oh for Christ's sake," groaned Manganaro, "shit for brains, that's all you are. We're not talking about unloading a couple of cartons of Luckies here."

"I just want to make some money," grumbled Utterback. His cigarette made an orange arc in the dark as he shot it into the pile of water crates.

"What about Thorpe?"

"Don't make me laugh, Eddie," said Utterback as he shoveled another cigarette in his mouth. "He doesn't know shit from shit."

"And Kinney?" said Manganaro.

"I think," said McManus, "I *think* I'll be able to handle him. He's a society boy, never got his hands dirty, never got into no trouble in his life."

"Really, Sergeant? I'd be interested to hear how you know that." A match flared like lightning, illuminating Lieutenant Kinney's handsome features. No one had heard him come through the French windows that opened from the hotel dining room onto the decrepit garden. All three noncoms jumped to their feet, each wondering the same thing: How long had he been there? What had he heard?

"Jesus, sir, you scared the shit outta me." All McManus could make out of him was a faint outline where the darkness was a shade darker, and the glow of a cigarette tip.

"Please, please, sit. This is a purely social call."

"We . . . we were just gassing, sir. You know, just—you know— *gassing.*"

"Gassing, I gather, about selling army material on the black market. That's what you were 'gassing' about, isn't it, Sergeant?"

"Oh well, you know. It's just, you know . . ." This is it, thought McManus. Investigation, court martial, detention. Manganaro was in deeper trouble. He would get nailed for his little mistake the other night. A legal term—accessory—shot into McManus's mind. He didn't know what it meant, but he had a feeling he was one. It was the end of his army career. It was the end of McManus's sorry life. He tasted fear in his mouth.

"Oh yes, Sergeant." Kinney drew on his cigarette. "I *know*." Kinney sat in one of the iron chairs and flicked the ash off his cigarette. "Aren't you going to offer me a glass of wine?"

"Cal, go get Fiorito to give you a glass for the lieutenant here." McManus didn't trust himself to go and get it—he was afraid that he would just walk out the front door of the hotel, go AWOL, and take his chances.

"And why don't you all sit down?" McManus and Manganaro sat, forward, uneasily, on the edge of the hard iron chairs.

"Let's not fool around here. You know I could put you away with what I've heard here." Kinney spoke easily, confidently. "One phone call, that's all it would take. You know that. I know that."

"Sir—"

"One phone call. I'd probably get a citation out of it. Not that I care."

Manganaro wasn't buying it. "Whadyou hear anyway? Three guys chewing the fat. Three guys. Your word against ours. That's how I see it." Eddie's gangster's brain knew its way around the narrow thoroughfares of criminal law, but he didn't know much about the Uniform Code of Military Justice.

"An officer against three noncoms, Manganaro. Three noncoms in a supply company. A supply company in a combat zone. I only just got here, Manganaro, why would I lie? And, by the way, could your activities withstand a thorough investigation?"

"What's in it for you, turning us in?"

"I don't want to." Kinney stubbed out the cigarette on the iron arm of his chair. "Believe me, I don't."

"You don't?" McManus felt a warm wave of hope. "You sure you don't?"

"How come?"

"Because, gentlemen, I want in."

There was a moment of silence while the two sergeants weighed Kinney's words. McManus was astounded. A serving officer in the Army of the United States of America was calmly suggesting that he join three noncommissioned officers in the commission of a crime. Just like that. McManus half expected the ground to start trembling and angry forks of lightning to split the serene, star-dappled sky.

Double-checking was a reflex action with a senior NCO. "I'm sorry, sir, I don't think I heard you right."

"What's the matter, McManus? Shocked?" Kinney chuckled. "You heard me right."

"Just what are you saying, sir?"

Manganaro answered the question. If they could have seen him, they would have noticed that he was grinning, a big, wide, happy grin. "The lieutenant wants to make some money. Hell, we all do."

Utterback returned with the glass and poured some wine for Kinney. The officer sipped. "I guess you didn't know that you aren't supposed to chill red wine."

"We're kinda ignorant about that kinda thing," growled Utterback.

Manganaro wasn't interested in such niceties. "Now we could turn *you* in."

"You could try," agreed Kinney. "I doubt that you'd get too far, though."

"No, probably not," said McManus. He knew that there were few things more difficult to pull off in the army than a successful prosecution of an officer on the word of an NCO—particularly if one of the NCOs ice-picked to death a civilian in a bad black market deal.

"Besides, why would you want to?" Kinney lit another cigarette. "We can all see the potential here; we all figured it out at the same time. This town is a mess. The army is pumping supplies into Rome—they tell me about five, six hundred tons a day—and no one can keep track of it all. As long as the front is supplied and the brass is taken care of, no one is going to miss a little wastage. All we have to do to have a nice little business is run off a fraction."

"Yeah, but how do we get set up?"

"Lorenzetti," said Manganaro. "He's the guy to see."

"Who's he?"

"He's a man with an organization. He runs this fuckin' town. He'll be interested in a deal. I guarantee it."

"A gangster?"

"A businessman."

"You know him? Can he be trusted?"

158

"I don't know him yet. I'm working on it."

Utterback scoffed. "Not getting too far, neither."

"Shut up, Cal."

"There are two elements here that make this plan foolproof," Kinney said.

"What?" asked McManus.

"Well, me, for one."

"I'm sorry, sir," said McManus, "I'm not getting this."

"I am," put in Manganaro. "The lieutenant is connected, right? You're the protection, ain't you, Lieutenant?"

"That's one way of putting it."

"So what's the other thing?"

"The Negro boys." Kinney pulled on his cigarette. "It was when I saw them that I realized the possibilities here."

McManus was still puzzled. "The Negroes? How come?"

"Yeah," said Utterback, "how come?"

"They do what they're told. And nobody likes them," said Kinney matter-of-factly. "They'll move the merchandise, do the work, take the risks on the street. If they get caught all we have to do is say, 'Well, you know the colored . . .' "

"Yeah," agreed Manganaro. "Who the fuck trusts niggers? The army sure don't."

"Me neither," said Utterback sourly.

"Won't we have to cut them in?" asked McManus.

"Pay the fuckin' melanzans? What? You crazy?"

"We can worry about that when the time comes," said Kinney. He ground out his cigarette and stood up. "I don't see a lot of risks here, men. Think it over. Good night."

Instinctively, even in the pitch dark, McManus saluted.

MISS MCNUTT, CAMILLO Sanseverio's long-dead nanny, had been a woman of equal but incompatible loyalties. Fiercely English, she spent her long years in Rome drinking tea and importing at great expense such delicacies as Fuller's Nut Cake, Robertson's Marmalade and Callard and Bowser Bonfire Toffee. Camillo remembered the toffee, the rarest of treats. Miss McNutt would dole out the hard candy, like shards of sweet glass, when he was very, very good.

In common with many English women of a certain class and age, Miss McNutt believed passionately in the promotion of the welfare of animals. Italian draymen were astonished to be set upon by a middle-aged *straniera* who berated them about the maltreatment of horses. She was an active distributor of pamphlets decrying vivisection. Had Camillo's father permitted it, she would have filled the courtyard of the palazzo with stray dogs. She did not, however, feed the cats in the Forum. That was the calling of a group of elderly, mad Italian women considered by Miss McNutt to be common, despite their good works.

For all her Englishness, Miss McNutt was adamantly Roman Catholic. She heard mass every morning at San Tomasso di Canterbury, the lone woman among a score of pink-faced, big-eared seminarians. The English fathers there called her "the Church Militant." The Italian priests at Santa Maria in Campitelli—where by bequest of the last Stuart pretender to the throne of England, prayers were said every Sunday evening for the reconversion of his rightful realm—were terrified of her. Miss McNutt acknowledged no English sovereign after James II.

It had been Miss McNutt, more than the hovering priests of Camillo's childhood, who had instilled in him an unbending sense of Catholic ritual. Without thinking about it, he attended mass or, at least, benediction, every day, and he did penance every Saturday, though he rarely had much to confess. He had done the Nine First Fridays so many times that a platoon of priests was sure to attend his death bed. Camillo's prayers on All Souls' were so voluminous and all encompassing that he had probably released each limb of his family tree from the pains of purgatory. Some of Miss McNutt's more peculiar strictures had fallen away—he no longer left room on his chair for his guardian angel—but his bedtime ritual had remained unchanged for sixty years.

Cleanliness was not merely next to godliness in Miss McNutt's mind, the two were inextricably linked, mystically, like the duality of Christ's person. Camillo's nighttime ablutions were not only hygienic but spiritual as well. They were as much a ritual as a beatification.

He drew himself a shallow, warm bath, undressed, washed carefully with a precious sliver of soap, dried himself, and then dressed again—shoes, socks, waistcoat, even his tie—before kneeling down at the priedieu in the corner of his spare bedroom.

Miss McNutt had always said, "You wouldn't speak to the Marquis of Bute in your bedclothes, so why should you do less for

God?" The Marquis of Bute was Miss McNutt's great hero: British, an aristocrat, hugely rich, and Catholic.

Camillo had only just dressed after his bath when his daughter-in-law knocked on the door of his room. He was glad he was clothed. He was always faintly uncomfortable in Gabrielle's presence, and he would have felt even more awkward if he had been surprised in his nightshirt. There was something about her beauty that always startled him.

The Sanseverio family had always been a handsome clan, as attested by the family portraits in the dining room and the small *salone*. Even discounting the natural tendency of painters to flatter their subjects, the gallery could only lead one to the conclusion that for generations the Sanseverios had produced handsome sons who married beautiful women who, in turn, produced pretty children.

Even Quinnie de Sayles, not known for his enthusiasm for the female form, had gone into raptures over the small portrait of the first Countess Lucia, in the headdress of an odalisque, which hung in the sewing room.

"Bellissima! Una vera Venere!" he had said in his fluty voice.

And now, here at the end of the Sanseverio line, came the greatest beauty of all. Nothing, it seemed, not the wear of war nor the torture of her husband's illness, seemed to dissipate Gabrielle's looks. Despite months of worry, her blue eyes remained sparkling and clear. Privation had thinned her, but her porcelain skin still glowed, her soft hair shone. Her character had hardened.

"Have you any money?" she asked.

"Yes. Some. A little. I should have quite a bit more when I get paid on Friday. I've done quite a bit of overtime." There was no Italian word for "overtime" and the English word sat at the end of the sentence heavy and immovable, like a boulder.

"We cannot wait that long. We've run out. We need some more." There was no need to name the commodity. Neither would say "morphine," as if by avoiding the word they could cure Sandro or, at least, lessen his pain.

"I have fifty lire." Camillo pulled out his kidskin notecase from his jacket and extracted five mauve-colored bills. "I'm sorry, but that's all I have."

Gabrielle frowned. "It won't do," she said crossly. "I need a hundred, a hundred and fifty at least."

"Perhaps you could give them this with the understanding that we will pay the difference when I receive my wages." That tradesmen would extend credit to members of the Roman aristocracy had once been a simple fact of life.

Gabrielle laughed unpleasantly. "You don't know these people."

"No. No, I don't."

"He's in pain."

Instantly, Camillo felt the hot jab of tears in the corner of his eyes. His son was in pain and he was powerless to help. "My poor Sandro, my poor son."

"My poor husband."

Camillo crossed the wide, cool room and opened the top drawer of his tall mahogony bureau.

"These belonged to my father." He held up an old gold pocket watch and a fat fountain pen. "I understand that they are quite valuable. The barrel of the pen is white gold." He looked lovingly at the old-fashioned objects. "They were gifts from my mother to my father. I remember Sandro used to sit on Papa's lap and beg to have the watch held next to his ear so he could hear the tick-tock." He smiled at Gabrielle. "Papa used to pretend that it was the most outrageous suggestion. 'Absolutely not!' he'd say. 'I cannot part with a single tick, never mind a tick *and* a tock.' 'Please, nonno, please,' Sandro would say. Papa always gave in, of course, and he would hold it to his ear and Sandro would listen as if he was hearing a symphony." The smile on Camillo's face flickered.

Gabrielle shrugged. "People don't want watches and fountain pens. You can't eat them. You can't spend them."

"I'm sorry. I don't have anything else."

"Do they work?"

"I believe so, yes."

"What about your American friends? Can't you ask them for money? They have lots of money." She thought of the soldier who had offered her twenty dollars.

"You mean . . . beg?"

"Yes. That's precisely what I mean."

"I couldn't."

Gabrielle took the watch and the pen. "If no one wants these then you may have to."

Camillo closed the door and lowered his old bones onto the priedieu and prayed until the tears came.

11

As the army reasoned—correctly—that the devil was particularly assiduous in the making of work for the idle hands of soldiers, the army saw to it that as many units as possible experienced, as frequently as possible, something Kinney called "regimented fun." When such fun took the form of concerts—Benny Goodman, Glenn Miller, Harry James—or comics—Jack Benny and Portland Hoffa, Burns and Allen—it was generally welcomed. Anything else—lectures, tours, serious plays, "long-hair music"—was considered chicken and to be avoided at all costs. The rumor that the army was going to inflict an opera on the men of A Company pleased no one.

Thorpe inspected his men and gave them their usual pre-fun instructions. They were to be polite and quiet and to remember at all times that they were representatives—"ambassadors" Thorpe called them—of the United States and its army. McManus had already passed along his own standing orders with regard to fun: shut up and applaud, even if they hated it.

"I would," Thorpe said to his men, "like to correct a mistaken impression. It seems that some of you think that you'll be attending an opera. That is not the case. Far from it."

There was a sigh of relief from men and NCOs.

"Instead, you'll be seeing a show called *This is the Army*, starring Mr. Irving Berlin." If the men of Company A were avid, or even lukewarm, fans of Irving Berlin, they failed to demonstrate it.

"*This is the Army* is an extremely popular show back home," said Thorpe. "In fact . . ."

Oh shit, thought McManus, he's getting chummy. McManus hated that and thought he had long ago cured his CO of such an annoying habit.

". . . in fact, when this show played on Broadway, people paid a lot of money to see something that you are going to see for free. Now, where did all that money go, you may ask? Well, I'm pleased to tell you that it went to the Army Relief Fund. In other words, it went to you men. In fact, Miss Kate Smith, whom I'm sure you all know, donated ten thousand dollars to the Army Relief Fund in return for just two seats to this show."

"Woman need two seats," whispered Jimmy Holt. Giggles swept through the two lines of men, like a breeze.

"Keep your fuckin' mouth shut," growled Manganaro. "Talking to you, Holt."

"Sorry, Sarge, but that Kate Smith got a big butt," Jimmy whispered.

"Ssst," hissed McManus, quelling the giggles.

"The performance will take place at the Royal Opera House," Thorpe continued. "That's probably where the confusion arose. Now, I know that you men will do nothing that will in any way bring dishonor on this unit or the United States Army. Sergeant McManus?"

"Sir!" yelled McManus. He rapped out orders. The men broke ranks and climbed into two trucks. Holt and Leacock swung up into the cab.

"Next stop the opera," said Jimmy.

In the lobby of the Royal Opera House each man was issued with a small carton of vanilla ice cream, a Hershey bar already oozing in the heat, and a pack of spearmint gum, the individual sticks stuck together.

"Army doesn't care what it costs," observed Leacock, trying to pry apart two of the fused planks of gum. "The American fighting man always gets the best."

To city soldiers, those who had been to the lavish movie palaces of New York, Chicago, or Detroit, the ornate faux baroque interior of the Royal Opera House was nothing more grand than they were used to. Some of them thought the red plush and gilding hopelessly old-fashioned and the lack of air conditioning unbelievably primitive. It was hot. The opera house had not been built for use in high summer—Rome's season, after all, ran from November to

March—so the six hundred soldiers packed into orchestra and balcony filled the humid air with the smell of sweat and with curses directed at the joker who had designed the place. Palls of cigarette smoke drifted through the air like the clouds of a gathering storm, counterpointed by the acrid smell of carpet singed by butts ground into the red broadloom by army boots.

Thorpe and Kinney left the seating of the men to the sergeants and went in search of their own places in the first three rows. The buzz of conversation and profanity dipped slightly when McManus led the men into the theater. Most soldiers were used by now to seeing blacks in their midst, but their appearance in any numbers always gave rise to an air of curiousity, lightly laced with hostility.

"Holy smokes!" shouted someone. "Smokes!"

There was a spattering of laughter.

"Searched 'em for razors, Sarge?" shouted a wag high up in the heavens.

"Welcome, as usual," grumbled James Holt.

"Settle down!" ordered an officer.

A sensitive soul in the USO had not consigned Thorpe's soldiers to the uppermost level of the four tiers of balconies, but their seats left much to be desired. They were extreme stage left, behind a complement of white soldiers, two of whom looked familiar to Stanley.

"Oh shit," he whispered, "Jimmy, it's them."

"Man, they are everywhere."

The Springboks were twisting around in their seats, staring at the Company. One of them shouted:

"Sus! But it stinks in here all of a sudden."

"Why don't you shut your fuckin' mouth, man?" yelled Jimmy.

"You going to come over here and make me, kaffir?"

"Holt," growled McManus, "your ass leaves that seat and I'm gonna break every bone in your body. Eddie, Cal, you keep 'em in line, I'm gonna stop this before it starts."

Manganaro and Utterback looked over at the South Africans, who were grumbling among themselves, their heads down like a spooked herd about to stampede.

"You gonna talk to Thorpe?" asked Manganaro.

"Shit on that. I'm gonna go talk to the Springbok NCO."

"Yeah," said Utterback, "leave the officers out of it."

McManus scurried across the theater and located the South African NCO, a sergeant major as brawny as McManus himself.

"Hey, Sarge," he said, "maybe we should have a little talk." McManus thrust out his hand. "Donny McManus."

"Coetzee, Nick Coetzee."

"Listen, Nick," McManus stage whispered, "I get the feeling there's some bad blood between your guys and my guys, but listen, there's a lot of brass here tonight, and Irving Berlin an' all, so let's you and me make sure they don't get out of line. I'll make sure my guys stay in line, you make sure your guys stay in line. What do you say? Deal?" He thrust out his hand again.

"Don't shake his hand, Sergeant," shouted one of the South Africans. "You don't know where it's been." There was a low rumble of laughter, like thunder. McManus glowered. "What is it with these guys, Nick? They want to start a riot or what?"

Coetzee shook hands. "No bloody chance, Sergeant. I don't want any trouble neither. My fuckin' CO is down front. They won't act up. And that one that shouted I'll take care of personally after."

McManus clapped the South African sergeant on the shoulder. "Thanks, mac, you're a pal." He darted back to his seat, reaching it just as the houselights were going down.

"What did he say?" whispered Manganaro.

"He said he'll keep 'em in line. Nice guy too."

"Good. S'fuckin' hot in here."

"So sweat," advised McManus. He hoped there wouldn't be any trouble. He liked Irving Berlin. *Yip! Yip! Yaphank!* was one of his favorite shows.

The orchestra struck up the overture and the show began and McManus figured he was home free. It was smooth sailing until the second act when a white actor in full blackface cakewalked on stage. He was dressed in a loud purple suit, white bucks, and a pearl gray derby with a wide brim like an eave. McManus felt the rustle of resentment in his soldiers.

"Ah ain'ts gonna jainin' no ahmy," the actor squawked. "Ah don'ts lahk de color a deah clothes."

McManus rubbed his forehead. "Oh shit," he whispered.

"You won't join, you fuckin' munt, because you're nothing but a fuckin' coward!"

"That man there!" shouted Nick Coetzee.

Hisses snaked through the theater.

A light-skinned black girl strolled on stage, greeted by whistles and catcalls.

"Kaffir hoer jong!"

The orchestra struck up and the girl started to sing a song to her boyfriend shaming him into joining the army because, as she told him, olive drab was "what the well-dressed Harlem man will wear."

"This," said Holt loudly, "is bull shit. I didn't join the army for no clothes."

"Holt, I'm warning you . . ."

"Hey kaffir! Kaffir! What the fuck are you doin' here with the white man?"

Holt jumped to his feet. "Hey, fuck you, jack!"

"Fuckin' munts!"

Shouts and yells were bursting out all over the theater now. A lit cigarette arched through the gloom; someone roared in outrage as the butt hit. Feet started stamping. The singer stopped singing and looked worriedly into the spots. The orchestra faltered, then ground to a halt.

Suddenly, Ernest Biggs jumped to his feet and yelled. "How come we always get the shitty seats? How come we always got to sit at the back of the fuckin' bus?"

"Yeah!" yelled the men of A Company.

"Jesus Christ, Biggs!"

"Because you're fuckin' animals, you fuckin' munt bastards!" Biggs pointed to the man. "Hey, fuck you, whitey!"

A mushy packet of ice cream sailed across the aisle and smacked Whiteside full in the face. "Hey!" he said. "Don't be doing that."

"That is enough!" shouted an officer, a South African. "This will stop at once!" But his voice failed to cut through the dense curtain of caterwauling.

The blacks and the whites were standing on their seats now, yelling and shouting, threatening, taunting. The NCOs of A Company, along with the full complement of sergeants from the South African outfit, had spilled into the aisle between the two factions, trying to keep them apart.

"For Christ's sake!" bellowed McManus. "All of you! Sit the fuck down!"

"Turn on the lights!" yelled Utterback.

167

A half a dozen officers came flying up from the orchestra seats along with a handful of American MPs and British Field Security Police, all adding their own loud voices to the fray. In among all the noise came the faint strains of music, the orchestra having struck up the "Star Spangled Banner," in a misguided attempt to bring the American soldiers in the theater to attention.

An MP smacked a South African with his billy, and that was all the spark needed to ignite the flammable situation. The hostile fumes in the air burst into flame. With a roar a couple of South Africans launched themselves into the fray, tumbling into a confused mass of black and white, officers and enlisted men. Punches were thrown. Billies swung.

Fights were breaking out all over the hall now as soldiers took advantage of the darkness and mayhem to settle some scores within their own units or to repay some slights, real or imagined, owed to soldiers of other outfits or armies. Ice cream, cigarettes, and trash rained down from the balconies, and screamed obscenities carried far in the perfect acoustics.

Holt, Leacock, Biggs, and all of the other men of A Company—except Whiteside—felt rage and release coursing through them, as if every slight and slap the army had ever administered had been distilled into this single, hate-charged moment.

"Come on, motherfuckers," yelled Holt. "We ain't afraid of you white bastards."

"Kaffir, I'm gonna donner you!"

"Assholes!" yelled Leacock. He hadn't forgotten his humiliation at the hands of the big white men—in front of his girl, too—and he suddenly realized how much he ached to get even.

Biggs was far more catholic in his hatreds. "Fuck you all!" he shouted. "Fuck the army! And fuck you too, man." He pointed at a South African lieutenant who was ordering him to sit down.

The houselights came up.

A squad of MPs poured into the theater, coursing down the aisles, clubs ready. The noise level dropped and suddenly everyone could hear the voice of an American MP captain. He was on stage, a microphone in his hand.

"Order!" The single crisp word boomed out of the loudspeaker. "Shut up! Now!"

Nervous Italian ushers scurried through the theater opening the fire exits. Cooler evening air flooded into the steaming theater.

There was a sudden abatement of tension, but violence still floated through the air. The thunderous shouting lessened slightly.

"Okay, listen up," said the MP captain. "We are going to clear the hall starting with this level. Every man will stay in his seat until told to move. That is an order. Any man disobeying this order will be placed under arrest."

A lowering roar of boos echoed through the theater. Already MP squads were marching A Company through one set of doors and the South Africans through another. More MPs were waiting outside to keep the two groups apart. Kinney and the sergeants moved quickly to reassert control over their unit.

"Get 'em in the trucks," ordered Kinney. "All of 'em."

"All of 'em, sir? Who's gonna drive?" asked McManus.

"I'll drive number one. Utterback—"

"Yessir?"

"Number two."

"Manganaro, McManus. You ride in the back. Any trouble and I want some names."

"Yessir!"

"Wait a minute, sir," said McManus, "the captain . . ."

"The last time I saw Captain Thorpe, McManus, he was deep in conversation with a colonel. Neither of them looked happy. Now let's get the hell out of here before there's any more trouble."

"Yessir!"

The men of A Company tumbled into the trucks, still high on adrenaline and with a delicious sense of victory. They laughed and shouted and stamped their feet all the way back to the depot. Manganaro and McManus didn't try to quiet them—let them scream all they wanted—knowing it was better to blow off steam, to get it out of their systems before the swift, sharp process of punishment began. And every man knew punishment was coming, but that was in the future. Right now, they had a moment to savor. Whiteside, however, was worried.

"We gonna get in trouble," he said sadly.

"Yeah?" Jimmy Holt shouted. "What can they do to us they ain't done already?"

"Right!" they chorused.

"What they gonna do, Sarge?"

"Don't know, Jimmy," said McManus.

"Bust us down?" yelled Holt. "Hell, we already as low as we can get. There ain't nothing as low as a nigger in whitey's army!"

"That's the truth!"

"What are they going to do? Pay us less?"

"No!" Biggs shouted. "They can't pay us less than they do already."

"Give us worse chow?"

"Can't get no worse!"

"Send us to jail? Hell no! I'm already in jail. We all are. We're in the goddamn army!"

Yes, all that was true, Leacock thought, but they could—and probably would—restrict the entire company to their barracks. Stanley shook his head sadly. He had a feeling it would be quite a while before Elena got to try on her new high-heeled shoes.

THE NEAR RIOT at the Royal Opera House sent bolts of energy through the synapses that bound the military body together. The USO complained to the commander of the American Forces Rome. In his office, the complaint bifurcated, one going down the chain of command to Thorpe, the other vaulting national barriers to land on the desk of the commander of British and Commonwealth Forces, thence downward to the South African company level.

The management of the Royal Opera House had recourse to the Allied Military Government. When the complaint came before the AMG head, Colonel Charles Poletti, the great khaki bureaucracy twitched. A formal apology was issued to the Royal Opera House, with an offer of restitution, thus taking care of the civilian, noncombatant side of things. Then Poletti turned his attention to the military.

Poletti felt that Rome and the Romans deserved a well-regulated militia, not just because it was necessary to the welfare of free peoples, but also because without it, Rome would be a madhouse. When Colonel Poletti heard about the events at the opera house, he damned near blew a gasket. Captain Thorpe and Lieutenant Kinney, along with Captain Van Zyl and Lieutenant Karstens of the Springbok Division, were summoned to Poletti's huge office in the Palazzo dei Conservatori on the Capitoline Hill to receive what the South Africans would call "a rocket" and the Americans "a chewing out."

Poletti did not greet the four officers cordially. They stood taut

170

in front of his desk while he riffled papers; then he returned their salutes with a glower and bid them, with bad grace, to sit down. They were not given permission to smoke.

Poletti stood, paced to the window, stared down at the ruins of the Forum and spoke like a judge handing down a sentence.

"We are the United Nations forces, gentlemen. The *United* Nations. It would not seem to me as if the display at the opera house was much of a show of unity. Any of you disagree with that assessment?"

The four officers said, "No, sir."

"As I understand it, racial epithets, obscenities, and remarks denigrating superior officers and the army in general were shouted on both sides. Is that correct?"

The four officers said, "Yes, sir."

"The performance, which featured one of America's—no, one of the world's—best-loved performers, was disrupted and damage was done to the theater. I can only be thankful that Mr. Berlin had not yet made his entrance, otherwise this story would be all over the stateside papers. That counts for something, I suppose."

"Sir—" began Thorpe.

"I'm not finished," snapped Poletti.

"Sorry, sir."

"I imagine I am safe in assuming that none of you reads the local papers?" Poletti unfolded a copy of that morning's *Il Messaggero* and tapped a boxed story, above the fold, page one.

"I'm afraid I don't speak a word of it, sir," said Van Zyl, speaking for all of them.

"Then I will read it to you. Please listen carefully." Poletti cleared his throat. "After the long night of Fascism, the flowers of culture looked with bright faces, full of hope, toward the Allied dawn. And yet, last night, in the heart of eternal Rome's great shrine to Terpsichore, a dark cloud passed across the glorious shining orb, the sun of our liberators. Men of skins of different hues profaned the temple of the Opera, doing battle over issues of race, distinctions we poor Romans thought forever banished with the eviction of the hated Germans and their lackeys . . ." Poletti tossed the paper aside. "It goes on from there. You can get the gist of what they're trying to say."

"Ah, excuse me sir . . ."

"You're Kinney, aren't you?"

171

"Yes, sir."

"What?"

"That was a news story, was it, sir?"

"That's how Italian papers sound," snapped Poletti. "Don't try and get smart with me, young man."

"No disrespect intended, sir."

Poletti ignored the apology. "I'll spell it out for you gentlemen. What *Il Messaggero* here is trying to say—a paper, by the way, read by the vast majority of the population—is that if there are racial divisions in the army of liberation, then what the hell is the difference between us and the bastards we just kicked out for them. In other words, we are being compared to the Fascists, and I don't like that."

Van Zyl spoke up. "Isn't that a little extreme, sir?"

"It doesn't matter. It's what they think that's important."

"Sir," said Thorpe, "I'd like to point out that my entire company has been restricted to barracks until further notice."

"As has mine," said Van Zyl quickly and, not to be out done, added, "And we're taking every possible step to root out the ringleaders so that we may punish them severely."

"As are we," said Thorpe.

Poletti looked disgusted. "I don't care what's going on within the army, gentlemen. My primary concern is for the welfare of the people of Rome and our relations with them. I understand, furthermore, that this disgrace in the opera house is only the latest in a series of incidents between the two outfits. So you'll keep them cooped up for a couple of weeks, resentment will build up, and the next time they encounter one another the situation will be that much more explosive. No gentlemen, not in my town."

"Sir," said Van Zyl, "we are expecting to be moved out of the city at some point . . ."

"When, exactly?"

"That has not yet been decided, sir."

"Then it's no solution, Captain. Besides, the question of punishment is not, to me, anyway, as important as demonstrating that this kind of race hate is not part and parcel of the allied cause. I want some kind of demonstration of amity, unity, a peaceful resolution of differences. I want to see something that will show the Romans that if there are differences among our men, there are ways beyond yelling and cracking heads. Now. Have you any sugges-

172

tions?" Poletti looked from one man to another. The four shuffled uneasily, like schoolboys caught by a pop quiz.

Kinney spoke first. "Sir, if I might suggest something . . ."

"You seem to be the only one with an idea, Lieutenant."

"Well, you've pointed out that the men under Captain Thorpe's command and those under Captain Van Zyl's do have differences of opinion, I was thinking that, perhaps, those differences could best be settled by means of something competitive but essentially nonviolent, sir."

"Like what, for instance?"

"Perhaps a sporting event, sir. Something open to the public. May the best man win and all that, sir. Sport is, I hardly need point out, inherently wholesome, not to mention all-American. That is, all-Allied, sir."

Poletti stared hard at Kinney, not sure if he was having his leg pulled or not. "Yesss . . . there might be something in that. It might be something that could work."

"Just a suggestion, sir," said Kinney modestly.

Kinney's opposite number, Lieutenant Karstens, mentally kicked himself for not having thought of it. Van Zyl would give him hell later, unless the suggestion was not adopted.

"Excuse me, sir," said Karstens, "no nation appreciates sport more than the Union of South Africa, but as I see it, there is one small problem. Just which sport did Lieutenant Kinney have in mind?"

"Baseball," said Thorpe quickly.

"South Africans don't play baseball," said Van Zyl. "How about cricket instead?"

"Americans don't play cricket," responded Thorpe. "How about football?"

"Is that what you yanks call soccer?"

"No," said Kinney, "it's what we yanks call football."

"Soccer and football are not the same thing," said Thorpe.

"Basketball," suggested Kinney.

"It's not played in South Africa," said Van Zyl. "Boxing?"

"No, no," said Poletti, "not boxing. Too violent. And besides, it's got to be a team sport. I want as much outfit as possible to participate."

Van Zyl thought of some of the big men under his command and decided to push for boxing. "We could have several fights, different weight classes, that sort of thing."

"That would still employ only six or eight men at most. Forget about boxing, captain."

"Rugby then," Van Zyl countered.

"We don't play it, sir," said Kinney.

"I suppose ice hockey is out of the question," said Thorpe.

"South Africans don't play it," said Van Zyl.

"And neither do American Negroes," said Poletti. "Besides, where would we get the ice?"

"Jukskei," said Karstens.

"What the hell is that?" demanded Poletti.

"It's a game, a South African game."

"Never heard of it. No . . ." Poletti looked out the window, deep in thought. "Maybe it won't work, good idea, though." The colonel seemed saddened that the United Nation forces didn't even have a simple ball game in common. Karsten, however, looked relieved.

"Ah, sir," said Kinney. "As I understand it, rugby is little more than a less developed game of football. Under the circumstances, perhaps our South African friends could learn the basics of our game and play that. The two do have quite a few points in common . . ."

"Ach man," said Karstens, "football and rugby have nothing in common. Use your kop."

"Karstens," cautioned Van Zyl.

"No, no, lieutenant," said Kinney with a smile. "I think you are still confusing soccer and football. What *you* call football, *we* call soccer. What *we* call *football* bears a strong resemblance to rugby. Correct me if I'm wrong, Lieutenant, but isn't rugby a game wherein an elliptical inflated ball is carried—not kicked—across an opponent's goal line for the purpose of accruing points?"

"Eh?" said Karstens.

"I can see the lieutenant's point"—Van Zyl said leftenant— "but if the games are similar, sir, why do we have to play by American rules? Why can't they play rugger?"

"Good point. Lieutenant?"

"Because I thought our South African friends and allies might be interested in playing a more highly developed form of the game, sir. I would have thought it would have been something of an education *and* a cultural exchange for them, sir."

"Hell, man, rugby is the national sport of South Africa," said Karstens, "we don't need another game."

Kinney addressed himself to Poletti exclusively. "All the more reason to play the American variety, sir. If, as Lieutenant Karstens says, rugby is a national mania in the Union, then Captain Van Zyl's men are likely to be avid rugby players. We, sir—and I think Captain Thorpe will agree with me—don't even know if our men play football."

"That's true, Colonel," said Thorpe, "I don't think I've ever seen my men play football. Or any variety of sports, sir."

"That's bad, Captain. It's a great morale booster."

"Couldn't agree more, sir," said Kinney. "But Captain Thorpe does have a point, relative to the inexperience of our men." Kinney looked remarkably earnest. "In the interests of fair competition, sir . . ."

Van Zyl could see that Poletti was wavering. The South African liked the idea of a sporting event and knew if rugby were chosen his men would prevail. Not that they were great athletes, or even great soldiers, but he found it hard to believe that a group of South Africans could lose a rugby match to a bunch of munts. Van Zyl had a brainstorm.

"Well, sir, I think we may have overlooked something in all of this. As you said before, quite rightly, this match is not so much about bragging rights between two fine units in the United Nations forces, but more about a display of good sportsmanship for the benefit of the Italian population."

"Yes, what of it?"

"Well, sir, you might not be aware of the fact, but Italy is far more a rugby-playing nation than an American-football-playing one, sir. I know for a fact that the Italians field a side in international play, or at least, they did before the war." Van Zyl did not add that he also knew for a fact that the team was abysmal.

"They do?" said Poletti with interest.

"Yes, sir."

"I always thought they played soccer."

"That is probably their first love, sir. But they have rugby in their hearts." Van Zyl decided to say no more as he was in danger of straying across the border from overstatement into outright lying.

175

"Is it?" Poletti stroked his chin. "Then rugby would make more sense to them, wouldn't it?"

Thorpe seemed paralyzed by this reasoning. Kinney did his best to counterattack. "It would make more sense, sir, but it would be to the detriment of one side, sir. It seems a little unfair, sir, to ask Captain Thorpe's men to play a game they don't know against a group of men who hail from a country where this sport is the national pastime. Might as well ask the South Africans to play baseball, sir."

"But Italians don't play baseball," said Van Zyl. "Think of it, sir, this game is, after all, for them. As you have said, sir."

Fuck the Italians, Kinney wanted to say. "Think of fair play, sir."

"Thorpe, what do you think?"

"I, well, oh, I think that there's, ah . . ."

"Okay." Poletti slapped his knee. "Rugby it is."

Van Zyl and Karstens exchanged smirks.

Kinney had one more card to play. "Sir, why not do the sporting thing? Toss a coin."

Poletti pointed at him. "Good idea. That is, if you gentlemen don't object."

Van Zyl and Karstens wanted to object strenuously but they knew that sportsmen never objected to a fair toss of a coin. Karstens looked at Kinney. When he got the smug, dapper American lieutenant into the scrum he'd wipe that smile off his face.

Poletti dug a coin out of his pocket. "Remember, gentlemen, even if you should win the toss you can still do the sporting thing and play the other fellow's game." Poletti flicked the coin in the air, caught it and slapped it onto his wrist. "Kinney, all this was your idea, you call it."

"Heads, sir."

"Heads it is. What'll it be, Lieutenant?"

Thorpe's smile vanished when Kinney said, "Rugby, sir."

"Damn good, Lieutenant! I knew I could count on you to be a decent fellow."

"It was the sporting thing to do, sir."

"That's the spirit! Now, I'll get on to our British allies and see if they can't second someone to your outfit to help with the training. That seems fair to me, doesn't it, Captain Van Zyl?"

176

"Oh yes, sir." He felt slightly uneasy, as if Kinney had something up his sleeve.

"By God, gentlemen," said Poletti, "this is the kind of spirit that wins wars."

As THORPE AND Kinney walked down the long, wide staircase, the *Cordonata*, that led from the Capitoline Hill to the Piazza Venezia, the captain said, tight lipped, "I can't begin to pretend to know what you were playing at back there, Kinney."

Austin Kinney drew languidly on his cigarette. "Well, sir, look at it this way. If we lose, we can claim it wasn't our game. No dishonor there. If we win—most unlikely—we can say we gave the Springboks every chance. Either way, we're in good with Poletti. We can't lose, sir."

"*You're* in good with Poletti," said Thorpe sourly.

"We're all in this together, sir."

12

Major John Howe was anxious to meet Lieutenant Manny Farfalla. He had been reading the evaluations on his new investigator and he was impressed. The army seemed to think a lot of Farfalla—dedicated and efficient not being pejoratives in Howe's vocabulary—and the young man had received a first-class education, all the more remarkable, Howe thought, seeing as Farfalla had no advantage of family or finance.

It was with considerable disappointment, then, that he recognized Farfalla to be the foul young man who had struck the infant on the Corso Umberto. Farfalla was not pleased either.

"You!" said Howe.

"Yes, sir. I'm afraid so."

"Well . . . you had better sit down, Lieutenant."

Farfalla sat stiff and upright in the chair in front of Howe's desk. The office had once belonged to a director of the state insurance company and it was operatically grand. Howe sat behind a desk of comically large size and behind him was a baronial fireplace complete with carved mantle and a deep inglenook. The fresco on the ceiling, a swirling stew of undraped bosomy women was, so Malinsky informed him, a depiction of Life and Fortune encountering Time. "The only actuarial iconography I have ever encountered. Sir."

"Well, Lieutenant Farfalla, I gather we shall be working together."

Howe assumed what he called his judge's mien. "I must tell you that I was disappointed in what I witnessed, Farfalla. I've read your

178

file and I am very impressed, though I find it hard to imagine a Harvard man committing such actions."

Action, Farfalla corrected mentally. And neither was he a Harvard man. Harvard men lived in Harvard houses. They got drunk at Locke-Obers and dated girls from Radcliffe, Wellesley, and Smith. They got punched for Porcellian, joined Hasty Pudding, and wrote for the Lampoon. They drove cars and went out for crew. They had money. They had names like Drew and Thad and Thatch. Austin.

Farfalla was a Harvard man in that he held a degree from Harvard College, but he had lived his four years with the family of his Uncle Iggy in East Boston. He didn't get drunk and he had had two dates in four years. One with the daughter of a neighbor of Uncle Iggy, a girl named Theresa, and one with a sophomore at Albertus Magnus College in New Haven, Connecticut. Farfalla joined nothing—wasn't asked, couldn't have afforded it if he had been—he rode the T, didn't go out for any sport, and had no money. As for his name, Farfalla was one of two Mannys in the class of '41, the other being Prince Manfred Von Hohenzollern.

"I do not understand it. I am at a loss."

Manny was tired of this. Yes. He had smacked the kid—no worse than Manny used to get once in a while from his own Pop—but he had said he was sorry and had paid the kid off.

"Sir, I regret what happened. I had a tough day. I'm sorry."

"And that child hadn't had a tough day? Scavenging in the streets for enough money to stay alive? It's no excuse, Lieutenant."

"There's another reason, sir, but I'm not sure you'll want to hear it."

"I'd be interested in anything you might have to say, Lieutenant."

"May I be blunt, sir?"

"Of course."

Farfalla leaned forward in his chair, smiling slightly. "There's something you should know about me here and now, Major."

"That being?"

"I'm an asshole."

"I beg your pardon?"

"It's true. Ask anyone."

"Lieutenant, I'm not sure . . ."

"I'm mean, sir. Ornery. Disagreeable. Grouchy. Or, sir, in Harvard man terms, fractious, querulous. I hit children in the streets. I send men to the gallows. I don't give up my seat on a street car to nuns or pregnant women. Sir, I'm a shit."

"Anything else, Lieutenant?"

"I'm not a gentleman, Major. I'm not a 'Harvard man.' I think you should know that."

"Do you have any good qualities you think I should know about?"

"Well, sir, considering the job I do, I'm not so sure that my disposition is a liability. However, you'll find that I'm efficient, hardworking, sober, and neat. I'm a stickler for detail. I don't have an open file in my career, sir."

"You always get your man, eh, Lieutenant?"

"Yes sir, I do."

Howe smiled. "Do you think you'll be able to work with me, Farfalla? I must warn you that in civilian life, both as a trial attorney and as a prosecutor, I lost a case now and then."

"Well, I'm young yet, sir. Plenty of time for failure. But yes, I know I'll be able to work with you."

"And how do you know that?"

"Because those are my orders, sir."

"Ah," said Howe, "orders. Orders are dangerous things, Farfalla. What if I gave you an order you were morally unable to carry out?"

"If it's in the Uniform Code of Military Justice, I wouldn't have any moral objections, sir."

"And if it wasn't?"

"I'd report you, sir."

"As easy as that?"

"As easy as that, Major."

"And risk doing damage to yourself in the process. I don't know a great deal about the army, Lieutenant, but I do know that it does not appreciate lieutenants informing on majors."

"If you ordered me to do something illegal, sir, I'd report you and take my chances with the army." Farfalla paused. "You don't have any plans to ask me to break the law, do you sir?"

"No. It's just that I'm not terribly comfortable with a . . . Prussian devotion to orders. Put not your trust in princes and all that."

Farfalla smiled sardonically. "No trouble there, sir. I don't trust anybody."

"Goodness. You really are an—"

"Asshole, sir."

"Yes." Howe frowned. "My first order to you, Lieutenant—and perhaps you'll take the trouble to find it in the Uniform Code of Military Justice—is this: you will not utter an obscenity in my presence again. It is the mark of a cramped mind. I do not believe you have a cramped mind. Is that clear?"

"Yes sir."

"Good. Down to business, then. I understand you are conducting a murder investigation. An open file."

"Not for long, sir. I know who committed the crime; it's just a question of finding him."

"And who is he?"

"A sergeant in the QMC."

"QMC?"

"Quartermaster Corps, sir."

"Of course."

"But sir, I believe that the murder is secondary to the larger issues embodied in this case."

"An issue larger than murder, Lieutenant?"

"Yes sir. The murdered man was a black marketeer. The murderer, I believe, was an American soldier. This whole thing could be a lead into the black market in Rome."

"How are you sure it was an American soldier?"

"I have a witness, sir. She places an American supply force sergeant at the scene." Manny shrugged. "It seems pretty straightforward to me, sir."

"And how many Quartermaster personnel are there in the city?"

"About sixteen hundred. Four hundred are NCOs."

"Four hundred suspects. How likely are you to be able to single out a murderer from a group that size?"

"It could be done, sir."

"Yes, but could it be done without disrupting the services of supply for the city and the front? After all, these people do have an important job of work to do. I don't know all that much about the armed forces, Lieutenant, but I do know that NCOs are the backbone of the service."

181

"Sir, you keep saying that. I know it's none of my business, but could you tell me how it is you came to be in the army?"

"I was asked by the Department of the Army. Apparently there is a shortage of jurists. An old friend of mine is in the Judge Advocate General's Office and he asked me to come in. My son is in the Navy. . . . It was a chance to contribute to the war effort." Howe smiled weakly. "I went from being an attorney to major overnight. I've never even fired a gun."

"Ah," said Farfalla, as if that explained everything.

"So, answer my question, Lieutenant. Can you carry on an investigation into this matter without disrupting the services of supply in the city?"

Manny shook his head. "No, sir."

"Then you must find another way, Lieutenant. No one is going to countenance anything that will undermine the war effort."

"Having an American soldier get away with murder, sir, does not seem to me to be contributing much to the war effort. It's a serious crime, an important wrong to redress. More important than, say, slapping a kid in the—"

"That's enough," snapped Howe. "I've been honest with you, Farfalla. I've told you of my lack of experience in military matters, and I've allowed you to speak freely, as an investigator must to a prosecutor or whatever it is the army calls my position—"

"Trial judge advocate," said Manny.

"Yes, thank you. Trial judge advocate. But I am still a major and you are a lieutenant. You will respect that difference in rank. Do you understand me?"

"Yes sir."

"As regards this homicide, I can only suggest you continue your inquiries as best you can." Howe opened another folder. "Capital crimes awaiting trial. A rape and a homicide, second degree. The Superior Military Court will be convened at the end of this month. Is there anything you need tell me beyond what I have here?" Howe tapped the folder.

"No sir. Full confessions in both cases. If they were being heard in civilian court I'd suggest mitigating factors in the murder, but—" Farfalla shrugged. It was a gesture that said, Well, that's the army for you.

Howe raised an eyebrow. "*You*, Lieutenant, you mitigate a sentence? That doesn't seem to be in keeping with your own description of your character. Why are you pleading leniency for a confessed murderer?"

"Because," said Farfalla, "it's not *right.*"

Howe knew the facts in the case. The soldier was almost an idiot, hardly aware of his actions, but there was nothing the major could do about that.

"I'm afraid my hands are tied. I'm confident that the defense will raise the matter at the sentencing, but I must prosecute to the limit of my ability. That's the law, Lieutenant, and that's what I'm here to enforce."

Farfalla nodded. Now it was clear. Soft-spoken, soft-hearted Major Howe, a man who worried about street urchins and was disturbed by obscenity, was an asshole too. Farfalla smiled.

"RUGBY," ANNOUNCED SERGEANT Rhys Jones of the Twenty-fourth, The South Wales Borderers, "is a game of thugs, played by gentlemen."

"And we ain't neither," said Holt out of the corner of his mouth.

"That man there!" yelled Lance Corporal Terence Llewellyn, the note of indignation ringing to the rafters of the depot garage.

"Are we in the American Army or the British Army?" grumbled Stanley Leacock.

"Shut your yap, Leacock," ordered Utterback.

Thorpe had delegated the rugby training of his men to Kinney, the prime architect of the plan. The lieutenant, standing on the loading dock with the two Welshmen delegated by the Eighth Army to assist the Fifth, stepped forward raising his arms, signaling for silence.

"Listen up," ordered McManus.

"Men, you are going to learn how to play rugby, that you already know. These two gentlemen have kindly volunteered to share their considerable knowledge of this fascinating game with you. During your training sessions Sergeant Jones and Lance Corporal Llewellyn will have authority over you. You will obey them as you would one of your own NCOs. You don't have much time to master this game, so I suggest you pay close attention to what these two men have to say. Sergeant Jones?"

"Sah!" Jones's voice was loud and penetrating, brass toned and leather lunged, but it issued from a bantamweight body. He was a short, wiry, red-faced man with darting brown eyes, bushy brows, and a bristly little mustache, like a dirty smudge on his lip. Jones wore the typical summer uniform of the British army—baggy shirt, baggy shorts, and big, heavy brown boots.

Rugby was his life and he loved the brutal game with a wild and unfettered passion. In his boyhood Jones had cursed the fates that had made him so small, rather than making him a great Welsh rugby player, a thundering tower of muscle and brawn. Throughout his youth Jones had spent his pocket money on linaments and exercise plans, "electricity belts," and odd pieces of muscle-building machinery, all advertised in the back of *Rugby Player* and *Rugby World*, but to no avail. By his late teens he had surrendered to his slight physique and played the game as hooker, the smallest man on a rugby side. He spent his time off the field thinking about rugby, analyzing and dissecting, until he became a canny and cunning brain truster of the game. Rhys Jones was what other Welshmen called "a clever bugger."

"A game of thugs, played by gentlemen, says I. And I heard one of you lads say you're neither. Now, that's where you're wrong. You might not be thugs, but you are gentlemen, gentlemen soldiers of the United States Army. I will treat you as such.

"Now then. The object of this noble game," he bellowed, "is for fifteen men to ground a very small ball beyond an opponent's goal line. As you might expect, fifteen equally determined men will try to prevent you from doing this." Sergeant Jones paused dramatically. "This, gentlemen, is a rugby ball." He drew the ball from a leather satchel and held it up as if it was a rare botanical specimen. There was some stirring in the ranks.

"That's a football," someone shouted.

"Shaddap," ordered Llewellyn. The lance corporal, Jones's junior by ten years, was exactly the physical specimen the sergeant had yearned to be when he was a boy. Llewellyn was a big, strapping man, muscled in the stomach like a cobbled street, with arms like pig iron and heavy legs which pounded like pistons. He was also a world-class rugby player, having represented Wales three times in Five Nations competition.

"No, no, no, gentlemen," said Jones. "This *is not* a football. It is a *rugby* ball. Make no mistake." Jones's eyes swept the two lines of men. He had already spotted Whiteside. The South Wales Borderers had taught Jones to think like a military man and he had slipped into the habit of applying military terminology to the game. Whiteside would be the block house, the fixed point for offense and defense. The backs, quarter, half, and full were the shock troops, interlocking fields of fire, sweeping the pitch, slicing through the enemy.

Holt and Leacock looked promising too. Tall, strong young men who, if they had any speed at all, would be difficult to catch.

"Now . . ." Jones climbed down from the loading dock and paced back and forth in front of the men. "There are three things that I will look for in the men I select: speed, stamina, and courage. You need speed to move the ball, the stamina to keep moving, and the courage to tackle and be tackled. Rugby, gents, is not a game for pansies."

"Fuckin' Knute Rockne," someone mumbled.

"Shaddap," said Llewellyn.

"You all know why this game is going to be played. The Springboks and you lot aren't seeing eye to eye and the brass can talk all it wants about good fellowship and sportsmanship but you and I know that's just a load of old codswallop."

"A load of *what?*" said Stanley.

"You heard the man," said Holt. "Codswallop."

"What's that?"

"Don't sound good."

"Shaddap."

"You lads are playing a grudge match and you want to win it. Is that not so, gentlemen?"

The company stared back at him.

"Am I right?"

"Yeah," they said more out of a desire to be polite, to avoid embarrassing the man, rather than any actual desire to win, or, for that matter, play.

"Am I right?"

"Yeah!"

"Good. Now, you, boyo, what's your name, then?"

"Alvin Whiteside."

"Alvin, what's the first thing I mentioned that I'm going to be looking for in my players?"

"Uh . . . speed, Sergeant."

"That's right. Speed. So let's see some. Lance Corporal!"

"Sar'nt!"

185

"We are going to take these men over to the racetrack and see how well they run, aren't we, Lance Corporal?"

"Sar'nt!"

There was a collective groan from the assembled men.

"Running? Shit!"

"It's a hundred degrees, Sarge."

"I ain't running no place."

McManus stepped forward. "Listen, any of you don't want to play this game, you don't have to. But you're gonna have to stay here and help out a little. You know what I'm saying? You gotta play the game or do the work. You choose."

"Thank you, Sergeant," yelled Jones. "At the double!"

"Company!" screamed Llewellyn.

With a clatter of boots and a chorus of curses, the men of A Company ran out of the depot and into the blinding heat.

THERE WAS NO hot training for Austin Kinney. By five o'clock that afternoon he was back in his hotel suite, enjoying a martini after his labors.

There was a soft, discreet knock at the door. Egidio, Kinney's pet concierge, had been glad to answer the summons to Austin's room. The young man always meant money.

"Good evening, sir."

"Yes." Kinney lolled on the plush sofa. His tie was undone and his shoes were off. He held his cold, clear drink in one hand. He did not ask Egidio to sit down.

"At your service, sir."

"Good. I need something . . ."

Egidio smiled. Whatever the young gentleman required, the concierge was sure he could supply it.

"Who's Lorenzetti?" Kinney swung himself upright, put down the drink and flipped a twenty-dollar bill—a real one, not scrip—onto the coffee table. Egidio looked longingly at the note.

"Go on, take it."

Egidio did take it, swiftly, with the skill of a prestidigitator, the bill vanishing into his striped waistcoat. "Why do you speak of this man?"

"That's none of your business, chief. I just want to know who this guy is."

Egidio took a deep breath, as if he was about to plunge under water. "Do you know what means *malavita?*"

Kinney hadn't paid too much attention to his prep-school Latin, but even he recognized the roots of the words for "evil" and "life." "Suppose you tell me what it means."

"It is all the bad things in Rome. The thieves and the murderers. Lorenzetti is like Al Capone." *Caponay*, he said.

"How do I meet him?"

"Cosa?" said Egidio in alarm. "Meet him? Why do you want to meet that man? He is a bad man, dangerous man."

"I have my reasons."

"You are the police?"

Kinney laughed. "What I am doesn't matter. Just tell me how to get hold of this guy Lorenzetti."

"I do not know."

"Sure you do." Kinney took another twenty from his billfold and dangled it in front of Egidio, taunting him with it, the way children tease puppies with a treat. "Sure you do. Don't you?"

"Perhaps," said Egidio hesitantly. "I think I know where you must go, but I'm not so sure."

"Not so sure isn't good enough." Kinney folded the bill and stuffed it into the breast pocket of his shirt. He took a long swallow of his drink.

Egidio looked pained. He wanted another twenty dollars very badly, but to get involved in the business of the *malavita*, even indirectly, was madness. He struggled with himself a moment—he already had twenty dollars and no harm done—but like a gambler unable to cash in his chips while only modestly ahead, he went for the bigger score. "Yes," he said with a little gasp, as if he had been holding his breath, "I know a place."

Kinney smiled his dazzling smile. "See, I told you you knew. All you had to do was think a minute."

Egidio looked grave. Dealing with the *malavita* was no laughing matter. He uncapped his fountain pen and scribbled on a piece of hotel stationery. "There is a cafe in Monti. Do you know where is this?"

Kinney shook his head.

"It is near the Colosseo. Not nice. Bad place."

Kinney took the piece of paper. Caffè dei Goti, it read, Via dei Serpenti.

"Via dei Serpenti means the street of the serpents. Now, maybe you know why."

"Slippery character, this guy Lorenzetti, huh?" Kinney handed over the other twenty. "Spend it wisely."

"Thank you, sir," said Egidio gravely. He closed the door.

Almost immediately, however, there was a knock. Kinney, the piece of paper still in his hand, answered to find the concierge standing there.

"Changed your mind, chief? Too late."

" 'Scuse, please." Egidio took the paper from Kinney's hand and carefully tore off the Excelsior letterhead. Then he shrugged. It wasn't the Roman shrug, but it was no less eloquent. It said, You can't be too careful.

13

Now and then, Warrant Officer Haley took a drink. Every so often, he took more than one. Once in a while, he got blind, stumbling, falling-down drunk, and he had done so the night before. He had had no intention of making a night of it when he went off duty, but on his way back to his billet, shared with a couple of gloomy guys from graves registration, he ran into a pal of his who invited him to a card game. The cards turned to craps and the craps turned into a party and the party became a nocturnal crawl through a hot, crowded tunnel of night clubs. Two drinks of dago red became five and then a whole bottle, then two; and then one of the meatballs who ran one of the joints pulled out a bottle of grappa which tasted like liquid gunfire.

A bunch of limeys came in with some girls and for once everybody was happy, no interservice bickering. They sang songs, a sort of contest. The Brits sang "Tipperary." The Yanks responded with "Roll Out the Barrel." The Brits sang "Run Rabbit, Run Rabbit, Run, Run, Run." The Yanks came back with the Maine Fight Song, although their drink-thick tongues had trouble with the line "To the Gods, to the Fates, to the Rulers of Men and their Destinies . . ."

Then they belted out some obscene songs: "The Fucking Machine of Madame Pauline," "The Engineer and the Cunt of Steel," and a song Haley didn't get set to the tune of "Indian Love Call," which had something to do with a one-armed flutist. He found it hilarious nonetheless.

They all sang the unofficial anthem of the Italian campaign:

We're the D Day dodgers out in Italeeee
Always drinking vino, always on a spreee

It was like the newly instituted practice of singing the national anthem before a ball game. Haley couldn't be sure but he thought he may have shouted "Play ball!" after the last line of the song: "Some of us D Day dodgers'll die in Italeeee . . ."

Then the girls got to work.

Seated at his post in the Insurance Company the next morning, a sticky wave of nausea and guilt broke over him as the scenes from the butt-end of the evening flashed through his aching brain. He had groped some girl in a dark corner of the club, mauling her thin breasts and raking his fingers between her legs. She had gotten hold of him and yanked, inexpert but eager to please. It was like she had been playing a slot machine.

Now, though, with painful clarity, he could see what he hadn't the night before. Beneath the caked makeup and the whore's vocabulary, she had been a kid, some kid no older than his son Steve. He looked at his thick fingers and rubbed them together. There had been hardly any hair *there,* and he had been too blind drunk to notice or, worse, care.

Haley thought—he couldn't quite remember—that she had sucked him off, right there in the bar. More guilt flooded through him. He lowered his hot forehead onto the cool marble of the counter.

But that hadn't been the worst of it. He remembered staggering down a street—who knew where?—and sitting down for a moment, just to see if he could stop his head from spinning, and the next thing he knew he was being nudged awake by the blunt end of some MP's billy. Dawn was breaking.

The cop had been good about the whole thing, though. He pointed Haley in the right direction and told him to go home and get cleaned up. On the steps of his hotel, Haley realized that his wallet was gone. Twenty-seven bucks.

"Eighteen years in the service," he whispered to the marble counter, "and I get rolled by some doxy."

"Hey, Haley!" shouted another sergeant arriving for duty. "Didja hear?"

"Stein," growled Haley, "you're late."

"Nope." He consulted his watch. "Just made it," said Sergeant Stein.

"Yeah, well, watch it next time."

"Anyway, didja hear?"

"Hear? Hear what?"

"Bates got it. Somewhere up north. Stepped on a mine and ka-boom! No more Bates."

"Who the fuck is Bates?"

"You remember," said Stein, "*Bates*. Bates in Naples."

"Oh yeah, Bates." He had been a company clerk that Haley had come to know when his unit and Bates's were quartered in the same transit camp down south. He didn't remember much about Bates—he could barely recall what he looked like—but in his present mood, the death of Bates struck Haley as yet another unbearable tragedy. "Aww shit. Poor Bates. Poor fucking Bates."

Haley was not happy to see the Duke. Haley hated Italians and Italy that day, almost as much as he hated himself.

"Good morning, Mr. Haley."

"Yeah, mornin' Duke," the warrant officer mumbled. He picked up some papers and stared at them hoping he was giving the impression he was too busy to talk. But the Duke persisted, lurking before the counter.

Gabrielle had managed to sell the fountain pen and the watch, but they had fetched little, not nearly enough to pay for a vial of morphine. Sandro was in agony from the pain of his injuries and craving for his drug. Camillo steeled himself to speak. "Mr. Haley, I wonder if I could have a moment of your time? Only a moment, please."

"Yeah? What is it?"

"I'm embarrassed to have to ask you . . ."

'What? Shit or get off the can, Duke.'

'Shit or get off the can' went into the Duke's store of Americanisms.

"I . . . I am experiencing a slight problem of—of money. I was wondering, perhaps, if you might be able to make me a small loan. You know, of course, that I shall repay it the instant I receive my wage." He paused a moment. "I would not ask, except there is, you see, something of an emergency in my home." He cleared his throat. "You know," he said carefully, "that I am good for it."

Haley stared at him through bloodshot eyes. He thought about

191

the whore, his wallet, and the grinning dago barkeep. And Bates. "Some of us D Day dodgers'll die in Italeeee . . ."

"Hey greaseball. Eat shit."

"Oh!" said the Duke, taking a step back.

"We come over here and fuckin' die for you sons of bitches and how the fuck do you fuckin' thank us? Fuckin' whores and beggars and thieves and pimps, that's all you fuckin' eye-talians are. Fuckin' scumbags."

"Oh!"

Haley was on his feet now. His face was bright red and the veins were standing out on his powerful neck. He spat as he yelled. "So get the fuck out of my sight, you fuckin' wop, guinea, greaseball, fuckin' dago pimp!"

"I beg your pardon, Mr. Haley," whispered the Duke. "I am so sorry."

"Fuck you, mac, just fuck you!" Haley's voice echoed in the marble halls, but no one paid much attention to him. Someone at the Insurance Company was always chewing out a Benny.

WHEN MANGANARO WALKED into the dark Caffè dei Goti and smelled real coffee, he knew he had come to the right place. He bellied up to the bar and leaned on his elbows, eyeing an equally suspicious bartender who was half hidden behind a gleaming, old-fashioned espresso machine that chuffed and hissed like a locomotive in a siding.

Manganaro slapped the bar. "Hey, paisan. Vino!"

The barman grunted, placed an unstemmed glass in front of Eddie and filled it with wine from a straw-covered flask. Manganaro sipped and looked around him. At the few tables in the gloomy recesses in the room sat elderly men, caps on their heads, their white shirts buttoned up tight to their collars. They were playing cards—*scoppa, briscola, tre-sette*—and each man had a tiny cup of coffee at his elbow. No one spoke. No one looked in his direction. Eddie smiled at the bartender.

"The only bar in this whole city that don't got any whores or soldiers. I like that."

"Non capisco inglese."

"Ne puttane, ne soldati."

"Si," said the bartender making it clear that the conversation was at an end.

Manganaro did like the place. It reminded him of the old Mustache Pete social clubs in Little Italy, East Harlem, the Village.

"Hey, paisan, c'mere." Eddie beckoned to the bartender.

"Desidera?"

"I need to talk to the boss."

The man jabbed a thumb into his own chest. "Sono io il padrone."

Manganaro shook his head. "No, no, I mean the real boss." He lowered his voice. "Lorenzetti."

"Chi?"

Eddie nodded knowingly. "Yeah, yeah. You gotta say that. I admire that really. I could be anybody. Just tell Don Lorenzetti that a friend of his American friends would like a word with him."

This was a shot in the dark. Manganaro didn't actually know if Lorenzetti had any American "friends," but he figured that the Rome mob couldn't be all that different from the Sicilian and Neapolitan versions and God knows *they* had American friends.

The man nodded, left his post, and whispered in the ear of one of the card players, a man who seemed to be the oldest person in the room. He was also the only one not wearing a cap, and he did sport a somber dark tie. To Manganaro he looked about as impressive as somebody's grandpa.

Lorenzetti glanced at Manganaro and then down at his cards. He played one and nodded. The bartender gestured to Eddie and pulled out a chair. Silently, the other two card players at the table folded up their hands and walked away to join games elsewhere in the room.

Eddie Manganaro knew the routine. Before he sat down, he said in his best Italian, "Don Alfonso, I am honored to shake your hand." Mustache Petes, he knew, went for that kind of shit. At least, they were supposed to.

"Don't call me Don. That is for peasants. For Sicilians. For terroni."

"Yeah, whatever you say," mumbled Manganaro.

"What is your name?"

"Eddie. Eddie Manganaro."

"And who are your American friends?"

Manganaro named a number of the better-known New York gangsters of his acquaintance.

"Siciliani," said Lorenzetti dismissively.

Manganaro wondered what the hell Lorenzetti had that made him so goddamn superior. All the top guys in New York—in the whole country—were Sicilian. No one was Roman—who the hell ever heard of a *Roman* mobster? The action was in the U.S.A. and the Sicilians owned it. Still, Manganaro refused to lose his temper.

"Listen, Lorenzetti, I think we can do business."

Lorenzetti scratched the white, old-man's stubble on his chin. "Business? What kind of business?"

"Look, I know who you are."

"Who am I?"

"You're the capo who controls the borsa nera."

"I don't know what you mean." Lorenzetti went to pick up his cards again. Manganaro put his hand down, his hand covering Lorenzetti's.

"Who you gonna play with, Alfonso? There's no one at this table to play with except me."

"And what is your game, Manganaro?"

"Food. Gas. Clothes. Cloth. Liquor. Drugs. As much as you want."

Lorenzetti smiled faintly. "How do I know I can trust you?"

"Because I'm like you."

"And what am I?"

"Like me. A businessman who does his business outside of the law. You don't ask for their protection; you don't need their rules."

"How do I know you are outside the law? How do I know you aren't the law yourself? How do I know the Americans didn't send you here to trap me, an innocent old man?"

Manganaro sat back in his chair. "I killed Falcone."

Lorenzetti's slightly rheumy eyes betrayed nothing. "It was you?"

"Yeah."

"Why?"

"The guy was no good. Couldn't be trusted."

"How do you know?"

"Trust me. I know."

"He was stealing from me," said Lorenzetti.

"What did I say? So what do you think? Want to do some business? You will make money. I guarantee it."

"Let us talk for a moment, Manganaro, and then we shall see."

"Talk? Okay. So talk."

BENNYS WEREN'T ALLOWED to use the canteen on the second floor of the Insurance Company, but they were permitted to enter it to pick up snacks for army clerks too lazy to make the trip themselves. The Duke hated running such errands. It was demeaning to have to fetch a Baby Ruth bar for a corporal fifty years his junior, but he could not ignore the advantages that frequently came with the menial task.

If he was sent to the canteen in the hours after lunch one of the cooks might give him a buttered roll or a bowl of soup or a leftover hamburger "with all the trimmings." Once he had been tossed a whole loaf of fresh bread—Wonder Bread it was called—and he had carried it home in triumph to Sandro and Gabrielle. It was poor stuff though, as soft as the bread his daughter-in-law received at the food distribution centers. Camillo thought the Wonder Bread was "off," as Miss McNutt would have said, but Gabrielle ate it all without ill effect.

No one gave him anything that morning when he went to pick up a cup of coffee and a doughnut for a Pfc in the typing pool. Still reeling from Warrant Officer Haley's unkind words and wracked with guilt and distress at Sandro's plight, Camillo stood in line waiting his turn, his head down, like a slave. He felt old and tired and helpless. He had sunk as low as he could ever imagine himself sinking. He had been foully, cruelly abused by a man he considered his inferior. His world, his values, were in ruins. If death had come to him that minute, he would have welcomed it.

He was not listening to the babble of English around him but somehow, a single sentence stood out. He heard someone say, "Say, you wouldn't happen to know where I could rent an apartment, would you?"

The Duke looked up. Sitting at a table a few feet away were two young American officers. The one who had asked the question was puffing on a cigarette. Both men had mugs of coffee.

"An apartment? You gotta be kidding. Housing's so short in this city the eyeties are sleeping ten to a bed."

"Jeez," said Austin Kinney, "that's too bad." An apartment was was an important part of his plan.

He had been sent to the Insurance Company to represent

Thorpe at the weekly sit-rep meeting convened for operational support units in Rome. The lieutenant with him was involved in settlement, billeting, and relocation. Together they had spent a boring morning listening to guys from the AMG tell them how terrible everything was. As if they needed to be told.

"What's the matter, Kinney," said the guy from housing, "don't like your billet?"

"No, it's fine. I just wanted someplace I could go to get away from all the brass. Kind of cramps a fellow's style, you know?"

"You mean you're afraid you might lose a broad to all those majors and colonels at the Excelsior."

"Right," said Kinney and both men guffawed.

"Damn right!"

Kinney stopped laughing. "You sure you don't know anything? I'd be willing to pay a little something."

The housing officer shook his head. "You could be paying in silver dollars, Kinney, and you wouldn't be able to find anything. It's driving me bats. And I'll tell you something else, if you *did* happen to find some housing, I'd be over there so fast with a couple of my guys to requisition it, hell, you wouldn't have time to memorize your address."

"Things are that bad?"

"Worse. It's like the AMG guy said. There are a million refugees in this city. The relief services are serving four hundred thousand meals a day."

"Beats the hell out of me where they're finding the supplies," said Austin.

"Luckily, that's not my problem."

CAMILLO WAS WAITING in the corridor outside the canteen, doughnut and coffee in hand, when Kinney passed by.

"Excuse me, sir . . ."

Kinney stopped. "What is it?"

"I could not help hearing that you were interested in a flat."

"That's right."

"I have something that might be suitable. My home."

Kinney looked around him quickly to make sure that the housing lieutenant was not around, then peered down at the Duke. "Your home?"

"Yes," said the Duke quickly. "It's quite large and only I, my son, and his wife, my daughter-in-law, live there."

Kinney held up his hand like a cop stopping traffic. "Sorry. I'm not interested in sharing a place."

"Well . . ." Camillo gestured helplessly with the doughnut in his left hand. "It's not quite like that. You would have all the room, all the privacy you need, sir."

Kinney shook his head. "Nope. Sorry. I can't use an apartment that already has people in it."

"Actually," said Camillo desperately, "it's not an apartment, not in the sense you think. It's not an apartment at all, really."

"Not an apartment? Then what the hell is it, really?"

"A palace," said the Duke.

AUSTIN KINNEY WAS no stranger to opulence, so the worn grandeur of the Palazzo Sanseverio did not impress him as much as it might have had he come from a less gilded background. For creature comforts, Camillo's ancestral home could not compare with the Kinney family apartment on Park Avenue. That thirty-five-room sprawl, fully staffed, was a mansion in the sky. Nor was it as imposing as the "big house," the Kinney estate on Long Island built by Kinney's grandfather and still inhabited by his crotchety grandmother who loathed her entire family, except for her fair-haired grandson. Even the Kinney "camp" in the Adirondacks was better appointed than the palace.

But Kinney liked it and, more important, it suited his needs. The Palazzo Sanseverio was big and it had what the lieutenant from housing would have called "class."

Kinney's seniors—captains, majors, and colonels who, in civilian life, lived dull lives, working boring jobs in drab towns—would be dazzled by the family portraits, the gilt and brocade. They would marvel at the extravagant ceiling fresco, they would probably even pretend to appreciate its artistic merits. The long gallery with its marble floors and the vast dining room with the carved table as long as a runway and the two great chandeliers dripping from the coffered ceiling would make them feel important, above the common herd. If they could swill champagne in a palace, a real, honest to God palace, then they would forget for a moment that come the peace they would have to go back to being bank managers or undertakers in places like Auvasse, Missouri, and Gladewater, Texas. And although they would tell people that war was, indeed, hell, they would secretly consider these the best days of their lives. That little glow, compliments of the lieutenant, wouldn't hurt Lex Kinney's boy a bit.

Camillo led Austin through the apartments, showing him a dozen bedrooms and six antiquated baths.

"Pretty old-fashioned, Duke."

"Unfortunately so." In Camillo's old world, the ordered, neat prewar world, it would never have occurred to a gentleman to comment on a bathroom. Hangdog, he followed Kinney down the corridor.

"What's in here?" Kinney put his hand on a big brass doorknob and turned it.

"No, no, Lieutenant. Please." The Duke hurried to the door and put his weight against it. "Not that one," he whispered. "That is the bedroom of my son. He is an invalid and cannot be disturbed. Please." He ushered Kinney away from the door.

Kinney nodded. The son was probably the in-bred idiot of the family. All these old European aristocratic families had at least one. He could only wonder at what kind of drooling, chinless freak lurked behind that door. It gave him the creeps.

"An invalid? Are you sure I'm going to get this place to myself? I don't like the idea of having an invalid around."

"I assure you that there will be no trouble. You shall see. There is another floor, upstairs, the old servants' floor. We shall move up there. I promise that you will not be disturbed." Camillo heard his own voice and it disgusted him. Eager, suppliant, it was the voice of servants, pimps, and panderers. He was telling a stranger that Sandro would not be a bother in Sandro's own house. But Camillo was desperate for the money. He had to have it. When times improved he would show this ill-mannered young man the door. In the meantime, the Sanseverios would not be the first noble Roman family to move to the attic and let the *piano nobile* to some rich foreigner.

Kinney clicked his tongue and shook his head as he appraised the kitchen, which seemed to his eye medieval. There was a giant wood-fired stove and a smaller, slightly more modern, gas range. The sink was as deep and as rough as a horse trough. A refrigerator stood in one corner, an old-fashioned one with a large condenser on top, like a white enamel goiter. It would be adequate for making ice and chilling wine.

Camillo stood and fidgeted next to the lieutenant, thinking that he should show off some of the features of the room, but he didn't know where to begin. His knowledge of kitchens, even his own, was limited.

"There are knives and forks and . . . other things."

"Well, Christ, I hope so."

The green baize door which separated the kitchen from the rest of the house swung open silently and Gabrielle entered. She had just returned from a frustrating day of standing in line, her half-filled string bag all she had to show for her labors. She was hot and tired and irritable, but to Kinney's eyes she looked cool and neat, clean-limbed and lovely.

"Oh." She looked at Kinney and recognized him as an American. "I did not realize that you were at home. Or that we had a guest." She spoke in English, her words nestled in a soft French accent.

"May I present the Baronessa Sanseverio," said Camillo stiffly. "This is Lieutenant Kinney."

"How do you do?" asked Kinney. They touched hands briefly. They looked each other in the eye.

"How do you do," said the Baronessa.

"If you would excuse us a moment, my dear," said Camillo, "we were just discussing a matter . . ."

"Of course. Good day, Lieutenant."

Kinney bowed a short, stiff little bow from the waist, just as he had been taught in dancing school. He was rewarded with a smile.

When she had left, Kinney turned to the Duke, handed him two fifties, American, and smiled. "Duke," he said, "I'll take it."

The Duke insisted on giving him a receipt.

14

"Wipers don't work," said Utterback. "And I thought it wasn't supposed to rain in this town, anyhow."

"Raining now," observed Manganaro.

"Yeah," said Utterback, "thanks."

It was a typical midsummer Roman rain: an hour of high winds, a few minutes of dramatic thunder, and then a cloudburst, a great sheet of water which turned the dust in the streets to mud and overwhelmed the storm drains. Then came a long, soaking drizzle which fell from a low sullen sky as heavy and as fine as chain mail.

The wiper arm scraped across the windshield of the jeep like a dull razor. Utterback, at the wheel, glanced in his mirror and saw James Holt and Stanley Leacock, following in their two-and-a-half-ton truck, staring back at him. Obscured from Utterback's view, behind Holt's truck, was another six by six, manned by Alvin Whiteside and driven by Ernest Biggs.

"What you tell the coons?" Utterback had to raise his voice to be heard over the engine and the rain thrumming on the canvas roof.

"I didn't tell them anything. What's it their business?"

"Holt's trouble."

"Listen, Cal, you should know by now that there's no trouble a melanzan can make for a white man, 'specially in the army. It's like the lieutenant says, the army don't trust Negroes."

"Niggers," corrected Utterback.

"We go out with them this once and then after that they go out alone. They do the dirty work; they take the risks. We get the money."

"How do you know they won't steal from us?"

"They won't."

"How do you *know?*"

"First of all, 'cause they won't. They'll be too scared. And second of all, there's not going to be any money changing hands, not on the drops anyway. I'm going to meet Lorenzetti once a week and pick up the take. Just like it was a legit business, you know?"

"You're letting this little greaseball run a tab? What are you? Crazy?"

"Cal, Lorenzetti's a big businessman. He's not going to stiff us. He needs us. You gotta learn to trust people."

Utterback grumbled. "Trusting Holt I don't like. I hate that fucker. What you choose him for anyway?"

"I didn't pick him, he rostered up. Next time it'll be someone else. We're gonna be using the whole company. Don't worry about Holt, for Christ's sake."

"Me? Worry about him? You're fuckin' crazy. He doesn't worry me."

"Cal, you been running your yap about Holt from day one. What he ever do to you, huh? He fucked your sister or something? Knock her up? Is that it?" Manganaro grinned. "What? You got a little black Utterback running around back home? That it?"

Utterback paled slightly and his thin lips set in a tight line. He spoke slowly and did not raise his voice any more than he needed to be heard. "Eddie, don't ever, ever, fuckin' make a joke like that. Ever. *It is not funny.*"

"I didn't even know you had a sister," said Manganaro meekly.

"*Ever.*"

They rode in silence for a moment.

"She cute, your sister? Big, you know, fun bags?"

"Jesus Christ!" shrieked Utterback. "Eddie! You're always pissing me off. You're always giving me a hard time and I'm sick of it. Sick up to here."

"Sorry, Cal."

"Yeah, you say that. Just *fuck you.*"

"Fuck *you.*"

"Well fuck you, Eddie. Dumb bastard guinea fuck. Where the fuck we going anyway?"

Manganaro consulted the neatly folded map in his lap. "Relax.

201

Just relax. We're doing fine. Just keep going straight. I'll tell you when to turn."

The small convoy rumbled past an MP patrol jeep parked in the middle of an intersection. The two policemen huddled under the dripping soft top glanced at them but with little interest. Utterback, however, got nervous.

"They saw us."

"Course they saw us, jackass. We're about six tons of machinery, you know. What? You think they give a shit? Cal, this whole fuckin' town is full of trucks. Jeez."

"When we gonna get there?"

"Soon, for Christ's sake."

They were in a nondescript section of Rome, a faceless zone of tall dilapidated apartment blocks, between the railway station and the Porta Maggiore. It was the least charming part of the city, developed late in the nineteenth century and meant to be Rome's proud answer to the Paris of Baron Haussmann and Napoleon III. The buildings were old but not antique, the streets wide but far from majestic. The only monuments to be seen were statues in drab squares, memorials to the few Savoy kings, their politicians and courtiers. It was the development of this area that had cost the Sanseverios so dearly. A dull, nameless quarter, it was a perfect place to do business with Lorenzetti.

Manganaro leaned out into the drizzle, craning his neck to catch sight of a street sign. He consulted his map. "Hold it, Cal. Yeah. Slow down. Yeah. Left."

Utterback turned left and, obediently, the two trucks behind followed. The growling of three powerful engines echoed off the buildings.

"Now what?"

"Now we look for the guy. Slow down."

"Guy? What guy? Lorenzetti?"

Manganaro looked pityingly at Utterback. "No. Some other guy."

"Who?"

"I don't know yet. I'll know him when I see him."

"Sheesh," said Utterback.

The rain had washed the beggars and the loiterers from the streets so the contact was not hard to find. A young man stood leaning in the doorway of a warehouse and he nodded almost imperceptibly as the jeep and trucks approached.

"There's our man."

"Good. Let's get this over with and then get the fuck outta here."

"Relax, Cal."

The wide warehouse doors swung open and the young man beckoned to Utterback, waving him in, but Cal hit the breaks, bringing the jeep up short. Holt braked late and the truck bore down on the jeep until Utterback's mirror was filled with a close-up view of the wide, toothy grill of the two-and-a-half and the word "Chevrolet" in olive drab paint.

"Fuckin' close, asshole," muttered Utterback, though not even he could bring himself to blame Holt for the close shave, not completely anyway.

"Turn on the lights, Cal," said Manganaro quietly. "Let's take a little look-see." The map slid to the floor. Nestled like a cat in Eddie's lap was a gleaming, oily .45 Colt.

There were blackout shields on the headlights of the jeep, but the narrow yellow beams caught three men. One of them Manganaro recognized as one of the elderly card players from the Caffè dei Goti. It was he who motioned the convoy forward.

"What do you think?" said Utterback.

"Oh what the hell. What did I just finish telling you? You gotta trust somebody, right?" Manganaro's hand closed around the gun.

In the cab of the lead truck, Holt only had to take one look at the men and the gloomy, empty warehouse to know what was going on. "I don't believe what my eyes are seeing," he said quietly.

"What you seeing, Jimmy?"

"The black market," said James Holt.

LORENZETTI WAS WAITING in a small, dark room far to the rear of the warehouse. He wore a suit and tie, a blindingly white shirt, and a snowy panama hat. He was smoking a cheroot, the acrid smoke reminding Eddie of the old guys down in Little Italy. Lorenzetti was every inch a Mustache Pete, a dinosaur already extinct in New York, Chicago, Cleveland, and Detroit, but alive and well and living in Italy, impervious to change in its natural habitat.

"We will wait," said Lorenzetti, "while my men inspect the merchandise you have brought."

"Inspect? What's to inspect? That's grade-A U.S.-government-issue stuff. What's the matter, Al, don't you trust me?"

Lorenzetti smiled faintly. "We have a saying: 'It is good to trust but—' "

" 'It is better not to trust.' Yeah, I heard that one. My old man used to tell it to me all the time. But listen, if we are going to be doing business, maybe it's better if you started trusting me. You think you could do that?"

"At the beginning, I think it is better if we understand one another."

"I understand. I understand you asked me for food. I got two truckloads of food out there." Eddie waved towards the warehouse. "And not rations. There's canned ham, canned fruit, like peaches and pineapples and stuff like that. Beef stew, pork and beans, hash—"

" 'Ash?" said Lorenzetti.

"It's like a kind of meat," said Manganaro uncertainly. "You'll like it."

Lorenzetti grunted. He would not be eating the foodstuffs supplied by Eddie Manganaro. He preferred fresh food gathered in the farmland beyond the city. It was costly, but Lorenzetti was a rich man.

"There's flour, sugar, and then you got your canned vegetables. Peas, potatoes, carrots, beets, spinach. Beans too—string, green, navy, lima. Good stuff. Powdered eggs. Klim. You said you were in the market for food. I got food." Manganaro folded his arms across his chest. "Jeez," he said in English, "I get tired of you guineas sometimes."

"C'è caffè?"

"Yeah, there's coffee. Two hundred and forty pounds of Chase and Sanborn in forty-pound bags. You'll have to break it down smaller." He added in English, "Me, I just deliver the shit."

One of Lorenzetti's men leaned into the office. They spoke rapidly in an Italian dialect that Manganaro could not penetrate, though he could guess at the meaning of the exchange.

"Your man says okay, right? Everything just fine, am I right? Good. Now that you've had a chance to inspect the merchandise, I want a chance to inspect the money."

Lorenzetti nodded, pulled open a drawer in the desk and withdrew a brick of soiled bills tightly bound with thick rubber bands.

He dropped it in front of Eddie, as if tossing a bone to a dog. Manganaro looked at the money, but he didn't touch it. Then he looked at Lorenzetti.

"You know," he said slowly. He stood and wagged a finger. "You know . . ." He circled round the desk until he stood next to Lorenzetti. "You know, Alfonso, you really are a piece of work."

Lorenzetti shrugged. "Non capisco inglese."

Eddie Manganaro smiled and pinched the cigar from the gangster's lips, dropped it to the floor and slowly ground it out with the heel of his boot. "And you are beginning to piss me off. I don't know what I ever did to offend you. I came to you with a business proposition—good for you, good for me—and all you ever do is treat me like dirt."

"Ho detto che non capisco inglese." From the open drawer of the desk he took another cigar and a box of matches.

"Don't smoke now." said Manganaro in Italian. "We'll both have a smoke when we're finished talking business." He added in English, "A nice friendly smoke."

"Mi insulta."

"No. No, Alfonso, you, you are insulting me. You need me. So let's forget this big man stuff you always pull on me. See, Alfonso, I'm not stupid. I got what you want. You, you got money. Alfonso, everybody in your business got money. The other guys, Vaccani, Pellegrino, Calvo. They got money. Lorenzetti isn't the only guy with money."

Manganaro sat on the edge of the desk. "But you see, Al, there is something you don't know about me. I, personally, like you. I want to help you. You treat me right, I'll treat you right. No more acting like you're the big shot, un pezzo di novanta, and I'm the pezzo di merda. Got it?"

Lorenzetti stared fixedly at him.

"See, 'cause if you don't understand this, I'll just head out and find myself another partner and that would be a shame for you, no? This war won't last forever, Al, so let's make some money while we can, okay?" Eddie picked up the money and placed it in Lorenzetti's hand. "Now. Hand me the money. With manners. Polite. Partner to partner. Nicely. Understand me, Alfonso? I'm not one of your boys, I'm not your servant. You treat me with respect, I treat you with respect. And that way, everybody is happy, okay?"

Lorenzetti's hand closed around the money. For a moment

Eddie was afraid that the Roman would take his brave words at face value and send him out to find another partner. Lorenzetti smiled thinly. "Take the money with my thanks, my most esteemed friend Signor Manganaro."

Eddie smiled. He took a cigar from the case and placed it between Lorenzetti's teeth, lit it, and waved out the match. "That's better, Al. That's a lot better. Now we understand each other."

"Davvero," agreed Lorenzetti. "D'accordo."

"D'accordo," said Eddie and he laughed the laugh of a man who makes easy money.

"RIGHT THEN," SAID Sergeant Rhys Jones. "You're going to get the ball. Let's see what you can do with it."

The fifteen men Jones had selected, plus Lance Corporal Llewellyn, had been divided into two eight-man squads. They faced off in the center of the Circo Massimo. It was the first fun the men had had in their training, the first break in Jones's iron regimen of runs, windsprints, calisthenics, and drills built around central rugby plays: scrum, maul, tackle, line out. They were hot, tired, and bored, itching to get their hands on the ball.

The team assembled daily at the racetrack, the men having been excused from two hours of duty a day to make room for these training sessions. At first they thought this was a good thing, but after their first encounter with Jones's rigid discipline some looked back with fondness on their army duties. Loading and unloading several tons of supplies daily was less onerous than the strenuous paces the Welshmen put them through. The hardest part to endure was the endless circuits of the track, long hot runs under a glaring sun. McManus sent out buckets of water to them and they drank it down although it was as warm as tea.

Jones worked his men hard for one reason. He had made some inquiries and found that the Springboks, confident of victory, were not training hard.

Lance Corporal Llewellyn set the ball for a placekick and booted the ball cleanly, charging through the kick, leading his men down the field.

James Holt circled under the ball, caught it, dashed forward a few yards, saw Llewellyn bearing down on him, stopped, and set.

"Stanley!" Holt launched the ball, a long graceful forward pass that landed like a pillow in Leacock's outstretched arms.

"Ya!" Stanley whooped in satisfaction. He tucked the ball into his stomach and charged, chewing up the gravel in his wake. He danced around the company clerk, Humphrey Joyce, and outran a big driver called Sam Crosby. He sped down field and planted the ball on the opposing team's goal line, right where the goalposts would stand. A cheer went up from Stanley's team. Holt hollered and whistled.

"Beautiful, man, just beautiful!"

Jones did not look pleased. "All right you lot," he yelled. "Gather round me." The team fell to the gravel at Jones's feet.

"Guess we know how to play this game, Sergeant Jones."

"It ain't so hard."

"Bring up them Africans."

"Shaddap!" suggested Lance Corporal Llewellyn.

"Kicked your ass too, jack," cackled Ernest Biggs.

"Silence!" bellowed Jones. "Now then, gentlemen, you have just witnessed an excellent example of how not to play the noble game of rugby."

"Hey! What you talking about?" demanded Holt.

"Yeah," protested Joyce, "that was a perfect touchdown, Sarge. Jimmy landed it just where he was ought to."

"For one thing, Mr. Biggs, you don't score a touchdown in rugby. One scores a try in rugby. Three points."

"Whatever you call it, Sarge. Stanley scored one. A good one."

"So you all think that was a good pass, do you?"

"Shit, yeah!"

"And in what direction did Mr. Holt throw that fine pass? How about you Mr. Crosby?"

"At Stanley," said Sam.

"Yes, but where was Stanley going?"

"To score a . . . a what you said. A try."

"And where was that?"

Crosby pointed. "Over there."

"Incorrect, Mr. Crosby. Mr. Leacock was going forward. Mr. Holt, here, threw a forward pass."

"So where was I supposed to throw it? Backward?"

"Precisely, boyo. Rule number one, gents: there is no forward pass in rugby."

"Hey," protested Stanley. "How you s'posed to get the ball up the field?"

"You run it up, Stanley," said Jones. "It's really very simple."

"So what happens if you get tackled?" demanded Crosby. Crosby was a big man—though not as big as Whiteside—and tackling was what he did best.

"Mr. Crosby asks a very good question. If you are tackled while carrying the ball, there is only one thing to do. You pass."

"Backwards?" asked Holt.

"Precisely, Mr. Holt. Once the ball is in play you'll form an attacking line. The lead man carries the ball. If he is in danger of being tackled, he must pass it to the man behind him, to his left—or right, depends—and that man advances with the ball. If he is in danger of being tackled, he passes, and so on down the line."

"But if the guys running with him are doing their job," said Whiteside, "he won't have to pass."

Jones looked puzzled. "How do you mean?"

"They'll be blocking for him."

"Knocking the other fuckers out of the way," Biggs explained.

Jones shot a glance at Lance Corporal Llewellyn and they both shook their heads. "Lance Corporal Llewellyn . . ."

"Yes, Sar'nt?"

"Tell these good men rule number two."

"In the game of rugby," Llewellyn shouted, as if he was on the parade ground, "the only man who can be legally tackled is that man in possession of the ball."

"What?" shouted Holt. "That's a joke, right?"

"No joking here, gents, this is a very serious matter. You only tackle the man in possession of the ball. And when you tackle him, gentlemen, make sure he's tackled good and proper because in this noble game if you merely knock the man down he can get up and start running again. He can pass the ball from the floor, if he can manage it. Play, gents, in rugby is almost continuous. That's why you have to be fit. It's not just enough having brass balls, boyos, you've got to have wind."

"Wind?"

"I don't want you running out of breath."

"How many time-outs?"

"None."

"How many substitutions?"

"None."

"What if someone gets hurt and can't play?"

"Then you play a man short."

"How long you play this game?"

"Two halves. Forty minutes each."

"There halftime?"

"Not more than five minutes. We'll have time for a little chat, get a drink, slash, and change ends."

"Slash?"

"Piss," translated Llewellyn.

Nevertheless, the fifteen members of the newborn rugby team looked at the two Welshmen as if they were speaking a foreign language.

Finally, James Holt spoke for all of them. "This sure ain't football," he said, shaking his head.

Jones grinned. "Precisely. Now, let's try it again, shall we?"

They spent another two hours charging up and down the field, attacking and defending. They were clumsy and awkward, their lines ragged. The reverse pass did not come naturally to them. They cursed when they made a mistake, punched the air in frustration. They exhorted and berated each other. They never stopped trying or running.

Jones was pleased. They hadn't a snowball's chance in hell of defeating a competent South African side—his brave words about winning had been nothing more than words; no coach gained anything by dwelling on defeat—but with enough time and enough hard work he was confident that he could avoid an embarrassingly one-sided game. Jones liked the men of Company A. They were scrappers—a quality Welshmen always admired—and some of them were gifted athletes, strong, fast on their feet, and quick-witted.

The raw material was there, all right. Leacock and Joyce were fast, faster, Jones reckoned than the hulking South Africans. Holt had good speed and a deadly accurate pass. Ernest Biggs was tough and he had the fire in his belly. Crosby was big, slow but determined. And there was Whiteside. He was not fast or nimble but his enormous strength made up for that. If Whiteside tackled the man with the ball, that man would remain tackled, no matter how great his skill or stamina. And Whiteside would be awesome in the scrum.

Jones had been given more talent than he had hoped for and as a good, pessimistic Welshmen, that was more than he had expected.

Enzo's broadway bar on the Via Palermo, Biggs's discovery, was one of the few drinking places in Rome where a black man felt welcome and where the sight of a white man, except Enzo himself, was rare. Why Enzo's had been adopted by the American black troops garrisoned in the city no one could say.

Enzo had named his three cellar rooms after the Great White Way simply because he believed that the association would strike a pleasant chord in the minds of American troops—no matter their skin color, Americans were much prized among Rome merchants for their riches relative to their European comrades in arms. For every Piccadilly Bar and King's Pub, there were half a dozen New Yorks, Hollywoods, and Wild Wests.

One of the Broadway's rooms was given over to a dance floor, the other two furnished with belongings left to Enzo by his mother and to his wife by hers. This collection of furniture, perfectly at home in the apartments occupied by the late old ladies, looked distinctly out of place in a serviceman's drinking establishment.

A phalanx of heavy, overwrought sideboards and end tables jostled for space with whatnots and corner cupboards, ponderous armchairs, spindly gilt chairs never meant to be sat upon, and lumpy Victorian sofas that reeked of long Sunday afternoons.

Enzo was a man without sentiment, so the treasures which once ornamented the two drawing rooms now decorated the Broadway Bar. Two cabinet clocks disputed the time between them and chimed the hours but could only be heard during the lulls in the music screaming from the big radio. Two flocks of ceramic geese flew up opposing walls toward two damp spots that looked remarkably like clouds; two collections of stuffed birds gazed from their glass mausoleums at the fantastic sweating soldiers through astonished artificial eyes.

Under the benevolent smile of Pio Nono sat James Holt and Stanley, Elena at his side, with Ernest Biggs and Alvin Whiteside. All of them, except Whiteside and Elena, had glasses of Enzo's wine. Stanley winced after every acid sip.

"You don't like that," said Biggs, "why don't you get one of them sweet drinks, like Alvin here."

"No thank you," said Leacock emphatically. "No thank you very much."

Biggs laughed.

Stanley riffled through the pages of the dictionary he always carried when he went out with Elena. "Hey, Elena, bevanda?"

Elena smiled. "No, t'ank you, Stanley."

Enzo and his wife dispensed their wares from behind an ornate dining table, pouring wine into a variety of vessels—blood-red Murano glass goblets, a souvenir of an in-law's long-ago holiday in Venice; china teacups, a wedding present; ornamental tankards purchased during the brief enthusiasm for the Pact of Steel; jars that had held preserves; and straight kitchen beakers that had served Enzo's family for a generation. Breakage was so frequent that it was apparent that before the occupation ended Enzo would have to find more glassware.

Like other establishments of its type, the Broadway Bar served wine, red and white and grappa, as well as the "sweet drinks," an odd collection of cordials salvaged from the cabinets of the old ladies: chartreuse, crème de menthe, Kirschwasser, Benedictine, ouzo, Galliano, Tía María, blue curacao, and cloying, minty syrups from North Africa brought as gifts by relatives returning from colonies in the Italian empire. Enzo's father had been an enthusiastic collector of beverages made in monasteries, distilled liquors of paralyzing alcoholic content created from petals and grasses and tasting as if they should be applied, rather than taken internally.

None of these was much in demand, except when the wine ran out, and that happened with depressing frequency. It was not unusual, therefore, for desperate soldiers to reel out of the Broadway, sick from sampling the sweet dusty drinks and from suffocating cigarette smoke.

Alvin Whiteside was the only man who chose to drink any of these, his preference being for a nutmeggy cordial from Ethiopia. James Holt had induced him to try it, telling him it was nonalcoholic. Whiteside sipped it from a delicate little gold-stemmed glass the size of an egg cup.

"Man," said Jimmy, "this whole thing just gets stranger and stranger. Here we are in fuckin' Italy. We're learning to play rugby and we're working the black market."

"I like that game," said Stanley, "but it's tough." Below the level of the table, he squeezed Elena's hand. She smiled and squeezed back.

"The game is okay," said Jimmy. "Jones is okay. It's the other shit I don't like. It's crazy."

"That's the army," said Biggs. "Crazy."

"Amen," said Whiteside.

"You bored, Elena?" Stanley looked through his dictionary. "Noia?"

"No, t'ank you, Stanley."

"Take your girl out on the floor, Stanley," said Biggs. "Show her a good time. He don't know nothing about women, does he miss?"

Elena had no idea what he said, but she smiled nonetheless.

"Leave her alone, Biggsy. Your ugly face scaring her."

Holt wasn't in the mood for fun. His sipped his drink. "The sergeants are going to make a fortune and what the hell is going to happen to us? What do we get? Nothing. Zero."

"What we don't get," said Whiteside, "is trouble. We do as we're told and we stay out of trouble."

"Hey, look," said Stanley, "it's Rufus. Rufus!" He waved at a black man who had come into the bar. He was the oldest soldier in the room.

"How you all doin'?" asked Rufus. "Who's this, Stanley? She your girl?"

"Elena, this is Rufus."

" 'Ow you do," said Elena.

Rufus laughed. "How do you do, miss."

"Hey Rufus, how things in the catering corps?" asked Biggs.

"Fine, Biggsy, just fine. It's a nice easy life."

"All you are is a servant, Rufus," grumbled Holt. "Put on your white coat and serve whitey."

"And what do you do all day long, Jimmy? You serve whitey too, you just pack and load and drive and pack and load. Break your back all day long. At least I work where it's nice and clean."

"Man's got a point, Jimmy," said Biggs.

"Yeah, but it's the way you got to do it. Doesn't it bother you? Acting like a darkie for the white man."

"That's what they expect, James. And like you say, it's just an act. You shuffle a little, doesn't hurt. They leave you alone. You stand up to them, you end up in the stockade. What's the point of that?"

Holt shook his head in disgust. "So you're another one. I'm trying to talk sense to these guys here and they keep saying that they don't want no trouble. Well, trouble is what I'm trying to miss, too. Like we took six tons of army supplies to the black market the other day. Crosby told me he done the same thing yesterday only this time no Manganaro, no Utterback. They just told him an address and told him to get going. You know what that means? That means if Sam gets caught it Sam's ass. Any of us get caught, then it's our ass."

"But we're just doing what the sergeant says," protested Biggs. "It's orders."

"C'mon Biggsy, use your head. There ain't no orders. Nothing written down. The army catches one of us driving that shit and the sergeants are gonna say they didn't know a thing about it."

"Maybe we should go to the captain or to that new shavetail, Kinney," said Stanley.

"Kinney?" said Rufus. "He about so high. Look like a movie star?"

"That's right. You know him?"

"Served him his dinner last night. He's got his own place over, hell, I don't know where it is, but it's quite a spread. Me and two of my waiters we got orders from the major himself to go and help this Kinney. He was throwing a big party in this big house he got. Guess it's some kind of R & R for the brass. Girls, booze, everything. One of your guys brung in the stuff, you got a guy named Harris in your outfit? He come in with food and stuff, and then some eyeties showed up. Meat, eggs, even brung up some champagne."

"See," said Holt, "Kinney's in on it too."

"Now you don't know that," said Biggs. "Could be like Rufus says, could be something for the brass."

"So why would Kinney be running it? It's his show, right, Rufus?"

"Sure seemed to me," said Rufus.

"Can't trust nobody," said Holt emphatically. "Not the NCOs, not the officers. We are being set up."

"But what can we do, Jimmy?"

Holt lowered his voice. "I think we deserve to get paid for our trouble. There's no reason why we shouldn't. I don't see any other way."

"But that'll make us just like them," said Stanley.

"But we are just like them, Stanley, as far as the army is concerned. Am I right, Rufus, you been in the army a long time? You ever heard of a black man reporting an officer and getting away with it?"

"No," said Rufus, "but stealing army property, Jimmy, that carries 'bout twenty years."

Biggs whistled. "Man, that's a long time."

"And who's running the risk? Not them. You think they'll do time if *we* get caught?"

Gravely, the men shook their heads. Elena could tell that the tenor of the conversation had changed. She looked worriedly to Stanley.

Jimmy leaned forward. "It's real simple. If we get caught then the army is going to find us guilty. It'll be no good us saying that we didn't get nothing out of it. The army won't believe a word we say, not if it's us against three white NCOs and an officer. So all I'm saying is that if we're taking the risk anyhow then a part of the take is ours 'cause if something goes wrong it adds to the same thing."

"So how you gonna get a share for us?" asked Biggs.

"Simple, I'll just go to Manganaro and ask the man for what's ours."

"Oh, just like that he'll start paying out? Manganaro is a bad man, Jimmy, you don't need me to tell you that. And that Utterback." Stanley didn't have to say any more.

"A bad man," said Alvin.

"That's right," said Biggs.

"He a little runty guy?" asked Rufus.

"Yeah, that's him."

"Sergeant?"

"Yeah."

"And this other one, is he big like a barn? Got a red face and sweats a lot?"

"Naww, that's McManus."

"Well, they was both up to this house, this Kinney's house. Last night, brought in some boxes. They didn't put 'em in the kitchen, though, where most of the stuff goes. Took it down the hall."

"What for?" asked Biggs. "I didn't think the NCOs did any hard work."

"So, they're storing shit up there, stuff they don't want any of us to see," said Holt. "They aren't stupid. Probably valuable stuff, more valuable than just canned ham and shit like that."

"Oh, Jimmy," said Alvin, "I don't like this."

"Don't worry about it, Alvin."

"So you're gonna go to Manganaro, just like that?" Stanley wanted an answer.

"That's right. He'll realize that if he pays us something then he'll keep his little business going."

"Jimmy, you could get us all in trouble."

"How?" challenged Holt. "If he don't make room for us then *he'll* be the one in trouble."

"Oh yeah? How's that? You already said we can't go to the officers. You said no one will believe us."

"Maybe the trucks'll break down. Maybe some of the drivers'll take sick. Maybe there'll be some kind of trouble down at the depot."

"That's for sure."

"No, think about it a minute. We can't lose. Think about it. They can't report us for *not* driving their shit around. They're going to have to cut us in."

"Or maybe take over the driving themselves," said Biggs.

"Fine with me. The thing that burns my ass, Biggsy, is that they're making money and we're the ones in danger. They want to drive, fine, God bless 'em—let 'em make all the money they want. But don't ask me to stick my neck out and don't give me nothing for it. That is bullshit."

"You're right, Jimmy," said Rufus.

"Maybe yes," said Stanley, "but I hope you know what you're doing, that's all."

"All we have to do is stick together, like the sergeants do. The whole outfit got to stick together on this."

"Oh Jimmy," said Alvin, "I don't like this one little bit."

"How can it go wrong, Alvin?"

"I don't know, but it will."

"No it won't. It's a sure thing."

Over the next few days, James Holt spoke to the men of his company, moving among them like a politician canvassing for votes. News of the sergeants' involvement in the rackets was widespread and none of them liked it. Hesitant at first, most, like Alvin and Ernest, expressed concern about getting into trouble, but all resented being used so cynically by their superiors. None was outraged by the thefts themselves. The army had taken them from their homes, discriminated against them, held markers on their lives. Plunder, in return, seemed more a right than a crime.

And like a politician, Jimmy found himself making promises. By the time he had made his rounds, he had vowed that every man in A Company would receive twenty dollars a week from the pocket of the syndicate. It seemed fair.

RUFUS AND HIS mess waiters were only brought to the Palazzo Sanseverio on special occasions, when Kinney was having an exceptionally large function, but servants—permanent staff—had reappeared in the palace. Maria Romana, a cook; her husband, Giorgio, butler and factor; and Maria Romana's friend and ally, an ageless crone named Alba, who did the heavier cleaning, had been hired by Kinney on the recommendation of Egidio of the Excelsior, and they answered to Austin Kinney's command and no other. When he was about the palazzo, Giorgio smiled and scraped, Maria Romana clucked maternally and insisted on making him coffee and serving him pastry, Alba laughed and hid her gums behind an old hand, veined on one side and callused on the other. When the lieutenant was not present they were more businesslike.

Roman servants always assume a measure of their employer's rank—the servant of a prince thinks himself a prince among servants—so these three servants saw fit to ignore or be outright rude to lesser mortals, like Camillo and Gabrielle. Maria Romana, Giorgio, and Alba had a servant's instinctive sense of power—who possessed it and who did not—and saw that a rich, young, handsome *tenente* of a conquering army far outweighed in importance a broken-down count, his mad son, and a foreign woman.

Maria Romana ruled the Sanseverio kitchen with the iron will of an absolute monarch. She was a tall, thin woman with a long, pinched face divided by a sharp nose like a ship's rudder. When she thought her authority questioned she raised that nose and stared at the transgressor, the beak and the steely gaze being more than enough to cow her husband and to drive Camillo from his own kitchen. Gabrielle, slightly more stalwart, could stand her ground in Maria Romana's realm long enough to prepare small meals for herself and her father-in-law, and, when she thought he might take it, some broth for Sandro.

The three servants waited in icy silence for her to perform her tasks, but as soon as Gabrielle had borne away her tray and the baize door had swung shut, Maria Romana and Alba recommenced their gossiping. It was an endless skein of backbiting and invective spun in deepest Romanaccio and in which Gabrielle—her looks, her clothes, her manner, her accent, her cooking skills, her weight, her parents, the interior of her womb, the state of her breasts and genitals, and who did she think she was, anyway?—figured prominently.

Theft, like gossip, was a natural perquisite of domestic service and the thievery in the household was attended to, in the main, by Giorgio. As butler he saw to the smooth running of the house, but to his great resentment he was not given a role to play in the majordomo's most treasured preserve, the household accounts. As there was nothing in the shops worth buying, no money was ever dispensed, thus denying Giorgio the delights of patronage—the favoring of one butcher over another, this wine seller over that one—a system carrying with it authority and prestige, not to mention fine opportunities for graft, kickbacks, bribes, and gifts from suppliant suppliers.

Food was delivered by surly black soldiers who complained about the stairs and the weight of the crates and sacks all stamped with black block army lettering. They brought staples—flour and sugar, rice, tea and coffee, canned goods—and many of the luxuries, like liquor, wines, meat, and candies. The real treasures though, were lugged into the kitchen by Italians, plainly blackmarketeers, taciturn fellows bearing the few fruits of the ravaged countryside: pasta, fresh vegetables, frothy milk, and sweet cream.

With no money to embezzle and no bribes to collect, Giorgio resorted to simple theft. In the beginning of his employment, before he had taken the measure of his patron, Giorgio's pilfering was petty: a few slices of leftover meat, some bread, a handful of rice or spaghetti, some wilted lettuce from the bottom of a salad bowl, the dregs in a bottle of wine, bruised fruit. These small acts of brigandage went unnoticed or at least unremarked. As the extent of Kinney's wealth became apparent, Giorgio, emboldened, took more—whole chickens; a dozen eggs; a bottle, sometimes two, of wine—secure that the American had so much that such morsels would never be missed.

If in need of further justification Giorgio told himself that he had only to look at the waste at Kinney's table to realize how unimportant such thefts were. The young *tenente* frequently entertained his comrades in arms and their beautiful Italian whores, and one could tell at a glance which plates had been set before the men and which before the women. The officers hardly touched their food, taking only a forkful or two before pushing it away. Giorgio was deeply shocked, once, to discover a cigarette mashed out and broken in the middle of a pearly risotto alla pescatora. Even the cigarette was only half smoked. The whore's plates returned to the kitchen clean. Americans ate so well, so often, that not even Maria Romana's fragrant creations could tempt them.

Still, the deliveries of food came, whole hams and turkeys, delicately marbled pieces of beef; and fish, unseen since 1940, was always in plentiful supply even though it never seemed to be popular with Kinney's guests. Fruit from the south, honey, jams, and confits, luxuries unknown for years, flowed into the Palazzo Sanseverio and in such abundance that Giorgio, Maria Romana, and Alba could only be amazed. Now at last, neither they nor their families were hungry, and on Sundays, at mass, Maria Romana gave thanks for having been sent such a magnificent benefactor.

On the upper floor, the Duke smelled the musky cigar smoke and heard the hoarse laughter, the soft rustle of cards, and the click of dice. He shut his ears to the muffled squeals coming from the bedrooms. Camillo reminded himself that the state of Kinney's soul was not his affair, though the defiling of his family home made him queasy. But Sandro needed Kinney's money. Gabrielle burned with a variety of hungers.

AUSTIN KINNEY DID not actually live in the Palazzo Sanseverio. Rather, like the Roman grandees of the past, he lived in one palace and took his relaxation in another. He preferred the more modern luxuries of the Excelsior for day to day, and saved the palace for his pleasures. The study of the Palazzo Sanseverio, however, a wood-panelled room which held the remains of the family library, was devoted to business, the unofficial headquarters of Kinney's black market enterprise. Stacked around the room were crates and boxes and bolts of cloth, all taken from the company warehouse, things too valuable to be stored there.

Kinney worked at the desk of Camillo's great-grandfather surrounded by packing cases filled with cigarettes and cigars, wooden crates stuffed with scotch and Irish whiskey, bourbon and gin. There were rolls of silk, cotton, and wool, cases of rare champagne still in their prewar wrappings. Stacked in a corner were fifty boxes of morphine syrettes and an equal amount of the new drug penicillin.

Around the Excelsior, the Grand, the Flora, the Hassler, and the Russie, the Palazzo Sanseverio was known as Kinney's Cathouse, an Americanism not yet part of the Duke's lexicon. Austin's "do's" varied in size, from six men and their girls for drinks and cards to full-scale dinners for fifty. At any affair, Kinney was always the most junior officer present, but no one ever pulled rank on him. Austin was always respectful towards his superiors. The captains, majors, and colonels treated him like the brilliant younger son of an extended family, to be indulged and teased and chaffed, but never rebuked. Kinney laughed at their jokes, made jokes of his own, and snapped his fingers at Giorgio when he noticed an empty glass. Austin's superiors puffed on his smokes and took the women he provided to the beds he furnished, and not one of them worried about the cost. Austin Kinney had class. And everyone knew his old man was loaded.

Kinney's old man *was* loaded, but Austin wasn't; the munificent paternal purse had snapped shut. In Austin Kinney's short past, there were too many expulsions from expensive schools, too many wrecked cars, a number of girls to be got out of trouble. Through Kinney's teens and early manhood, Lex Kinney had paid out quite a bit to extract his son from scrapes and to keep the family name out of the papers. The Kinney bequest to the Widener Library had ensured Austin's entry into Harvard, and the Kinney Chair in Old Church Slavonic kept him there.

The family millions could not keep Austin in the good graces of his first posting in the army, New York's prestigious Seventh Regiment. While Kinney père did pay to correct the "misunderstanding" over the company funds entrusted to Austin's keeping, he could not pay to keep him in one of the few U.S. units that carried any social cachet. Lex Kinney told his wayward son that he hoped the army would do him some good and closed his checkbook until after the war. To Austin's horror, the army had consigned him to the remote and inglorious service corps. And worse than that, he had been broke.

No longer. Locked in the desk was his syndicate's capital, thick wads of bills now totalling $15,000. It represented just three deliveries, three tiny fractions from the army's vast supply. As Giorgio stole from Kinney, Kinney stole from the army, secure in the knowledge that no one would ever notice or care. By the end of the month, he estimated that the $15,000 would be $50,000; by the end of the summer, a quarter of a million. Not bad.

The bills themselves were worn and sweat-stained, dirty, frayed at the edges. They had been carried by GIs through mud and snow, steaming heat and monsoons, in boots and packs and helmet liners. The bills trickled into the hands of Lorenzetti's pimps and bar owners and thieves—it was said he even controlled the shoeshine boys—and at the confluence of these different streams, a river of cash formed, flowing through the gangster's hands and into Kinney's. Austin had never paid much attention to economics in his various schools but there seemed to be a formula here that one of his august professors might have taught. Lorenzetti sold sex and rotgut cheap, in large quantities, to buy a more valuable commodity, food, which he sold dear. And Austin reaped the rewards, hardly lifting a finger. It was like making a killing in the market.

He was interrupted in his reverie by a knock at the study door. He closed the cash drawer and locked it.

"Who is it?"

"Gabrielle Sanseverio."

Kinney smiled as he opened the door. "Baronessa," he said, "this is a pleasant surprise. Are you and your family comfortable in your new quarters?"

"Are you," she asked, "in yours?"

"Very nice," said Kinney. "Very nice indeed."

Gabrielle tried to look over his shoulder into his study. "I wonder if I might have a word with you?"

"Of course, but let's not talk in here." Kinney stepped into the hall and locked the door behind him. "This way, please," he said, as if Gabrielle were a visitor.

They picked up Giorgio in their progress and he scurried ahead of them, opening doors, bowing them through, then rushing to overtake them again.

One of the most delightful rooms in the palace was also one of the smallest. Camillo's wife had called it her sewing room, and she had appreciated the light from the lofty French doors that opened onto a small terrace. From there one could look down on the Piazza Margana or up at the Capitoline Hill. Off to the left, looming above the ochre rooftops, the huge dazzling white monument to Vittorio Emanuele II seemed to hang in the sky like a cloud bank. The walls of the room were a pale blue. The ceiling was frescoed, not grandly like the *salone*, but with figures of Aglaia, Euphrosyne, and Thalia set with garlands and flowers. Over the small fireplace was the tiny portrait of the Countess Lucia in the headdress of an odalisque.

Kinney did not notice the art. He never took his eyes off Gabrielle. She settled on a sagging Louis Quinze sofa, Austin taking an armchair nearby, the chair in which Camillo used to sit reading aloud while his wife tatted. Giorgio hovered in the background, unhappy.

Austin stole a glance at his watch. He was not entertaining that night but he did have plans and he needed to bathe and change. But there was plenty of time—besides, he had been meaning to get to know the baronessa.

"May I offer you something? It *is* just about time for cocktails."

"No. I mustn't stay."

"Please. I insist. An aperitif, perhaps."

"No, I must go back upstairs. I only wanted a moment."

"I'm sure there can't be anything terribly pressing. Giorgio."

Giorgio jumped as if pinched. "Si, signore?"

"Bring a bottle of gin."

"Subito, signore." And then, delighted to have a chance to show off his small store of English, "One martini cocktail."

"Yes, that's right."

"Subito, tenente." He left but did not close the doors behind him.

Gabrielle smoothed her dress over her knees. "I have come to speak to you about that man," she said, businesslike. "All of your servants, in fact."

"Have they bothered you? Have they been rude?"

"Yes, but that is not the matter."

"What is, then?"

"They are stealing from you. They are stealing from you and boasting of it in the neighborhood."

"Stealing? My goodness."

"I suppose it does not matter to you. You seem to think it is funny."

Kinney's smirk broadened into a smile. "No, I just don't think it's terribly important. And it really is nothing for you to worry about." He leaned forward, his cigarette case open like a pair of jaws. "Would you care for a cigarette?"

She took one and Kinney lit it for her. "I assumed they would steal. Servants always do, don't they? All the more so if they happen to have the misfortune of living in a starving city, wouldn't you think? I'm much more concerned about you. How have they been rude?"

"It doesn't matter."

"Oh, but it does. Please tell me."

"They seem to forget that this is not their house. Or yours, for that matter."

Kinney flicked his own cigarette. "Gabrielle, you are absolutely right. I'll see to it that it stops at once. Are you getting all you need, by the way? There's lots of food. As you may have noticed, I entertain quite a bit. I hope it doesn't disturb you."

"Not at all." Gabrielle still felt a slight shock at his casual use of her first name. Camillo would have been outraged.

"And *are* you getting enough?"

"We have our rations."

"Rations! How on earth can you live on rations?"

"We manage. Your Colonel Poletti has just raised the bread ration to three hundred grams a day."

"And cut meat, milk, and sugar. No, you must take what you need. There's plenty for everyone. Even with thieving servants."

"I'm not sure Maria Romana will give up a crumb, not on my word she won't."

"Is she the tall, thin one with a face like a foot or the short one with the mustache and no teeth?"

Gabrielle smiled. "The tall one."

"I'll tell her."

"Really? In what language?"

"I'll make myself understood."

Giorgio returned with a tray. He did not like what he saw. Gabrielle was sitting back, relaxed in the sofa, her legs crossed, smoking one of the *tenente's* cigarettes. They were becoming

222

friends. Giorgio set the tray on a small table and began fussing with the gin bottle, the ice, and a small jug of vermouth.

"Stop that," said Kinney. "I'll do it. He never makes them dry enough."

Giorgio affected not to have understood and dropped some ice into a pitcher.

"Giorgio!"

"Si, signora!" The manservant swung around as if scalded. He couldn't quite look Gabrielle in the eye.

"Il tenente ha detto basta!"

Giorgio looked from Gabrielle to Kinney. Austin smiled. "I think you better do what she says, Giorgio." Kinney motioned toward the door. "I'll see to the drinks."

Giorgio frowned, bowed, and walked from the room with all the dignity he could muster, acutely aware that the reign of the kitchen was at an end.

Kinney chuckled as he mixed the drinks. "Well, you seemed to handle him without any trouble."

"His wife is the real terror."

"I don't envy him. Here." He handed her the cold beaker of ice-blue gin.

She took it, but hesitantly. "I'm not used to drinking, not since the war began."

"It'll do you good. Besides, it's time to get yourself reac-climated, I'd say. The war is all but over."

Gabrielle sipped and shivered. "Is it?"

The state of military affairs didn't interest Austin Kinney much, except as they concerned him, but he felt he should say something martial, if only to establish his bona fides as a soldier. "The invasion of France . . . the whole thing could be over in a couple of weeks."

Gabrielle raised an eyebrow and smiled questioningly. "Weeks?"

"Months, then." He realized that the way to Gabrielle was not as a warrior covered in glory or even opinions. She cared about the war even less than he did. "How's your drink?"

"Delicious."

"How's your husband?"

"Bedridden."

"Poor fellow. You must tell me if there's anything I can do to help. And where did you learn to speak such excellent English?"

"English! Americans and Englishmen always ask that question. It's because you don't know how to learn the languages of others, or you don't bother, that you can't imagine anyone being able to learn yours. I learned English where one is supposed to learn things, in school."

"Not just in school, surely?"

"In school and later, in London."

"I've just come from London. Did you like it there?"

"The weather is bad and the food is filthy, but the city is quite pretty."

"The English would say that the French pay too much attention to food. What did you think of the men?"

"Many of them are very charming. Some of them smell like damp dogs."

Kinney laughed. "I've never heard that before. What do American men smell like?"

"I couldn't really say."

"Guess."

"I suppose they smell like children, like money, like chewing gum. Perhaps they smell like the cinema."

"That's not very good . . . better than damp dogs though. How did your husband become bedridden?"

"He was tortured by the Fascists. In one of their prisons. He was gone a very long time."

"And now it's as if he's still gone."

Gabrielle looked hard at Kinney, trying to read his face. But he showed nothing beyond his usual look of bland self-confidence. It was as if he had done nothing more than speak lightly of her fine command of the English language. "I don't know what you mean."

"It doesn't matter." Kinney sipped. "He must have been a hero."

"I think," said Gabrielle evenly, "that he was a fool."

"Well, he must have had his reasons."

"Yes. Foolish ones. Honor. Somewhere in his mind I think he quite welcomed the idea of martyrdom."

"How old are you?" asked Kinney suddenly.

"Thirty-one. How old are you?"

"Twenty-two."

"A baby," she said. "A boy."

"No I'm not." He put down his drink and kissed her. There was a moment of resistance and then her mouth opened and her smooth tongue bitter with gin and tobacco speared his mouth. Their lips were sealed against one another. He ran his hands up and down her body, along her ribs, feeling her twist and curl under his touch.

She pulled back, spots of color in her pale cheeks. She studied his face for a moment, then raised her lips to be kissed again. Kinney fumbled with the buttons of her linen blouse and then slipped his hand to her breast, clutching at her brassiere, digging to find his way to her soft skin. She pushed him away.

"Wait," she said.

"What for?" There was a catch of anger in his voice.

Gabrielle unbuttoned her blouse, tossed it to the floor and then reached behind her and unclipped her bra. It fell forward into her hands. Kinney looked at her for a moment, her breasts white and full and pink-tipped, and then leaned forward. He kissed one nipple, then the other. They stiffened and rose in his lips. Gabrielle's arms snaked behind his neck and held him close in the warm fold between her breasts. She fell back, carrying him with her.

His knee was between her knees and she spread her legs without thought, her skirt riding up. Kinney tugged at the waistband of her loose silk panties, and she raised her buttocks an inch while he stripped the flimsy garment from her. She braced a foot against the arm of a sofa and dropped the other foot to the floor, open to him. Kinney brushed his fingers through the soft tuft of hair and then bent and slipped his tongue into her, tasting the matted, musty oil, sweat, and sex. Her pelvis thrust forward hard, as if shocked, as if he had bit her, and her hands snaked behind his head. He bore into her with his tongue and lips, like an animal feeding on the soft parts of prey.

Then he broke free, sat up, unbuckled his pants and pushed them down to his knees. She saw his penis only for an instant, heavy, fat, and powerful, and then he jerked it into her, slicing through the slick, soft folds, and pressed deep. Gabrielle's legs buckled like a belt behind his hips and her hands dove into his shirt, stripping buttons, her fingers playing on the hard plates of his chest now oily with sweat. She heard his breath hot in her ear.

Gabrielle pushed him back and raised her head, curling toward him to look down between their bodies. She watched fascinated as he thrust into her and she raised to meet each thrust. She felt warm and wanton, open and filled, seared by the great luxury of sex. She reached down and closed her hand around the root of his penis, feeling her own fist mash against her. Her fingers slipped to his balls, they were loose and viscid, and she played with them and felt him buck in response. She thought, This is what whores do, this is what he wants.

She gasped when he came and dug her heel into the small of his back, twisting under him, grinding into him as the flood backed up and he became loose in her. Kinney collapsed onto her chest and combed his fingers through her fine hair. Hopefully, she thrust at him, but felt only softness, moisture, and a living, humid heat. Gabrielle's knees were trembling and her toes were curled in her sandals. She was drenched in sweat, her own and his, and their breathing seemed quite loud in the still room. She rocked her hips to rouse him.

Kinney pulled off her and yanked up his pants. He stretched across the sofa to reach his drink, the glass cold and wet with condensation. He sipped and leaned back and touched the silvery, oily foam and rolled her clitoris between his fingers. Her lips parted and her eyes closed, she shivered, and he stopped.

"No more now," he said.

Her skirt was gathered at her waist, as narrow now as a belt. She pulled it down over her thighs and swung her leg to the floor, sitting up. She took his hand and raised it to her lips.

"Later, then?"

"Yes."

"Where?"

"Here. In a bed. There are lots of them, you know."

"And them?" She glanced toward the ceiling.

"You said he's bedridden. And Camillo's just an old man. You shouldn't find it too hard to give him the slip."

"Where are you going?"

"Out."

"Where?"

"Just out," he said firmly.

"And what should I do while you're gone?"

Kinney smiled. "Why don't you have something to eat?"

After he had left and she had returned to the chaste upper floor, Giorgio, Maria Romana, and Alba went into the sewing room. They examined the rumpled sofa with dismay and sniffed the air like a trio of setters.

15

"Gentlemen," said Rhys Jones, "the scrum." He tapped his chin and stared out over the Circo Massimo, looking at, but not really seeing, the ruins of the palace on the Palatine. It was the tenth day of practice and the team was dressed for the first time in their uniforms, their "kit," Jones called it. He had scrounged a pile of red and white jerseys, black shorts, thick blue woolen socks and a pile of boots from the British army recreation services. They looked like rugby footballers and, more to the point, they were beginning to perform like a team. Jones had discovered that they were having informal practices on their own, tossing the ball and talking tactics late in the day when the sun was cooling.

The almost genetic imprint of football had faded somewhat, and the men of A Company had come to appreciate rugby's clean continuous play and the potent mixture of subtle strategy and raw strength. The fifteen were seated at Jones's feet and paying closer attention to him than they ever had to a teacher in school.

"The scrum," he repeated. "If you think of the eighty minutes of rugby as the entire war, the scrums are the individual battles in that war. Win them and you win the war. Like El Alamein."

"Any battle you want, Sarge," shouted Sam Crosby, "except Anzio!"

The team laughed nervously. For many of them Anzio had been a baptism of fire, and that protracted struggle had taken its toll. Seven members of Company A had died in the shelling.

"Actually, Sam," said Jones, "Anzio is a very good example. Mr Leacock, Stanley, what happened at Anzio?"

"We sat on the beach and got the shit kicked out of us for eight weeks," said Stanley.

"Ah. Yes. But why?"

"Germans. They were in the way."

"They was strong, Sarge," shouted Biggs.

"Strong and—? Anybody?"

"Mean."

"Tough."

"Dug in."

"Desperate."

"Yes. All of those things, but I'm looking for something else." Jones stopped speaking for a moment and looked from face to face. "The jerries were strong and *determined*, gentlemen. At Anzio you had two strong armies locked together, head to head." Jones laced the knuckles of both fists together and pushed. "Back and forth. You pushed. They pushed. We wanted to get to Rome and the signorinas, they wanted to push us into the sea. Two strong, determined forces, pushing. And what happened?"

"We won!" shouted Biggs.

"We pushed harder," said Holt. "And *then* we won."

"Right!" Jones clapped his hands. "And so it is with the scrum. Two interlocking forces, strong and determined, pushing one another. It is a fist made up of eight men, a one-ton punch, your fist against the fist of the other team, driving against each other for possession of the ball. Right. On your feet, boyos."

The front line of a rugby scrum is made up of two large men, the props, supporting between them a smaller man, the hooker. Behind them are a row of four strong men, supporting that forward line. Behind them is the anchoring point of the scrum, the eighth man, a position that fell to Alvin Whiteside.

When deployed on the field, the scrums of the two teams are locked together, eight men yoked by the front line. Cheek by jowl—literally—the two forces intertwine and the ball is thrown through the tunnel of legs. The opposing hookers attempt to hook the ball out of the scrum and feed it to their own scrum half, who is then free to run down the field toward the enemy goal line. Scrums are dirty, hot, dangerous, and brutal. As a former hooker, Jones thought them the most exhilarating part of the game.

The first few attempts at scrums were failures, with sixteen men—Llewellyn pitched in—going down in a tangle of arms and legs. But as the afternoon wore on, they got the hang of it, the mass of men groaning and grunting, pushing and straining, scrabbling for a toehold in the field. As expected, Alvin Whiteside dug in and locked his scrum into position.

At the end of practice, Jones blew his whistle. "Right, All Blacks, gather round." Llewellyn tossed him the ball. "Three days before the game I want you lot to stop shaving. You see, when you get in the scrum and your cheek is up against one of those bastards, it won't feel nice for him, not at all. I'll square it with your CO that you'll be excused shaving."

The team was frowning at him and Jones was puzzled. Usually they appreciated hearing about little tricks that would discomfort the enemy.

"What's the matter, lads?"

"What did you call us?" asked Holt.

"Call you? I didn't . . . oh. All Blacks." Jones laughed. "Sorry, Jimmy. The greatest rugby team in the world—excluding the Welsh, of course—is called the All Blacks. They're from New Zealand and they are brilliant. You don't get any better."

"Why they called that?" asked Stanley. "Are they colored?"

"No, I don't think so. Sorry, lads, just got into the habit of calling you lot that in my mind. Didn't mean any harm. Terry, you know why the All Blacks are called the All Blacks?"

"They wear black kit, Sarge."

"Yes, but is that why?"

"Dunno, Sergeant."

"That's a good point, though," said Jones. "You lads ought to think of a name for this team, give it an identity, like."

"The lions," shouted someone.

"Tigers."

"Bears."

"Hey, Sarge, what are the Welsh called?"

"Well . . . they're not called anything, really. The Welsh. The Taffs."

"The Taffs?" That was immediately rejected as not nearly belli-cose enough.

"What's wrong with the All Blacks?" asked Stanley. "Sarge says they're the best. And it fits us." Stanley grinned.

"He said they're the best after the Welsh," said Biggs. "But I don't go for the All Black Taffs. Sounds stupid. What the hell is a Taff anyway, Sarge?"

"It's a river, Biggsy."

"A river?"

"Hey, Sarge," yelled Jimmy. "The Welsh got an animal, like the Americans got the eagle?"

"Oh yes, Jimmy, we've got a dragon. It's the national symbol." Along with a daffodil and leek, but he didn't think either would appeal to his young team.

"The All Black Dragons," said Jimmy. "I like it."

"THERE WAS THIS guy in Brooklyn," said Eddie Manganaro, "pissed off the wrong people, you know what I'm saying?"

"Yeah," said McManus. He sipped his wine, looked up into the starry sky, and sniffed the sweet evening air. The membership of Father Mousecat's Home for Children were enjoying their relaxation after a hard day of work. Ever since they were surprised by Kinney they kept a lantern lit low, and the three sergeants had turned their chairs around, facing the French doors as if expecting a cabaret show.

"What was the guy's name?" asked Utterback. He always enjoyed Eddie's stories about his gangster days.

"Nicolosi," said Manganaro. "We always kidded him that his name was Nicoloski, like he was a Polack, you know. Fuckin' hated that." Manganaro chuckled. "Anyway, he pissed off the wrong people and lands up dead, right?"

"What happened to him?"

"Got shot. They found him in the trunk of a '35 Chrysler Airflow. That was his car."

"Nice car," said Utterback.

"I had a Locomobile, once," said McManus. "Used, of course. But *that* was a nice car. How come they named it that? Always thought that was a lousy name for a car. Studebaker had a Knute Rockne. That's a lousy name. Hupmobile, lousy name. Terraplane, lousy name. Pierce-Arrow, *that's* a nice name for a car. Stutz Bearcat. That's a good name."

"Shuttup, Donny. Eddie, who shot Nicolosi?"

"I dunno, some guys. Anyway, there's this new prosecutor, a kid, pain in the ass, and he gets a real hard-on for this pop, says he's gonna find out who killed Nicolosi, like anyone gives a rat's ass. Anyway, the cops come around and they pull a couple of us in—not arrests, you know, just for questioning, bullshit, and I'm down there—"

"Down where?"

"Precinct house. And I know most of the cops, right, and they're asking me questions, but they know it's bullshit because why would I pop Nicolosi and they know he's a piece of shit, so who cares? But they gotta because of this prosecutor, so they're asking me where I was last Tuesday and I'm saying at my mother's or some shit like that and then in comes this prosecutor." Manganaro sipped his wine.

"Nice kid, you know, college boy. With the glasses and the big Adam's apple and he's dressed like a fuckin' undertaker from the whadyacallit, Brooks Brothers, and he's all serious and he says, I swear, 'Mr. Manganaro, we took this from the dead man's wallet and I wonder if you could identify it. And guess what he shows me.''

"A love letter," said McManus.

"What?" said Utterback.

"Photograph. I look at it and you know what it's a picture of?"

"Pussy," said Utterback.

"A streetlight! A fuckin' streetlight! Can you beat that? That Nicoloski!" Eddie laughed.

"I don't get it," said McManus.

"Me neither."

"So this Nicolosi is a gambler, right? Runs a crap game somewhere in Brooklyn, I don't know, Coney Island maybe, and he carries around a picture of the streetlight he runs the game under. Like some guys carry around pictures of their girl or the wife and kids, Nicolosi got a picture of his streetlight."

"Yeah, so what happened?"

"So the prosecutor, DA, whatever the hell he is, is saying all serious, 'Can you identify this for us, Mister Manganaro?' And so I tell him and the fucker doesn't believe me! The only time in my life I tell the bulls the fuckin' truth and he don't believe me. Can you beat that?" Manganaro drank some more wine and laughed. "Those were the fuckin' days."

"Ever get arrested?" asked Utterback.

"Yeah, coupla times. They never made anything stick, though. I never done no time, which I used to think was a shame because if I had done time then they wouldn't draft me and I wouldn't be here talking to you two bozos. But with that pile of cabbage the lieutenant is holding for us, the army suddenly don't seem so bad."

"I don't know how come we can't have *none* of the cash now."

"Forget about it Cal," said McManus. "The lieutenant's right. We divvy now and we're liable to get caught. When the time comes to go home we all get one quarter of the pie. Nice little nest egg to get started in the real world."

"I guess. . . . How do we know he won't take off with all the money?"

"He won't. Relax. Eddie picks up the money once a week so we know how much is going into the kitty. It's like having stock in the phone company or Con Edison or something solid."

"Yeah," said Utterback with a grin. "But how do we know we can trust Eddie?"

"*That* we gotta worry about," conceded McManus.

"I put you two birds onto the sweetest deal in the whole fuckin' army and this is the thanks I get? That's gratitude."

"Someone's coming," said Utterback alarmed. "It's that fuckin' Holt."

"Jimmy, what do you want?" McManus put down his wine and sat up.

"Need to talk, Sarge."

"What about?" demanded Utterback.

Holt took a deep breath. "It's about them deliveries we been making."

"What about them?" snapped Utterback.

Manganaro and McManus exchanged glances.

"You want some wine, Jimmy?" Manganaro shoved the bottle across the cast-iron table. "Sergeants don't mind fraternizing with the enlisted men once in a while."

Utterback appeared to mind.

"No thanks, Sarge."

"So what about these deliveries, Jimmy?" Manganaro drew on his stogy.

"We were wondering what was going on, Sarge."

"What do you think is going on, Jimmy?"

"We think something is going on. Maybe there's a little money being made here."

"You fuckin' nig—"

"Shut up, Cal," ordered McManus. "Jimmy, what the hell are you talking about?"

For a moment, Holt was afraid he had made a mistake and that McManus didn't know what his two colleagues were up to.

"I think we all know what's going on here," said Manganaro pleasantly. "Take some wine, Jimmy. Have a seat. You smoke cigars? You want a cigar? They're good cigars."

"No thanks, Sarge." Holt remained on his feet.

"Then sit down, you're giving me a stiff neck you standing like that."

Holt sat, perching himself on the edge of one of the rusting metal chairs.

"That's better." Manganaro leaned forward and tapped lightly on Holt's knee. "Hey Jimmy, you wouldn't be trying to shake us down, would you? You niggers haven't organized yourself to shake down your old sergeants, have you? Jeez, I really hope not." Manganaro sounded almost reasonable.

"Sergeant, what you-all do is your business—"

"Fuckin' A," said Utterback.

"But how you do it, that's another thing."

"It is? How so, Jimmy?"

"You think we don't see what's going on, Sarge? You're using us. We think we ought to get something for our trouble. We get caught doing your business then we're in trouble just as if we were in business for ourselves."

"Don't worry about it, Jimmy, don't worry about it." Manganaro tapped the ash from his cigar. "You boys get in trouble then you just tell 'em that big, bad, mean Sergeant Manganaro put you up to it."

Jimmy shook his head slowly. "That's not gonna work, Sarge, and you know it. Because if we get in a jam and tell 'em what you're up to then you'll deny everything and seeing as this is a white man's army we po' colored boys are going to be in deep shit up to our ears for nothing, Sergeant." He looked Manganaro in the eye. "Just because I'm in the army doesn't mean I'm stupid."

Manganaro leaned back in his chair and puffed on his cigar. Then he took a sip of wine. "You're a New York boy, ain't you, Jimmy?"

"Yeah."

"Harlem boy?"

"I'm nobody's boy, Sergeant."

Manganaro laughed and shook his head. "Jimmy, I'm sorry. I don't mean it that way. You know, someone younger than you, you just call 'em boy. Sometimes, shit, I call Utterback boy. Besides, I hear that Jones always calling you guys boy."

"He says 'boyo.' That's just the way them Welsh talk."

"Yeah, well. Just answer the question. You're a Harlem . . . fella, right?"

"Yeah."

"East Harlem?"

"No."

"You ever been to East Harlem?"

"You mean where the dagoes live? Yeah, I been there once or twice. So what?"

"Well, I got this friend lives up there, lived up there his whole life in the Italian section of East Harlem. Got a business up there. Nice business. Makes a lot of money. And you know what he does, Jimmy? He runs numbers in Harlem. Nigger Harlem. He sells junk to the niggers, he sells nigger cooze to white guys which personally makes me sick, but you know how it is, to each his own, am I right, Cal?"

"You're right, Eddie."

Manganaro drew on his cigar and blew across the tip. "Then one day a couple of the niggers works for my friend, they get big ideas. They say, hey, we're the ones running the numbers, we're the ones pushing the junk, we're pimping the gash, so maybe we should take over." Manganaro took a swallow of wine.

"Now my friend didn't like this. He didn't go for this idea at all. No, sir. And so he did something about it. And you know what he did, Jimmy?"

"I can guess," murmured Jimmy.

"Now there, my friend, you are wrong. I don't think you can guess. 'Cause what happened to them was horrible, truly horrible. Two niggers got stuffed—alive—into building furnaces, another gets killed and they find him with his pecker cut off and stuck in his mouth, and another they make him put his tongue on the third rail at 116th Street and Manhattan Avenue." Manganaro slapped his hands together as if cleaning them off. "Hey presto-chango! No more trouble with the niggers. You gettin' all this, Jimmy?"

"You're not scaring me, Sarge. I know you ain't gonna kill us."

"This is wartime, asshole," sneered Utterback. "Ain'tcha heard? People get killed in wartime."

"Simmer down, Cal," said McManus.

"Jimmy, no one said nothing about killing anybody. I just told you that story because I thought maybe you'd find it interesting. But let me put it this way. You're privates. We're sergeants. You're colored. We're white. Ask yourself, Jimmy, who got all the cards?" Manganaro smiled affably. "So listen, why don't you go back to your friends and tell 'em you talked it over with me and I personally guarantee that there ain't gonna be no trouble." Manganaro leaned forward until his face was only inches from Holt's. His voice hardened and there was fury in his clenched jaw. "So you should keep your big, flat, nigger fuckin' noses out of the white man's business. Okay? So get the fuck outta here before you get me mad. Got it, boy?"

"Scram, sambo," said Utterback.

Holt stared coldly into Manganaro's eyes, then shook his head slowly. "Sergeant, you're a hard man to do business with. I'll just have to think of a way to convince you that I'm an easy man to do business with."

"Don't fuck with me, Jimmy," said Manganaro softly. "Don't make the mistake of fuckin' with me. I'll be watching you."

Holt stood up. "Sergeant, I don't plan on making any mistakes." He left quietly, closing the French doors behind him.

Manganaro poured himself some more wine and coaxed some smoke out of his cigar butt. He thought he had handled the situation well. He hadn't lost his temper, he had made his position clear, and he figured that he had scared Holt into changing his mind. Of course, a guy like Jimmy had to exit on a brave line, but that was just talk. Manganaro was pretty sure that this was the last he would hear of that particular problem. It was like being a don. Manganaro liked that.

Utterback, of course, was apoplectic. "How do you like that? I told you, Eddie, I told you both, I always said that nigger was trouble."

"There's no trouble," said Manganaro evenly. "It's all been taken care of. Hey, Donny, you're pretty quiet tonight."

McManus sighed heavily and shook his head. "I don't know, Eddie, I don't like this. . . . How much money you say the lieutenant got in the kitty?"

"Fifteen large," said Manganaro with a grin.

"Hot damn!" exclaimed Utterback.

"That's a lot," said McManus.

"Yes, indeedy."

"Then," said McManus, "I think you oughta cut 'em in."

"Jesus H. Christ! Eddie, you hear that? Donny wants to give our fuckin' money to the niggers! You must be outta your dim-bulb mick brain. Son of a bitch!"

"Eddie," pleaded McManus. "Who's it going to hurt? A hundred a month, two hundred a month, it's peanuts. It's overhead, wastage. It's just the cost of doing business."

"Would you listen to this shit?" Utterback screeched. "Fuckin' mick nigger lover. That's a first in my book. Donny, you are some poor fuckin' excuse for a white man."

"Cal, for once in your sorry goddamn life would you shut your fuckin' mouth? Think, both of you, for a couple of hundred a month you buy peace and quiet. No trouble with the niggers, then no trouble with the business. Eddie, who's it going to hurt?"

"Who's it gonna hurt? Me, that's who. And you. And Cal. You can't ever give anything away in this business. Not to the niggers, not to nobody, never to niggers. Believe me, you start giving in, cutting deals, you're outta business."

"Yeah," said Utterback. "I'm with Eddie."

"I don't know . . . What if they start gettin' ideas? What if they start acting up?"

Manganaro had already considered this problem and had a solution.

"If they get outta line—which they won't, guaranteed—then we'll do what we have to do."

"And what's that?"

"Kick a little ass, Donny."

"Amen," said Utterback. "A-fuckin'-men."

PROVENANCE

I'm waiting in an office up at Avery Hall up at Columbia University, cooling my heels until Adam Malinsky can get around to seeing me. I have an appointment and all, but his secretary tells me he's running late. How does an art historian get so busy, you ask? I don't know.

So I'm sitting there, right? Right outside his door and his secretary is answering phones and doing the kind of things secretaries do and I'm paging through a copy of that boring *Burlington* magazine but I'm looking at the secretary because she doesn't look like a college department secretary. She's really pretty, but that's not it, it's because she's dressed up very expensive, very tasteful, with the jewelry and everything and then it hits me. She's not doing this job because she needs a job, she's some rich young woman who's taken this job to be near Malinsky, be close to the master.

And the office doesn't look like a college office, either. I mean, how many college offices have what looks to me to be an Albert Pinkham Ryder and two, count 'em two, Maurice Prendergasts. I didn't know that Malinsky was into American art; I mean, I didn't think he admitted there was a painter after David. Then the secretary stands up to go look up something in the file cabinet and I see she's not even sitting in a normal desk chair, it's a Shaker chair, which I imagine must be pretty hard on the *tuchis* day in day out. Suffering for your art, right?

So I say to her, "That's a nice chair. Shaker, isn't it?"

And she looks me in the eye and goes, "Yes, note its simplicity of line."

I had to laugh.

Malinsky's office wasn't just nice like his reception room, it was

238

really nice. The walls that weren't, as they say, book lined, were paneled in some dark wood and carved with an acanthus frieze around the top. It looked like something Malinsky had bought from a stately home before it got knocked down.

There were only two paintings—very spare, you know, very reserved—but what paintings! Behind Malinsky's desk, facing you so visitors could see it, was an honest-to-God Poussin, *Rebecca at the Well.* And on the other wall was a beautiful Claude Lorrain, one of his great landscapes with classical ruins. A knockout, really.

That Malinsky. He's so rich. The books, his TV show, and the real money, the fees he gets from dealers like Peony for authenticating his paintings. If Malinsky says it's a Raphael, it stays a Raphael. I'm telling you, the guy should sell franchises.

All over the place, on the desk, on the bookshelves, are these photographs in silver frames. Malinsky with Bernard Berenson, with Meyer Shapiro, with Frederick Hartt, with Pevsner, Panofsky, Sir John Pope-Hennessey, Anthony Blunt—we are talking the A team of art history here.

Malinsky was short and he had swept-back white hair, sort of like Leonard Bernstein, and these beady little eyes behind silver-framed glasses. He had this way of looking at you like he had just blown his nose and looked in his hanky and there you were. It was nothing personal, you understand, Malinsky was like this with everybody. I mean, he had every reason to be nice to me—Peony would probably get him to authenticate the Chapman Reni, more money for him—but he had a reputation to maintain, so he wasn't.

"I've heard of you," he said, when I came in, raising himself in his chair just as much as he needed to in order to shake my hand. "You got that Crivelli back for the Cropton Collection."

"That's right." My biggest case. It's a long story. "Thanks for taking the time to see me, I appreciate it."

"Peony said it was important. A Reni, or, at least, an alleged Reni." Translation: When Peony has me over, fills me with champagne and plovers' eggs and presses a big, fat check into my hand, *then* it'll be a Reni. "Did you bring photographs?"

"No, professor, I didn't. Peony will be handling the authenticating. I'm working on provenance and I came across your name by accident."

Malinsky looked skeptical. Translation: How can you be in the art racket and come across Adam Malinsky's name by accident? It's like being in the religion game and hearing casual mention of Jesus Christ.

"Let me try and clear something up here, if you don't mind." I took the Chapman file out of my briefcase. "Now, I took the liberty of looking you up in *Who's Who,* sir, and I see that under military service the entry reads: "Lieutenant, Fine Arts and Monuments Office, 1944–46.""

"Em-hmm. They used to call us the Venus chasers. Frederick Hartt was one of the first into Florence, lucky devil."

"But here in an army file from 1944 I have an entry typed by a Corporal Adam Malinsky of the Judge Advocate General's Office. Is that you or is this just an amazing coincidence?"

Malinsky looked upset. He sighed and was silent for what seemed like half an hour. He put his hand out to the phone, as if he was going to call his lawyer, then stopped. Finally he said, "Oh God, yes. That's me."

You know, it wasn't like I had found out he'd committed a war crime or anything like that. So he was a corporal. So was Napoleon, wasn't he?

"Have you ever been in the service, Mr. Leblanc?"

"Yes."

"Horrible, isn't it?"

"No day at the beach, professor."

"I was drafted in 1944 and I assumed I would go into the Fine Arts and Monuments Office, but like a fool I admitted that I knew how to type and some ox of a sergeant told me that the army needed clerks more than Venus chasers. I was shipped to Metairie, Louisiana, and put through army clerk school. They taught me shorthand. It was the purest chance that I was sent to Italy, although I was thankful for that. The Judge Advocate General's Office was a terrible bore, but I held tight there until I was rescued by some of my FAMO friends."

"Lucky break."

"Yes. I ached to join the FAMO. I don't know how much you know about our activities, Leblanc, but we weren't a group of rear-echelon aesthetes, you know. We were right up there with the fighting forces. We had to be, to get in and protect things, protect the treasures. A couple of armies tramping through Italy can do quite a bit of damage, you know."

"I can imagine."

"You can't unless you were there to see it," he said.

Well, I was sure I could imagine it, but never mind. I showed him the paragraph from James Holt's files. "Does this mean anything to you?"

He read it quickly. I've always admired that. I read very slowly myself. Malinsky just glanced at it and seemed to get it all at once.

"Well, I remember Farfalla, of course. And Howe. He was a lawyer of some kind, Howe was. Very southern as I recall, very parochial, hadn't a clue about art. Probably never read anything more demanding than a magazine. I dimly remember . . ." Malinsky screwed his eyes tight. "Some summer day in a church in Rome . . . San Clemente? San Giovanni e Paolo? No, I can't remember, but the man couldn't tell a fresco from a fishstick. He was a boob."

"And this other one? Farfalla?"

"Very tough. An investigator. We all hated him. Worked himself—and everybody else—around the clock. He had some terribly derogatory nickname. I can't remember what it was, though."

"Do you have any recollection about these incidents and these dates? I mean, what were Farfalla and Howe doing so interested in James Holt?"

Malinsky laughed dryly. I bet he practiced that laugh, used it to make grad students feel like morons. "Farfalla was interested in everything, Mr. Leblanc. A real"—you could hear the quotation marks—" 'buttinsky,' that's what the other men called him."

There are people who would say the same about me. "As an investigator that would have been his job, professor. You can't remember anything about this particular incident? You can't remember why they interviewed Holt?"

Malinsky raised his hands, as if I was asking the impossible. "It was some time ago, Mr. Leblanc." Then, "Is this Holt fellow, by any chance, black?"

"Yes, he is. Was. He's dead. He died a couple of weeks ago."

"Yes, I vaguely . . . Some nastiness. We were a criminal prosecution unit so there was always a fair amount of nastiness around. Murder, rape, theft, that sort of thing."

"Yeah, but you can't . . ."

"You're sure Holt was black and not just involved in the black market? That seems to ring a bell."

"Couldn't he be both, black and black market?" I tried a shot in the dark. "If you dealt with a lot of black market cases, couldn't there have been a black market in art?"

"Ha. Would that there had been, Mr. Leblanc. You might have been able to pick up some bargains. Rome was in very dire straits. People wanted food, fuel, medicines, not art."

"Well, couldn't someone have traded food for art?"

Malinsky gave me that "look what I've found in my hanky" look. "I rather tend to doubt it. No common soldier would have traded commodities for art. How could they know what they were handling? It would take a most *un*common soldier, if you ask me."

"Well, what about that guy down in Texas, the one they just found with all that stuff that had been stolen from Germany?"

"He was set to guard it, Mr. Leblanc. One assumes that the FAMO people had already certified it. In any case, even if they hadn't, if the Nazis had gone to all the trouble of hiding it, he must have known it was valuable."

"Well, how about this, then. What if Holt was dealing on the black market, and whenever someone offered him a piece of artwork he had some FAMO guy look it over, sort of like Duveen and Morgan, or Berenson and Isabella Gardner."

"Don't be ridiculous," he said, very testy. "No FAMO officer would get involved in anything like that. We were the only people in the whole blessed U.S. Army who were doing anything positive. We were protecting the heritage of mankind, Mr. Leblanc. We didn't destroy things, no matter how worthy the cause. I'm not saying the fighting soldiers weren't doing a good thing, they were. You've been in the service and I think you'll agree that the prevailing attitude is 'it's a nasty job, but someone has to do it.' Not among the Venus chasers. We loved what we did. We couldn't wait for the dawning of each new day. To suggest that any one of us could have been involved in . . . monstrous."

I hadn't meant to piss him off. I guess I shouldn't have mentioned Berenson. These old guys are awfully touchy. "It was just a theory, sir."

"You see, we'd made our life's work the study of art, and the prospect of war destroying all those masterworks, well, it made us sick. I was in Naples when word came of the bombing of Monte Cassino. I was in the Galleria and all of a sudden a great cheer went up. Cassino had been bombed! I didn't cheer, Mister Leblanc. I put my head down on the table of the café and wept."

This I had trouble imagining.

"We were scholars. I think, until the war, we were all more or less resigned to a life spent in museums and archives and classrooms. In the FAMO we were *doing* something, Mr. Leblanc. It's difficult to explain but I felt—we all felt—as if we were reaching back over time, to Piero, to Raphael, to del Sarto, and giving them a helping hand. We might not have painted *La Primavera,* but we gave it life. It was quite the most important work of *my* life."

Translation: And that's something coming from me, buddy boy, considering how much important work I've done.

"Professor Malinsky, James Holt at the time of his death was in possession of a very valuable painting. He was a Pfc in a trucking outfit. How do you suppose he could have gotten hold of a Guido Reni?"

"If it *is* a Guido Reni."

Well, look, I wanted to say, it *is* a Guido Reni, but I didn't. See, if Malinsky got annoyed, he might decide, just for the hell of it, that it wasn't. And when Adam Malinsky decided your Guido Reni wasn't a Guido Reni, it stayed not a Guido Reni. Bad for the Chapmans, bad for Peony, bad for me.

"Let me put it this way, then. How could you explain how a black Pfc, no more than twenty years old, came to own a late 16th-century Italian painting?"

"Maybe he was an art lover and he bought it."

Of course, no one had considered this, not even Randall.

"But . . ."

"You have to admit that it's a possibility." Malinsky's eyes were glittering and I could tell he was just aching for a chance to call me a racist. Like he had a *ton* of black graduate students.

"Yes. But his family tells me that he showed absolutely no interest in art." Well, they hadn't said that specifically, but they didn't mention that Holt was an art lover. "I'm interested in discovering if his acquisition of the painting had anything to do with the events mentioned in the report you typed in Rome in 1944."

"I'd be interested, too, Mr. Leblanc. But I'm afraid I just don't remember anything about that report." He glanced at his watch and I glanced at mine. I had only been there twelve minutes. I figured I deserved a little more time. "Any idea where I might find Major Howe?"

"I'd check cemeteries in the south, Mr. Leblanc. He was close to sixty in 1944."

"And Farfalla?"

"I imagine he's probably still alive. He was about my age. If I were to guess, I would say he became a lawyer or a policeman."

I hope so. Lawyers, doctors, and cops are the easiest people in the world to track down. "Beyond that, you don't remember anything about him? Where he was from? Where he went to school? Anything?"

"I'm sorry, Mr. Leblanc. I had my mind on other things. I prayed daily for my transfer into FAMO."

"You wouldn't happen to have any diaries, letters, notebooks from that period, would you, sir?"

"Nothing germane, Mr. Leblanc." Translation: Wait for my memoirs.

"I'd appreciate it if you could review them in the off chance there's something . . ."

"I will, I promise you." Translation: The hell I will.

"Thank you, sir."

"And if there's anything else I can do, Mr. Leblanc, please don't hesitate to ask." Translation: Don't ask.

16

The big Chevrolet truck edged down the Via dei Delfini, the narrow beams from the headlights darting ahead, probing the dark of Piazza Margana. Holt cut the engine and the truck rolled to a halt in front of the great stern gate of the Palazzo Sanseverio. He and Stanley swung out of the cab, Jimmy hauling a gunny sack after him. Biggs and Crosby clambered down from the bed of the truck while Alvin Whiteside stood on the tailgate tossing heavy cardboard boxes to them, lightly, as if they weighed practically nothing at all. When the truck was unloaded, Whiteside jumped down and the five men stood silent, staring up at the lighted windows of the *piano nobile*. Shadows moved across the curtains, and the sounds of talk and laughter drifted through the windows and down into the still square. The judas gate in the portal stood open to accommodate latecomers to Kinney's party.

"I don't know," said Whiteside, "that place is fulla people. We're gonna get caught."

"No," said Holt. "No, we won't. Lieutenant's having a big party, that's what Rufus said, lots of brass. Kinney can't raise a big stink in front of them. Remember, he's the one who stole this shit in the first place."

"What if somebody sees us?"

Jimmy opened the sack and pulled out five white jackets, the type worn by servants in an army regimental mess. Whiteside's jacket was several sizes too small, his broad shoulders stretching the seams to the breaking point, the sleeves ending just below the elbows.

"Rufus said there'll be at least three mess waiters in there. Anybody sees you, just act like them. You've seen 'em, just act like Pullman porters."

"What if Kinney sees us?" whispered Biggs.

"You think he knows what you look like, Biggsy? He don't even know your name." Holt took a deep breath. "Let's go."

Like most Roman palaces, the Palazzo Sanseverio was built around a courtyard, a secular cloister. The five men crossed it, eschewing the grand main staircase for the narrow, dark back stairs which ran up into the house like a shaft in a mountain mine. It led directly to the servants' entrance to the kitchen.

Hardly a day passed that a black soldier didn't appear in the palace kitchen with some kind of delivery, so Maria Romana and Giorgio were not surprised to see them. True, deliveries had never been made at night before and the bearers never wore white jackets, but the two servants knew nothing and cared less about the uniform policy of the United States Army. As for the nocturnal delivery, Maria Romana and Giorgio were too busy to pay it much mind.

Kinney's party that night was a large one. Paris had fallen to the Allies a few days before and some fifty guests had been invited for a long frolic to commemorate this monumental milestone on the road to victory. Gabrielle, acknowledged now by everyone, save her father-in-law, to be Kinney's mistress and châtelaine of the palazzo, was sparkling, happy, and falling in love with her handsome young lieutenant.

Dinner had ended, coffee had been served, and Rufus and his two subordinates were serving brandy, whiskey, and port. Soon the fun would shift into high gear. There would be dancing in the *salone,* cards and dice in the drawing room, and passion in the bedrooms.

Around midnight, Maria Romana and Giorgio would serve a buffet with cold champagne and beer, to cool the dancers and fornicators and to calm the gamblers.

The two Italian servants scarcely looked up when Holt and his companions came into the kitchen. Maria Romana pointed a carving knife at a spot in a corner and told them to stack the boxes there.

Rufus was loading his tray with brandy snifters and crystal ashtrays. He looked nervous.

"Hey, Jimmy."

"How's it going, Rufus? How's the party?"

Rufus glanced at the baize-covered door and swallowed hard. "Swingin'. I hope you ain't going to be making no trouble for me, Jimmy."

"Don't worry, man. Don't worry. How do we look?"

Rufus stepped back and looked at the five, shaking his head and clicking his tongue. "You are the sorriest bunch of stewards I ever did see."

Holt grinned. "We're kinda new to the job, Rufus. Everybody ready?"

His four companions nodded.

"Okay." Holt started for the green baize door.

Giorgio looked up from the turkey he was carving. "Ma dov'è vai, eh?" he asked sharply.

"We gotta report to the lieutenant," said Holt. "He wants to talk to us."

Giorgio understood only one word—lieutenant—but it was enough. He grunted and returned to his task.

"Now let's go." The hallway ran the length of the first floor of the palace. It was wide and tiled, checkerboard fashion, in white and dark blue marble. Three chandeliers blazed, but the light failed to penetrate a few elaborately framed but rather murky landscapes hanging on the brocaded walls. To their left, a set of double doors opened into the *salone,* and the sounds of good cheer, louder now, echoed along the corridor.

The door to the study was locked. Holt pulled a short crowbar from the deep pocket of his fatigue pants and inserted the edge between the door and the frame, level with the lock, and leaned on the lever. The old wood creaked.

Leacock glanced nervously over his shoulder, toward the sound of the merrymaking.

"C'mon, Jimmy, c'mon."

Holt rocked the steel bar in the jam. "Alvin, you do it."

Whiteside stepped forward and put his full weight on the crowbar. The wood creaked, then shrieked and splintered. The five men froze and listened for footsteps. There were none.

"Okay," whispered Holt, "let's move it." They dashed into the room, Jimmy closed the door behind them, careful not to slam it, and then snapped on the lights. For a moment all the five men could do was stare dumbly at the abundance.

"Holy shit," whispered Holt.

"Lookit all this stuff."

"Man . . ."

"We can't take it all, Jimmy," said Sam Crosby. "We'll be here all night."

"No." Jimmy surveyed the boxes and bales. The liquor was too heavy, too bulky, too hard to conceal, as were the bolts of silk and cotton. Cigarettes were light but in relative abundance in the city. Too easy to replace. The drugs. They were packed in boxes no bigger than egg crates. Each man could take an armful of them.

"The morphine." Jimmy knelt down and quickly counted the boxes. "An even fifty. We'll take that. That'll make them sit up and take notice."

Biggs protested. "Morphine? What the fuck we do with morphine?"

"We ain't gonna do shit with it," said Holt quickly, "but *they're* gonna sell it. Worth a fortune, Biggsy, lot of hurt people out there. Listen, I can't explain now."

"What about this other stuff?" said Crosby. "Peni . . . peni . . ."

"Should we take that, Jimmy?" asked Stanley urgently.

"I don't know. If it's here it must be valuable." Holt teetered on the edge, indecisive, unable to make up his mind.

"It'll mean two trips," said Stanley.

"Too dangerous," said Biggs.

"Okay, forget it," said Holt. "Okay. This is the plan. You take the stuff down the front stairs to the truck. Then you come back up and we go out through the kitchen the way we come in. We gotta let them eyetie cooks see us leave."

"Let's get started," said Leacock. "I want out of here. Jimmy, what the fuck you doing?"

Holt was tugging at the drawers of the desk. "What's it look like? I'm breaking into this desk, that's what." He levered open the cash drawer, the old lock not putting up much of a fight. It pulled out of the wood like a rotten tooth. When he saw the money, he blinked, then whistled slow and low.

"What is it, Jimmy?"

"Money. A lot."

All at once the enormity of the black market struck him and he felt a sudden chill of fear. He hesitated a moment, his hand poised over the nest of bills.

"How much is there, Jimmy?"

"A lot. Thousands."

"Take it man," urged Crosby.

Holt jammed the bills into his pocket. Under the layer of money was a gun, an officer's heavy Colt .45. Without hesitating this time, he grabbed that, too, pulling up his shirt and nestling the gun between his belt and skin.

The other four were loaded and ready to go, heading for the door. Leacock, his arms filled with boxes, peered out, surveyed the long hall, and then darted, Biggs, Crosby, and Whiteside right behind him. They stopped at the top of the stairs.

"I'm gonna wait right here. Lookout. When you come back I'll let you know if the hall is clear."

"Right," whispered Leacock and led the way down the stairs.

"Jimmy!" whispered Biggs. "I can't hold 'em!" A box of morphine was sliding off the bulging pile he held in his broad arms.

Holt caught it. "I'll bring it. Move it."

Holt watched as they padded down the steps and then realized for the first time that he was panting, sweat was running down his face. He leaned against the cool wall and tried to slow his hot breathing and hammering heart.

Sounds of the party had traveled down the hall, but they had changed in pitch and tempo. The voices were dispersed through a number of rooms now, and louder, charged with liquor. There was lots of laughter.

A door opened at the far end, the party end, of the corridor and Holt had a split second to dart a step down the stairs and out of sight. Two people were coming down the hall, a man and a woman. The man was leading the woman by the hand. She was giggling. Holt could smell her scent and his cigar smoke.

"Come on, babe," said the officer, opening the door to a bedroom. "Time for a little exercise." He slammed the door behind him. Holt allowed himself to breathe again.

"Sssst, Jimmy . . ." The men were back, crouching on the stairs.

"Listen," whispered Holt, his voice hot and urgent, "gotta get the fuck outta here. There's an officer in the room across from Kinney's office. The party's spreading out. Half a dozen of 'em could come down here any minute. Gotta be quiet."

His four comrades nodded. They crept forward, stealing toward the kitchen door, Jimmy bringing up the rear. At the kitchen door he stopped and slapped his forehead.

"Shit, I forgot that box of morphine. It's on the stairs."

"Leave it," whispered Leacock.

"Can't. You go down to the truck and pull it round the corner. If I'm not down there in fifteen minutes, then scram."

"Got it," said Stanley.

Holt turned and tiptoed back the way he came. Just as he reached the top of the stairs a bedroom door opened.

"Boy."

Holt jumped and spun around. Standing in the doorway was the middle-aged officer Holt had narrowly avoided in the hallway a few minutes before. He had stripped to his underwear, a pot belly slung over the waistband of his OD skivvies. His dogtags nestled in a thick mat of wiry hair on his chest.

"What you doing here, boy?"

Holt's jaw clenched. "Nothin' sir . . ." He cast down his eyes.

"C'mere."

"Yassir." James Holt shuffled along the hall.

"You weren't spying through the keyhole, were you boy?"

Holt looked up and shook his head. "No, *sir.*"

"You're all sweaty, like you're worked up."

"I bin workin' in de kitchen, sir. I was goin' downstair for some fresh air, sir."

"Well shit on that, soldier, you're on duty, aren't you?"

"Yassir."

"Then go and get me a drink." The officer leaned into the bedroom. "Hey honey, you want a drink?"

"Si," said a muffled voice.

"Go and get me a bottle of bourbon and some ice. At the double, soldier."

"Sir, I ain't no steward, sir. I'm just for cleanin' up de dishes, sir. I'll send the steward, sir."

Anger streaked across the officer's drink-reddened face. "Jesus Christ! That's always how it is with you goddamn darkies! Always trying to avoid work. Lazy sons of bitches. No sir, soldier, *you* go and get me that whiskey and *you* bring it back. Got that?"

"Yassir."

"Move it." The officer stepped back into the bedroom and slammed the door.

Holt stormed back along the hall toward the kitchen. "Son of a bitch!" he hissed. "Shit!"

"Jimmy!" Rufus cried, "where you been?"

"Never mind, man, never mind. Just set me up a bottle of bourbon, an ice bucket, and two glasses. Shit!" He slammed his hand against the wall.

"Ma che cosa stai facendo?" demanded Maria Romana.

"Jimmy, what you playin' at?"

"Just do it, man, okay?"

"Jimmy," said Rufus plaintively as he filled the order, "I said I didn't mind helping, but you gotta to leave me cut outta the trouble. You hear?"

"Don't worry about it, Rufus. Just don't worry about it." Jimmy picked up the tray with both hands and backed through the baize door. At the entrance to the bedroom, he braced the tray against the door frame and tapped lightly with his free hand.

"Your drink, sir. I leave it out by de door, sir."

"Bring it in."

The low bedside lamp didn't cast much light, but there was enough to see the man stretched out on the bed. A woman lay next to him. She had tousled dark hair, and her big brown eyes were woozy, unfocused by the liquor she had already consumed, a cigarette drooped from her red lips. She had the sheet pulled up to cover her breasts, but a white bare leg was thrown out languidly.

"Evenin', ma'am."

"You keep your eyes to yourself, boy."

"Oh yas*sir.*" He put the tray down on the table on the officer's side of the bed.

"Okay. Now scram. And no more goldbricking."

"No, sir. Goodnight, sir."

Back in the hall, Holt dashed to the grand staircase, grabbed the box of morphine and headed, once again, for the kitchen. He skidded to a stop at the door and pressed his ear against the prickly green cloth. Beyond, muffled but recognizable, was a familiar voice. Kinney was in the kitchen, yelling at Rufus.

". . . all over the colonel's uniform," he said.

"Yassa, sorry. Won' happen agin, suh."

"Damn right it won't, Rufus. I do not want that man here again, do you understand me?"

"Yassuh, he gone, suh . . ."

Jimmy couldn't walk through the kitchen, not with a box of morphine in his hand. Maria Romana and Giorgio had seen a group of black men leave. It didn't matter if it were four or five; Holt doubted they were keeping track. He would go down the front steps and out.

At the top of the main staircase he stopped and listened just to make sure his escape path was clear. It wasn't. Footsteps were coming up the steps, towards him. Panic almost overcame him. He couldn't go back the way he came. He couldn't linger in the hall. Jimmy looked up the staircase to the next floor and then bounded up, taking the stone steps two at a time. He charged into the first room he found.

It was dark there, but enough moonlight came through the narrow windows for him to make out the outline of a huge bed. Exhausted and streaming with sweat, Jimmy Holt sat down on the edge of the bed, put the morphine on the floor at his feet, and put his head in his hands.

THERE WAS NO overtime for the Duke that night, not that he needed it now that Kinney paid him for the use of the palace; and while the rent was good, it was not enough to allow him to quit his job as a Benny. Besides, he needed the work, not just for the money it provided, but also to reassure himself that he was earning an honorable wage, doing his duty like a good paterfamilias, rather than just trading on a family legacy. And yet he was uneasy. He could not banish the feeling that, somehow, he was pimping.

Camillo paused on the *piano nobile* and cocked his head down the long hall, listening for a moment to the sounds of revelry. In a bedroom nearby he could hear a muffled squeal and a rhythmic thump as a headboard bumped against a wall. He shook his head and trudged wearily up the last flight of steps.

The Duke always looked in on Sandro before retiring. He

opened the door to the bedroom and turned on the low light. Holt jumped to his feet.

"Jesus Christ!"

"Who are you? What are you doing here?"

Sandro lay ashen and asleep in the middle of the large, wide bed. His left hand, stripped of nails, was hooked over the counterpane, his fingers split and tortured. The right side of his face was crumpled where his jaw had been broken and his teeth knocked out. His eyes were sunken deep and dark ringed, the skin thin and pale, so tight across his forehead that it seemed that the shadow of skull could be seen beneath.

"Who's that?"

"Be quiet," hushed Camillo, "you'll wake him."

"He looks sick. Real sick."

"He is very ill," whispered Camillo urgently. "You must go." He tried to push Jimmy toward the door, felt the gun in his belt and stepped back.

"Listen, I don't know who you are but I'm guessing you don't have anything to do with that cathouse downstairs . . ."

"Cathouse . . . ?" Camillo nodded. "Yes. You guess correctly," he said stiffly.

"But I have to get outta here and I can't go downstairs the way I came up. There another way out of here?"

"Are you a thief?"

Holt looked at the Duke. "Yeah. I'm a thief who steals from other thieves."

"What do you steal?"

"This." Holt picked up the box of morphine.

The Duke was tired after a long, hot day at work. His English failed him. "Dio mio . . . la morfina . . ."

"Yeah. Now how the hell do I get out of here? I'm kinda in a hurry."

The Duke could not take his eyes off the drug.

"I get it," said Holt, "you need some of this for your boy." Jimmy tore open the box and held out a half a dozen Syrettes. "Here, take these, man."

The Duke reached for them and then pulled his hand back. "I cannot take them. I haven't enough money."

"Fuck it, man, I'm giving it to you. I don't want money. You need 'em, take 'em."

Camillo took the little vials and put them on the night table. He squared his shoulders and extended his hand. "I am Camillo Sanseverio. Thank you, sir."

Holt took Camillo's thin hand and shook it. "Yeah, whatever you say. Now I gotta blow, man."

"Wait." The Duke fished in his jacket pocket and found one of the last of his calling cards, printed before the war. With an American-army-issue ballpoint pen he drew a slash through the small coronet printed in the lower right-hand corner of the card. "Take this, please."

"Fine." Holt jammed the card in his pocket with the money. "Now let's get going."

"There is another staircase," said Camillo. "I will show you to it."

At the servant's staircase, Camillo shook hands again. "Will you tell me your name?"

"You gonna turn me in?"

"Certainly not."

"My name's James Holt." He started down the stairs, then stopped. "But don't tell nobody."

"I give you my word."

"Good enough, man," said Holt, descending into the gloom.

Camillo listened to his footsteps and thanked God that at least one honorable act had been performed beneath his roof that night.

STANLEY LEACOCK AND the rest had just about given up hope when Holt appeared.

"I thought they got you, man. I thought you were dead for sure."

"I'm fine. Everybody okay?"

"Yeah," said Crosby.

"Where you been, Jimmy?"

"Long story, Alvin. Now let's get the fuck outta here."

The truck roared through the night, Jimmy wrestling the big vehicle down the narrow back streets. A few minutes later the five of them, bundles of morphine in their arms, presented themselves at another palace.

Lady Molly did not seem at all surprised to see them. "Dear boys," she said, opening the door. "Do come in. Put your parcels on the table. Heavens, there do seem to be a lot of them. You're just in time for some scotch I took off some fathead in the Guards. You know, I think he may have buggered my brother at school. Or perhaps the other way round. Vice versa, if you see what I mean. Never mind. Doesn't matter. Earl will be delighted to see you."

"What?" said Biggs.

"Hey, Molly, what's this?" Holt produced the *carte de visite* that the Duke had given him.

She held it close to her nose. "This is a visiting card, dear boy. Given you to you by Count Camillo Sanseverio. I don't think we know that one, do we Earl?"

"No," said Earl. "I don't think we do."

"But what's that little mark he made on it? Acted like it was a big deal."

"And so it is, dear boy. Striking the coronet like that means he's put himself on an equal footing with you, that his title doesn't matter. It's quite the mark of friendship, you know."

"Huh," said Holt. "I hardly met the man."

"You must have made quite an impression. Now do you all want drinks? Good. No, Alvin? Can't tempt you. Very well. Have you heard, my darlings? Paris has been liberated. Earl and I were saying perhaps we should go back, but I don't think we shall. Too many ghosts. And the French are such a sour lot and of course they're going to be far more sour than they ever were now the English and Yanks have pulled their fat from their fire once again. You know how they feel about us. And they'll be madly revising history, too; the most terrible scum will float up and say they were madly *anti-boche*. Still, it's nice to know one could go back if one chose to. They were always rather fond of Earl there, though, weren't they, darling?"

"Yes," said Earl.

"What did she say?" asked Crosby.

"Don't worry," said Alvin Whiteside. "She always talks like that."

17

When the last, sated, satisfied officer tottered down the stone steps of the Palazzo Sanseverio, Gabrielle and Kinney sat in the sewing room, discussing and dissecting the evening like a pair of social climbers or an ambitious couple plotting the husband's rise in the firm. Kinney was still annoyed that a glass of port had been upset on Colonel Hunnolt's uniform. Kinney had made a great fuss at the time even though the colonel had laughed it off. Hunnolt, in civilian life an insurance salesman, was not comfortable around servants and had wished that Kinney had not gone on so.

"He'll remember," grumbled Kinney, "and it makes me look bad."

"Don't be ridiculous, darling. It was an accident." They were sitting on the sofa, Gabrielle nestled under his shoulder. "He hardly noticed. It was nothing, he said so himself."

"He noticed."

"Everyone seemed to have a good time."

Kinney refused to be cheered. "Of course they had a good time. They always have a good time. That's the object of this exercise."

"You don't suppose they ever wonder how you manage it? They don't get suspicious?"

"They don't want to know. Besides, it's widely known that I come from quite a rich family. I suppose they imagine that my dear old dad sends me a little spending money from time to time."

"Charlie Hamilton told me that he had just written to your father telling him what a swell guy you are. That's what he called you, a swell guy."

"Charlie Hamilton wants to get in good with my father." He looked at her, smirking a little. "And why shouldn't he tell him I'm a swell guy. So I am."

"Of course, darling." She sat up and stroked his hair, but he pushed her hand away. He sipped from his snifter of brandy. It was Italian, not bad, but not French. "I can't wait till we liberate Cognac."

"Maria Romana is a wonderful cook, a genius. We never had a cook as good in the old days." Now that Gabrielle had reassumed her rightful place in the household she could afford to be magnanimous. "We must keep her on."

Kinney knew, instinctively, that the "we" didn't refer to the Sanseverio family as constituted in "the old days"; he also heard Gabrielle's unspoken "after the war," but he let it go. If Gabrielle thought he'd be taking her—ten years his senior, foreign, and, presumably, divorced—home to meet the family, she was mistaken. Dad was sure to think his son considerably less swell.

She yawned and stretched. "I supposed I'd better go and see to . . ." She pointed toward the ceiling.

"Yes, do that."

Gabrielle stood, corraled a stray wisp of hair, and sighed. "Oh, what a bore he is."

She presented her forehead for a kiss. Kinney brushed his lips across it, softly, tenderly. The gesture was curiously intimate and innocent. For a moment, she thought he might actually love her. He patted her cheek. "Don't fret, my sweet," he said.

Sandro was stirring restlessly in his bed when she entered his room, not quite awake, but far from his usual leaden stupor. When she turned on the light, his eyes fluttered open.

"Gaby . . ." he whispered and smiled his crooked, tortured smile. "There were people in my room. Here. Papa and another man." His eyes, usually dulled, showed sparks of life. She tried not to look at him, fussing with the bed clothes.

"You must have had a dream. You must sleep."

His hand sought hers. It was damp and cold, like a beef tongue on a butcher's slab. "Will you stay with me? Will you lie beside me for a while?"

Gabrielle fought to stop herself from drawing her hand away from his grasp. She forced herself to lean over him and kiss his cheek. His skin was damp too, his cheek lightly stubbled. Camillo bathed and shaved Sandro every morning; he brushed his teeth as well, but it seemed to do no good. His gums were discolored and bled slightly, his teeth decaying, part of the degenerative effects of doses of morphine. His breath was meaty and fetid, and her gorge rose when she smelled it, vaporous and clammy in her face. Instinctively, she pulled away.

"You must rest." She took a syringe from the drawer of the night table. Then she caught sight of the syrettes, standing in a row like toy soldiers. Gabrielle picked up one and held it to the light, gazing at it in wonderment. At first she felt joy, relief that Camillo had taken upon himself the procurement of his son's solace. It was the last of Gabrielle's duties and she would gladly give it up.

She pulled the protective sheath from the needle and prepared to plunge it into Sandro's arm.

"Wait," he pleaded, "I want to stay with you for a moment. I just want to look at you. My wife."

"You are in pain, Sandro, you must take this."

"No!" he said like a child refusing to eat his vegetables.

"Sandro," she said crossly, "it is very late. I am very tired."

As she took his arm, he said, slowly, "You are my wife."

"I am very tired," she said, spearing the vein.

CAMILLO HAD ALMOST objected when Kinney had chosen as his bedroom Sandro's own, but fearful of losing his tenant he had held his tongue. Austin liked the big sleigh bed with its high headboard, the ebony bureau, and the tall *armadio*. A cool night breeze always blew off the terrace.

Kinney was lying in bed, naked, lazily smoking a cigarette, when Gabrielle returned to their room.

"What's this?" She held up a morphine syrette.

"It's a morphine syrette. The latest thing. Drug and needle in one piece. Use then throw it away. Where did you get it?"

"The old fool found six of them somewhere." She put the vial down and reached behind her to unbutton her black silk dress. Kinney liked this moment, when the silk rustled to a soft pile at her feet and she stood almost naked in the warm, soft light. A stream of smoke trailed from his mouth. Then he sat up abruptly.

"Jesus Christ!"

"What is it?"

"Jesus Christ!" Kinney sprung out of the bed and pulled on a dressing gown. He scrabbled in the change and money clip on the dresser searching for his keys.

"What is it?"

"I've got to check something." He jammed his keys into the pocket of the bathrobe and pounded down the hall.

He didn't need the keys. When he turned on the lights he stopped, as the drivers had done, and stared dumbfounded. Then he ran to the desk.

"Jesus Christ!"

He met Gabrielle in the hall. "Austin, what is going on? What is the matter?"

He seized her by the shoulders and shook her. "Where does the old fool sleep?"

"Upstairs."

"Show me."

"Austin, what is happening?"

"We've been robbed, Goddammit."

Kinney didn't bother to knock. He pushed into Camillo's room, snapping on the light. The Duke awoke at once.

"What? What? Sandro?"

"Where the hell did you get the morphine, the syrettes?" Kinney grabbed Camillo by his nightshirt and yanked him upright, half pulling him from the bed. The Duke groped myopically for his glasses, but Kinney slapped them away.

"You don't need those, where the hell did you get it?"

"I . . . I found it."

"Don't give me that bullshit," Kinney yelled. "You stole it!"

"I am not a thief." He looked past Kinney to Gabrielle.

"I . . . I heard shouting," she stammered.

"Lieutenant Kinney," said the Duke, "I must ask you to leave this house at once."

"Never mind that, old man, tell me where you got this stuff."

"I told you. I found it."

"Yeah? Where?"

"On . . . on the steps."

"Jesus Christ." Kinney sat down on the bed. There had been close to twenty thousand in the desk, and who knew how much the morphine was worth.

"Why are you wearing my son's clothing?"

"Shuttup."

259

"Lieutenant Kinney, I don't think you have heard me. You must leave this house at once. Do you understand me?"

"Listen, old man," said Kinney, "I paid for this place, remember? If I leave, you'll have nothing. If I go, the AMG housing officer will find out you got room here for a few dozen people and that you've been renting space at black market rates, and I can prove it—you're the one who insisted on giving me a receipt, remember? You'll go to jail and what'll happen to your precious freak of a son then? So shuttup and let me think . . ."

A few minutes later he was at the phone in the study, dialing rapidly. "C'mon," he growled into the mouthpiece as the telephone rang ten then twenty times. Gabrielle stood in the doorway watching him, afraid of his anger.

"Lemme speak to Manganaro!"

A very sleepy Signor Fiorito found himself jolted to full wakefulness. "Manganaro, si. Sergente Manganaro, si, subito."

A full three minutes passed before Kinney heard Manganaro's angry voice come down the line. "This better be good," he croaked, "whoever the fuck you are."

"You listen to me, Manganaro, don't mess with me because if I found out you're behind this then you are a dead man, you understand me?"

"Who the fuck is this?"

"Listen, don't give me—"

"Lieutenant? Is that you? What the fuck is going on, sir?"

Kinney was silent a moment. "You don't know what I'm talking about?"

"On my mother's grave, sir."

"Well then brace yourself, Sergeant. We've been robbed."

On the third floor of the Hotel Palatino Splendido, Jimmy Holt heard Manganaro's anguished scream, "Jesus Christ!"

"RIGHT, THEN," YELLED Jones. "In a few days you gentlemen will be defending the honor of your company on the rugby field. Today, however, we are going to take a little peek at the skills you have already acquired. Together, for the last few weeks, we've learned the basics of this noble game. Today, you put them all together. Gentlemen, I have the honor to present to you the first fifteen, The Twenty-fourth, The South Wales Borderers."

Fifteen Welshman stared at fifteen black Americans.

"How are you, Yanks," said the captain of the Welsh side, a small man named Evans.

"Fine," said Whiteside.

"They don't look so tough," whispered Crosby.

"Mr. Holt, as Captain of the All Black Dragons, you have the privilege of tossing the coin. Lance Corporal Evans, as visiting captain, will make the call."

"Heads, Sergeant."

Holt flipped the coin high in the air and let it fall to the ground.

"Heads it is. Mr. Evans?"

"We'll receive the kickoff, Sergeant."

"Right, then!"

Just before the kickoff, Jones and Evans had a brief exchange.

"Don't worry, Sergeant," said Evans, "we'll go easy on your lads."

"Quite the opposite, Evans. They're good lads, but they need seasoning. Give them everything you've got. Play hard. Don't feel obliged to play fair. The Springboks won't."

"Righty-oh, Sergeant," said Evans in his sing-song voice. "I feel sorry for the buggers, then."

The All Black Dragons scored two tries and converted both for a score of ten points. The Welsh scored six. Final score: All Black Dragons 10, South Wales Borderers 30.

"THE WAY I see it," said Manganaro, "it's gotta be one of three things. Lorenzetti—"

"I never trusted that fuckin' guinea," spat Utterback.

"Why would he pull a crazy stunt like that?" asked Kinney.

"Yeah," put in McManus, "he's got a sweet deal with us. He pulls a thing like that and he's gotta know he's ruining a good thing."

"Maybe he knows something we don't. The AMG raised the bread ration, you know. Maybe this whole black market thing is over before it got started."

"Impossible, Manganaro," said Kinney flatly. "The bread ration was raised because it had to be raised. I heard last night that it cuts the AMG reserves to a three-day supply. They cut the milk ration to kids three to five and gave it to one- and two-year-olds. They're afraid of food riots. There's a confidential report out of Colonel Bizozero's office saying a fifth of the population has tuberculosis.

261

You know what aggravates tuberculosis? Malnutrition. Christ, the infant mortality rate is ten in a hundred."

"Jeez," said McManus.

"The black market is just starting in this town. Things are going to get a lot worse before they get better."

"Then who?" demanded Utterback. "Eddie, you said there were three possibilities."

"The niggers."

"I knew it! Those fuckers!"

"Oh come on, Sergeant. They wouldn't dare. There were twenty-five senior officers at my place last night. They wouldn't have the guts."

McManus put a cigar in his mouth and started chewing on it nervously. "Remember what Jimmy Holt said? He can be pretty determined when he puts his mind to it. I *knew* we shoulda taken care of the guy."

"Where is he? I'll fuckin' kill him!"

"You can't be serious, McManus."

"Besides, Eddie," said Utterback, "you guaranteed it wouldn't happen. You said it definitely would not happen."

Eddie shrugged. "So he's got bigger balls than I thought. I can't help it he's a nervy buck, can I?"

"Wait a minute," protested Kinney. "You can't tell me that some of the men broke into the palace and stole all the money and fifty crates of morphine while I was in the other room with twenty-five senior officers. Impossible."

"Shit's gone isn't it?"

"Yeah," said McManus, "and if they took it, where the hell is it? They couldn't have moved it into the billet last night without someone seeing something. Hearing something."

"What about maybe they sold it?"

"Oh for Christ's sake, Cal, *we* couldn't sell fifty crates of morphine without help from Lorenzetti. Naww, they got it stashed someplace."

Kinney was still unconvinced. "If they have it at all," he said.

"Maybe we oughta go and have a talk with that fuckin' Jimmy Holt."

"Cool down, Cal. We gotta stay cool."

"That fuckin' nigger wisenheimer."

"I'll talk to him," said Manganaro. "Just him and me."

"No rough stuff, Eddie," cautioned McManus. He hadn't forgotten the visit from the CID man on the first day they were in Rome. He didn't want another one.

"Naww, nothing like that."

"Sergeant, you said there were three possibilities. What's the third?"

"Maybe it was an inside job," said Manganaro evenly. "Maybe a certain lieutenant I know double-crossed us."

Kinney laughed. "Now why would a certain lieutenant you know want to do a thing like that?"

"For the money."

Kinney shook his head. "From the very start we've known one thing about this little operation of ours: that it was safe, virtually foolproof. It would be madness to jeopardize it for a few thousand dollars."

"Try fifteen," said Utterback, who had trouble imagining any sum greater.

"Gentlemen," said Kinney, his voice soft with sincerity, "I assure you, I had nothing to do with this."

"That's good enough for me," said McManus, who, despite an NCO's knowledge of officers, still trusted them, even a tainted one like Austin Kinney.

There was a timid knock at the door, Thorpe leaning just enough of his body into the room as was absolutely necessary. The four men stood.

"Good morning, sir," said Kinney, "we were just going over the disposition of supplies, sir. We're ah . . ."

"Don't let me interrupt you, Lieutenant. I wonder, could you find time to deal with this?" He proffered a piece of paper.

Kinney took it. "Yes, sir."

"That's all. As you were, men."

Kinney sat down and glanced at the piece of paper. Without looking up he asked, "McManus, how many units of morphine in the haul we lost?"

McManus rubbed his chin. "Let's see . . . fifty boxes. That's about seventy-five hundred."

Kinney sighed. "We're going to have to get them back, somehow. The sooner the better."

"What is it, sir?"

"An audit notice. Routine it says."

263

"Oh brother . . ." said McManus. "When it rains, it pours. That's my motto."

"ALL RIGHT, LADS," said Jones, "you've seen how rugby is played and you did well. You scored two tries against an experienced, hard side. Much better than me and Llewellyn expected. Isn't it, Terry?"

"Marvellous, Sar'nt."

"Sarge," said Leacock, "those guys played dirty. In the scrums they was kicking and even biting. What the hell kind of game is that?"

"That's rugby, son. Now this is our last practice before the game. Let's make it count. On the field, boyos."

A COUPLE OF hours later, James Holt and Stanley Leacock were back in their room in the Hotel Palatino Splendido. They had showered and put on clean uniforms and were heading out for the night. Manganaro knocked on the door. He was not unexpected.

"Have a word with you, Jimmy? You got a minute?"

"What you want to talk to me for, Sarge?"

"Just a friendly chat, like. Beat it, Stanley."

"I'll hang around, it's okay with you, Sarge."

"I said, beat it."

Stanley looked at Holt, who nodded. "That's okay, Stanley, I'll catch you later at the Broadway."

Manganaro sat on the bed, slapping his cunt cap against his knee. "So," he said, "tomorrow's the big day. How you feeling? Feeling good? You gonna have a good game? You gonna win? I got a sawbuck riding on you guys, you know."

" 'Preciate it."

"I hear there's gonna be a big crowd. Lots of our guys, lots of their guys, lots of guineas. Gonna be a big day for you guys."

"Yeah."

"Just one thing bothers me . . . something I'd like to get cleared up before, you know."

"What's that, Sarge?"

"What you think, Jimmy? You're a bright boy. Sorry, bright man. Fella. Why do you think I want to talk to you? Got any ideas, maybe, Jimmy?"

"Nope."

"Why don't you look me in the eye when you say that, Jimmy? C'mon, look me in the eye."

Holt looked him in the eye, his gaze steady and unafraid.

"I don't know why you're here, Sarge."

Manganaro giggled. "The balls on this kid! *Sure* you do, Jimmy. You know, I gotta tell you, you're sorta playing with fire here, you know. What you done, where I come from, the people I do business with, a guy like you, lands up dead."

"Yeah? What did I do exactly?"

"But you see, 'cause I'm an understanding kind of guy and because you're young and inexperienced and all, I'm gonna make you a deal. You give back all the shit and all the money and we'll forget the whole thing ever happened. No hard feelings. Now, I consider that pretty reasonable. What you say? Deal?"

"You saying I stole something from you? Is that it? Man, you are crazy."

Manganaro's short fuse had burned its length. He sprung off the bed and pushed Jimmy back against the wall, his fist under his chin. "Don't fuck with me. Don't fuck with me, nigger. I know you stole the shit. You mess with me and you'll end up in a fuckin' box. You understand what I'm saying?"

Holt pushed away Manganaro's fist. "You listen to me. I'm done taking shit from you, fuckin' two-bit gangster. Do you get that, man? You are done fuckin' with me. With us."

"Big man, oh, big man. What you gonna do, Jimmy? Fuck me up? Put me in the fuckin' ground? You better make sure you got the balls for making threats. I know it was you, Jimmy. Now tell me where the shit is before I lose my temper."

"How do you know it was me?"

"What was it the man said? Just because I'm in the army doesn't mean I'm stupid. You said that, Jimmy. Works for me too, you know. Coupla days ago you come and talk about being cut in. Then our shit gets stolen. Who else could it be, you fuck?"

Holt shoved Manganaro away, but Eddie kept at him, standing over him like a hectoring parent. "Can't think of an answer to that, huh, Jimmy? No snappy comeback from this nigger. Don't want to talk to your old sergeant? What's the matter, Jimmy. Stuck?"

"I ain't stuck, Sarge. I'm ignoring you."

"You little fuckin'—" Manganaro threw himself at Holt and almost immediately wished that he had not. Jimmy was stronger and younger and just as determined. Eddie tried to butt him with his head and got two swift, iron-hard jabs to the stomach in return. Manganaro doubled over, wretching and gagging. Holt leaned down until his mouth was level with Eddie's ear.

"Okay, Manganaro, listen up. You want your shit back? This is the deal. We keep half the money. You get all the morphine back. We don't want it. Every man in the depot gets an extra fifty a week. And you'll get the fuck off our backs. No more coons, no more niggers, no more darkies. We're your partners now."

"Go fuck yourself. You go and fuck yourself." Manganaro managed to stand upright. His eyes were dull with hatred and pain. He cradled his stomach as if holding a baby.

"Think about it," said Holt. "Talk it over with the other guys. You tell me your answer after the game tomorrow." Holt opened the door. "You know, I'm looking forward to that game. Kicking whitey's ass could get to be a habit with me."

"Fuck you!"

"Awww sarge, that's no way to talk. Ain't you gonna wish us luck?"

18

Word of the rugby match had spread throughout the city, so by game time a crowd several hundred strong had assembled at the Circo Massimo. Supporters of the All Black Dragons were assembled on the grassy verge on the right of the track, Springbok supporters on the left.

Sergeant Jones had seen to it that his own South Wales Borderers were there in force to cheer on his side, and large portions of the other American black units in the city had shown up, too. Poletti would have been gratified by the number of Italians present, curious and starved for any kind of entertainment. The crowd was further swelled by dozens of American soldiers with no money, but plenty of time to kill on an August Saturday afternoon.

Jones had cajoled the British Army into erecting goal posts and had managed to get the field marked. Officials came from a Lancashire regiment. The Americans contributed a brass band, some folding chairs, and a squad of military police.

A few Italian vendors worked the crowd, selling melting ices flavored with white sugar stolen from the various armies in town; there were squadrons of shoeshine boys, beggars, and whores. There was a marked difference between this crowd and the men who had assembled a few weeks before in the Royal Opera House. Being out of doors at a sporting event made the throng less restless, less belligerent; and even the flagons of wine being passed from hand to hand seemed to make the crowd festive rather than bellicose. The brass band ground and puffed like a steam engine through "The Trolley Song," though the Welsh, preferring their own music, were attempting to drown it out with throaty renditions of "Abide With Me," and "Men of Harlech."

Thorpe and Van Zyl sat on the sidelines chatting amiably, both relieved that the cloud that had hung over their careers and their units was about to lift. Lieutenant Karstens, suited up to play, was disappointed to see that Kinney was not.

"You're not playing?"

"Don't be absurd," snorted Kinney.

JONES GATHERED HIS team around him. "Right then," he said, "try to remember everything I've told you, but if you forget it, just remember this: Attack! Attack! Attack!"

"Got it," said Holt.

"If you get the ball close to their line, get it to Whiteside and let him break across. All right? Wait a minute." He looked at the circle of faces. "Where the fuck *is* Whiteside?"

WHITESIDE HAD BEEN the last to leave the hotel. He had gotten into his kit and clattered down the street toward the racetrack. As he passed the depot, Utterback emerged.

"Hey, Whiteside. Get over here." He slurred his words slightly—he had been drinking. Utterback's usual first stop on his way to work in the morning was the wine shop of Via Buccimazza. He had a gun, Manganaro's gun, thrust into his belt, and he toyed lightly but clumsily with a crescent wrench.

"Can't, Sarge. I'm gonna be late for the game."

"Fuck that. Get in here, I got a little job needs doing. And I think you're just the man for the job."

"Sarge, the *game*." Far off they could hear the thump and crash of the brass band.

"Over here! At the double!"

Whiteside gritted his teeth and ran into the garage. "I gotta hurry, Sarge. Sergeant Jones'll be awful mad if I'm late."

"Don't worry about it, Whiteside." Utterback tapped the wrench in the palm of his hand, like a cop itching to use his billy. "I just wanted to talk to you, boy."

"Don't you want to see the game, Sarge?"

"Sure . . . sure . . ." He moved in close. "Whiteside. That's a funny name for a big buck like you. I always wondered, just which is your white side, Whiteside?"

Alvin smiled nervously.

"I asked you a question. Which is your white side, Whiteside? Ain't you gonna tell me?"

"Don't know, Sarge."

"Doan know, Sarge," mimicked Utterback. "You ain't too smart, are you?"

"Sarge, the *game* . . ."

"I said, you ain't too smart, are you, boy?"

Whiteside looked down at the oily floor of the garage. "I guess not, Sarge."

"But you're smart enough to tell where the shit you niggers stole is, right?"

Whiteside shook his great head. "I don't know what you're talking about, Sarge."

"I doan know what you talkin' 'bout, Sarge," moaned Utterback. He shoved Whiteside hard, pushing him back into the depot.

"Hey!"

"C'mon, c'mon." Teeth clenched, Utterback poked Whiteside in the stomach with the handle of the wrench. "You gonna tell me? You gonna do the smart thing for once in your life?"

"Why you picking on me, Sarge?"

"I want to know where the money is."

"I don't know nothing about no money."

"You don't, huh?" Utterback jammed the wrench savagely into Whiteside's stomach. "Sure you do."

"You hurtin' me, Sarge."

"Hurt you? Fuck no! I'm not hurting you. Nothing hurts you fuckin' niggers." He thrust the wrench into his belly again. "That don't hurt, does it boy?"

"Sergeant, please!"

"Sergeant, please!" squealed Utterback. "That don't hurt. "This'll hurt." He slammed the wrench lengthwise into Utterback's stomach. The blow staggered the big man.

"Owww, Sarge. Cut it out, *please*, Sarge."

"Now tell me!" Utterback raised the long wrench like a club. Whiteside threw up his hands to protect himself.

"I don't know nothin', Sarge, please . . ."

Utterback swung, hitting Alvin a glancing blow on the shoulder. As he struck a second time, Whiteside's hand shot out and grabbed the wrench, stopping it in flight, and pushing Utterback away. The sergeant stumbled a few steps, slipped in a pool of oil scum, and tumbled to the concrete floor. He came up laughing.

"Oh, oh, oh, you done it now, boy. You done it now. You know what you done? You just struck your superior. Six years in the stockade, you know that? That's what's coming to you."

"Sarge," pleaded Whiteside, his voice high and tight with fear. "You hit me with the wrench. I just pushed you. Please, Sarge . . ."

"You are in trouble now. Now *tell me.*" His voice echoed off the parked trucks.

"I don't know nothin'."

"That's really too bad, Alvin, it really is. 'Cause if you'd told me, I guess I would just forget about what you just did."

"I didn't do nothin'." Whiteside began to cry, big round tears, fat like grapes, rolled down his cheeks.

"Big fuckin' baby. C'mon." Utterback shoved him toward the rear of the warehouse. "C'mon. Move it."

"What you doin', Sarge?" said Whiteside through a veil of tears.

"I'm putting you in custody till I can get an MP to put you under arrest."

"What you doing this for, Sarge? Please, Sarge . . ."

Utterback pulled the pistol from his belt and pointed at Whiteside's head. "March, soldier."

"This ain't right."

"Shuttup and move."

"Please, Sarge."

Utterback yanked open the door of the freezer. Frigid air streamed out, clouds of condensation billowing. "Come on. Get in there."

"Sarge . . ."

Utterback cocked the gun. "Am I gonna have to blow your head off? You sit in there a while, while I think about whether or not to hand you over to the MPs. Get in. It won't kill you. You do some thinking too. You think about what you want to tell me. Get in!"

Alvin looked into the freezer as if into a tomb. "You ain't gonna call the MPs?"

"I don't know, I'll think about it. Get in."

"What about the game?"

"Get in. I'll be back in a minute."

Alvin Whiteside took a tentative step into the freezer, bending down to avoid striking his head. Utterback shoved him hard and slammed the door.

"Sarge, please." Whiteside's voice was muffled. "Please, Sarge. It's dark in here." There was a long paused. "Sarge, the *game* . . ."

"Fuck the game," mumbled Utterback. He walked out of the garage, rolled down the heavy metal door, and locked it.

THE BRASS BAND had run through its repertoire and was back on "The Trolley Song" again. The once-happy crowd was growing restive now. Thorpe and Van Zyl had run out of things to say. Thorpe wanted a drink. Van Zyl looked as if he wouldn't have minded one either. Catcalling had broken out.

"The fuckin' munts took one look and are so scared they won't take the field."

A Welsh private cupped his hands around his mouth and yelled back. "That's because they were promised a match with human beings, not you fuckin' apes." The South Africans were, almost to a man, bruisers.

"WHO SAW HIM last?" demanded Jones.

"No one was really paying attention, Sarge."

"Fuck! Look, I'm going to go have a chat with the ref. Jimmy, you run back to the billet and see if you can find him. Did you have any kit left over?"

"There's some. What for?"

"Because if you can't find Whiteside I'm going to ask the ref if we can play Llewellyn. You game, Terry?"

Llewellyn looked over at the South Africans and nodded. "Yer."

"Good lad. Off you go, Jimmy."

Holt raced across the Circo Massimo towards the depot. Utterback had just reached the edge of the playing field.

"Hey, Sarge. You see Alvin?"

"He ain't with you?" said Utterback innocently.

"No."

"Took a powder, I bet."

"Damn." Holt kept running, down the Via di San Teodoro and into the Via Foraggi, passed the depot to the Hotel Palatino Splendido. Fiorito, no rugby fan, was slumped behind the reception desk reading that day's *Il Messaggero*.

"You seen Alvin?"

Fiorito looked over the top of his newspaper. "Cosa?"

"Alvin, man, Alvin. You know, big like this? Tall? Oh fuck it!" Jimmy charged up the stairs and into the room Alvin shared with Ernest Biggs. Empty. He raced back into the hall and stopped.

"Alvin!" he shouted. "Where the hell are you?"

ALVIN WHITESIDE PUT his shoulder to the freezer door and slammed his weight against it. There was a dull boom, but the heavy door didn't budge. Not even Whiteside's great strength could dent it.

"Oh mama," whispered Alvin. The tears froze on his face and crackled like glass.

THE BRASS BAND was doing its best, improvising "Little Brown Jug," when Holt got back to the playing field. There were over a thousand people now crowding the sidelines of the Circo Massimo. The Welsh soldiers had abandoned hymns and were singing, to the tune of "Onward Christian Soldiers," "Lloyd George knew my father . . ."

"No sign of him, eh?" said Jones, "well, ref says we've got five minutes to field a side or forfeit." He grabbed the rugby clothes from Holt and tossed them to Llewellyn. "Come on, Terry, time to get your togs on."

"I guess we ain't the All Blacks anymore," said Stanley Leacock.

THERE WAS A loud, rousing, extended cheer when the two teams finally took the field. Holt and Karstens met at the halfway line and the ref tossed the coin. The All Black Dragons were considered the home team, so Karstens called.

"Heads."

The coin, a heavy British half crown, thumped and bounced on the ground.

"Tails," shouted the ref. "All Blacks?"

"We'll receive the kick, Sergeant," said Holt.

"Right then, gentlemen," said the ref, a British sergeant major with a Lancashire accent so thick you could ice skate on it. "Fair play. Shake hands."

Karstens and Holt shook hands. "Good luck, you fuckin' munt bastard, you're going to need it."

"Eat shit, whitey. I hope you already got all the babies you want, man, 'cause after the first scrum there's just going to be a bloody hole where your dick used to be."

Karstens turned bright red. "Fuckin' kaffir!"

"What did you do with Whiteside, man? Scared of him, huh?"

"I'm not scared of any munt bastard."

"None of that," roared the ref. "I'm not having that. You two lads want to be sent off now? Right then. Get on with it."

A great shout went up at the kickoff. Jimmy Holt, playing fullback, caught the ball deep in his own territory, near his goal line. He raced forward ten yards, a great herd of South Africans lumbering toward him, his own attacking line fanned out to his left. Then he slammed on his brakes, set, and cocked his arm as if to throw an American football forward pass.

"No!" shrieked Jones from the sidelines. "Not forward!"

But Jimmy didn't throw. He dropped the ball behind him to Stanley Leacock, who scooped it up and, with the entire right side of the field as empty as a prairie, danced down the sideline and planted the ball under the Springbok goal line.

The All Black Dragon crowd erupted, screaming, yelling, shouting. The Springboks, along with Jones, Llewellyn, and the officials, just stared.

"What the bloody hell was that?" shouted Jones.

"Statue of Liberty!" yelled an American serviceman in the crowd.

Sam Crosby took the kick and converted the try. All Black Dragons 5, Springboks 0.

ALVIN WHITESIDE PACED back and forth in the frigid black. His teeth chattered and his breathing was labored. His skin felt dry and course. He shook his head to clear it of an overpowering drowsiness. His arms and legs felt as heavy as anchors.

Hopefully, he said, "Sarge? Please let me out."

THE FIRST SCRUM was a stew of sweating bodies, foul breath, and curses. The men, yoked together like teams of oxen, grunted and spat. Unshaven cheeks rasped rough like wire brushes. A callused white hand reached out of the mess and grabbed at the All Black hooker, Humphrey Joyce, snatching at his balls.

"Fuckin' homo!" screeched Joyce.

Holt, prop, kicked out at the wall of shins in front of him. The hard toe of his boot struck bone.

"Aynah!" yelled one of the opposing line. "Jou swarte tater!"

"Fuckin' assholes!"

"Ek jou bont en blou slaan, kaffir."

"Fuck you, jack."

"Doodmak!"

"Eat shit, whitey."

The ball was released into the narrow channel of legs and the great beast heaved. The South Africans surged, bullying over the Dragons. Llewellyn dug in as eighth man.

"Hold them," he growled, "fuckin' hold them, All Blacks . . ."

But they couldn't. The Springboks bore down and broke the American scrum, which collapsed.

"Skrumskakel!" shouted Karstens.

The South African scrum half shot the ball to his attacking wing and the offensive line formed and charged. While Holt and the rest of the team tried to sort themselves out, Terry Llewellyn was up, off and running. He caught the Springbok wing just ten yards from the All Black goal line. His arms encircled the attacker's legs and brought him down. The South African's legs jerked, kicking out, catching Llewellyn's jaw. They hit the ground together and the Welshman saw his chance to hit back. His sharp elbow speared the wing in the stomach. The ball popped out of the man's grasp and rolled out of bounds.

"Fokin' kaffir boettie."

"Cunt tooth."

"Eh?"

"Line out!" shouted the ref.

The two teams lined up at right angles to the touch line, two unruly queues. Elbows jerked out like wings.

"Jimmy," ordered Llewellyn, "you take it."

Holt faced the two lines of men. The rugby line out is not unlike the basketball tip-off. The ball was to be thrown in, shaded, if possible, toward one side. The air would be filled with hands scrabbling for the ball. Instead of the usual rugby toss, slung low from the belt, Jimmy cocked his arm behind his head, football style, and fired a deadly accurate pass to Ernest Biggs at the end of the All Black line. Biggs scrambled a yard or two downfield before being stopped, going down in a welter of South Africans. Someone stepped on his hand and someone else kicked him in the side. He brought his knee up sharply until it connected with solid flesh.

The ball was gone. A Springbok back was racing downfield, Holt and Leacock on his tail.

"Gaan! Gaan!" screamed a South African.

"Stop 'im!"

Holt caught up, but was smashed away by a murderous handoff from the runner. He pitched forward on his face. Leacock dove but grabbed only two wide armfuls of air and then hit the ground. He saw only the ball carrier's heels power him across the goal line. Stanley pounded the dirt.

"Son of a bitch!"

The pressure that Holt and Leacock had put on the runner had forced him to ground the ball in the extreme right-hand corner of the All Black goal. The conversion would have to be attempted at a tricky oblique angle twenty-five yards out.

"Stelskop!" yelled Karstens.

"Pressure," bellowed Jones. "Pressure, All Blacks."

They lined up behind their goal line as a burly South African placekicker bore down on the ball. The instant his toe touched the ball, the All Blacks rushed forward. Stanley jumped as high as he could and managed to get a finger on the ball, deflecting it an inch or two—enough, though, to alter its flight a crucial fraction. The ball bounced off the goalpost and caromed out of play.

All Black Dragons 5, Springboks 3.

"LOOK AT THEM boys," said McManus gleefully. "They can fuckin' *play* this game. They're really in there fighting it out with them fuckers. Can you fuckin' believe it?"

"They don't like to be called boys," said Manganaro.

"Yeah, well, you know what I mean."

"I hope they get creamed," said Utterback.

LADY MOLLY, AN elaborate, feathered hat on her head, looking like an exotic bird, stood on the sidelines with Earl Talker, who leaned on a shooting stick. They passed a flask of Pimm's between them.

"You know, Earl, I haven't a *clue* what's going on."

"YOUR CHAPS ARE certainly doing well," said Van Zyl graciously through clenched teeth.

"Yes," said Thorpe. "To be quite honest with you, I'm quite surprised."

"Ja," said Van Zyl. "So are we."

KINNEY STIFLED A yawn and glanced at his watch.

SOMETIMES THE SYMMETRY of life surprised Farfalla with its odd order. Sports did not interest him, but the last sporting event he had attended bore a curious relationship to this one. It had been a junior varsity game at Harvard Stadium, the Crimson versus Dartmouth. He had gone because his Uncle Iggy, with whose family Manny roomed in East Boston, had said he wanted to see a football game, to see the college boys play. Iggy had been in the United States for thirty years, but sitting in the stands he looked as if he had just stepped off the boat.

He wore a dark suit, a white shirt buttoned up to his chin, and a beret. He puffed a Perodi throughout the game, turning to his nephew periodically to ask complex questions about the sport in a thick Sicilian dialect, questions Manny could not have answered in any language.

Iggy had enjoyed the game and conceived a love of Harvard teams that would last for the rest of his life. Farfalla had been cold and bored, but apart from Iggy he remembered two things about the game. One was Dick Harlow, the patrician head football coach. On hearing a flood of invective issuing from the mouth of a Harvard player—muffed catch—Harlow had turned to his assistant, Henry Lamarr and said, "Henry, Henry, that *can't* be one of our boys, could it?"

The other thing that Farfalla remembered was that Austin Kinney had been there, looking warm and prosperous on the sidelines. He wore a camel-hair coat, smoked a cigarette, had a fresh-faced blonde on his arm and a silver flask in his pocket. And here he was again, at a sporting event four years and half a world away from that crisp Cambridge fall. Kinney was standing a few yards away from Farfalla, as oblivious to his existence now as he had been in 1940.

ALVIN WHITESIDE SAT in the dark, his big legs drawn up to his chest, as if he was trying to make himself as small as possible. His fingers were so numb he couldn't feel them. Frost had formed in his hair. His ears ached in the cold. His eyes drooped in a suffocating fatigue and his mind wandered, ambling through sleepy dreams and fond, fuzzy thoughts of home.

THE SHOCK OF being behind in the score to a bunch of black men, the shock of being even scored on by blacks, the shock of even *playing* blacks, was beginning to wear off. The Springboks were settling down now, flexing their muscles and their greater skills, dominating the midfield and punching holes in the All Black Dragon defense.

Llewellyn drop-kicked a return, and a big but nimble South African took the ball back to the halfway line before being brought down. Jimmy knew this man was trouble. He wasn't slow like the other big men; his strong legs whipped like sprung steel. Jimmy tackled him a little higher than was strictly necessary, managing to land a good mashing shot in the man's testicles. He toppled and curled.

"Aynah! Teelbals! Fok!"

There was an outraged roar from the South African spectators and a huge, delighted cackle of laughter from the Welsh.

"That's taught him!"

The ref blew his whistle and he came running up to Holt, red-faced. He spat the whistle out. "What the fuck are you playing at, lad?"

"Rugby," said Holt.

"You deliberately—"

"I tackled the man. If I didn't do it right, don't blame me. I never played this game before."

"Send him off!"

"Kill the kaffir!"

"I'm warning you," said the ref. "I'll be watching you. Any more of that nonsense and you're off!"

"Yeah, sorry about that."

When it became apparent that Holt was not going to be ejected from the game a howl of indignation sprang from the South African ranks.

"Skeidsregter kaffir boettie jong!"

The Springbok left center pointed at Holt threateningly. "Jou gaal sal waai, kaffir."

"Talk English, motherfucker."

"Hy is 'n kind des dood," yelled the right wing.

"Fuck you, piece of shit."

"This will stop!" ordered the ref. He blew his whistle. "Resume play."

They were back in the scrum now. Joyce and the South African hooker dueled for the ball, slashing kicks and bruising shins. A hand snaked around the head of Sam Crosby, grabbing one of his ears and twisting it.

"Motherfucker," said Crosby to the other prop forward. "Let go."

"Jy sal dit kry, kaffir."

"Oh yeah," growled Crosby, "try this on for size, white boy." Crosby slammed his own hard head into the face of the prop forward. Joyce hooked the ball, Llewellyn took it, and the scrum broke. When the rubble of arms and legs cleared, Crosby's victim was lying mid-field, holding his face, blood streaming through his fingers. The ref looked suspiciously at Crosby as he trotted by.

"He slipped," Crosby explained.

Llewellyn was tackled twenty yards from the Springbok goal line, but before he went down he got the ball off to Holt, who charged upfield. He was doubled over the ball, football style, slipping it to Leacock, a perfect quarterback reverse. Holt was tackled.

"Hey! Ref!" Holt raised his empty arms. "I don't have the ball. Get off me, man." He shoved his tackler aside.

"Waar is die bal, kaffir?"

"He's got it." Holt pointed to Leacock, all alone, running across the Springbok goal line. All Blacks 8, Springboks 8.

MANNY FARFALLA KNEW all about Austin Kinney; most Harvard men of that year did. Farfalla was fascinated and appalled by him, loathing his easy charm, his money, the absence of struggle in his future or want in his past.

Manny had worked hard to get to Harvard; study and perseverance were second nature to him. The first time he had heard of

Harvard he had determined to be educated there, working at it single-mindedly, against the jibes of his classmates, the brown uncomprehending eyes of his mom and pop, and the gentle discouragement of his teachers, who warned him against "setting his sights too high."

To go to the best college in America meant you were the best. It meant joining a brotherhood of scholars in a bastion of achievement. Of course, he was not naive, he knew all about "college boys," but they were the stuff of jokes and comic songs by Fred Waring and the Pennsylvanians. There would be some at Harvard, of course, but they would be disdained by the men who deserved to be there, be your name Farfalla or Finkelstein or Phipps.

The truth had come as something of a shock. Farfalla, a brain, was removed from the stuff and sinew of the school, by his name, his accent, by his own excellence. He would hear about, but never meet, the Saltonstall who had a barber's chair in his living room in Claverly Hall, the Lathrop who swallowed that first lore-inspiring goldfish, the Lodge who smoked a hookah. Of all the gilded youth, Harvard, class of '41, none was so brightly burnished as Austin Kinney. His drinking, his money, his girls, even his car—a sixteen-cylinder Marmon—were legendary. Farfalla watched him in the classes they shared—Sorokian's sociology, Matthiesen's lit, Hauge's econ and stat. He lolled and smirked and scraped by with C's.

They spoke once. Manny, hearing that one of the downtown Boston clubs, the Bruce, needed part-time banquet waiters, had gone to Louisburg Square in search of employment. Kinney was emerging as Farfalla innocently presented himself at the front door. Austin, in poor humor after his twice-yearly lunch with Lex, who was in town to confer with the black-suited bankers of State Street, had scarcely glanced at him.

"Domestics round the back," he had said.

THE BLOOD SEEMED thick and turbid in Whiteside's veins and his heart beat slow and faint. He felt a calm, resigned well-being, a slow passage of care. Gradually, he fell into a deep, serene sleep.

IN FIFTEEN SHORT minutes, the game changed dramatically. It was as if the All Black Dragons' initial enthusiasm for the game had evaporated. Three times they lost the ball in confused, disorderly, bloody scrums and three times the South Africans scored and converted.

Score at the half: Springboks 23, All Black Dragons 8.

JONES HAD FIVE minutes to rally his forces. He was not the kind of coach who screamed and berated. His voice was calm.

"You've played bloody well, better than anyone could have expected. I'm bloody proud of you, but there's still forty minutes of rugby left. Now, there are three things you're going to have to do. Are you listening, boyos?"

"Yeah," they said.

"One, get the ball to Terry as much as you can. He's the fastest wing out there. He's a professional, remember. They're getting tired and slipshod, but he isn't. Get the ball to him and he can score. Two, Jimmy, you know any more American tricks? The first one gave me heart failure, but it worked."

"I been thinking about that. How 'bout this. You know how we're supposed to pass the ball down the line when we're rushing? Well, there's nothing in the rules that says I can't throw a lateral along the line, not to the next guy, but to Terry or Stanley at the end of the line. The fuckers are going to be going for the second or third man, not the end, see?"

"Bloody dangerous, Sarge," said Llewellyn, "the ball in the air like that."

"You just be ready, man. It'll work."

"What's the third thing?" asked Crosby.

"You've got to provoke a penalty. Those fuckers are browned off, see. They expected it to be a walkover, but it isn't. They may be winning, but they wanted to slaughter us. They haven't. When you're close in goal get a penalty, make them angry, see, make them make a mistake. Karstens looks pretty bothered, try him. Okay?"

"Got it, coach."

"You all right, Humphrey? You're doing all right in the scrum?"

"One of them grabbed my balls, Sarge, right in the scrum."

"Next time, use your knees, bach. Knee him in the bollocks, push them up his throat. Don't wait for him to do it to you."

"Okay, coach."

"Right then, gentlemen. Let's play rugby."

THE TEAMS TOOK to the field, drawing thunderous applause from both sides. The crowd was bigger now, over two thousand strong, a huge mélange of forces and units, whites and blacks.

The South African fullback received the kick and blasted upfield. He passed off to the fly half, who rocketed the ball over to his inside center, who ran smack into Sam Crosby. It was like running into a parked truck. Both men went down, the ball wobbling free.

Llewellyn was right there, on the ball. He wheeled and started for the Springbok goal, Holt, Leacock, and Joyce fanning out beside him.

"Aanvrag!" shouted Karstens, running in hot pursuit.

Llewellyn didn't pass off, he didn't have to. There was no one in front of him. He flat-handed Karstens and burst across the Springbok line. Crosby converted.

Springboks 23, All Black Dragons 13.

MANNY FARFALLA HAD maneuvered his way through the crowd until he was standing right next to Austin Kinney. At the score, he turned to him.

"Quite a game, eh, Lieutenant?"

"If you like this sort of thing," said Kinney.

THE NEXT SCRUM was brutal, a seething, flailing mess of grunts, punches, and kicks. As soon as Humphrey Joyce bent down to lock heads he brought his knee up sharply, feeling the satisfying squash of the opposing hooker's genitals.

"Aynah!"

"Fuckin' homo."

Joyce hooked the ball to the scrum half who whipped it to Holt who faked a pass to Stanley. Jimmy dug in and ran five, then ten, then fifteen yards. Karstens brought him down, kidney-punching as he went. Holt got up slowly. He noticed a wedding band on Karsten's ring finger.

"Hey Karstens. I fucked your wife."

"What!" screamed Karstens.

"You know what? She just loves to suck black cock. She told me, 'Jimmy, I just love to suck black fuckin' choad.' She's probably down there in Africa doing it right now. Lot of black dick in Africa, but not enough for your fuckin' wife. Horny bitch."

Karstens forgot where he was. "You bastard," he yelled and

swung a wide roundhouse right at Holt. Jimmy pulled just enough of his body out of range, catching only a small piece of the punch, but went down with a great, theatrical show of pain.

The South African crowd groaned. Karstens had just punched an opposing player in front of a couple of thousand witnesses *and* the ref. Jones screamed apoplectically from the sidelines.

"Ref! Ref! Did you see that! Send the bastard off!"

The referee came pounding over to Jimmy, like the cavalry, his whistle tweeting like a deranged sparrow. He pointed toward the sidelines and spat out the whistle.

Holt smiled in the dust and cradled his head. "Owwww," he wailed, writhing on the ground.

"Off!" barked the ref. "Get the fuck off my pitch!"

"But ref . . . but ref . . . He insulted my wife."

"I don't give a damn! Off!"

Karstens hung his head in shame and trotted slowly for the sidelines. As soon as he was off the field, Holt sprung to his feet and dusted himself off. Jones was delighted. They were a man up on the Springboks and within field goal range.

"Penalty kick," ordered the ref. Llewellyn took the easy kick and scored.

Springboks 23, All Black Dragons 16.

THE GAME BECAME the athletic equivalent of trench warfare. Ruck, maul, and line out—neither side seemed to be able to get the advantage of the other. As soon as the ball was in play and a yard or two gained, there would be a thunderous tackle followed by a turnover of the ball. Time was drawing short; players on both sides were in pain, limping up and down the field. Noses bled, skin flayed off knees and knuckles. In the scrums ears were twisted and bitten, punches smacked ribs. Shins were kicked skinned.

Twice Terry Llewellyn broke from the pack and twice he was brought down by bone-juddering tackles. Play was sloppy, off-sides and knock-ons were spattered throughout play. Ground gained was reconquered almost immediately. The Springboks, with their lead, slowed down the ball, dogged the play, waiting for the clock to run out.

Holt decided it was time to make a move. "Stanley. Next play. Statue of Liberty."

"Check, Jimmy."

"Got that, Terry?"

"Right, Jimmy."

In the scrum, Humphrey Joyce hooked the ball to Llewellyn who passed off to Holt. Jimmy barged upfield, stopped, and dropped the ball to Stanley, who was away in a flash, headed for the goal line.

"It worked!" Holt yelled. "I don't believe it! It worked again!"

The Springboks, caught off guard, yelping in frustration, pursued, but there was nothing between Stanley and a score. The nearest Springbok was ten yards behind him, far too far away. The crowd was on its feet now, yelling, shrieking in delight as Stanley pounded off the yardage. A score and conversion would bring his team to within two points of the Springboks. With ten minutes to play, anything could happen.

Then he was tackled.

A huge bloodcurdling roar went up. Stanley got to his feet, the ball still cradled in his arms. He was staring at Karstens, who had leaped from the South African sidelines to bring him down.

"What the fuck you doing, man?"

"Fuck you, kaffir!"

Stanley threw the ball—it bounced off Karsten's forehead—and then threw himself onto the man. Jones was racing onto the pitch, screaming at the ref. Holt turned to the South African player nearest him and socked him squarely in the jaw. It was the general signal for attack. The game forgotten, the players fell on one another, fists flying. Then the South African supporters charged, met by the Welsh and the black American units. Police whistles shrieked. An MP, wisely, went to call reinforcements. McManus waded into the melee.

Lady Molly grabbed Earl's shooting stick and whacked the nearest soldier, an American private.

"You cad!" she shrieked.

LIKE A CLOCKWORK toy winding down, Alvin Whiteside's great heart beat slower and slower and then, presently, stopped. He gave a great settling sigh, like a sinking ship, and died in his cold sleep.

19

By eight o'clock that night, the mess at the Circo Massimo had been sorted out. The police had cracked some heads to restore order and a number of arrests had been made, but the military authorities released those taken into custody. There was no point, it was determined, in punishing a few for the actions of many.

As to the question of who actually won the match, that was a far thornier issue. The Springboks had been leading at the close of play and, therefore, insisted that they were the victors. Partisans of the All Black Dragons pointed out that Leacock would surely have scored and with time still to play the outcome was in doubt. Furthermore, the Springboks had cheated and, therefore, forfeited the match. The issue was never officially resolved but was debated for months—the Welsh are almost incapable of bringing an argument to a satisfactory close—with both sides maintaining their positions.

In consequence of that and the still-unexplained disappearance of Alvin Whiteside, the All Black Dragons' victory celebration was subdued. The entire company gathered in the depot to hear Thorpe make a little speech to which no one paid much attention until he mentioned beer.

"Lieutenant Kinney and I thought you deserved a little refreshment after your grueling day, so the lieutenant managed to secure two cases of beer. I don't know how you do it, Lieutenant."

"Wasn't easy, sir."

"So, in a moment, we'll drink a toast to the finest rugby team in the United States Army!"

Jones had a few words to say. "I'm not much at making speeches, lads, but I wanted to say that I've never coached a finer group of men. You played well, you gave it your all. It's been a privilege. I don't know how Lance Corporal Llewellyn and I are going to be able to go back to our routine—the war's going to seem mighty dull after you lot. Let me just say that you're a damn fine bunch of chaps. I wish I had another two months with you, then I'd play you at Cardiff Arms Park. No joke, boyos. Now, about that beer, eh, Sergeant McManus?"

"Three cheers for Jones and Llewellyn!" shouted Stanley. "Hip-hip!"

As the cheers rang in the rafters, McManus, the refrigeration expert, hefted the two cases of beer. At minus ten degrees he figured the bottles would need only a minute in the freezer.

When the last cheer died away, there was a glassy crash from the rear of the depot. McManus reappeared, beer splashed on his pants legs and soaking his shoes.

"Sir," he said, his voice unsteady, "a word with you, please Sir . . ."

IT WAS EASIER for Farfalla to go to Company A than for the company to come man-by-man to him, so Manny took over Kinney's office, stationed Salapska outside the door to regulate the flow of witnesses, and parked Malinsky in a corner with a steno pad to take down statements. Had Whiteside been hit by a bullet, killed in the combat zone, his death would have generated no inquiry and a page or two of paperwork, concerned chiefly with the disposition of his remains and his GI insurance policy. A death in an army freezer required investigation and inquest.

Before calling in Thorpe, Farfalla settled in Austin Kinney's desk chair and looked at the desk like a field marshall surveying a map of a battlefield. There was a sheaf of army forms, a stained blotter, a carousel of rubber stamps, an in tray and an out tray, both empty.

There were only two items of any interest. The ashtray of choco-late-colored glass was filled with the butts of cigarettes, half smoked. He picked one up. Farfalla had never heard of the brand, and the length of the ends suggested that Kinney was an unen-thusiastic smoker or that he had been suffering from a bout of nerves. Perhaps he had been upset by Whiteside's death. Maybe the lieutenant had been working hard, laboring conscientiously to do his part in the great crusade. Neither case seemed to fit the Austin Kinney Farfalla knew, or thought he knew.

The other object that Farfalla examined with interest was Kinney's coffee cup. It was not the standard stainless-steel half-pint canteen mug that sat on the desk of every desk jockey in the service under the rank of colonel. Rather, it was a large but delicate cup and saucer, royal blue china edged with a fine gold band, a family crest painted in the depression where the cup sat in the saucer. It was flanked by a heavy silver teaspoon. Identical, Farfalla imagined, to the one Kinney had found in his mouth the day he was born.

Manny picked up the cup and looked at the underside. Then he felt Malinsky staring at him.

"Something wrong, Malinsky?"

"No. Sir. I'm just surprised. I didn't know you were interested in Limoges."

"Limoges?"

Malinsky inclined his head and raised his eyebrows as if trying to get them to point at the cup. "The china. Sir. Quite a fine piece. Although," he added modestly, "I'm no expert. But it's Second Empire. Any damn fool could see that. Sir."

"Valuable?"

"In its set. Sir. It would be quite valuable. A single piece like that, less so. But still not something you would pick up in a junk shop. Sir. Not unless you were quite lucky."

"How do you know it's part of a set?"

"China usually is. Sir."

"Yeah." Farfalla lost interest in the cup. "Well, let's talk to the captain."

THORPE WRUNG HIS hands and said that Whiteside's death had shocked him. "A terrible thing. A tragedy." He sounded like a prep school headmaster who had lost an unpopular scholarship boy to a hazing prank. How would it affect the reputation of the school?

"Yeah. Any idea how it happened?"

Thorpe looked from Farfalla to Malinsky. "I . . . Well, I thought everyone knew how it happened."

"Suppose you tell me."

"Well, eh, Private Whiteside entered the refrigerator to cool off and, ah, the door closed behind him. And because we were down the street at the, uh, game, no one heard his cries for help. Poor fellow."

"Yeah, Poor fella."

"EVERYBODY KNEW WHITESIDE liked to sit in the icebox," said McManus. "It cooled him off. Bet every guy in the outfit's done it one time or other. Heck, I done it myself. Whiteside started it, though."

"Sitting *in* the refrigerator."

"Yeah. Well no, not exactly. Not *in* it. On the step. Letting air, you know . . ." McManus made wafting motions with his meaty hands.

"So why did Whiteside get *in* the freezer this time?"

"Beats the heck outta me, sir."

"Me too."

"Shouldn't happen to a dog."

"HE WAS A good kid," said Manganaro. "Never caused no trouble."

"What was he doing in the freezer?"

"Well, I'da guessed he was cooling off."

"And somehow the door closed on him?"

"Yeah. An accident."

"An accident?"

"Yeah. Tough, huh?"

"AN ACCIDENT," SAID Utterback. "Could happen to anybody. A lot worse has happened to other guys in this war."

"You don't seem too upset by this, Sergeant."

"You get used to anything in wartime, Lieutenant," said Utterback like a grizzled old campaigner.

"Did you like Whiteside?"

"Like? Yeah. I guess he was okay."

"But you don't like the colored, do you, Sergeant?"

"No crime in that. I don't think mixing is such a hot idea. We're us. Them's them."

"And never the twain shall meet, right?"

"Not if I can help it, sir."

"IT WAS—" Leacock's lip trembled and his eyes filled with tears. "I'm sorry, sir."

"Take your time, soldier."

Stanley buried his head in his arms and sobbed.

"IT WAS AN accident," said James Holt. He looked straight ahead of him, staring at a spot on the wall just to the left of Farfalla's head. "An accident. That's all."

"CIGARETTE?" said Kinney.

"No thanks."

"Do you mind if I . . ." He lit up, not noticing, or, perhaps caring, that Malinsky was grimacing and swatting at the curls of smoke with his steno pad as if trying to drive a bat out of the room.

Kinney exhaled through his nostrils. "Funny us running into each other at the game and now here under these tragic, tragic, circumstances."

"Yeah," said Farfalla, "tragic."

"What can I do for you?"

"Just a couple of questions."

"Fire away, Lieutenant," said Kinney, as if he were older, wiser, and busier, but being generous with his time.

"No one on duty yesterday at the depot. Is that correct?"

"I'm afraid not. The men not actually on the team wanted to see the match, of course. It seemed unfair to make some of the men stay behind. Of course, I realize now, too late . . . well, Captain Thorpe and I, we blame ourselves."

"You do, huh? That's funny, Thorpe didn't mention that to me."

Farfalla consulted the autopsy report on the desk in front of him. The army coroners were installed in Rome now, but they had little to do, violent death being quite rare in the city. More to pass the time than out of zeal, they had done a very thorough job on Whiteside's corpse. "Says here there was severe bruising on his right shoulder. Where do you suppose he got that?"

"From trying to batter down the door? Private Whiteside was rather, quite a, um, large boy."

"Yeah, says so here. And you know what? He's got bruising on his left shoulder too."

Kinney stubbed out his cigarette. "There. You see, he changed ends. Er, sides. Shoulders."

"Yeah, that's probably it." Farfalla studied the document a moment longer. "Trouble is 'bruising in the region of the right shoulder follows a pattern consistent with attempts to open the door through the use of bodily force. Bruising on the left shoulder of unexplained origin, as is a pattern of similar contusions in the lower abdomen.' So what do you make of that? I mean, Whiteside wasn't likely to run into the door stomach first, was he?"

"No, I suppose not. Of course, who can say what a fellow might do in a situation like that?"

"Yeah, but it's pretty strange, wouldn't you say?"

"I really wouldn't know, Lieutenant."

"Manny. Call me Manny."

"Manny," said Kinney.

"So you figure it was an accident?"

"A tragedy."

"Yeah."

"Well, if that's all . . ."

"I guess. Unless you can think of any reason why he might be murdered."

"Murdered! Why on earth would anyone want to murder someone like Private Whiteside?"

"Not *like* Whiteside. Whiteside."

"Yes, well, I meant . . . Anyway, I'm sure that no one had any reason to kill him. What makes you think he might have been murdered?"

"Dunno. These bruises, it's like . . . oh well, I don't know." Farfalla stood up and thrust out his hand. "Well, thanks. Great to see you again."

"Again?"

"Since yesterday."

"Oh yes, of course. See you round, Manny."

"You'll let me know if you hear anything. Anything that might . . . you know, if Whiteside had any enemies. Maybe someone had a grudge. Someone, I don't know . . . Anything you might hear. Anything."

"You're, ah, not closing the book on this?"

"Naww, not yet. Rome's pretty quiet. It'll give me something to do, you know. Good practice. Nose around a little."

"Well, it's your time, Manny."

Manny made a gun out of his index finger and thumb. "Can't hurt, right?" He winked. "See you round the campus, Austin."

KINNEY PUT AWAY his sincere smile and hurried to find the sergeants. Until his meeting with Farfalla he really had thought Whiteside's death had been an accident. Now he prayed it had been.

McManus was alone in his office, looking pale and worried. He jumped as the door crashed open.

"Where are the others?"

"Uh, around, sir. Cal's in his quarters, I think. Did you, uh, you know . . ." He glanced through the windows. Groups of drivers and loaders were standing in little knots. Some stood in front of the refrigerator, talking and glancing at it, the way people linger in front of a burned-out building long after the last fire engine has pulled away. "Did you talk to the lieutenant? Did he mention our, you know, business?"

"Does the death of Whiteside have anything to do with it?" asked Kinney sharply.

"No."

"I hope so, McManus."

"What about the audit? You found any to make up for the shortfall?"

"I'm working on it, Sergeant."

"What are you going to do, sir?"

"Call in some favors, Sergeant. But don't worry about that now. This Whiteside business, it *was* an accident, wasn't it? I mean, you know that for a fact."

"Aww sir, it's gotta be. No one would be stupid enough to pull no bull like that."

Kinney chewed his lower lip. An acute sense of self-preservation told him he was heading for trouble. His mind shifted to high gear as he addressed the question of how to extricate himself.

"I want to see you three. We've got to do some serious planning."

"Yessir. I'll round up Cal and Eddie and come on up to your office."

"Don't be an ass. When you get off duty come to the palace."

"Yessir."

"And McManus," Kinney raised an admonitory finger. "Mouths shut."

"THEY KILLED HIM, Jimmy. You know that." It was all Stanley could do to keep his tears down.

"We gotta do something," said Biggs. "We gotta give their shit back. That way—"

"That way Alvin died for no reason. No reason. We give the stuff back and they win," said Holt.

"Who gives a shit?"

"I do, Stanley, I do. You think we're going to be safe if we give them the stuff back? As long as we have the morphine and the money we got insurance."

"Didn't do Alvin no good. No insurance on Alvin."

"You said no one would get hurt," said Biggs.

"I'm sorry. I didn't know," said Holt quietly. "I didn't think they . . ."

"We gotta go to the law," said Biggs urgently. "We gotta go to that CID man, Faloopa or whatever his name is."

"Biggsy, man, you know what we look like right now? Right now we look more guilty than whitey. There is no justice in this army, not for us. You understand? You go to that CID man and we're fucked for sure. A bunch of niggers with a lot of money and a mess of morphine? They'll say it was us killed Alvin. Sergeants and Kinney, they won't even get their names in the papers. We'll get the rope."

"So what we do, Jimmy?"

"We stick together. No going out unless you're with a couple of other guys. This'll die down. We sit tight and wait."

"Wait for what?"

"Wait till we can make our own justice, that's what."

HOWE READ FARFALLA'S preliminary report on Whiteside's death, taking only a moment or two to digest the few terse paragraphs.

"An accident," said Howe.

"Private Whiteside was known to refresh himself in the freezer unit. The door was on a spring catch, quite a stiff one. He entered

291

the freezer, forgot about the door. It snapped shut. He tried and failed to batter his way out. He died," said Farfalla.

Howe repeated, "An accident."

"Nope. He was murdered."

Howe leaned back in his chair. "All right, Lieutenant, why don't you explain it to me."

"There were two types of bruising on the body, sir, one consistent with his attempts to get out of the freezer. The other suggests two sharp blows to the body. Sir, I think Whiteside was forced into the refrigerator. In my mind, sir, the bruising is probable cause that a crime was committed."

"To what end, Lieutenant? According to the statements you collected, Private Whiteside was well liked. He was never involved in any trouble in, or as far as we know, outside of, the army. And, as regards the bruising, I understand that the deceased was a football player."

"Rugby, sir."

"Rugby, then. A very bruising sport, I understand."

"I checked into that, sir. He's been playing rugby daily for weeks now and there wasn't another mark on him, nothing. No old contusions, no scarring. Not a scratch."

"Then why put him in a refrigerator? If we've learned anything from this war, Lieutenant, it's efficient ways of killing people."

"That's simple, sir. To make it look like an accident."

"Motive?"

"None yet. It'll come."

"Suspects?"

"Ditto, sir. I need your permission to continue."

"You think that it is worth your time, Lieutenant? It's pretty difficult to convert an accident into a murder, you know."

"It's even harder to make murder look like an accident, sir."

Howe smiled. "Well, someone's done a pretty good job here. Apart from a few bruises which *can* be explained, this does look remarkably like an accident."

"Yes," said Farfalla, "that's what intrigues me."

KINNEY WAS ON the phone when the three sergeants filed into his study at the Palazzo Sanseverio. He waved them in and went on talking.

"Yes, I know. It's a bitch. But anything you could help me out with . . . You know, Marty, I never forget a friend. Yes. Well, so long." Kinney put down the telephone and reached for a cigarette.

"That was Naples. Guess what? No morphine. Aversa, same story. I spoke to Foggia, nothing doing. Seems we're going to take a crack at the Gothic line and all reserves are being called up to the front. That means not only do we have this goddamn audit, it means we might actually get a call to disburse. We'll be getting it from both sides."

"Jeez," said McManus.

Kinney puffed on his cigarette. "We're going to have to get that stuff back. Does anyone have any idea where it is?"

"That's what I was trying to figure out," said Utterback. "How was I supposed to know a nigger as big as that would croak from the cold."

The three men gaped at him.

"Christ Almighty," said Kinney quietly. "What did you say?"

"Jeez. Fuck, Cal."

Utterback shrugged. "Yeah, well . . . I was trying to help."

"You dumb, fuckin' . . . son of a bitch!"

"Yeah, well fuck you, Eddie. What about that guinea you popped right when we got here? Huh? What about him?"

"What?" shouted Kinney.

"Nothin' sir, don't worry about it."

Kinney ran his hand through his hair and stubbed out his cigarette. "Look, this is getting a little too hot. I think we better dissolve this partnership. Lay low until things cool down a little."

"Hold it," said Manganaro. "Not so fuckin' fast. Hey, Lieutenant, didn't you say as how we needed you? You're supposed to be connected, right? You're supposed to be the protection, right? So protect us."

"I can't protect against murder, you jackass. Nobody can."

"Then what the fuck good are you?"

"Don't you talk to me like that, Manganaro."

"Fuck that shit!" yelled Manganaro. "Don't come that crap with me. You're down here with us, Kinney. We go down, you go down. We walk, you walk. We ain't takin' the fall for you, college boy. So you and us, we gotta figure a way that gets us all off the hook. All of us."

"Right," said Utterback.

"McManus?"

293

"I'm with Eddie and Cal, sir."

"Christ!" Kinney pounded the desk, then reached for another smoke.

"Now just relax," said McManus, soothingly. "It ain't all that bad. The CID guy, he's gonna think it was an accident because everyone really thought it was an accident." He looked balefully at Utterback. "Now we know. It wasn't. So what? As long as we keep our yaps shut, no one's gonna be any wiser, right?"

"Makes us accessories," said Manganaro. "Accessories after the fact on a murder rap. On the outside that carries hard time. Army's probably a lot worse." He clapped Utterback on the shoulder. "Thanks a lot, pal."

Utterback shook off the hand. "Fuck you, Eddie," he said but with little of his usual brio.

"Okay, okay, forget that. We keep quiet about Whiteside and the CID is gonna believe it was an accident."

"And what about the morphine? The audit is in two days, Sergeant, for God's sake."

"That's the easiest part, sir," said McManus. "We make the deal. We make the deal with the drivers, like I said we should all along. None of this shit would have happened if you'da listened to me."

"Not a fuckin' chance," said Utterback.

"Shuttup, Cal," said Manganaro.

"I don't see what else we can do," said McManus. "We get the morphine back, we give 'em half the money. That way we make it through the audit and in a little while we can go back to making money. Makes sense to me."

"Jeez, Donny," said Manganaro, "me dealing with a bunch of spooks? I mean, how's it gonna look?"

"It looks a lot better than the inside of the stockade at Leavenworth, Eddie."

"You got a point, Donny, I admit that."

"Uh-uh," yelled Utterback. "I ain't goin' along with it. No dealin' with the niggers!"

"What you want to do, Cal? Kill 'em all?"

"Fuckin' wish I could, Donny, you fuckin' nigger lover."

"Cal, would you for Christ's sake be reasonable?"

"What about you, Eddie? You believe this? You're not going

along with this, are you? You gonna let 'em deal the fuckin' niggers in? You said you'd never do that!"

Manganaro shrugged. "What we gonna do, Cal? The melanzans got us. What can I say . . . ?"

"Cal," said McManus, "you want to make some money? Fuck the money! You want to stay alive?"

"Yeah," said Manganaro, "seems to me you got the most to lose outta all this, Cal."

"Like you didn't do nothin' to that eyetie, Eddie."

"I beat that. No one gives a shit about him. He's dead and buried. Nothing connects me to him. It's forgotten."

"Christ!" yelled Utterback in frustration.

"It's agreed," said Kinney briskly. "I want you to talk to them. Get the morphine back. That's number one. Then the money. Manganaro, McManus, you two square it."

"Can do, Lieutenant."

"What about me?"

"Utterback," said Kinney sternly, "you will stay the hell out of sight. You keep to the depot. You do your job and you shut up. When Manganaro and McManus meet with Holt you are going to be miles away, do you understand me? You are not part of this."

"Sold down the river," mumbled Utterback, "and by white men, too."

"Sergeants, fix it."

"Yessir."

"Tonight."

"Don't worry about it. We'll go talk to them in this nigger bar they hang out in."

"Use your head, McManus, don't do anything in front of witnesses. Not *in* the bar."

"We'll be careful, sir," said Manganaro. "We all want to get this thing over and done with."

WHEN THE SERGEANTS had left, Gabrielle brought the martini things into the study and made drinks for both of them. She sat on his lap and smoothed his hair and kissed him gently. He tried not to push her away.

"Please," he said.

"Why are you so unhappy with me? It's because of those drugs, isn't it?" She laid a cool, reassuring hand on his brow. "I'll give back the drugs he has." She glanced toward the ceiling.

"Six syrettes? What the hell good are six syrettes going to do?"

She didn't mention that there were only three left. Soon she would need more.

"Besides, doesn't beloved Sandro need them?"

"It wouldn't matter." She embraced him, squeezing him close, holding his head to her breast, a curious, maternal gesture. "One day this will all be behind us, Austin."

"Yes . . ." For all Kinney's power, for all the right people he knew, there was no chance that he could arrange a posting home. A transfer, though, shouldn't be too difficult to manage. Something that smacked of the heroic. Something close to the front. But not too close.

PROVENANCE

Like I said, cops, doctors, and lawyers are the easiest guys in the world to find, if they're not hiding, I mean. See, they have bar exams and boards and certificates and professional associations to join, and these professions have directories and listings and *Who's Who* up the wazoo. I mean, it's not like looking someone up in the phone book, but if you know what you're doing it's pretty easy. Rare is the lawyer, for example, who's not in a big fat set of books called Martindale-Hubble. It's arranged by state, which is kind of a pain in the ass, then by towns within that state. I started with New York because when I'm looking for someone I don't know where, I always start with New York. Sometimes it works out. Farfalla wasn't in New York. Sometimes it doesn't work out.

But remember me? Methodical? It was in all the papers recently that California was the most populous state in the country so I tried that next, figuring I had a one in nine chance of finding him there. That's what the census said, anyway. So I started with Los Angeles, the most populous city in the most populous state. No Farfalla. So I try San Diego, which my almanac tells me is the number two city in the state. No Farfalla. So on to number three, which is San Francisco, and bingo. It's not always this easy.

Farfalla, V. E., was born on the nineteenth of December, 1922, which meant he was spitting at seventy. He was admitted to the bar in November of 1949. The Martindale-Hubble numerical codes told me that Farfalla held a B.A. from Harvard and his law degree, an LL.M., was from Boalt, which turns out to be the law school of the University of California, Berkeley, one of the best in the country, so they tell me.

Then: "Admin. Law Judge, US Dept. of Labor." Farfalla was a judge. Lucky guy. I've always thought that being a judge must be a great job.

You don't hear much about Administrative Law Judges, but there are lots of 'em, hundreds, maybe thousands, attached to the federal government. In the Department of Labor, like Farfalla, or Health and Human Services, Interior, Commerce, Treasury—most of the federal agencies have ALJs to adjudicate laws pertaining to their department. It's not the most glamorous side of the law, but a judge is a judge, you know? Farfalla had a good salary, the prestige of being a judge, the robes, and people had to call him "your honor." Martindale-Hubble told me that the Office of Administrative Law Judges handled workers comp cases, mostly workman's longshore and black lung.

Those few lines in Martindale-Hubble told me a lot. I could see it. Farfalla gets out of the service and like a lot of other GIs looks into the crystal ball and sees that the future is in California, so he takes his 52-20 and his other GI benefits and heads out West.

And you know, it really is pretty good out there, even now. Cops I know who moved out there—not Oakland or L.A., obviously, but places like Pismo Beach and Ventura and Santa Barbara—they wouldn't come back to New York for anything. Those California towns, they love to hire New York cops. They treat 'em good, which is more than you can say for New York. Anyway, Farfalla goes out to California and goes to Boalt—him being a Harvard man and a veteran I guess he could more or less go wherever he wanted—and sets up. After a distinguished private practice (I'm guessing now) he gets the call to the OALJ. Okay, so it's not the Supremes, but it's not bad. Manny Farfalla had done okay.

I called Peony and told her I was going to San Francisco and that my airfare and hotel would be showing up on the bill I was going to be giving her when all this was done. She didn't mind that I was flying business class, but she grumbled a little when I told her I'd be staying at the Mark Hopkins, which is really swank and expensive.

"Harry," she said, "*I* don't stay at the Hopkins when I go to San Francisco." Which is true. She stays with her Aunt Tess, who has a place in Pacific Heights that makes the Hopkins look like a Motel Six. Rich people are funny about money, but I guess you heard that.

Peony didn't ask me why I was going to San Francisco instead of calling Farfalla on the phone. She's smart. Peony knew that if I called him from New York and said Guido Reni, James Holt, Rome in 1944, blah, blah, blah, then he *might* have said, "Oh yeah, well this is what happened and this and such with the painting and Holt and this guy Howe," and the whole thing might have been cleared up in a phone call. Cost Peony maybe fifteen bucks.

But maybe he wouldn't. Maybe he'd get all tight-assed on me and say, "I don't know you from Adam and leave me alone," and then I would have to go to California anyway and begin all over again and put up with all his yelling about calling the cops. And like I say, a judge is a judge, even an ALJ, and it's better if they aren't mad at you. If I called him from the nice respectable Mark Hopkins and said "Judge, I've come all the way from New York to talk to you," that was better. I also like to talk to people face to face in matters like these.

Besides, I like San Francisco. There are those beautiful jades at the Asian Art Museum, and the Art Institute is always good for a chuckle. Peony was paying, so what the hell.

Anyway, I got to San Francisco on a Tuesday afternoon, and as soon as I got to the hotel I put in a call to Judge Farfalla. I knew I wouldn't get him the first time—you almost never get anyone the first time—and of course, his secretary asks me, "What is this in reference to?" This is always kind of a difficult question to answer; I mean, you don't want to give away anything, but at the same time if you just leave your name and number then they might not—probably won't—call you back. Especially a judge. They're busy people, and I'll bet if you deal with workman's comp cases you get a lot of crank calls from people who want to know how come you turned them down for benefits.

I told her that I was doing research on the Army Provost Marshall's Office and the Judge Advocate General's Office in Italy, during the war. Which sounds sort of scholarly, and it was kind of the truth, too. Farfalla's secretary said that she would have him call me back and she said it in that nice San Francisco way that almost makes you believe he will call back.

And don't you know it, he did. Late Wednesday afternoon he calls and he's all business just the way you'd expect a judge to be. Also, the guy's about seventy but he didn't sound it—he sounded a lot younger—and another thing, maybe he'd been in California for forty years and maybe he'd picked up some of that kind of rounded California accent, but you could hear the city, or maybe Jersey, in his voice.

Farfalla wasn't exactly suspicious, but he wasn't a blabbermouth either.

"Are you writing a book?" he asks me.

"No sir, I'm compiling a report."

"On what?"

I told him what I had told his secretary.

"I was a very small cog in that machine, Mr. Leblanc. I can't imagine I'd be much use to you. What are you? A historian?"

I decided it would not be too politic to lie to a judge. "No sir, I'm an investigator. I was a detective with the New York Police Department for fourteen years."

"And you're compiling a report on the APMO and the JAGO, in Rome, forty-five years ago?"

"Well, sir, I'm looking into one particular incident and your name came up. You know Adam Malinsky? He suggested I get in touch with you." You notice that I didn't say, You remember Adam Malinsky? See, here I think I'm dropping an important name. I'm in the art business, right? And to me, Adam Malinsky's a big name, a door opener, and I figure it's going to cut a lot of ice with Farfalla. But it's obvious to me that Farfalla has never heard of the guy, not in an art context anyway. I'll bet there are guys in the lumber business or the wholesale kitchen-supply game who'd look at you as if you had eight heads if they mentioned the big guys in their field and you hadn't heard of them.

Farfalla says, "Adam Malinsky? I haven't heard that name since '44 or '45. How the hell did you find him?" Malinsky would just shit if he heard that.

"Well, sir, he's not all that hard to find if you know where to look."

There was a long silence on the other end of the line, then a sigh. "This is about Kinney, isn't it? Austin Kinney."

Austin Kinney? Who the hell was Austin Kinney? Still, I tried for a shot in the dark. "The Kinney case could have bearing on this, Judge."

"The Kinney case? I'd have thought it was called the Sanseverio case."

"Well," I said, "that too." Who the hell was this Sam Severio?

"Look, Mr. Leblanc, how long are you going to be in town? I'm in court all week."

"I'm going to be here as long as it takes, Judge."

"Okay, can you come out to the house this Saturday? Saturday morning? We'll talk. Away from the phones."

You know, it was funny. I got this feeling that Austin Kinney and this Severio character weren't things Farfalla wanted to talk about and yet it was like he thought he *should* talk about them.

"That would be great, Judge. I appreciate it."

He gave me an address in Berkeley and hung up.

Now, I don't know a lot about what they call the Bay Area, but everybody's heard of Berkeley—you know, hippies and drugs and radicals and People's Park and Patty Hearst. Not a place you'd expect to find a judge.

Well, I rented a car and headed out to Berkeley Saturday morning and found out that there's Berkeley and then there's Berkeley Hills. They are not similar. Euclid Avenue is up in the Berkeley Hills and it is plush. Up there, above the town, high above the flats where the radicals and the students and poor people live, you'll find a very nice neighborhood. Big houses, lots of trees, lawns, great views—like grandstand seats for San Francisco Bay. The only thing that tells you you're near the other Berkeley is that all the Mercedes and Volvos and Lexuses have politically correct bumper stickers.

Judge Farfalla had this nice house at the top of a steep driveway. Nice white house with a kind of tower on one corner, built, I'd guess, in the thirties. There was a pretty, wide patio and a smallish swimming pool and down the hill a ways was a tennis court, but you couldn't see it all that well because someone had grown ivy up the fence that kept the balls in the court.

Farfalla was about my height—say five-ten—but he was kind of stooped in the shoulders. He was thin and the skin on his cheeks was sunken. It made his big nose prominent. His mouth was turned down like he was never in a good mood. He didn't look like the kind of judge I'd want to face if I was a lawyer with a shaky case.

There was coffee on the patio. From the tennis court came that bonk-bonk sound of a game in progress and every so often a feminine squeak or two.

"My daughter," said the Judge, "and a friend of hers."

I sipped the coffee, which was really good, and said polite things about the view, which was really good too. Then:

"Would you mind, Judge, if I taped this?" I pulled out my little tape recorder.

"Just a minute," he said, and got up and went into the house. I wondered, what? Was he calling the police? His lawyer? What? He came back a minute later with his own little recorder—wasn't nearly as good as mine—and put it down on the table. "Do you mind if I record it too?"

"Not at all." We turned on both recorders at the same time, like duelers cocking our guns or Ferrante and Teischer or something.

"Judge Farfalla, I appreciate your taking time out to see me. I know you don't know me from a hole in the ground—"

"Sure I do. I know you were a policeman"—well, hell, *I'd* told him that—"that you went to John Jay and NYU, that you spent fourteen years in the stolen-art squad, and that you are now working for yourself in the art security field . . ."

The little sneak! He'd checked me out! Like I said, cops, doctors and lawyers.

"But I'm not involved in the art world at all, Mr. Leblanc, never have been. So why don't you tell me what this is all about?"

"I was just getting to that, sir." I took the precis of James Holt's statement out of my briefcase. I talked while he read it. "The estate of James Holt was found to contain a very valuable painting, sir, and I'm supposed to find out where it came from—if he acquired it legally. You wouldn't happen to know anything about that, would you, Judge?"

Farfalla kind of chuckled and nodded. "I couldn't say for sure, but I could guess."

"You could? Does it have anything to do with the incidents mentioned in this report?"

Farfalla was silent. On the tape you can just make out the bonk-bonk from the tennis court.

"Mr. Leblanc—" said the Judge.

"Harry," I said.

"Harry, you got some time?"

"Nothing but, Judge."

"Then let me tell you a story."

And so he did. And it was a doozy.

20

A light rain fell that early evening, a Roman presage of autumn, but it had stopped by the time Jimmy, Stanley, and Elena came out of the Broadway. It was close to eleven o'clock but the streets were still damp and the military traffic rushed along the dark streets, the tires making sounds like bacon sizzling or calico tearing.

In the Broadway, the three had drunk little and spoken less, the two soldiers wrapped in their own sadness. Elena had been made to understand that Alvin Whiteside had been killed and she shed a tear for him as she would have for any death, but she had grown bored with her glum companions. Twice she had tried to coax Stanley onto the dance floor, but with no success.

She had pouted for a while but then, because she was a loving soul, had tried to cheer her boyfriend, stroking his cheek and kissing his neck, and she had said soothing things to him in Italian. But Stanley refused to be comforted.

Jimmy Holt and Stanley Leacock were out simply because they could not stand to be in, back at the barracks. They were together because they could not face being alone. The gaiety, the music, and the laughter at the Broadway, though, only depressed them further.

After an hour, Holt could stand it no longer. "Let's get the fuck out of here," said Jimmy abruptly, not even waiting to drain his drink.

"Yeah," said Stanley. "Elena, we gotta go. A casa. I'll walk you home."

Elena was glad to go. She was not by nature a glum person, but the low spirits of her companions were contagious.

They walked the wet streets, from Via Palermo along Via Panisperna to Piazza Magnanapoli, passing the brawny brown bulk of Trajan's Market at the top of the Via Quattro Novembre.

"Ci sono fantasmi qui," said Elena, unhappily, nodding her head at the ruins.

Stanley didn't bother with his dictionary. "You tell me some other time, okay?" It was her habit to explain the legend and lore behind every monument they passed.

"Som' udder tame," she parroted, and hugged him close, as if for warmth.

In the curve of the Via Quattro Novembre there is a wide, dark flight of steps that leads from the high ground of Trajan's Market to the Piazza Foro Traiano and Trajan's great column, rising like an ivory tusk from a thicket of splintered gray marble pillars. At the base of the steps stood McManus and Manganaro.

"Hi, Jimmy. Hi, Stanley. Evenin', miss," said McManus.

The three stopped midway down the staircase and the two sergeants climbed up a few toward them.

"Stanley," said Jimmy quietly, "you better get Elena out of here."

"Jimmy," said McManus soothingly, "there's nothing to worry about. We've just come to talk to you . . . Relax."

"Yeah, Holt, relax."

"I don't think we've got anything to talk about."

Manganaro smiled. "You know, Donny, he's right. The man is right. We don't have anything to talk about." Eddie opened his arms wide, as if in welcome. "Jimmy, you've won. We give up."

"Won what?"

"Don't trust 'em, Jimmy," cautioned Stanley.

"The war," said Manganaro. "It's over. You wanted in the syndicate? You're in. You guys want fifty bucks a week, you got it. You want half the money? Hey, it's yours."

Elena looked from Stanley to Jimmy. "Stanley, che successo?"

"Aww man," said Holt, "what do you take me for?"

McManus came a few steps closer. "Jimmy, Eddie, he's on the level. Believe me . . . I've always been straight with you. You can believe me, right?"

"All we want back is the morphine and half the money, just like you said. And when we get rolling in again, you and your boys are there. Fellas, I mean. From the first buck. It's gonna be a beautiful partnership, believe me."

"That was before Alvin, Manganaro. The money, the drugs, that don't matter anymore."

"Look at this, the guy is changing the rules on me. Can you beat that?"

"Jimmy," pleaded McManus, "you gotta believe us. That had nothing to do with us."

"Oh c'mon, McManus! You think we believe all that shit about an accident? Man, you keep on making the same mistake. You keep on thinking we're fuckin' stupid. What is it with you guys?"

"It wasn't us," shouted McManus. "It was Utterback."

"Like there's a big difference," said Jimmy.

"Utterback," said Stanley. "Jesus Christ!"

"Cal fucked up. He did it all by himself, he did it without telling us. All he was trying to do was trying to find out where you guys hid the stuff. It was a mistake. We admit that. Cal fucked up. What can I say? No more anybody getting hurt. We can settle this, Jimmy. Be reasonable."

Holt advanced on Manganaro, coming a step or two toward him. "Be reasonable, the man says. Be reasonable! You make money off our backs, you fuck us out of our share. You kill my friend. And when things get hot, it's *us* who have to be reasonable."

"Listen, Jimmy, listen. Utterback was out of line. If we'da known, then it never would've happened. Jimmy," said McManus, "you gotta trust me."

"What for?"

"Because you got to, Jimmy," said Manganaro, "it's as simple as that. Right now, all we got is each other. Now we gotta work together or we'll all end up in the shit."

"And Alvin? Where's he?"

"That I can't do nothing about," Manganaro mumbled.

"Yes you can! Utterback's your boy. You settle him."

"C'mon, Jimmy, be realistic. What am I supposed to do, huh?"

"Oh, I get it. The Negro boy dies, well that's just too bad. The white boy, he just walks away. Is that it?"

"Jimmy, that's the way it's always been. You're a smart kid. You known a long time now it's a white man's world. Jesus, Jimmy, Whiteside's gone. No reason we should all follow him."

"And the next time?" yelled Holt. "The next time someone's got to die? Gonna be one of us again? Is that it?"

"Jimmy," pleaded McManus, "let it go, he's gone."

"No. Not this time. Face it, Eddie, you two are dog shit without us. Without us, you're dead men."

"Eddie?" said Manganaro. "Eddie!"

"So what you want, Jimmy?" shouted McManus. "If you want we should kill Utterback, you're crazy."

"Yeah, we can't kill one of our own," said Manganaro.

"One of *my* own died, Eddie. Seems fair to me."

"Fair ain't part of it," said Manganaro. "It was never part of it."

"Look," McManus wiped sweat from his face. "Look, how's about he gets a transfer? I can fix that."

"A transfer? What the fuck you take me for, McManus, a fool? A transfer? Why don't you just fix it that the motherfucker gets the Silver fuckin' Star? You gonna fix a transfer, why don't you fix one for me? Or Stanley? Or any of us? A transfer? A *transfer* is supposed to make up for what he done to Alvin?"

"A transfer to the front. To Normandy. We're losing a lot of guys up there."

"Yeah," said Manganaro enthusiastically, "that's like the guy's gone already. France is a fuckin' slaughterhouse. It's like he was put in the ground already. Jimmy, he's a dead man. Like it was meant to be. We get him outta here and chances are he'll be dead in no time. Utterback and Whiteside, they can figure it out with the big man upstairs."

"Vengeance is His, that's my motto."

"No deal," said Holt.

"Jimmy, please, man . . . We're doin' our best here."

A low cry came out of the shadows, a mixture of hurt and howl, outrage and pain. It ended in a spate of barely articulate words. Elena clutched at Stanley.

"You fuckers," said Utterback, "all you fuckers . . ." He stepped into the moonlight, an M-1 Garand rifle held out in front of him. It was a stiff-arm, fixed bayonet pose. The snout of the rifle swept from McManus to Manganaro, then traveled across Stanley and Elena to point at Jimmy. Then, abruptly, it swivelled back to Eddie.

"You sold me out." Utterback whipped his gun to McManus.

306

"A transfer. Jesus, Donny"—his voice was tight and hot, teary—"you sold me out to the niggers." He shook his head. "I thought we were pals."

McManus stepped toward him. "Cal . . . it's not like that . . ."

"Aww fuck it," said Utterback and fired twice. Both rounds slammed into McManus's chest, the two bullets picking him up and tossing down the steps. By the time he hit the ground, his shirt was a mass of blood. He lay very still.

Elena screamed. Manganaro fired, diving behind Stanley for cover.

"Stanley!" Jimmy screamed. "Stay down!"

"Elena!"

Utterback fell into the darkness, firing wildly. The staircase seemed to be alive with howling, angry bullets trapped in the narrow space. A round smacked into Stanley's neck, and his eyes grew wide and frightened and he grasped at the spot as if stung by a bee. A great gout of blood surged through his fingers. He opened his mouth to cry out but there came only a terrible rasping sound, a desperate viscous sucking at air. Elena was no longer screaming.

Utterback's rifle came clattering out of the darkness, tumbling down the steps. Then came the sounds of running as he charged up the staircase to the street. Very calmly, or so it seemed to Jimmy, Manganaro raised his .45 and fired at the retreating footsteps. The big gun bucked in his hand as he fired. But the boots clattered on, away.

Jimmy raised his head. Stanley's blood was running down the steps, as if from a fountain. Elena had a slash of blood across her white cheek, like a bruise or a birthmark. Her legs were doubled under her as if she had fallen heavily. McManus lay sprawled at the bottom of the stairs. Jimmy felt as if hours had passed since those first two shots.

Manganaro turned to Holt, his gun raised. "Fuck it," he said, "I might as well do you too." He pulled the trigger. The smash of the hammer against the empty chamber sounded louder than any gunfire. Holt looked down the barrel and into Manganaro's empty eyes and ran.

JIMMY'S SUDDEN ACTION seemed to rouse Manganaro. He shook his head like a boxer clearing his mind after a punch and then started up the stairs after Utterback. He tripped on something, falling hard to the stone steps. He groped around his feet and found a high-heeled shoe, which he hurled into the night.

"DEAR BOY," SAID Lady Molly opening the door. "Whatever has happened? You do look a fright, doesn't he, Earl? As if you're being chased by banshees or rather like my brother did when he was caught with that sailor. Do come in."

Jimmy staggered into the apartment and sank into one of the velvet sofas. His breathing was shallow and he felt a crushing fatigue.

"Drink, James?" asked Earl. He was wearing a long, quilted silk dressing gown. He clutched a beaker of scotch in one hand. Jimmy took the glass and gulped, choking for a moment on the bruising liquid, and then knocked back more, draining it. He coughed and held it out to be refilled. Earl and Lady Molly looked on in silence.

"Stanley's dead."

Molly put her hand to her mouth. "Oh dear God."

"What? What happened?"

"He got shot. Utterback, or maybe Manganaro. I don't know. There was a lot of shooting. McManus is dead. So's Elena." Jimmy looked up. "You don't know them. There's a lot of trouble. You could get in trouble, me just being here."

"Don't worry about us," said Earl.

Lady Molly peered through her own drink at Jimmy. "This wouldn't have anything to do with that mass of parcels you've left in our spare room, would it?"

"Yeah. Yeah, it does."

"Perhaps you'd best tell us about it."

"It's the black market," said Jimmy. "Them sergeants were involved. We just wanted our share and now Stanley's dead, Alvin's dead. McManus, Elena." Holt's eyes filled with tears. "Stanley . . . he trusted me. He was my friend." A great, cold breaker of sorrow broke over him. He closed his eyes tight. "And Alvin . . . And McManus. He wasn't such a bad guy."

Earl poured more scotch into Jimmy's glass. He drank and cried, great wrenching sobs that shook his whole body. His arms jerked and the scotch slopped. Molly sat down next to Jimmy, took the glass from his hand, and held him close.

"You poor thing," she said softly into his ear. "You poor, poor boy . . ."

MANGANARO FOUND UTTERBACK huddled at the base of the Torre delle Milizie. He was jammed up against the old brown bricks, shivering though the night was warm. There was a wild, desperate look in his pale eyes.

Manganaro squatted down next to him. "Hey, Cal," he said gently. "Cal, buddy, we gotta talk. The shit is going to start flying and we gotta be ready to duck, you know?"

"You tried to kill me, Eddie."

"Yeah, well, fuck you, you tried to kill me." Manganaro chuckled. "Cal, you are a lousy shot."

Utterback turned his dirty tear-streaked face to Manganaro. "Is Donny . . . ?"

"Yeah. You croaked him. Hey but forget about it, Cal. Everything's gonna be okay. In a way, this is about the best thing that coulda happened."

"What?"

"Yeah. See, you and me, we're gonna go have a few drinks, see, like everything's copacetic. Not a care in the world. Tomorrow when the shit hits the fan we're gonna say, 'Who? Us?' "

"But . . . the morphine. The audit. I mean, what's gonna happen?"

"Cal, don't you see? It was all McManus. Him and Stanley, *they* were dealing, they were the syndicate. Right under our fuckin' noses! How do you like them apples? They messed around with the wrong people, they land up dead. Happens every day. Okay, so you, me, Kinney, we'll get a little slap on the wrist. It's Thorpe who'll catch the shit, but who cares? All we gotta do is shut up and we're home free."

Utterback's eyes opened wide. "You think so? Really?"

"Sure," said Manganaro, "trust me."

21

The Duke awoke in the dark of that summer morning in a brown miasma of memories. He had been dreaming of his youth, vivid dreams and yet curiously remote, like a series of tableaux acted out for him, his own role played by an actor. There was Miss McNutt and his father and mother, his wife—even, for some reason, a man named Silvio who had once been gatekeeper to the palazzo but had died before the dawning of the century. They were not dreams filled with omen and portent or fantastic happenings. He had been shown the events of dead days gone as if someone was trying to tell him that somewhere in time or history the days of his life were replayed again and again, endlessly down the ages. Everyone seemed so happy there. It was a depressing beginning to his day.

Camillo rose, bathed and dressed, then descended the stairs to the street. The sun was up, but night still lurked in the church of Santa Maria Campitelli, patches of black crouching in the dusty corners and behind the tombs of Camillo's ancestors. There were eight or ten old women at mass, as usual, and when the equally ancient Monsignore D'Onofrio creaked onto the altar, it was all these old women could do to rise to their swollen feet.

The priest hunched before the altar whispering the words of the mass as if the prayers were a secret, maybe even a bit of scandalous gossip, to be kept at all costs from the eager, eavesdropping ears of the congregation. The Duke's eyes followed the mass and he mechanically stood, knelt, sat, as regular as a pump, but his mind attended to his own prayers, no less routine.

His thoughts to God traveled in a well-worn groove, like a

prisoner pacing in his cell, calling on the Almighty to grant respite to his son, to mend him, body and soul. Camillo asked that Gabrielle not stray, that his family be preserved. To show God that he was not wholly self-centered, he sought guidance and long life for Pope Pius, prayed for the souls of the fighting men who had died during the night and mentioned, in passing, the welfare of Italy, the people of Rome, refugees, and the men and women of the religious orders. This brought him, like a train into a station, back to his own intentions again. He paused here, trying to think of something he had to bargain away in return for God's favor. But he had nothing, he knew, that God wanted that He didn't have already, his love and fealty.

During the Confiteor, Camillo found himself wondering if God ever tired of hearing his prayers, day after day, the same whine of want, a constant chant of supplication. Why, he wondered, did He not grant his prayers, if only not to have to hear them anymore, the way a parent will give into a mewling child, purchasing peace.

With a little start, like an electric charge, Camillo wondered if God was deliberately ignoring him, as if he had been suddenly shut out of a club, a club in which he thought himself to be a member in good standing. He blinked at the miraculous painting of the Madonna over the altar. Could it be that his prayers went unanswered simply because they had not been heard, like a letter left unopened? Camillo prayed a random prayer, not to God this time, but to Miss McNutt, addressing it like a telegram, asking her—for *she* no doubt was in the bosom of the Lord—to intercede on his behalf.

But there was no happy response from Miss McNutt or God that morning. Camillo had always wondered why it was that in the early days of his religion, when the sound of the footsteps of Christ and the Apostles could almost still be heard, when saints abounded, when the faith was shining and new, there were so many miracles, so many answered prayers. Now, with the tarnishing of the centuries, with a world at war, prayers needed, *demanded*, to be answered, miracles *had* to be worked. Camillo's requests, he thought, were not unreasonable. But it was as Saint Theresa had said: It is no wonder God has so many enemies, considering how badly He treats His friends.

It was Camillo's habit to return to the palace after mass to see to the bathing of Sandro. Since the arrival of Kinney, he also had a cup of coffee.

He climbed the steps to the first floor and made his way along the passage towards the kitchen. He stopped in front of the door to Kinney's bedroom and impulsively, suddenly, without thinking, put his hand to the handle and opened it. There had been another raucous party the night before and the silence of the bedroom had a sleep-heavy, leaden, hung-over air. Kinney lay asleep with Gabrielle. She lay on her side, naked, a cool linen sheet drawn up just over her haunch, her lovely blonde hair spilling onto the pillows. Kinney was stretched beside her, an arm draped proprietarily over her waist.

The Duke felt a physical stab of pain, a rage that trailed nausea in its wake. He stared at Kinney, his eyes burning. This scoundrel was young and whole, healthy and handsome. A swaggerer, a braggart, who slept in Sandro's bed and had his wife like a whore, paying in food and drink, as if she were nothing more than a sutler to soldiers. Camillo closed the door and staggered a few steps back into the hall. He leaned against the wall, God's fool and mocked by Him.

JAMES HOLT AWOKE that morning in the high-ceilinged bedroom in Earl and Molly's apartment. He lay still in the bed, an old creaking bed with a headboard like a tombstone, and looked around him. Stacked neatly in a corner were the boxes of morphine, the opened one on top, the money and the gun in a paper bag nearby. The pain of the previous night was still there, undulled by sleep and alcohol and set with jagged memories: Alvin, Stanley, Elena. But in the night, as if worked on by the corrosive whiskey, his grief had rendered down to a small, sharp, nugget of hate.

UTTERBACK AWOKE LATE to the aching, open-wound memory of too many desperate drinks and dead bodies. Manganaro was standing over him, his uniform blouse fresh and starched, his cheeks scraped close and clean, a model soldier. He handed Utterback a mug of strong coffee, hot and bitter.

"Cal, it's morning. The shit's in the air. Don't fuck up, okay? You okay?"

"Yeah, yeah," said Utterback.

"Holt's AWOL. It's gonna be bad. That dick from the CID is gonna be here any minute, like the fuckin' airborne. You sure you're okay?"

Utterback thrashed under the sheets as if checking to see that his legs still worked. He farted and rubbed his face. "Yeah, yeah. I'm fine, Eddie. Jesus Christ."

"Don't fuck up and we'll be okay."

"Yeah."

"Get cleaned up and get on duty like nothin' happened. Act normal. And then act surprised. Got it?"

"Jesus Christ, Eddie. Would you fuck off and leave me alone, please. What are you? My fuckin' mother?"

"Just don't screw up."

"Okay, already."

Utterback staggered down the hall of the hotel and threw himself under the shower, feeling edgy and coughing nervously. Anxiousness tremored through his body. How could Manganaro be so calm?

" 'Cause he's a hood," said Utterback into the stream of water. Then: "Need a drink."

The wine seller on the Via Buccimazza knew Utterback; he stopped in every morning. He set up a glass and poured just as Utterback stepped in from the blaze of the hot street. There was a sepulchral gloom in the briny-smelling cavern, which soothed Utterback's aching eyes. He drank down the wine at a gulp.

"Gimme another vino."

The Italian refilled the glass, then retreated to a dark corner of the bar. Utterback drank off half the glass and felt better, less jittery. He put a cigarette to his lips and lit it.

"Everything is gonna be okay," he mumbled. "Everything is gonna turn out okay." He tossed off the rest of the sour wine and slapped his gut. "Bar-keep, one for the road."

"Un altro?"

"Gimme another."

The wine seller poured, then looked beyond Utterback. A figure stood in the string curtain of the door.

"Hey, Sarge . . ."

Utterback turned, glass in hand, and squinted at the figure backlit by the bright sun, framed in the door.

313

"Who's that?"

"Me, Sarge," said Jimmy Holt. He raised the pistol and fired once.

"WE MEET AGAIN, Austin," said Farfalla.

"Yes. Screwy isn't it?" Kinney was sweating and that interested Farfalla. He didn't think people like Kinney ever perspired.

"What's going on in this outfit, Austin?"

"Damned if I know, Manny."

"You sure? Who do you suppose killed McManus and Leacock? Never mind Whiteside and the girl."

"Well, *I* didn't." He did his best to smile at Farfalla. Kinney realized that, for the first time in his life, he was afraid.

Farfalla's eyes were hidden behind his dark glasses. "Never said you did."

"It was a joke."

"What do you think happened?"

Kinney shook his head. "I really couldn't say. Maybe an argument or something. I don't know."

"Black market? Maybe it was a bad deal, maybe they pissed off the wrong people. That a possibility?"

"I suppose."

"Any thefts in your unit?"

"Not that I know of."

"You're supposed to *know*."

"Everything is accounted for."

"Where's Holt?"

"AWOL, so Manganaro tells me. *He's* the one you should be looking for."

"I'm working on that."

"MOLLY, EARL, I need a car. And you have to drive it for me."

"I could do that," said Earl.

"No, not you, Earl. A black man'll attract attention. A white woman can go anywhere. And I need a suitcase, a big suitcase."

"Well," said Molly, "that's no problem. We have lots of suitcases. Franco, he's the *portiere*, he has a motorcar. I'm sure he'll lend it to us. He's done it before. It's a question of petrol, though, you see."

"Petrol?"

"Gasoline," said Earl.

"And where am I supposed to drive this motorcar?"

"I'll show you."

"And where will you be?"

"In the back. Under a blanket."

"Heavens, how madly cloak-and-dagger."

Molly and Earl watched Jimmy pack all the morphine in their old suitcase. The last box, the open one, he tossed aside. "This is for you. This stuff should be worth something."

They squinted at it. "Well, James," said Molly, "we're not dab hands at selling things of this sort."

"Perhaps Bianchi could dispose of it," said Earl.

"Yes," said Molly uncertainly. "Perhaps . . ."

Holt pulled a handful of bills from the paper bag, a wad of tens and twenties. He thrust them into Earl's hand. "Here, Earl, buy yourself a piano. That's from Stanley and Alvin. And me."

Lady Molly drove the doorman's battered old Fiat through the streets erratically, calling out to soldiers she passed, "Hello, hello . . ."

315

22

When Manganaro heard Utterback was dead, he stood up, locked his desk, and without a word to anyone, got in his jeep and drove away. There was only one man in the city who could help him now.

He crossed the city quickly, weaving the jeep in and out of long, green columns of military machinery. He scarcely braked and he muttered and cursed when an MP held him up on the Via Labicana while the great, drab behemoths of a tank recovery unit rumbled by. He crossed Via Merulana and zoomed along Via Emanuele Filiberto, through Piazza Vittorio and into Via Balila.

The lookout, the young man Manganaro had seen the first time he visited Lorenzetti's warehouse, lolled against the garage door. He seemed to have no other job than to observe the street for his master. He nodded at Manganaro as if they were both inhabitants of a small town meeting on Main Street.

"Devo parlar' col padrone," said Manganaro.

"Perchè?"

"Never mind why, sonny, just tell him I'm here."

The man gave Manganaro a long look and then opened the garage door, just enough for Eddie to get under and in. He started toward the rear of the building, to Lorenzetti's office, but the lookout stopped him, putting a firm hand to his chest.

"Attenda," he said and went in search of his boss. Eddie stood motionless in the middle of the garage. The old gangster took his time emerging, keeping Eddie waiting as he might a menial. Manganaro did his best to control his temper.

Lorenzetti appeared, two men, bodyguards, trailing him like

gun dogs. Despite the warmth of the day, Lorenzetti was dressed, as usual, in his suit and tightly knotted tie. He stood in front of Eddie, his arms folded across his chest.

"What do you want?"

"I'm coming to you with a problem, Alfonso."

"What is the problem?"

"I have an enemy."

Lorenzetti shrugged. "We all have enemies, Manganaro. A man should be able to take care of his enemies."

Manganaro smiled. "Oh, I will, Al, don't worry about that. I'll take care of him. There's one problem: I can't find him. He's hiding."

"Wait until he reappears. Then deal with him. It is simple."

"I don't have that kind of time. I got to find him and finish things now."

"I am sorry to hear you have troubles, Manganaro, but I'm not sure how this concerns me."

"I want you to find him for me."

"Io?"

"You, your people. This is your town, Don Alfonso. If he's hiding you can find him. You have people on the streets, you have informers, you probably have people in the police, friends of yours who would be glad to do Lorenzetti a favor."

"You overestimate my power."

"No I don't. Do this for me and I'll give you anything you want. I'll cut my prices. I'll cut my prices in half. You'll make double what you're making now. You'll be richer than you ever thought."

Lorenzetti nodded, his mouth turned down, as if weighing the pros and cons of the deal. "And who is this man?"

"He's a black man. A soldier. A man named James Holt."

Lorenzetti turned and looked at his bodyguards. " 'Olt," he said. "Well, that's quite easy."

Jimmy stepped out of the gloom. "How you doing, Eddie?"

Manganaro looked from Holt to Lorenzetti. "You fuckin' dago! You fuckin' sold me out! To a melanzan!"

"You are finished, Manganaro. It is over. There will be no more business, no matter what you say. I will be lucky to get out of this." Both bodyguards had guns trained on Eddie now.

Manganaro felt a sharp bolt of fear. "Christ! Jimmy, Jimmy, what kind of deal did you cut with this fuckin' greaseball?"

Holt walked toward him. "All the money, Sarge, and all the morphine." He stopped in front of Manganaro. "For you."

Manganaro laughed and shook his head. "You have got to be shittin' me. Cal always said you were trouble. Poor son of a bitch, for once in his life he lands up right."

"He's dead."

"Yeah, I know. So what you gonna do, Jimmy? Kill me?"

"Yeah."

"Oh." He put out his left arm, his right arm snaked into his pocket. "But first, c'mere . . . I want to tell you something. A secret." He pulled Jimmy close. Eddie's hand shot out of his pocket, clutching the ice pick. He threw his weight against Holt, both men tumbling to the ground.

"You fuck! You fuckin'—"

The ice pick flashed, and as Holt threw up a hand to protect himself, he felt the icy shaft enter his hand, puncturing his palm like a single stigma. His skewered hand curled like a claw and his knee came up and jammed into Manganaro's ribs. He grunted and fell sideways. Jimmy tore the pick from his hand and swung at Eddie, catching a fleshy fold of skin, his jowls, and tore open his cheek, laying bear a row of yellow, then red, teeth. Manganaro screamed and clutched his face. Jimmy kicked him again, dropped to his knees, and grabbed Manganaro with his bloody hand. His nails dug into Manganaro's flesh, snatching at his trachea as if to tear it from his throat. Then he drove the ice pick straight into Manganaro's astonished right eye.

Holt felt snappings and tearings along the short shaft and Eddie's screams were high pitched and feral, a long, tortured wail. His legs swept and scythed and his chest heaved. His hands scrabbled, trying to rip himself free. Jimmy was down and on him, bearing down hard on the ice pick, working it into Eddie's head, as if trying to pry open Manganaro's skull. Warm blood enveloped them both, spraying in a fine haze when Manganaro screamed, his blood-coated tongue slithering in his ragged mouth. Jimmy pushed until the shaft would penetrate no further, until the handle of the ice-pick was nestled in the bone crib, the socket where Manganaro's eye had once been. Now it was an eggy, gluey mass welling around the handle and slipping through Holt's fingers.

Jimmy rolled off Manganaro and lay flat on the floor, his mangled hand beneath him. He panted for a minute or two, then slowly raised himself to his knees, coughed, and hocked on to the concrete. He got to his feet, unsteady. He looked at Lorenzetti and his bodyguards. "Thank you," he said.

THE LOG FOR Military Police Post Six on the Via Arenula near the river recorded that at 5:41 P.M., that day, Private James Holt turned himself in, answering the charge of Absent Without Leave. The log further stated that he was injured, his left hand having been bandaged. The prisoner had $2.63 on his person and claimed that he had been drunk for the last two days. He was transferred to Regina Coeli prison, where he was remanded pending investigation of his case the next morning.

FARFALLA DIDN'T WAIT for morning. As soon as the report came in he and Howe went to the prison and had Holt brought down from his cell.

"You know me, don't you soldier?" asked Farfalla.

Jimmy Holt nodded. "Yes, sir."

"But you don't know the major, do you?"

"I don't know any majors, sir."

"I'm Major Howe, son, and we want to help you. You're in quite a bit of trouble. You understand that, don't you?"

"I'm a AWOL, major. Guys go AWOL all the time."

Malinsky was busy scribbling in a corner.

Farfalla stood up and paced the small room. Regina Coeli prison is set in a depression next to the Tiber, with the Lungotevere, the river road, running along a bank at about the height of the prison's second story. As Farfalla stared out the window he could see only the ankles and heels of passersby, as if he was in a cellar room.

"Holt, AWOL is the least of your problems," he said. "I have reason to believe that you are implicated in the deaths of five, possibly six, people. They are: Alvin Whiteside, Stanley Leacock, Sergeant Calvin Coolidge Utterback, Sergeant Donal McManus, and an Italian national named Elena Grillo. I further believe that you are responsible for the death of an Italian national named Arturo Falcone. Private Holt, as sure as I'm standing here, you are going to hang for one or all of those murders."

"No, sir."

"No?"

"No, sir."

"Private Holt," said Howe, "you have been AWOL since last Sunday. During that time these deaths—these murders—have occurred. And you tell us you had nothing whatsoever to do with them."

"Yes, sir."

"How's your hand?" asked Farfalla.

"Fine, sir."

"What happened?"

"Cut myself, sir."

"How?"

"Was drunk, sir. I fell down, sir."

"Where?"

"In the apartment."

"Apartment? What apartment?"

"My friend's apartment, sir."

"The medical report says that you've sustained a deep puncture wound. Not the kind of thing you'd get if you fell down and skinned your hand. It's a kind of stab wound." Farfalla leaned over Jimmy. "Who stabbed you, Holt?"

"Nobody stabbed me, sir. I fell."

"Fell? You couldn't fall and make that kind of wound."

Jimmy caught Farfalla in his stare. "You could if you fell on a piano, sir."

"Piano? What the hell are you talking about?"

"The piano at my friend's house, sir. Got these wires, sharp too. I was drunk and I fell on them, sir."

"What apartment?" said Farfalla. "Where is this apartment?"

"It's Earl and Molly's apartment, sir. I been there since right after Alvin died. I went there and they gave me something to drink. I've been drunk ever since. I was in their apartment. Ask them."

"You did not leave the apartment for two whole days? You never left it, not for a second?"

"No, sir."

"Impossible!"

"No, sir. Earl and Molly, they did it for years. When the Germans were here, sir. They never left for three whole years."

"Nonsense. How is it possible?"

"Well," said Holt, "it's quite a big flat, you know, and there's a terrace. Quite secluded. Of course, the whole neighborhood knew

320

I was there. There are no secrets on a Roman street, you know."

"What? What the hell are you talking about, soldier?"

Malinsky smirked.

Howe put out his hand as if to steady his subordinate. "Private Holt, did you kill these people?"

"No, sir."

"Do you know who killed them?"

"No, sir."

"Do you know why they were killed?"

"No, sir."

"Do you know anything about the black market?" ask Farfalla sharply.

"No, sir."

"What about Lieutenant Kinney?"

"What about him, sir?"

"Do you know of any involvement the lieutenant might have in the black market? Did he and the sergeants ever . . . did they ever talk about it? Did you ever observe any funny business at your depot?"

"No, sir."

"Jesus!" Farfalla slapped one hand into the other. He paced a little more, then turned on Holt again. "Where were you on the Sunday after I questioned you about Whiteside?"

"I went to Molly and Earl's. I was down, sir, because of Alvin. They gave me some whiskey."

"And you did not report back to your barracks that night. Is that correct?"

"Yes, sir."

"You went AWOL?"

"Yes, sir."

"Why?"

"I told you, I was blue, sir."

"And Leacock? Where was he?"

"He was with Elena, sir. That's his girl."

"You didn't go out with them?"

"No, sir."

"You two were very close friends."

"Yes, sir."

"But you didn't go out with him Sunday night?"

"No, sir."

"Why not?"

"He went out on a date, sir. You got all the company you need on a date, sir. You and your girl."

"Where did they go?"

"I dunno, sir."

"And you were at this, this Molly and Earl's?"

"Yes, sir."

"Where were you Monday morning?"

"At Molly and Earl's, sir."

"And Monday afternoon?"

"Same place, sir."

"And then you turned yourself in?"

"Yes, sir."

"Why?"

Holt looked unblinking at Farfalla. "Cause I didn't want to get in any more trouble than I already was in, sir."

"When you were in this apartment, you were with Earl or Molly the whole time?"

"Yes, sir."

"They were with you the whole time? Neither of them ever let you out of their sight?"

"One or the other. Except when I went to bed, sir. They didn't see me sleep."

"And when was that?"

"Midnight. Maybe one. I don't know. I was drunk."

Farfalla smiled grimly. "And that was about the time the murders took place."

"I never killed no one. You ask Earl and Molly. They'll tell you."

"Oh I intend to, soldier. Bet on it."

"I'm not a gambling man, sir."

"Not even on a sure thing?"

"Private Holt," said Howe, "do you like Lieutenant Kinney?"

"No, sir."

"Why not?"

"He's an officer, sir."

Howe smiled faintly. "I mean, apart from that. Do you dislike him personally, I mean?"

"Yes, sir."

322

"Why?"

"He's a white man, sir."

"So, if you knew something incriminating about him you'd volunteer that information to me and Lieutenant Farfalla?"

"No, sir."

"You wouldn't?"

"No, sir."

"Why not?"

"Because you are officers and white men, sir."

"I'm warning you, Private," said Howe sternly, "this is no laughing matter."

"I'm not laughing, sir."

"You would withhold information to protect Kinney. Everything you've said here already could be a lie."

"Could be," said Holt, "but it ain't."

"And Kinney?"

"He's never done nothing to me, sir. I don't like him because of what he is. Excepting that, I don't have no problem with the lieutenant. He's your problem, sir."

"What makes you think he's a problem?" snapped Farfalla.

"You do, sir. You got something against Lieutenant Kinney, sir, not me."

"But you just said you don't like him."

"And I said why, sir."

Howe took off his glasses and rubbed his eyes. "You wear your skin like a uniform, Private."

"It's the only uniform I got, sir." He looked into Howe's blue eyes. "It's the only one I can trust."

LADY MOLLY WAS not surprised in the slightest to see Lieutenant Farfalla at her door.

"Do come in, Colonel. Earl and I were just having a drop of . . . what is it, Earl?"

"Prosecco," said Earl.

"Of course, very refreshing. It's rather like champagne without all the fuss and funny hats."

"I'm Lieutenant Farfalla. I'm with the APMO, that's Army Provost Marshall's Office, CID. I'm an investigator."

"Heavens! You're all that? Goodness, how grand. My uncle was a KCMG and a KC and, right at the end, an OM, but he was much older than you. I expect you'll catch up. Do sit down. Lovely name, Farfalla, don't you think so, Earl?"

"Wine, Colonel?" asked Earl.

"No thank you. And I'm a lieutenant."

"Oh well, never mind," said Lady Molly. She and Earl looked at Farfalla, pleasant but uncomprehending smiles on their faces, as if Manny was the friend of a friend who just happened to be passing through Rome.

"Do you have any idea why I'm here?"

"No," said Molly, "but I expect you'll get to it eventually. Are you sure you wouldn't like something to drink?"

"No thank you, ma'am. Am I to understand that you're friends of James Holt?"

"That's right," said Molly.

"A fine young man," put in Earl.

"Have you seen him recently?"

"Seen him? My dear boy, James practically *lives* here. He's one of our closest friends. Isn't he Earl?"

"Yes," said Earl.

"When did you see him last?"

"When was that, Earl?"

"Just this afternoon. He spent the weekend with us. Or part of it."

"When did he arrive here?"

"On Sunday afternoon. He came to stay with us after that beastly business with his poor friend, the big lad. What was his name, Earl?"

"Alvin. Another fine fellow."

"He arrived Sunday afternoon and he stayed with you until this afternoon?"

"That's right. He could have stayed longer but he said he had to get back to the army. It needed him apparently, but I said what nonsense, it has bags of soldiers, what difference would one more make. Poor fellow, he'd been on the most terrific bender, you know, it was all Earl and I could do to keep up. He was quite *distrait.*"

"And he hurt his hand," said Earl.

"Yes, the ass. Took quite a tumble. He was well away, of course, could happen to anyone. Almost happened to me once. We'd been in Venice seeing Archie and Belinda Partridge. Do you know them, Lieutenant? They're Americans. They had the most lovely place in the Ca' Mocenigo—Byron and all that you know, which rather appealed to Archie because he wanted to be a poet; terrible drivel, but he was fun in a dim sort of way and Belinda was splendidly beautiful, exquisite, and as bad a sculptress as he was a poet but luckily *her* family *and* his were quite ferociously rich, you know, so it really didn't matter what they did. We were up there visiting—years ago, now; of course, everything seems years ago to me now—in the depths of winter, and you know there isn't much to do in the winter in Venice except drink; not all that much to do in the summer if it comes to that—and after luncheon I was a peg too low from all the drink and just as I was getting into our motoscafo I went ass over tea kettle on the dock and would have fallen in the canal if it hadn't been for the ganzier. He's the johnny who holds the boat. Do you remember, Earl?"

"Yes," said Earl. "I remember." He sipped his wine and smacked his lips. "Those were the days."

"Gone too, I'll be bound, now, with this silly war and all that talk about world government and so on. You know, I have the feeling that the world is going to be quite drab from now on. We're all being hoisted on our own petard, too. Quite silly, really. I admit it, we used to sit about chatting about the rights of the common man and so on, but that's quite easy to do when you're doing your jawing at the Roc in Antibes, or Juan les Pins, or wherever the hell it is. Now it's going to be all workers' housing and model villages and overalls. Not in the least bit fun. I don't think so at any rate, do you Earl?"

"No, not me. I'd turn the clock back if I could." He raised his glass as if in toast. "The twenties!"

It seemed to Farfalla that they had completely forgotten he was there. "May I?" he said. He stood and opened the piano case. The jagged wires stuck up like stakes at the bottom of a pit.

"He fell on that?"

"Yes. Frightful. Blood everywhere. Pulling him off was absolutely gruesome, wasn't it, Earl?"

"Horrible."

"He claims he was in this apartment, never left it, from Sunday until this afternoon. Is that true?"

"Yes, that's right."

"You never saw him leave?"

"No."

"What about when he went to sleep?"

"Well, he went to sleep, didn't he?"

"He could have pretended to go to sleep and then left the apartment and returned later in the night. He *could* have done that, right?"

"But why on earth would he want to skulk about in the middle of the night?"

"He was free to come and go as he pleased, you know," said Earl. "He wasn't being held against his will."

"Of course, we wouldn't have seen him if he had. We are usually a bit up the pole when we go to bed, and when I sleep a squadron of Mons angels couldn't rouse me."

"Up the pole?" asked Farfalla.

"Tipsy," said Earl.

"So, for several hours, Holt could have been outside the apartment, is that right?"

"Yes, that's right."

Farfalla stood, smiling. "Thank you very much. Would you two be prepared to testify to this in a court of law?"

"Of course, wouldn't we, Earl? Though I haven't a thing to wear."

"And you know the penalties for perjury?"

"Well, not offhand, but I'm sure they're positively devilish."

"I've taken up too much of your time."

"Nonsense, we have lots, don't we, Earl? I'll see you out . . . Oh, just a moment . . ."

Farfalla was already on the landing. "Yes, ma'am?"

"You know, as regards James's nocturnal skulking, you might want to have a word with Franco. That's our portiere. The doorman . . ."

"Why?"

"Because he sits by the door all night. His wife sits there all day. In a little sort of glass box thing. If James had gone out, Franco would have seen him. In fact, he couldn't have gotten out unless Franco let him out. He locks the big door at ten and only he has the key. He gets quite shirty if you come in or go out after that. Do ask him. He'll tell you for sure."

Farfalla's shoulders slumped. "I'll do that. Does *he* know the penalties for perjury, by any chance?"

"Oh, chapter and verse, I'm sure. There you are, then. Do come again."

23

The Duke passed a few days in grief, scarcely speaking to Sandro and shrinking away from Gabrielle as if she were diseased. He went mechanically about his tasks at the Insurance Company, performing so badly that he was rebuked countless times for sloppy work. Only one thing did he do with any clarity and that was to consult the Army Post Office directory, the listing of every unit and every soldier based permanently in Rome. Three days after discovering Gabrielle with Kinney, three days without Mass, he walked out of the Insurance Company in midafternoon, never to return. First he went home; then he went to the Hotel Palatino Splendido.

Holt had been transferred from Regina Coeli—Howe had recommended company punishment—and had his brief interview with a very agitated Captain Thorpe. He received his 15-2 but in the absence of any supervising NCOs he was confined to his barrack until such time as punishment could be carried out.

The company was in turmoil. With McManus and Utterback dead and Manganaro listed AWOL (it would be some days before his body would be found in the reedy shallows of the Tiber, downstream, near Magliana), the running of the unit had fallen to Thorpe, Kinney, and a couple of corporals. It was, in Kinney's view, not such a bad thing. The morphine audit had been delayed a week and Kinney's request for a transfer was well in hand. Colonel Hamilton had been quite moved when the young man had asked him for help in moving closer to the fighting. After all, Kinney could have remained, honorably, in the rear echelons, rather than volunteering for more hazardous duty. Hamilton had decided to throw Austin a going-away party.

SIGNOR FIORITO DIRECTED the Duke to Holt's room on the second floor. The few soldiers around the hotel assumed he was one of the elderly residents who made the Hotel Palatino Splendido their permanent home. No one noticed the tube he carried wrapped in newspaper.

Holt was lying on his bed, staring at the ceiling, when the Duke knocked. Wearily, he swung upright and opened the door.

"What are you doing here?"

"You remember me?"

"Yeah, sure. You're the one who got me out of Kinney's place. You gave me that card. Lady Molly told me what that little mark meant."

"It means I regard you as my friend."

Holt sat down on the bed and looked at the Duke with hollow eyes. "I don't have no friends . . . I'm on company punishment. You ain't supposed to be here."

"That does not matter to me," said the Duke.

"That night . . . that night you came to my home . . ."

"Your home? I always thought that was Kinney's place. What about it?"

"You had morphine and you had a gun."

"Yeah?"

"I need them. I need them both."

"I don't got 'em any more."

The Duke sat down on the bed next to Holt. He took off his glasses and rubbed his red-rimmed eyes. "Dio mio . . . ," he said with a sigh.

"It's your boy again, isn't it? You need some morphine for your boy?"

"Yes, yes. It is very important. It is vital . . ."

"How much you need?"

"Five, perhaps six, of those little glass . . ."

"Syrettes."

"Yes."

"I think I know where you can find some. With a friend of mine."

"And the gun?"

"What do you want the gun for?"

"Please, sir, that is my affair." Camillo slipped the string off the newspaper-wrapped cylinder and unrolled the small portrait of the Contessa Lucia in the headress of an odalisque. "This is for you, as payment."

"I don't want it."

"You must take it. It is a question of honor. I can no longer take without paying. It is not worthy of my family. Please understand me."

"Listen, old man, you want that shit, I'll tell you where to go. But I don't want no goddamn painting. Just forget it, okay?"

The Duke rolled up the painting and tied it with a neat little bow. "Please take it as a mark of friendship and esteem. It is important to me."

Jimmy groaned. "Friendship. I told you. I don't have any friends. You want that shit, go and take it. But you take your painting too. I don't need it."

Camillo opened a dresser drawer, placed the painting inside and closed it with an air of finality. "I don't need it either, Mr. Holt. It is not important."

LADY MOLLY RECEIVED Camillo with the same good humor she showed all visitors, known to her or not. She tried to press a glass of gin on him, told a lengthy anecdote about attending a temperance meeting in Ireland, then gave him the rest of the morphine and the gun—"glad to see it go, horrible thing"—and then saw him off with her customary "do come again."

Back in the living room, she said, "Earl, what do you suppose is going on?"

THE DUKE SAT by Sandro's bed and stroked his son's hand, thinking of days gone by. Sandro had been a serious boy with bright eyes, prone to sudden fits of high spirits and deep pools of sadness. Camillo remembered Sandro running through the *gran salone*, through shadows and light, laughing. He remembered Sandro twelve years old, in the mausoleum of the Scipios, still and quiet, in thought, and finally asking if it was true that he was sitting at the tomb of his ancestor.

Camillo remembered Sandro on the Sermonetta's tennis court,

effortlessly playing an elegant game. He was tall and strong then, probably eighteen, perhaps twenty. Camillo had heard two women watching his son—he seemed to recall that they were Pecci-Blunts —exclaiming at his handsomeness and bearing and then whispering, "Such a pity they haven't a penny."

The last time he saw Sandro, the real Sandro, he was descending the stairs of the palazzo with the Fascist secret policemen, the thugs from OVRA. They were stealing his son away from him forever. Sandro's nose had been crinkled in disdain.

Camillo leaned over the bed and kissed Sandro on the cheek. "Goodbye, my son," he said softly. "Please forgive me . . ."

Then he injected six vials of morphine into Sandro's atrophied arm. And then he sat with him, holding his hand until he slipped away.

THE DUKE ENTERED the Excelsior Hotel just before eight that hot summer evening, walking past the MPs with a bearing so proud they didn't think to stop him. Egidio, the concierge, responded instantly to Camillo's imperious snap of his fingers.

"The Conte Sanseverio to see Lieutenant Kinney."

"I am so sorry, Eccellenza," said Egidio, "but the lieutenant is at dinner. Some of his brother officers are giving him a small farewell—"

The Duke looked the man up and down. "You will fetch him at once."

Egidio swallowed. "Si, Eccellenza, subito." Egidio rang for a page, who scurried off in search of Lieutenant Austin Kinney. The Duke sat stiffly in one of the lobby chairs, calm and composed, his gray eyes flicking over the officers and their women. They stood laughing in the lobby, trying to decide where to go next.

"Hey! It's the Duke!" yelled Captain Goodyear. "How ya doin', Dukie? Where does a guy go to have some fun in this town?"

The Duke looked at him with distaste. "Go away. Get out of my sight."

"Huh? What?" Goodyear gaped.

Kinney appeared at the top of the stairs. He was in dress uniform, a black bow tie at his perfect wing collar. He was wreathed in sweet cigar smoke. He trotted down the stairs.

"What's up, Duke? What the hell you doing here, you old jackass?" Kinney had been drinking.

Camillo drew the pistol from his jacket pocket and caught a satisfying look of fear in Kinney's handsome blue eyes.

"Hey, Duke . . ."

"I am a Count," said Camillo and fired. The bullet slammed into Kinney's chest and threw him through a potted palm and up against the wall. Camillo advanced on him and fired again, a shot to the head. "I am Conte Sanseverio," he whispered.

PROVENANCE

So I'm sitting there in business class listening to my little tape recorder through my headphones and there's this girl next to me, eighteen maybe, can't believe her luck—she's been upgraded. She's cute, too, real cute, which is probably why the guy at the TWA desk at JFK upgraded her, like she's going to go to Europe for two weeks and when she gets back she's going to go to the airport and find that guy and say, "Thanks for upgrading me, and just to show my appreciation, I'm going to have sex with you," because you know that's what the guy was thinking, right?

Now normally I'd be happy to have this cute girl sitting next to me because, you know, I'm human too, and usually I sit next to complete lunatics. Like this one time a couple of years back, I'm on my way to Chicago—not business class—and I'm sitting next to this numerology nut and all kinds of other weird stuff and he tells me, you know, that JFK was abducted by aliens and that Elvis's grave is empty and that the Lindbergh baby was an angel and that Billy Joel was Martin Luther in another life—the usual, right? He also told me that John Lennon was killed by the KGB, and I hate to say it but after he explained it to me, it kind of made sense. But anyway, the guy is a complete wacko and he asks me what I do, so I mention the art world and he gets all interested and tells me that he's a painter-sculptor-printmaker-fabric-designer-performance-artist-photographer-jeweler and how he's looking for a New York gallery and could I recommend someone. So here's the perfect opportunity—what dealer did I hate so much I wanted to inflict this guy on him? So I told him about this hip place downtown and I tell him the dealer's name and tell him to tell the guy that Bernard Berenson sent him.

You know, when I thought about it later, I figured I'd made a mistake because this guy probably ended up with that gallery and he's headed for a big career in the art world. I half expect to see this guy's stuff in a big ad in *Art in America.* You know, "Works on Asbestos" or something like that.

Anyway, I'm on my way to Rome and this girl would normally be a pleasant companion to pass the time with—it's her first trip to Rome and she's already quizzed me about how to get into the city from the airport, how much do hotels cost, and do I know any good restaurants, and normally, like I say, this wouldn't bother me. But today it does because I'm listening to the tape I made of Judge Farfalla and I can't keep my ears off it.

"I remember Howe saying to him, 'You wear your skin like a uniform,' and he said that it was the only uniform he could trust. And I *knew* just then, in that moment, what had happened. I knew that this kid, what, twenty years old, James Holt, he went out and killed two people. I didn't know about Manganaro then, not yet, but it was a cinch he killed Utterback. And you know why? Because he knew the army wouldn't help him bring the killers to justice. He knew there was no justice in the army, none that applied to him, anyway. He was on his own . . . But I couldn't blame him for taking the law into his own hands. I didn't get mad. I tried to bust his alibi because it was my job, but Holt had us cold. Nailed." On the tape you can just make out the tennis game. It sounded so, I dunno, so peaceful, girls playing tennis on a warm California Saturday morning.

"I wanted to get Kinney," Farfalla was saying, "I really wanted to bust him. And Holt was the only person who could give him to me. And he *wouldn't.* You know why? He told me. He said that Kinney was my problem. The white, college-educated, officer class. Never mind that Holt couldn't tell the difference—or didn't care that there was a big gulf separating Kinney from me—he saw things in, well, black and white. He more or less said to me, 'You created Kinney. You get rid of him.' Holt had taken care of his own. What happened after that was not his problem.

"And that problem got taken care of. Kinney was a lot closer in class to Camillo Sanseverio than I was to him. The upper classes settled this between themselves."

"And Sanseverio," I asked, "what happened to him?"

"Oh well, Kinney's father made a big stink. I mean, there's no doubt it would go to trial, but we tried to mitigate it. Fix it so Camillo would get life. We really played up the emotional Italian thing—although that wasn't Camillo Sanseverio—his son cuckolded, his family dishonored. But Kinney's father got the word out in Washington and Camillo got the rope. In the military prison in Aversa, July 1946. The last thing he said to me was, 'You have been very kind.' Like I had helped him fix a flat or something."

"Forty-six?" I said. "What took so long?"

"Oh, we kept appealing it. Not that Camillo cared. His son was gone, so he didn't give a damn. Though he did reconcile with his daughter-in-law, Gabrielle, her name was. She was a beauty. I always figured Camillo killed his son—mercy killing, really—but there was no way we could prove that. Not that I wanted to. I was on Camillo's side. See, even if we had gotten Kinney, the powers, the money, the old-boy network would have gotten him off. The whole thing damn near turned me into a red. So Camillo did what was right. That's why we worked so hard to get him off."

"We? You keep on saying we. Who's we?"

"Me and Major Howe. He gave up being a trial judge advocate to work on the defense. He stayed in the army a year longer than he had to. I was sorry when he died, in the sixties. I saw it in the *Reporter.* It was because of him I became a lawyer . . ."

Cindy, that's the girl sitting next to me, asked me what I was listening to and I told her language tapes. She said she wasn't worried about language because she spoke some Spanish and figured that was pretty close to Italian.

A COUPLE OF days before I left New York, I called a friend of mine in Rome, a guy named Osvaldo Biagione, who's attached somehow to the Hertziana Library there on Via Gregoriana. It's one of the great art libraries of the world, the Hertziana, and you can usually find Osvaldo there doing research on some obscure subject or other. Osvaldo is one of the last eighteenth-century kind of guys—he gets an income from somewhere, family money, I guess, and studies all the time, writing these little monographs on jewel-engraving in Renaissance Mantua or theatrical set-decoration in Venice before 1705 (which means before Goldoni, he tells me), and then he has them printed and bound and gives them to libraries or to friends as Christmas presents. Nice guy, knows everybody, knows art, do anything for you, but he can get to be a little boring if he's got a bee in his bonnet about, I don't know, the fresco cycle at San Pudenziana at Narni or something.

Anyway, when I got to my hotel—the Inghilterra, that Peony is a doll—there's a message for me to call Osvaldo. So I call him and we arrange to have dinner that night at a great restaurant called Al Vogher, and after Osvaldo bends my ear for a while about his latest bit of research (the Villa of Herodes Atticus on the Appia Pignatelli) he tells me what I want to know. He's tracked down the last little piece of the puzzle. I go back to my hotel real proud of myself because I'm going to finish this case and also because I used a little Rossi/Conti on my cab driver who, I could tell, was real impressed.

YOU KNOW MIAMI Beach? Imagine Miami Beach without the beach and smaller and the buildings not as tall and you've got Parioli. That's a part of Rome on the other side of the Borghese Gardens, a very snooty suburb, virtually all modern buildings, ugly as sin I think—I mean, who the hell would want to live in some concrete thing put up in the sixties when you could live in beautiful downtown Rome? A lot of rich people, it turns out, who want air conditioning and better plumbing than you get in the old buildings, although Osvaldo says it's still pretty terrible, even in Parioli.

The address Osvaldo gave me was on Via Elenora Duse and he said I was expected the next day. I showed up on time.

A maid let me in, said something in Italian which I took to mean "The signora will be with you in a minute," but which turned out to mean "Follow me, the signora is waiting." The apartment was nice, not nice like Peony's, but it had marble floors and a lot of old furniture and some paintings I wished I could have had a closer look at, land-scapes mostly, and some portraits.

The old lady was sitting in a faded tapestry chair in the corner of a big drawing room, Peony would have called it. The heavy curtains were half-closed, so it was kind of dim in there, but I could make out the old dame just fine. She sat up straight and had very blue eyes. Her hair was as white as—okay, snow—and her skin was smooth and clear, maybe a little, sort of, old-lady-ish, but she didn't look like an old suitcase, if you know what I mean. She extended a frail hand and her jewelry rattled, good stuff, but more modern than I would have expected. She wore a gold crucifix around her neck.

"Mr. Leblanc? Is that a French name?" She said it like it was French. Luhblonk.

"That's right, ma'am."

"I was French once," said Gabrielle Sanseverio. "I won't get up. It takes too long and it is such a bother getting back down again."

"I appreciate your taking the time to see me, ma'am."

"I wasn't sure I would see you. All of that was a long time ago."

"I can understand that, ma'am."

"People always think that old people want to talk about the past. Perhaps that's true of some, but not me. I keep my mind on the present. I like to watch television and read the newspapers."

"I apologize if we're going to be going over some painful ground."

Gabrielle waved her hand and her jewelry rattled again. "Better to sort all this out now."

"Do you mind if I tape this?"

"Not at all."

I set up the recorder and took some pictures out of my briefcase. They were really good color shots that Peony had made of the painting.

"Do you recognize these, ma'am?"

Gabrielle fumbled for her glasses and angled the pictures toward the light. I watched her closely. You could see that she had been quite a dish once.

"Ahhh . . . ," she said. "Oh yes. I remember this lady. Beautiful, isn't she?"

"She sure is."

"This is the Contessa Lucia Sanseverio. An ancestor of my late husband. This picture hung in a little room at the Palazzo we called the sewing room. A very pretty room . . . A very pretty room." She looked away from the pictures and toward the windows, and she winced, or sort of jumped, as if she had been pricked by an old memory. I felt terrible.

"This painting, ma'am, was found in the possession of a man who died recently in New York City. A James Holt. Does that name mean anything to you?"

"An American?"

"Yes, ma'am."

"We had quite a few Americans to dinner at the Palazzo during the war. Soldiers. Myself and . . . a friend, we were very active socially."

"I doubt he would have been one of your guests, ma'am. He was not an officer."

"We only had officers."

337

"So this painting was a Sanseverio family possession, and yet for some reason I have not been able to figure out, this work passed into the hands of Mr. Holt. Mr. Holt's daughter, a Mrs. Chapman, has engaged a firm of art dealers in New York City to sell the painting on the open market. I represent the dealers. I have to tell you, ma'am, that this painting could turn out to be quite valuable."

"Of course. It's a Reni."

"I need to know if you, as a Sanseverio heir, would attempt to block the sale of this painting."

"And why should I do that, Mr. Leblanc?" She looked at me with those clear blue eyes and I knew she could be a tough customer if she wanted to. Sometimes you can just tell. Peony has that look. Some cops I know have that look. Me, I don't have that look.

"Well, as Mrs. Chapman's possession of the painting is unclear, the Sanseverios would have a pretty good claim to it."

"This is about money, is it not?"

"Yes ma'am." In my experience, most things are.

"I have no interest in money. I was terribly poor once upon a time and not for terribly long, but I am no longer. When my father-in-law died he bequeathed the Palazzo and all it contained to me. We had not been on the best of terms but the circumstances of his death were such that he wished . . . I am thankful that we were friends at the time of his death. The Palazzo wasn't worth much after the war." Her eyes glittered. "But it is now. I still own it and I rent out flats. To foreigners mostly. Ten million lire some of them cost. A month! Madness."

That was not bad money. Ten million lire was just about nine grand.

"So you are prepared to confirm Mrs. Chapman's possession of this painting."

She was silent a long time, then she leaned forward. "Is she poor, this Mrs. Chapman?"

"Well, she's not rich, ma'am."

"Then let her have the painting. I'm not going to tell you any more than this, Mr. Leblanc, but during the war I was a wicked, wicked woman. I am seventy-seven now. I must look to the state of my soul."

I gave her one of those sly looks you give old bats when they tell you how fast they were in their youth or when they think they've said a naughty word like "buttocks."

But she wasn't taking that from me. "Don't make fun of me, young man. If I say I was wicked, I was."

I realized then, horrified, that her old eyes had filled with tears. I wanted to say, "Okay, okay, you were wicked."

Instead I took a paper out of my briefcase that Peony's lawyers had drawn up. "Would you sign this document stating that the painting was acquired legally and that you renounce any claims on it?"

"I will. My son, the present count, is a lawyer. He shall have to look it over."

My stomach lurched. A son! And a lawyer! That meant trouble. Maybe the old lady was making a fortune off her property, but her son wasn't quite so close to death that he would say no to a big pile of cash dollars. She must have read my mind.

"Don't worry, Mr. Leblanc. Sandro will do as I tell him. This is Italy and in Italy sons still obey their mothers."

"No, it's just that I didn't know you had a son. I'm surprised, that's all."

Her old hand snaked out and took a silver-framed photograph off the table next to her. She handed it to me. "This is my son. It was taken when he was thirty. He is forty-six now. He has three sons of his own. The line will live on. That was very important to the old count."

I looked at the picture. Sandro Sanseverio was standing in front of a tennis court, in whites. He had blond hair and deep blue eyes and an almost pretty face. There was a self-confidence in his eyes that made me uneasy. I hoped the old lady could handle him.

"Very handsome," I said.

"All the Sanseverios have been handsome," she said in a faraway voice.

WELL THE OLD bat did it. The next day the release was delivered to my hotel, signed by Gabrielle Sanseverio and countersigned by her son. I called Peony and she whooped down the line.

"You are a genius, Harry. A genius!"

"Yeah, I know."

"What are you going to do now?"

"I'm going to take a little vacation here in Rome."

"Yeah? Well turn off the meter."

That Peony. She slays me.

But it had been fun. And I felt good. I decided to go and see the Raphaels at the Farnesina. I love them. That's *art.*

339